"We can't deny that there's chemistry.

"Or maybe I'm misreading the signals?"

"You're not misreading anything," Jason said.

Holly looked up at him, putting her mouth mere inches from his. Was she *trying* to drive him crazy? Or did it just come naturally?

"I think we'll agree that anything beyond friendship would be a bad idea," she said, so close he could feel the heat of her breath on his lips.

It took everything in him not to kiss her. To keep his libido in check. The only thing giving him the will to resist was the drowsy child lying limp in his arms. He was a much-needed buffer. "Are you always this brutally honest?"

"If we have any hope of making this work, if the boys and I are going to live under your roof, we have to be honest with each other. Even if the truth hurts a little."

Holly was still watching him, waiting for a response. If she wanted honesty, that was what he would give her. "The truth is, I really want to kiss you."

* * *

Demanding His Brother's Heirs
is part of Mills & Boon® Desire™'s No.1
bestselling series, Billionaires and Babies: Powerful
men...   fingers

DEMANDING HIS BROTHER'S HEIRS

BY
MICHELLE CELMER

Published in Great Britain 2015
by Mills & Boon, an imprint of Harlequin (UK) Limited,
Eton House, 18-24 Paradise Road, Richmond, Surrey, TW9 1SR

© 2015 Michelle Celmer

ISBN: 978-0-263-25273-6

51-0815

Harlequin (UK) Limited's policy is to use papers that are natural, renewable and recyclable products and made from wood grown in sustainable forests. The logging and manufacturing processes conform to the legal environmental regulations of the country of origin.

Printed and bound in Spain
by CPI, Barcelona

Michelle Celmer is a bestselling author of more than thirty books. When she's not writing, she likes to spend time with her husband, kids, grandchildren and a menagerie of animals.

Michelle loves to hear from readers. Like her on Facebook or write her at PO Box 300, Clawson, MI 48017, USA.

To new beginnings

One

Holly Shay didn't believe in signs.

But as she tossed Devon's and Marshall's dirty clothes on top of the hamper, her wedding band, loose after she'd dropped the last of her baby weight, slipped off her finger and went flying across the room. Two carats of flawless princess-cut diamonds hit the wall at high velocity, leaving a dimple in the paint, and landed with a clunk on the nursery floor.

Maybe someone was trying to tell her something. That it was time to take it off. At this point she didn't have much choice.

The idea of hocking the ring broke her heart, but she had only a few weeks to find a new apartment. She had no job and not a penny to her name. Only after Jeremy's death last month had she learned of the considerable debt he'd sunk them into over the course of their ten-month marriage. She would be paying off his debts for many years to come.

But that's what addicts did, or so she had been told. If she had only known she could have helped him. It still astounded her that she had been so blind. She'd known deep down that something wasn't quite right with him. She'd assumed it was the stress of having twin infants. A new marriage—especially the shotgun variety—was a challenge in itself, but toss a high-risk pregnancy, then fragile preemies into the mix and things could get dicey. The boys had been born a month early and had had to spend nearly two weeks in the NICU. When they finally had come home it had been with machines to monitor their breathing and heart rate. It had taken a toll on them both.

But it wasn't until after Jeremy overdosed that she'd put the pieces of the puzzle together. Only then did she recognize the signs. She had been stupidly and irresponsibly blinded by love, by the fantasy of the perfect family she had always dreamed of having. When would she learn that for some people the happily-ever-after would never come? It just wasn't in the game plan.

It could have been so much worse. Holly had lost both her parents when she was a child, but she had been one of the lucky ones. Orphaned ten-year-olds typically were difficult to place in the foster care system, but she had been taken in by a really nice couple with two other foster kids. There never had been much money, but the essentials always had been covered. She'd had a hot meal every night, decent clothes on her back and someone to help with her homework. And though she and her foster siblings all lived at opposite ends of the country now, and her foster parents had retired to Florida, they still emailed and texted on a semi-regular basis. But it wasn't the same as having a real family.

The last pinkish whispers of dusk filtered through the blinds as Holly gazed down into the matching cribs at her sleeping sons. An overwhelming feeling of love filled the chambers of her heart. She'd never known it was possible to feel such an intense connection to another person. She would hands down give her life for them.

They would be three months old tomorrow, meaning Jeremy had been gone almost a month now. It broke her heart that they would never know their father. Her marriage to Jeremy hadn't been perfect, or easy, but the good relationships never were. She just hadn't realized how *im*perfect it actually had been.

Was it better that he had died now rather than in a year or two? Had not knowing him spared the twins undue heartache? Or would they go through life with a hole in their hearts that never would be filled?

Could you miss someone you'd never known?

Holly remembered all too well what it had been like after her parents died. She had learned to cope, but it was the sort of thing a person never really got over. It was always in the back of her mind. The unfairness of it. The deep feeling of emptiness. Knowing that she was truly alone. But now that she had the boys, she would never be alone again.

She walked across the room to where the ring had landed and bent over to pick it up. It had always felt clunky and heavy on her hand. Too big and flashy. That was Jeremy's taste, not hers. She would have been content with one carat or less. He'd refused to tell her what it cost, but it must have been thousands. Tens of thousands, even. Hopefully it was worth at least half that much used.

Instead of sliding the ring back on her finger, she slipped it into the front pocket of her jeans. The landlord had taken pity on her and given her an entire month rent-free to get her affairs in order and find an affordable place. She couldn't put it off any longer. Tomorrow morning she would load the boys in the stroller and take a trip to the jewelers to see what she could get for the ring. She'd run the scenario through her head a million times, and the outcome was always the same. She needed money, and the ring was the only thing she had left of any worth. She didn't even own a car. Which made hauling twins around a challenge.

The only question now was, even if she had the money to get a new apartment, would anyone give her a lease? The credit cards Jeremy had opened in her name were all maxed out and in default, and until she could arrange for some sort of child care, getting a job would be next to impossible. She had no family to help her, no friends willing to take on the task of twins full time, and conventional day care for two infants would be astronomically expensive.

In her chest she felt a tightness, a knot of despair that made it hard to breathe. She'd been through difficult times in the past, but never had she felt this hopeless, this sense of impending doom.

She peered into the cribs one last time, smiling when her gaze settled on the boys' sweet angelic faces. Then she turned on the baby monitor and backed out of the nursery, quietly shutting the door behind her.

She and Jeremy had seriously discussed moving but they'd never gotten the chance. Her morning sickness had been so bad the first four months Holly had spent half her time in bed, and the other half hanging over the commode. In her fifth month, just as she had begun to feel like a human being again, she had gone into premature labor. They'd stopped it just in time, but from that day on she'd been on strict bed rest. It hadn't been easy, but they'd managed. At least, she'd thought they had.

Jeremy had promised her that after the boys were born they would start looking for a house. He'd thought they would buy a fixer-upper in a small cozy town upstate. A place they could make their own. Now she knew that with all of Jeremy's debt, no bank ever would have given them a mortgage. Jeremy must have known it, too.

She felt torn between missing him and wanting to sock him in the nose for not being honest with her. Whatever their problems, they could have worked them out. Why hadn't he just talked to her? It was no secret he'd had trust issues, but they had run deeper than she'd realized. A foster kid himself, Jeremy hadn't been as lucky. He hadn't talked about his past much, but she knew he'd been in the system most of his life, bounced around between group homes and foster homes until he'd ventured out on his own at sixteen. Clearly his past had scarred him more than she'd ever imagined. As his wife she should have known. She should have seen what was happening, right? She could have saved him.

The question was had he wanted to be saved?

She stepped into her bedroom and switched on the light. Their neatly made king-size bed mocked her from across the room. She hadn't slept in it since she'd found Jeremy there. Other than straightening the covers, she hadn't touched it at all. She'd been avoiding the bedroom in general, only going in to grab her clothes, and only because there was no place else in the apartment to store them. She'd been sleeping on an air mattress that she'd first put in the nursery, and recently moved into the living room next to the sofa.

She looked around the room and sighed. She used to love this apartment. Now she could barely wait to leave. Since his death being here felt...wrong. It never would be a home again without Jeremy. His whole life, everything he'd owned in the world, was in that apartment. She was torn between wanting to keep it all and the need for a fresh start.

She grabbed her pajamas and pulled the door closed behind her as she stepped into the hall. It was barely eight o'clock, but these days she slept when the boys slept. That wouldn't be possible when she got a job.

She collapsed onto the sofa, letting her head fall back and her eyes slip closed. She must have gone out instantly, and when she roused to the sound of a knock at the door, it was nearly nine-thirty.

She assumed the visitor was her neighbor Sara from across the hall, who often stopped by after work to chat, so Holly didn't bother checking the peephole. She wasn't exactly in the mood for company, but it would be rude not to say hello.

She pulled open the door, but it wasn't Sara, after all. A man stood there, and though he was facing away, looking down the hall toward the stairs, something about him seemed eerily familiar. Something about the tall, solid build and broad shoulders. The thick, coarse black hair that swirled into a cowlick at the left side of his crown, and the stubborn little tuft that wanted to stand up straight. He would always have to use extra gel—

Her breath caught in her lungs and her heart took a downward dive to the pit of her belly. Oh, God. Whoever this man was, from the back he looked exactly like Jeremy. Except for the clothes. He wore a suit, and Holly had worked in retail long enough to recognize a custom fit when she saw one. The closest Jeremy had ever come to wearing a suit, custom or otherwise, had been dress slacks and a blazer, and then only because she'd forbade him from wearing jeans to the wedding of a good friend. And she'd had to go out and buy the stuff for him.

She'd barely completed the thought when the man turned, and as she saw his face, her world shifted violently. Staring back at her were eyes as familiar as her own, and though she could see his lips moving, his voice sounded muffled and distant, as if someone had stuffed cotton in her ears. Her vision blurred around the edges, then folded in on itself.

It couldn't be, she told herself. Either she was dreaming or having a complete psychotic break. Because this man didn't just look like her dead husband.

He *was* Jeremy.

Before Jason Cavanaugh could inquire as to the identity of the attractive blonde who'd opened the door to the apartment his lawyer claimed had been his brother's, the color leached from her face. Then her eyes went wide and rolled back into her head. He watched helplessly as she crumpled to the floor, her head barely missing the door frame as she went down.

He sighed and mumbled a curse. His prowess with women was legendary, but even he'd never had one fall to his feet in a dead faint.

As an identical twin, this wouldn't be the first time someone had mistaken him for his brother. Though he had never gotten this reaction before. Angry words, yes, and once he'd even had a drink thrown in his face.

He could only imagine what Jeremy had done to this poor girl. Had he charged up all her credit cards and then bailed on her? Slept with her best friend? Or her mother? Or her best friend's mother?

When it came to Jeremy the possibilities were endless. But all Jason wanted was to fetch his brother's belongings, if they hadn't been disposed of already, and head back upstate. He didn't know if there was anything worth keeping, and he wasn't normally the sentimental type, but he had so little left of his brother. Five years ago, after Jeremy had been through another wasted stint in rehab, their father had had enough. He'd disowned Jeremy, disinherited him and purged their home of anything that reminded him of his troubled son. For all the good it had done. And though he knew it was irrational, deep down Jason still blamed himself for Jeremy's downward spiral. Against his father's wishes, Jason had even set up a monthly allowance for his brother, who had no means to support himself. Maybe that had been a mistake, too.

Jason knelt beside the woman, whom he was guessing couldn't be more than twenty-two or three, and touched her cheek. It was warm and it seemed the color was returning to her face. Long brown hair with reddish highlights fanned out around her head and her T-shirt rode up exposing an inch or so of her stomach, making him feel like a voyeur.

"Hey." He gave her shoulder a gentle nudge and she mumbled incoherently. "Wake up."

Her eyes fluttered open, big and blue and full of confusion as they focused on his face. "What happened?"

"You passed out," he said, offering his hand. "Can you sit up?"

"I think so." She grabbed on, her eyes glued to his

face, containing a look caught somewhere between shock and horror. He gave her a gentle boost and though she wobbled a little, squeezing his hand to keep her balance, she managed to stay upright.

"Got it?" he asked.

She nodded and let go, still transfixed. "You look just like him. Except…" She reached up to touch his left brow, grazing it with the tips of her fingers. Her touch was so light it was almost provocative. "No scar."

"No scar," he responded.

She blinked several times, then yanked her hand back, as if just realizing that she was touching a total stranger. "I'm sorry. I just…"

"It's okay." However or wherever Jeremy had gotten the scar, it must have occurred in the past five years. Since the day they were born, it had been next to impossible to tell them apart. They were truly identical in every way.

Well, almost every way.

"Jeremy never told you that he had an identical twin?"

She shook her head, appearing dazed and very confused. "He told me that he didn't have *any* family."

Jason was living proof that he had.

"He lied to me," she said, still shaking her head in disbelief. She looked up at Jason, and in her eyes he could see anger and hurt and a whole lot of confusion. "Why would he do that?"

Jason had asked himself that same question a million times. His brother was dead, and Jason was still cleaning up his messes. He would make amends on Jeremy's behalf. As he had done so many times in the past.

"Maybe I could come in and we could talk," he said, as it was a little awkward crouched down, half in, half out of the apartment. They clearly needed to get a dialogue going so he could assess the damage. However Jeremy had wronged this woman, Jason would fix it.

"Yes, of course," she said.

He rose to his feet and held out a hand to help her. "Need a boost?"

She nodded and, clinging firmly to his hand, slowly rose. She was taller than he'd expected. Maybe five-seven or -eight, putting her at his chin level. She was also excessively thin to the point of looking gaunt, with dark hollows under her eyes.

Jason felt a twinge of reservation. Was she strung out and in need of a fix? Had she supplied drugs to his brother, or had it been the other way around?

Whoa. Wait a minute.

He took a mental step back. He didn't know anything about this woman. It wasn't fair to assume she was into drugs just because his brother had been. That would be guilt by association, of which he himself had been a victim.

She wobbled slightly and he gripped her forearm with his other hand to steady her. "Take it slow."

Still dazed and looking pale, she said, "Maybe I should sit down."

"That's probably not a bad idea." She teetered on long slender legs encased in distressed, figure-hugging denim as he helped her to the sofa several feet away. That was when he saw the mostly empty baby bottles on the coffee table.

Jesus. His brother had sunk low enough to prey on a *single mother*? She wasn't wearing a wedding ring.

The idea made Jason sick to his stomach.

He sat on the edge of the coffee table across from

her, close enough to catch her if she passed out again. "Have you known Jeremy long?"

"A little over a year."

"And you two were…involved?"

She frowned. "He didn't tell you that he was married?"

Married? *Jeremy?* That was truly a shock. "No, he didn't. I haven't talked to my brother in more than five years. Since our father cut him off."

"Then you don't know about the boys."

"Boys?"

"Our sons. Devon and Marshall."

Two

If Jason hadn't already been sitting, the news would have knocked him off his feet. As it was, he felt as if someone had stolen the breath from his lungs.

He'd come here hoping to find a personal memento that would remind him of his brother. An article of clothing, maybe a photograph or two.

Never in his wildest dreams had he expected to find offspring. "My brother had *children*?"

"Twins."

"How old?"

"Nearly three months."

Oh, Jeremy, what have you done? "I'm sorry. I had no idea."

"So the boys have a real family? Aunts and uncles and cousins?"

She looked so hopeful he hated to burst her bubble. From the shadows under her eyes, and her painfully thin appearance, he was guessing life hadn't been kind to her lately. "We have distant relatives in the UK, but I'm the only one of our immediate family left."

"Oh. I don't have family, either, so I thought…" Her obvious disappointment tugged his heartstrings. But then she took a deep breath and forced a smile. Maybe she wasn't as fragile as she appeared. "But they do have you to tell them about their father. You probably knew Jeremy better than anyone."

Most of the time he felt as if he hadn't known Jeremy at all. Not since they'd been kids at least. "What exactly did he tell you about our family?"

"He told me that he had no family. He said he was orphaned as a toddler and grew up in the foster system."

Foster system? Nothing could have been further from the truth. But that was typical for Jeremy.

Jason tamped down the anger building inside him. "What else did he tell you?"

"That he was sick as a child, and because of his illness no one wanted him."

Jason's hackles stood at attention. "Did he say what sort of illness he had?"

"Cancer. He always feared it would come back."

Jason ground his teeth and tried to keep his cool.

"Jeremy did not have cancer. Nor did he grow up in foster care."

They had been raised by their biological parents in a penthouse apartment in Manhattan. There was little he and his brother wanted that they hadn't received. Maybe that had been part of the problem. Jeremy had never had to work for anything.

"He lied to me?" she asked, looking so pale and dumbfounded he worried she might pass out again. "Why?"

"Because that's what Jeremy does." He paused and corrected himself. "Or *did*."

A flash of pain crossed her face, and he felt like a jerk for being so insensitive. She obviously had cared deeply for his brother. But if their marriage was anything like his brother's past romantic relationships, this poor woman didn't know the real Jeremy. "They determined that it was an accidental overdose?"

Teeth wedged into her plump lower lip, she nodded. Her voice was unsteady when she said, "It was a lethal mix of prescription medication."

Jeremy would ingest just about anything that gave him a buzz, but prescription meds had always been his drugs of choice.

"You don't look surprised," she said.

"His addiction was the reason our father cut him off. The arrests, the months he spent in rehab… Nothing helped. He didn't know what else to do." Their father had exhausted every connection he had to keep Jeremy out of jail, when incarceration might have been the best thing for him.

"Why didn't I see it?" she asked, and in her eyes Jason saw a pain, a confusion, that he knew all too well.

"He was good at hiding it."

"At first I thought he was sleeping." Her eyes welled and she inhaled sharply, blinking back the tears. "They tried to revive him, but it was too late."

"There was nothing you could have done. I know it's difficult, but please don't blame yourself."

"That's easy for you to say."

"No, it's not." The way Jeremy behaved was in fact partly due to Jason, and he would never let himself forget that. Although, parallel with the pain of Jeremy's death flowed the relief that he would never hurt anyone again. He wouldn't be around to break his wife's heart. His children would be spared the pain of watching their father self-destruct. His wife was young and pretty, so it was unlikely she would stay single for long. Though the idea of another man raising his brother's children burned like a knife in his side. If anyone was going to take on the responsibility of raising Jeremy's kids, it would be Jason.

He opened his mouth to address her and realized he didn't even know her name. Nor had he told her his. "In all the excitement we weren't properly introduced," he said.

That earned him a cautious smile. "I guess we weren't. I'm Holly Shay."

"Jason Cavanaugh."

He offered his hand and she shook it, hitting him with another confused look. "Cavanaugh? But Jeremy said his last name—" She caught herself, shaking her head in disbelief. "But it wasn't Shay, was it? That was a lie, too."

"You're not the first woman with whom Jeremy—" He hesitated, searching for the least painful explanation "—misrepresented himself."

"So our relationship, our marriage, it was all one big lie?"

Now she was getting the idea. "Have there been financial repercussions?"

She hesitated, but the brief flash of fear and desperation in her eyes was all the answer he needed. Cheating strangers was one thing, but to con his own wife, the mother of his children? "How much did he take you for?"

She lowered her eyes, and when she didn't answer he asked, "Did he leave you in debt?"

With her lip wedged firmly between her teeth, she nodded.

"Considerable debt?"

Again, no answer.

"You can tell me the truth. It isn't going to upset me or hurt my feelings. I accepted a long time ago the sort of man my brother had become. Nothing you can say will shock me." Sadly, that was the honest truth.

She finally looked him in the eye, chin held high, and said, "I'm devastated financially. The only thing of value that I have left is my wedding ring. If it's even a real diamond."

At the mention of a ring Jason sat up straighter. Could it be possible? "Can I see it?"

"I have it right here actually." She reached into the front pocket of her jeans and pulled out the ring. Jason's heart skipped a beat. And here he'd thought that was gone forever, too. Traded for cash or drugs or God knew what else. He'd be damned if Jeremy had had a conscience after all.

"It's definitely real," he told her.

"How can you tell?"

"Because this ring belonged to my mother."

Holly was so screwed.

That ring had been her only hope to claw her way out of this financial abyss, but knowing that it had belonged to Jason's deceased mother she couldn't sell it now. She wouldn't be able to live with herself.

"Jeremy was the oldest by seven minutes, so when our mother died it went to him," Jason said. "It's been in our family for generations."

And that's where it should stay.

With a heavy heart, she held out the ring to Jason. "You should have this back."

"You're Jeremy's wife," he said. "The mother of his children. It belongs to you now."

If only that were true. She may have been his wife, but she obviously hadn't had a clue who he was. "Please, just take it."

Looking uncertain, Jason took the ring. "Are you sure?"

"Absolutely."

The thick platinum band and enormous stones looked so small in his big hand. "Honestly, I figured Jeremy had probably sold it years ago. I never thought I would see it again."

He slipped it into the inside pocket of his suit jacket. With it went all of her hopes and dreams of a decent start for her and her boys. What would she do now? File bankruptcy? Go on public assistance? Live in a shelter? Or on the street in a cardboard box?

Jason must have sensed her distress. His brow furrowed with concern, he asked, "Are you okay?"

"Fine," she said, pasting on a good face, the way she had for Jeremy, who'd never questioned the sincerity of her words. He'd believed anything she'd told him if it meant keeping the peace. Especially near the end.

Jason was clearly not at all like his brother.

"You don't look fine," he said, studying her, his eyes and his face, even his expression, so much like Jeremy's, but different somehow. "If it's money you're worried about, don't."

Someone had to. And talk of her dismal finances was making her uncomfortable.

"My money issues are really not your problem," she

said, letting him off the hook, thinking that would end the conversation.

"I'm making them my problem," he said firmly.

Whoa. His look said he wasn't playing around, but neither was she. "That's not necessary, but I appreciate the offer."

It was as if he hadn't even heard her. "I'll take care of your debt and give you whatever you need to get back on your feet."

Nope, not gonna happen. From the time she'd left her foster home until she'd married Jeremy, she'd survived completely on her own. It hadn't always been easy, but she'd managed. It was clear now that trusting Jeremy with their finances had been a terrible mistake. One she wouldn't be making again with anyone else. For all she knew Jason could be like his brother. He *seemed* genuine, but so had Jeremy. "I can't let you do that."

He watched her intently for several seconds, as if he were trying to decide if he could change her mind. Apparently he didn't think so. "If that's what you want."

"It is." She would get by somehow. She always had. Of course, back then, she hadn't had twin infants to consider.

"At least allow me to cover the funeral costs," he said. "I owe Jeremy that much. And his children."

If she let him it would shave off a fair chunk of her current financial responsibility. And maybe it would bring Jason closure. Everyone deserved that, right?

She shoved her pride aside long enough to say, "That would be okay."

He looked both sad and relieved. He was extremely attractive, but of course she would think that since he looked just like her husband, whose chiseled features and long lean physique had caught her eye the instant he'd walked into the party where they'd met. She'd never slept with a man on the first date, but she had gone home with him that night.

The sex itself hadn't been mind-blowing, but it had been nice. What she'd really liked, even more than the physical part, was just being near him. She'd liked the way his lips moved when he spoke, the inquisitive arch of his right brow. She'd loved the feel of her hand in his. He'd made her feel safe.

At first.

Unfortunately, as her pregnancy had progressed and her condition had become more fragile, he hadn't been able to cope. Instead of taking care of her, assuring her that everything would be okay, she had been the one constantly soothing his anxieties and fears.

She'd convinced herself that once the boys were born, things would go back to normal. But even after the twins were home from the hospital and out of danger, Jeremy's temperament had continued to deteriorate until she'd felt as if she had three children and no husband. Some days he hadn't even gotten out of bed, and he'd begun to resent the twins for taking up all of her time. He'd even accused her of loving the children more than she loved him.

She'd kept waiting for things to change, for him to go back to being the sweet, sensitive and attentive man she'd married. How could she have known that that man had never existed?

"If you hadn't talked to Jeremy in so long, how did you know he'd died?" she asked Jason.

"I got a call from my attorney. For the first time in five years his allowance went untouched for over a month. I knew something had to be wrong."

Holly's jaw fell and her heart broke all over again. "He had an allowance?"

"You didn't know," he said, and she shook her head, feeling sick all the way to her soul.

She was beginning to wonder if Jeremy had told her the truth about anything.

"I apologize if I'm getting too personal," Jason said. "But where did you think the money was coming from? Did he have a job?"

"He told me that he had been in a terrible car accident when he was a teenager that permanently damaged his back. He claimed the money was from a lawsuit settlement. But there was no accident, was there? And no settlement."

Jason actually cringed, as if it pained him to admit the truth. "Not that I know of."

Had any of it been real? Had Jeremy honestly loved her and the boys? Had he even been capable of that kind of love?

"Will you be staying here, in the city?" Jason asked.

The idea of how and where she would find an affordable apartment without a job or money filled her heart with dread. "I—I don't know. Yet."

"I'd like the chance to get to know my nephews. They are the only family I have left."

"Of course. I would love that. I'm just… Suffice it to say that things are a little up in the air right now. But as soon as we're settled I'll let you know."

Though she tried to put on a good face, Jason's look of skepticism said he wasn't buying it. He studied her with the same stormy blue eyes as his brother. So alike, yet not. "You have nowhere to go, do you?"

She squared her shoulders and lifted her chin, saying with a confidence she was nowhere close to feeling, "I'll find something."

"You mentioned selling the ring. Do you have any other resources? Was there life insurance?"

If only. But that wasn't his problem. "We'll get by."

"I'll take that as a no." He sighed and shook his head, mumbling under his breath. "He left you with nothing, didn't he?"

No, he'd left her with something. A big old pile of debt and two very hungry mouths to feed. She lowered her gaze, clasping her hands in her lap so he wouldn't see that they were trembling. "We'll manage."

"How?"

She blinked. "Excuse me?"

"How will you manage? What's your plan?"

Good question. "Well… I haven't figured *everything* out yet, but I will."

When she'd met Jeremy she had just moved to New York and had been staying with the brother of a friend back home in Florida, where she'd been raised. At the time, meeting Jeremy had felt like destiny. But now, with her life in shambles, if it wasn't for her precious boys, she might have wished she'd never met him.

Though her tone conveyed the utmost confidence, Holly's eyes told an entirely different tale. Jason could see that deep down she was scared—terrified even—at the prospect of supporting herself and his nephews. But she was clearly in no position to support herself, much less twin infants. And he was in the perfect position to help her. If she would only let him.

His biggest hurdle would be her pride, which she seemed to possess in excess. But he had learned long ago that there was a very fine line between pride and irresponsibility.

He heard the wail of an infant and realized it was coming from the baby monitor on the coffee table. Then a pair of wails, like baby stereo.

Holly sighed, looking exhausted and overwhelmed, and Jason wondered how long it had been since she'd had a decent night's sleep. He could only imagine how difficult life had been for her lately, being a recent widow with twins. And then along he'd come to tell her that everything she knew about her husband was a lie.

Talk about rubbing salt in the wound.

"Would you like to meet your nephews?" she asked.

His heart jumped in his chest at the prospect of meeting twins who were now his only family. "Of course I would."

She pushed herself up from the couch, wobbling slightly before she caught her balance. She flashed him a weak smile and said, "Still a little woozy, I guess."

And who could blame her? He rose, prepared to catch her if she fell over or, God forbid, lost consciousness again, as he didn't have the first clue what to do with a screaming infant. Let alone two screaming infants. He followed closely behind her, and as she opened the bedroom door, it was obvious that both his nephews had healthy lungs. He never would have imagined that anything so small could make such a racket.

She switched on the light and Jason held his breath as he peeked over her shoulder into the cribs at his nephews. There was no doubt they took after his side of the family. It was like looking at photos of himself and his brother at that age.

Holly lifted one wailing infant and then turned to

Jason and held the little boy out to him. "Jason, meet Devon," she said.

Jason just stood there, unsure of what to do.

"He won't bite," Holly said.

Jason took the infant under the arms and he quieted instantly. He looked so tiny and fragile wrapped in Jason's big hands, his blue eyes wide. And he hardly weighed anything.

"This little complainer is Marshall," she said, lifting him from the other crib. She propped him on her shoulder and patted his back, which did nothing to stop his wailing. He must have been the feistier of the two.

"Marshall was our grandfather's name," Jason told her.

Holly turned to him, saw the way he was holding her son and smiled. "You know, he won't break."

"I've never held a child this small," Jason admitted, feeling completely out of his element. In business he'd dealt with some of the most powerful people in the country, yet he had no idea what to do with this tiny, harmless human being. "He looks so fragile. What if I drop him?"

"You won't," she said, and he hoped her confidence wasn't misplaced.

Noting the way Holly held Marshall over her shoulder, he set Devon against his chest, placing one hand under his diapered behind and the other on his back to steady him. But he realized as Devon lifted his little head off Jason's shoulder to stare at him, blue eyes wide and inquisitive, he wasn't as fragile as he looked.

Jason watched Holly as she laid Marshall, who was still howling, on the changing table and deftly changed his diaper, cooing and talking to him in a quiet, soothing voice, her smile so full of love and affection Jason kind of wished she would smile at him that way.

She's your sister-in-law, he reminded himself. But damn, she was pretty. In an unspoiled, wholesome way.

Women, as he saw it, were split between two categories. There were the ones who wanted the traditional life of marriage and babies, and those who balked at the mention of commitment. He preferred the latter. For some people, marriage and family just weren't in the cards.

Holly turned to Jason, held out her son and said, "Switch."

It was an awkward handover, and Marshall hollered the entire time Jason held him. It was hard not to take it personally.

"Would you like to help me feed them?"

"I don't know how."

"There's nothing to it," she assured him with a smile. After all she had been through, the fact that she still could smile was remarkable.

Feeling completely out of his element, Jason sat on the couch while his nephew sucked hungrily on a bottle and stared up at him.

Although not by choice, children had never been a part of his life plan, so he usually did what he could to avoid them. But if he was going to be a good uncle, he supposed he should at least try to learn to care for them. If, God forbid, something were to happen to Holly, they would be his sole responsibility. And then, if something were to happen to him, if his illness were to return, who would take them?

The idea was both humbling and terrifying.

This was the absolute last place he had expected to end up when he'd left home today.

Their bottoms dry and their bellies full, the boys fell sound sleep, and Jason helped her put them in their cribs.

"How often do you have to do that?" he asked Holly as she stood at the sink rinsing the empty bottles.

"Every three hours. Sometimes more, sometimes less. They've never slept more than a four-hour stretch."

That would be an average of eight times a day. Two babies, all by herself.

He had a sudden newfound respect for single mothers.

"How do you manage it alone?"

Her tone nonchalant, she said, "I've learned to multitask."

He had the feeling it was a bit more complicated than that. How was she supposed to get a job with the boys to care for? Day care, he supposed. Call him old-fashioned, but he wanted to see his nephews raised by their mother, the way he and his brother had been raised by theirs. He had nothing but fond memories of his early childhood. Life had been close to perfect back then.

Until it hadn't been anymore.

She finished the bottles and wiped her hands on a dish towel. "Thanks for the help."

"Anytime," he said, and he meant it. "In fact, I'll be back in the city next week and I was hoping I could spend some time with the boys."

"You don't live in New York?"

"After our father died I moved upstate." The lake house had been in their family for generations and had been his favorite retreat as a child.

"Jeremy used to talk about us moving upstate, getting a house in a small town. A fixer-upper that we could make ours. With a big yard and a swing set for the boys. I can't help thinking that was probably a lie, too."

Sadly, it probably was. Jeremy had preferred the anonymity of living in a big city. Not to mention the ease with which he could support his drug habit. Something told Jason that wouldn't have changed.

Jason always had been the one who'd strived for a slower-paced lifestyle. Ten years of working for his father had landed him on the business fast track, but his heart had never really been in it. Only after his father's death had he started living the life he'd wanted.

"You and the boys should come and visit me," he told her, surprised and hopeful when her eyes lit.

"I'd like that. But are you sure you have the space? I don't want to put you out."

At first he thought she was joking, and then he remembered that she knew virtually nothing about their family. Or their finances. Maybe for right now it would be better if he didn't bring up the fact that her sons stood to inherit millions someday. It might be too much to take all in one night. And though Jeremy had been disinherited years ago, he would see that Holly and the boys were well cared for.

"I have space," he assured her. Maybe once he got her there, once she saw how much room he had and how good life would be there for them, he could convince her to stay, giving him the chance to right the last wrong his brother would ever commit. He owed it to his nephews.

And to himself.

Three

Jason sat at the bar of The Trapper Tavern, the town watering hole, nursing an imported beer with his best friend and attorney Lewis Pennington.

"Are you sure you can trust her?" Lewis asked him after he explained the situation with his sister-in-law and nephews. "I don't have to tell you the sort of people with whom your brother kept company. She could be conning you."

Jason didn't think so. "Lewis, she was so freaked out she actually fainted when she saw me, and she seemed to genuinely have no clue who Jeremy really was."

"Or she's as good an actor as your brother."

"Or she's an innocent victim."

"With your flesh and blood involved, is that a chance you really want to take?"

Of course not. The day his brother died was the day the twins' happiness and well-being had become Jason's responsibility. "That's why, when she's here, I'm going to ask her to stay with me. Until she's back on her feet financially."

He'd left Holly his phone number and told her to call if she needed anything. She'd called the next morning sounding tired and exasperated, asking to take him up on his offer to visit, saying she needed a few days away from the city. In the background he could hear his nephews howling. He admired the fact that she wasn't afraid to admit she needed help. And he was more than happy to supply it. That and so much more.

"My point is that you know nothing about this woman," Lewis said. "Don't let the fact that she's the mother of your nephews cloud your judgment."

"With a brother like Jeremy, I've learned to be a pretty good judge of character."

"Maybe so, but I'd hide the good china, just in case."

Jason shot him a look.

"At least let me run a background check, search for a criminal history."

"If you insist, but I doubt you'll find anything."

"When is her train due in?"

Jason glanced at his watch. "An hour."

He'd offered to drive to the city and pick up her and the boys at her apartment, but she'd insisted they take the train. And when he'd tried to talk her out of it, she'd only dug her heels in deeper. Though he barely knew her, he could see that persuading her to do something she didn't want to do was going to be difficult, if not impossible.

"If she's so destitute, why not just pay her debt and set her up in her own place in town? What woman wouldn't go for that?"

The kind who was too proud for her own good. And

as much as it annoyed him, he couldn't help but respect that. "I offered to pay all the debt Jeremy left her with and help her get a fresh start."

"And?"

He took a long swallow of his beer, then set the bottle down on the bar. "She wouldn't take a penny."

Lewis's brows rose in surprise. "Seriously?"

"She wouldn't budge."

"She's independent?"

That was putting it mildly. "You have no idea."

"Attractive?"

Immensely. "That's irrelevant."

Lewis grinned. "Are you attracted to her?"

Hell yes, he was. Who wouldn't be? "She's my sister-in-law. My feelings are irrelevant."

"Not if you plan to live under the same roof with her. Feelings have a way of happening whether we want them to or not."

"My only concern is for my nephews."

"What if you ask her to stay with you and she refuses?"

"Obviously I can't force her."

"That's not necessarily true."

Jason frowned. "What do you mean?"

"You have leverage."

"Leverage?"

"Your nephews. You could threaten to sue her for custody."

"On what grounds? She seems perfectly competent to me." Not to mention the damage it would cause the twins, first losing their father, then being ripped away from their mother.

"If she's as destitute as you claim, the last thing she'll

want is a legal battle. The threat of one could make her more likely to cooperate."

Or put her right over the edge. He did worry that getting her cooperation would be difficult, but he couldn't imagine ever taking it to that extreme. However, if there was any validity to Lewis's suspicions, Jason could be downright ruthless if it meant keeping his nephews safe. But there was no need to jump the gun. Unlike his father, who had been quick to judge and considered anyone he didn't know well a potential threat, Jason preferred to grant people the benefit of the doubt. Innocent until proven guilty. But he knew he could never convince Lewis that she was telling the truth, so he didn't even try.

"How is Miranda?" he asked his friend.

Lewis sighed and rolled his eyes. "All whacked out on hormones again."

Lewis and his wife had been trying unsuccessfully to conceive a baby over the course of their three-year marriage. They had tried every method, be it Western medicine or holistic, with no success. They were now on their third IVF attempt in nine months, and it had been emotionally taxing on them both. Though more so on Miranda, Jason imagined. Lewis had a teenage son from a former relationship, someone to carry on his legacy.

Jason found it ironic that Jeremy, who'd lacked the integrity to care for his own sons, had had no problem at all conceiving a child, while good people such as Lewis and Miranda, who had everything to offer a son or daughter, were helpless to make it happen.

"When is the next procedure?" Jason asked.

"Next Friday," Lewis said, eyes on the thirty-year-old scotch that he swirled in his glass. "And regardless of the outcome, it will be our last."

"What?" Jason set down his bottle a little harder than he'd meant to. "You're just going to give up?"

"After three years the perpetual disappointment is taking a toll on us both. We've begun to look into foreign adoption instead."

"Another time-consuming process," Jason said and Lewis nodded.

"But when we're approved, at least there will be a light at the end of the tunnel."

"Have you considered a surrogate?"

"Only to have her change her mind after the baby is born? It would destroy Miranda."

Yes, it probably would. "I'm sorry, Lewis. I wish there was something I could do."

"We'll get through this."

Jason didn't envy their situation. Though it had taken years of introspection and soul searching, he'd come to terms with the fact that he would never have a family of his own. Now it would seem he'd earned one by default.

Longest. Trip. Ever.

Despite Holly's hope that the twins would sleep most of the five-hour train ride, they had fussed and complained, sleeping in fits and bursts, and generally making a nuisance of themselves. By the time Holly got them in the stroller and ready to depart the train, she'd expended the last of her energy and was running on pure adrenaline, wishing she had taken Jason up on his offer to give them a ride. But now as she sat in Jason's black luxury SUV, the boys buckled safely in the back, that adrenaline was wearing thin.

After today it was abundantly clear that if Holly was

going to make it as a single mom of twins, she was going to have to sock away her pride and learn to accept help a little more often. For the twins' sake. They were a handful now, but what about when they began to crawl and walk and get into things? Just the idea made her weary. She knew she should be in New York looking for a job and a place to live, and taking this vacation was irresponsible and selfish, but her sanity depended on it.

While Jason loaded their bags in the back, she looked over her shoulder into the backseat, peering into the boy's car seats. They were both out cold. She would have wept with relief, but she didn't have the energy.

"Rough trip?" Jason asked as he opened the driver's side door and climbed in, flashing her a smile. One she felt from the ends of her hair to the tips of her toes and everywhere in between.

Whoa. Where the heck had that come from? She turned away, pretending to look out the window at the station, hoping he wouldn't notice her conspicuously rosy cheeks. It wasn't helping matters that he smelled absolutely delicious, like some manly musk drifting on a warm spring breeze.

She tried to fight it, but it was hopeless. Ribbons of heat twisted through her veins, making her skin flush. Making her feel restless and aroused.

In all the time she had been with Jeremy, Holly had never experienced this intense physical reaction from a simple smile. To be fair, she hadn't had sex in over six months, though it felt more like a year. Or five.

Her cheeks burned hotter. She really shouldn't be thinking about sex right now. But the harder she tried not to think about it, the further her mind strayed.

"Everyone buckled and ready to go?" Jason asked her as the engine roared to life. She could feel his eyes on her; she had no choice but to face him. The alternative was to act rudely.

Willing away the heat rushing to her face, she turned to him, her gaze instantly locking on his stormy eyes. Though it was wildly bizarre, she didn't look at Jason and see Jeremy anymore. They may have been identical in looks, but his personality and disposition set Jason apart from his brother.

His brow wrinkled. "Are you feeling okay? You're flushed."

Aw, hell. "I'm fine. Really. Just tired."

Concern etching the corners of his eyes, Jason reached up to touch her burning hot cheek with his cool, surprisingly rough fingers, then frowned and pressed the back of his hand to her forehead, the way her mom had when Holly was a little girl. "You're warm."

No kidding. She was surprised her face hadn't melted off. And the fact that he kept touching her wasn't helping matters.

He was dressed much more casually today, in dark slacks and a white polo shirt that contrasted sharply with his deeply tanned face. Considering it was only the first week of June, she was guessing he spent a considerable amount of time outdoors. If she lived near a lake, she probably would, too. As a young teen one of her favorite pastimes had been going fishing with her foster dad and siblings. She had always hoped someday she would be able to share those experiences with her own children.

"We have to go through town to get to my place," Jason told her as he pulled out of the lot. "Do you need to stop for anything or would you prefer to go straight to the house?"

"House, please. How far is it from town?"

"Ten minutes, give or take. I'm on the far side of the lake."

Trapper Cove, which was indeed tucked back into a cove off Trapper Lake, was just as she always pictured a small upstate New York town to look. Quaint and clean and undeniably upscale. She rolled her window down and took a deep breath of fresh lake air. So different from the city.

As they headed down Main Street into the heart of the town, Jason gave her a brief history lesson on the various shops and businesses. They passed a marina and boat launch, and a members' only yacht club. On the water she counted at least a dozen of what her foster brother, Tyler, would have called "big ass" boats. He also would have commented on the luxury import cars lining the pristine streets. She wondered if the area had been this posh when Jason and Jeremy were kids. When Jeremy supposedly had been living on the streets and begging for food.

Just thinking his name made her heart hurt. It still astounded her how many lies he'd told, and how she had been married to a man she didn't even know. Looking back, which she had been doing an awful lot since she'd met Jason, she realized that life with Jeremy had never been a fantastic love story. They'd met and started to date, and three months later she'd found herself pregnant. When Jeremy had insisted on marrying her she'd thought the true love part would come later, when they got to know one another better. Clearly she had been wrong. She hadn't known him at all. The man she thought she'd fallen in love with didn't even exist.

Never in her life had she felt so betrayed.

As they drove slowly through the center of town,

people stopped to wave and shout hello to Jason, and she received more than a few curious glances.

"It's a beautiful town," she told him. "You seem to know a lot about it. And a lot of people."

"Jeremy and I spent every summer here as kids with our mom and grandparents. Our dad came up on weekends when he could get away from work."

She couldn't imagine a more ideal setting to spend her summers. Or her winters. Or springs and falls, as well. "So you live here year round now?"

"I do."

"Are you close to the lake?"

"About as close as you can get without living in a house boat."

She blinked with surprise. "You live *on* the lake?"

"Straight across from town."

She peered out the car window across the lake. She could barely make out the silhouette of homes tucked back against the thick forest bordering the shore; at this distance she could see very little detail. Among them, nearly hidden behind a row of towering pine trees, stood what appeared to be some sort of enormous and rustic-looking wood structure. Maybe a hotel or hunting lodge. It was too huge to be someone's home.

"Can you see your house from here?" she asked him, as they passed the Trapper Drugstore and The Trapper Inn. Beside that sat the Trapper Tavern.

"Barely," he said. "I'll point it out to you the next time we're in town."

He left Main Street and the town behind and turned onto a densely wooded two-lane road that circled the lake. Mottled sunshine danced across the windshield through breaks in the trees, and every so often she could see snippets of clear blue lake. The earthy scents of the forest filled the car. It was so dark and quiet and peaceful. She closed her eyes and breathed in deep, and like magic she could feel the knots in her muscles releasing, her frayed nerves mending. For the first time since Jeremy died she was giving herself permission to relax.

It felt strange, but in a good way.

After several minutes Jason steered the vehicle down a long and bumpy dirt road. "There's something you don't see in the city," Jason said, pointing to a family of deer foraging just off the road. They were almost close enough to reach out the car window and touch.

The trees opened up to a small clearing, and towering over them stood what she had assumed was a lodge, so deeply tucked into the surrounding forest, the dark wood exterior seemed to blend in with the vegetation. But as they pulled up to the front entrance, she could see that this was no lodge. This was a house. A really *huge* house.

She took a deep breath and willed herself not to freak out. She should have known. Most people of modest means did not spend their summers at the lake house. That in itself should have been her first clue that Jason's family was well-to-do. But she never would have guessed that they had done this well.

The summers that Jeremy had claimed he'd spent living on the street, begging for food, he'd actually been here, in a *mansion*?

Holly felt sick all the way to her bones. Any lingering traces of love or respect for her dead husband fizzled away. She had never been more deeply saddened or utterly disappointed in anyone.

Jason parked close to the door, cut the engine and turned to her, watching expectantly when he said, "Home sweet home."

Four

Holly peered out the car window, craning to see way, way, way up three floors of towering wood beams and glass. She had never seen a house with so many huge windows. The view from inside had to be incredible. The house somehow managed to look traditional and modern at the same time.

And here she had worried that being in close quarters with her brother-in-law might be awkward. "I guess you weren't exaggerating when you said you had room for us."

Jason winced a little. "It wasn't my intention to blindside you."

"You just didn't want to overwhelm me. I get it."

"You're not angry?"

She smiled and shook her head. How could she be? His intentions were good and his heart in the right place, and in her opinion that was all that mattered.

Besides, to learn the depth of Jeremy's lies in one huge dose would have been too much to bear in her fragile state. Spoon-feeding her small bites of the truth made it a little easier to digest.

The front door opened and an older couple stepped outside. After a brief moment of confusion, Holly realized that they must work for Jason. A dwelling this enormous would obviously require a staff.

They met her at the car door as she climbed out.

"You must be Holly," the woman said with a distinct New England accent, taking Holly's hand and pumping it enthusiastically. "We're so pleased to finally meet you."

"Holly, this is Faye and George Henderson," Jason told her.

If she had to guess, Holly would put the couple somewhere in their early to mid-sixties. "It's so nice to meet you both."

"Aye-yup," George said in a voice as rough and craggy as his weathered face. He was a huge man, even taller than Jason and impressively muscular for someone of his advanced age.

"Now let me see those little angels I've heard so much about," Faye said, rubbing her palms together, eyes sparkling. She was small in stature, but there was a sturdiness about her that said she wasn't afraid of hard work.

Jason opened the car door and Faye peered inside, gasping softly, tears welling in her eyes. "Oh, Holly, they're beautiful. Your parents would have been so proud, Jason. Wouldn't they, George?"

George peered over his wife's shoulder into the backseat. "Aye-yup. They surely would."

"Let's get Holly settled into her room," Jason said.

He and Faye helped with the boys, who didn't even rouse, while George took care of the bags. The interior of the house was open concept, and with all of those enormous windows, felt like an extension of the forest. With its massive stone fireplace and overstuffed furniture, the decor was an eclectic cross of country cottage and shabby chic. In the center of the first floor stood a staircase like she'd never seen before. At least five feet wide, with lacquered tree branch banisters, it wound its way up to the second floor. Holly followed Jason up, her legs feeling like limp noodles.

At the top was a large, open area with more overstuffed, comfortable looking furniture, its walls lined floor-to-the ceiling with richly stained bookcases, their shelves sagging under the weight of volumes and volumes of books. She had never seen so many outside of a library.

Another set of those enormous windows boasted a breathtaking view of the lake, and below, off the back of the house, a multi-level deck.

To the left was a hallway that led to the bedrooms and on the opposite side, another smaller set of stairs.

"This is incredible," she told Jason, who had lugged Devon, still sound asleep in his car seat, and the diaper bag up the stairs. "I can understand why you wanted to stay here instead of the city."

"I've always considered this my true home," he said, leading her down the short hallway to the bedrooms. As she peered in through each doorway, she could see that the rooms were spacious and tastefully decorated. Warm and homey and comfortable, but in a refined, upscale way.

"Which room is yours?" she asked, and the idea of

him sleeping just a door or two away made her heart jump in her chest. But he pointed up, to the ceiling.

"I'm upstairs in the loft."

Wow. *Another* floor? This was a whole lot of house for one guy.

"Here's the nursery," he said, shouldering the door open.

Nursery? Why would a single guy need a nursery?

The truth was she knew very little about his life. She knew he'd never been married and had no children. Whether that was by choice or circumstance she didn't know. But she could see that the furnishings in the nursery were far too modern and pristine to be anything but brand-new.

"You bought furniture," she said, and from the looks of it, every other baby accessory that she might possibly need. And there were two of everything. Two cribs, two chests of drawers. Even two closets. And lots of toys. A child would want for nothing in this room. "It's perfect."

He set the car seat on the floor next to one of the cribs. "I'd like to take credit, but Faye is the genius behind this. I didn't have a clue what you would need."

"It was nothing," Faye said, waving away the compliment with a flick of her wrist as she crouched down to unbuckle Marshall from his car seat.

"You did all this for one little visit?" Holly asked Jason.

He turned to her. "The first visit of many, I'm hoping."

He smiled, and something in his eyes, in the way he looked at her, made her feel all warm and gooey inside. They stood that way for several seconds, just looking at each other, and though it sounded silly even to herself, she could swear that for an instant time stood still.

"Why don't you show Holly to her room while I tend to the boys?" Faye said, lifting a passed out Marshall from his car seat and onto her shoulder.

Holly tore her gaze away from Jason. "I can get them."

"Nonsense," Faye said. "You're obviously exhausted. You get yourself settled while I take care of these little angels."

If she had been on the train with them, she might not be so quick to call them angels.

Holly started to follow Jason out, but hesitated at the door, looking back at her sons. Since they'd come home from the hospital they had barely been out of her sight. And though they were perfectly healthy now and growing like weeds, leaving them in someone else's care made her palms sweat.

"You go on along," Faye said with an understanding smile. "They'll be fine. I practically raised Jason and Jeremy."

Learn to accept help, she chanted, and forced herself to say, "Okay, thank you."

Her room was the next one over. It was enormous, with its own full bathroom and walk-in closet. The furniture was knotty pine, and the king-size bed was draped with a huge, hand-sewn quilt.

"I think this room alone is bigger than my entire apartment," she told Jason. "It's a beautiful house. Thank you for letting us visit."

"You're welcome anytime." He smiled and she got that warm squishy feeling again, as if her insides had started to melt and were getting all mixed together. It was difficult to look at him without getting caught up in the blue of his eyes. She couldn't recall Jeremy's eyes ever captivating her this way.

She was just tired. And confused. Things would be clearer after she'd had a few hours of sleep. She hoped.

Jason must have read her mind. "Would you like to lie down for a while?"

Oh, would she ever. She crossed to the bed and ran her hand over the quilt. It was so pretty that she was afraid she might damage it. "It will be nice sleeping in a real bed again. An air mattress just isn't the same."

He looked confused. "You don't have a bed?"

"I do, but that was where…you know, I found him."

He winced a little. "Sorry, I didn't realize."

"And there was no way you could have known."

"I guess we haven't really talked about that," he said.

No, but they probably should, just to get it out of the way. She sat on the edge of the bed. "There isn't much to tell, really. When I first walked in I thought he was just taking a nap. As I got closer to the bed I could sense that something was wrong. Then I…" She stopped to swallow the lump in her throat. "He was cold to the touch, so I knew it had been awhile…"

He winced again, as if hearing the events of his brother's death pained him. And why wouldn't that be the case? Despite Jeremy's shortcomings, they were still twin brothers, identical in almost every way.

"I'm sorry," Jason said. "I didn't mean to dredge that up."

Not a day passed—hell, not even an hour—when she didn't see in her mind the image of her husband lying there. Nothing he could have done, no lie he could have told, would make her wish him dead. And though his death still upset her, her feelings had changed so drastically since she'd learned the truth. Those first few weeks had been torture, and she had missed him so terribly, but then, in a small way, she had begun to feel almost relieved. Not that he was dead, but that she would no longer have to deal with his erratic mood swings.

"I knew," Jason said, sitting down on the bed beside her. "I could *feel* that something was wrong, if that makes any sense."

"That's not unusual for twins, is it?"

"I could *always* feel his presence. Even when we were thousands of miles apart. Then he was just... gone." He turned to look at her and there was so much sadness in his eyes she wanted to hug him, but that felt like crossing a line.

"Now it feels as though a part of me is missing. Like it's just, if you'll pardon the expression, *dead space*."

"I can't even imagine being that close to another person."

"It's the sort of thing you don't think about, or even notice, until it's not there anymore."

"I'm so sorry," she said, laying a hand on his arm. He glanced at her hand, then up at her face, and there was a look in his eyes like...well, she couldn't say for sure what sort of look it was, but she knew that it made her insides feel funny.

"The twins are asleep," Faye said as she stepped into the room. Holly snatched her hand from Jason's arm, feeling a bit as if they'd been caught doing something naughty. Which they hadn't been. At all. Still she felt compelled to explain. But she didn't.

"Thank you," Holly said and left it at that.

"Is there anything I can do for you before I start dinner?" Faye asked. "Anything you need?"

"Just a nap."

Faye smiled. "Make it a quick one. Dinner is in one hour."

When she was gone, Holly told Jason, "She's so nice."

"She's thrilled to have you here. So is George. He's just not as likely to show it."

He did look like the strong silent type, a lot like her foster dad had been. A gentle giant. Holly sighed and rubbed her temples, longing for rest, but she was too wired to sleep.

"Headache?" Jason asked her, and she nodded. "I think there's a bottle of pain reliever in the bathroom. Let me go look."

"I can—" Before she could offer to do it herself he was halfway to the bathroom. "—Or not."

Just to test out the bed, Holly swung her legs around and lay down, her head sinking into the pillow.

Oh. My. God. She'd never been on a mattress so comfortable. It was like a little slice of heaven. She dared to close her eyes for just a second, knowing she should check on the boys. And that was the last thing she remembered.

Bottle of ibuprofen and a glass of water in hand, Jason walked back into the bedroom, but it was too late. Holly was out cold and snoring softly. She was so pretty and wholesome-looking that it damn near knocked his socks off. And sweet. Far too sweet and earnest for her own good. Her marriage to Jeremy was proof of that. It was a relief to know that with him, she and his nephews would be safe and well taken care of.

He set the bottle and glass on the table beside the bed in case she woke and needed them. He took a quick peek in the nursery, but didn't go in. Both boys seemed to be sleeping soundly, and he didn't want to risk waking them.

His phone started to ring and he quickly stepped into the hallway. It was Lewis.

"I did the background check."

That was quick. He wondered if that was a good or bad thing. "And?"

"She is who she says she is. She has no criminal record. Hell, as far as I can tell she's never had so much as a speeding ticket."

Jason had expected as much, but it was a relief to know for sure.

"I also looked into her financial status."

Now this was the part Jason wanted to hear. *"And?"*

"It's bad."

His gut clenched. "How bad?"

"Credit cards, personal loans, student loans. And they're all in default. Her credit rating is in the toilet."

Jason cursed. "How much in total."

Lewis told him the sum and Jason cursed again. *Jesus, Jeremy, why? Why her?*

Jason knew what he had to do, and he wouldn't be satisfied, wouldn't be able to sleep at night, until he made this right. "Pay it off. All of it."

"I thought she didn't want you to do that."

"I don't care. Just take care of it."

"If that's what you really want."

"It is."

He hung up and headed downstairs to talk to Faye. He found her in the kitchen waiting for him. She stood with her arms crossed, foot tapping, wearing her exactly-what-do-you-think-you're-doing-mister face. She may have been a small woman, but she was a force to be reckoned with.

And though he had a pretty good idea why she was in such a snit, he shrugged and said, *"What?"*

"You know that I don't like to meddle—"

He laughed. "Yes, you do."

Since his mother had passed away, Faye had taken it upon herself to, as she put it, keep Jason honest. Not that it was ever necessary, as he was the twin who never went against the grain. He did exactly what was expected of him without fail, always going above and beyond the call of duty. It was his curse. He was the "good" twin. And now, the *only* twin. It was a blessing that his parents hadn't lived to see Jeremy completely self-destruct. It would have devastated their mother. She had blamed herself for Jeremy's behavior. Thought it was as much Jason's fault. More so, even.

"She's adorable," Faye said. "And sweet."

Yes, she was. Too adorable and sweet for someone like him. "You say that as if it's a bad thing. Would you prefer that she be unattractive and incorrigible?"

Faye gave him another look. "And obviously very vulnerable."

"And you think I would take advantage of that?"

"Not on purpose."

"I only want to help her, to make up for what Jeremy did to her. Her and the boys."

Faye wasn't buying it. "That's it, huh?"

"Why is that so difficult to believe?"

"Because I saw the way you were looking at her."

"No crime in looking." Faye knew he didn't do commitment. That he could never have a family of his own. Holly had already been taken advantage of by one Cavanaugh. He would never do anything to hurt her. At least, not intentionally.

Faye's deep frown said she didn't like his answer. "Are you still going to ask her to stay?"

"She has nowhere else to go. Jeremy put her so far into debt she'll never dig herself out."

Faye frowned. "How much did he take her for?"

Jason told her and Faye gasped, holding a hand to her bosom. "Oh, good lord. That poor thing."

"Don't worry. I'm taking care of it. She needs help, even if she won't admit it. My number one priority is the twins and seeing that they're raised properly. Someday my entire fortune will be theirs. They need to be prepared if they're going to carry on the Cavanaugh dynasty responsibly. They need the proper breeding and a top-notch education. I can provide that. Not to mention a stable and substance-free environment to raise them in. I refuse to let them turn out like their father."

Looking indignant, she said, "You're not suggesting that Holly isn't fit to be a parent because she doesn't have the right breeding."

He sighed. "Call it what you will. Wealth is a huge responsibility and at times a terrible burden. And as we've learned with Jeremy, it can easily be misManaged. I want them to be prepared for whatever life throws at them."

"As long as you remember that Holly is their parent and no decisions can be made without her approval."

"I realize that." Of course he would never try to undermine her authority, but he also knew what was best for his nephews, and he would make Holly see that.

Five

Holly woke slowly from her nap, feeling so cozy and comfortable on the firm mattress that she could easily have drifted back off to sleep. She almost did, but snapped herself awake. The boys would be waking soon to be fed and she should think about eating something herself. If she lost any more weight she was going to look like a skeleton. She reached for her phone, and checked the time. 8:07 p.m. Well, she'd probably missed dinner, but that was okay. Faye struck her as the type who might keep a plate of leftovers warm.

Holly sat up and blinked herself awake, surprised by how well-rested she felt after only a few hours of sleep. She got up and walked to the window. The water was clear and calm and—

Hold on. Where the heck did all the boats go? And why was the sun on the wrong side of the lake?

She looked at her phone again and realized it wasn't

eight in the evening. It was morning, and she had slept *all night*!

The air whooshed from her lungs as if she'd been punched in the stomach. She rushed to the door and yanked it open, startling Jason, who was on the other side, fist raised, about to knock.

"Well, good morning. Faye sent me up to tell you that breakfast…" He trailed off, concern in his eyes. "You look like you just saw a ghost."

Nope, just hyperventilating. "Where are the boys?"

"In the kitchen with Faye."

"They're okay?"

Jason looked confused, as if he thought she might be a little loony. "Of course they are."

She was so relieved she had to grab the door frame to keep her knees from buckling.

"What did you think I would do, sell them on the black market?"

She *hadn't been* thinking, that was the problem. She'd just reacted. "No, of course not. It's just that we haven't been apart much since they came home from the hospital. They are almost never out of my sight. I only just started sleeping in the living room instead of on their bedroom floor."

"Take a deep, slow breath," he said.

She took three, then another, until she could feel the knots in her stomach unwinding, her pulse slowing. This was not the way she had hoped to start her morning. This trip was supposed to be fun and relaxing. They were supposed to be getting to know one another.

"Better?" he asked.

She nodded, feeling steadier. And pretty darned ridiculous for overreacting. "I panicked. I'm sorry. I didn't mean to be so rude."

"You weren't rude."

"It's just that they were so fragile when they were born, and though I know that now they're just as healthy as any other child their age, I always feel as if I'm waiting for the other shoe to fall."

"Holly?"

She looked up at him. She couldn't look his way without getting caught up in those ocean-blue irises. And the way he said her name made her insides feel warm and soft.

He laid his hands on her shoulders, giving them a reassuring squeeze. "You're safe here. I'm not going to let anything happen to you or the boys. I give you my word."

She believed him.

She barely knew this man, but she knew in her heart that he meant every word he said. And she was rational enough now to realize how nice his hands felt on her shoulders. A little *too* nice, in fact. There was nothing rational about *that*.

"You all right?" he asked, his hands slipping lower, to the tops of her arms.

More like confused. He was standing really close, and he smelled so good. It would be so easy to reach out and touch him...

No, she really shouldn't do that.

"I'm fine. Just a little disoriented."

"You missed dinner last night. You must be starving."

"I am," she said.

He dropped his hands from her arms and she was both relieved and disappointed. And clearly not thinking straight.

As they stepped into the hall she could smell bacon and freshly brewed coffee.

"How does a walk around the property sound after breakfast?" he asked as she followed him down the stairs.

"I'd like that." God only knew she could use some fresh air.

"I thought that we could go into town this afternoon."

"I'd love to."

The kitchen was huge and outfitted with top-of-the-line appliances that any chef would drool over. Faye stood at the stove stirring what looked like scrambled eggs, Devon on her hip, while Marshall squealed happily and kicked his chubby little legs in his car seat on the kitchen table. Holly needn't have worried, they looked happy and perfectly content in Faye's care, which Holly was ashamed to admit had her feeling the tiniest bit jealous. She was used to doing everything on her own.

Faye smiled when she saw Holly. "Well good morning, sleepy head. Are you hungry?"

Her mother used to call her that, and to hear it again made her smile.

"Starved," she said, lifting Marshall into her arms for a snuggle, tickling him under his chubby chin. He giggled and kicked and fisted her hair in his soggy hands. It occurred to her just then that she hadn't brushed her hair, or her teeth for that matter, and if that wasn't bad enough, she was wearing last night's clothes. She sneaked a look at her reflection in the stainless steel refrigerator. Her ponytail was a bit askew, and her clothes were wrinkled. But it wasn't as if Jason hadn't already seen her at her worst.

His cell phone rang and he pulled it from his pants

pocket. He checked the display and frowned. "Excuse me. I have to take this."

When he was gone, Faye asked Holly, "How did you sleep?"

Holly tried to straighten her hair but Marshall kept grabbing at it. "Like the dead. I didn't even hear the boys wake up. I'm a little surprised that they slept all night."

"They didn't," Faye said. "They woke up around dinner time and had a bottle. Then Jason and I played with them for a while. They conked out around ten and slept until about 2:00 a.m."

"Why didn't you wake me?"

"Jason asked me not to. He said things have been rough for you and you needed rest. He's a good man, you know."

Holly hiked Marshall up over what used to be her hip, but now was just a knobby bone. "I've noticed."

"After what happened to you with Jeremy…" She shook her head, looking so sad. "I just want you to know that Jason isn't at all like his brother."

"I can see that."

"I wish you had known Jeremy when he was younger. He used to be the sweetest boy. I wish I knew what happened, why he changed the way he did." She held out a plate of bacon and offered Holly a slice. "You must be famished."

Holly took a piece and bit into it, her mouth watering. Bacon was one of those things that always tasted better when someone else made it. "It's delicious. Thank you."

"You're all skin and bones. We need to fatten you up."

She had always been naturally thin. She'd only gained twenty pounds when she was pregnant with the twins. But Faye was right: now she was *too* thin.

She finished that slice and reached for another, dodging Marshall's sticky hand. "Do you and George live here in the house?"

"We live in the caretakers' cottage," Faye said, gesturing out the window above the kitchen sink. Holly craned her neck to see. The small dwelling had the same dark wood exterior as the main house and was set back several hundred feet in the forest. It blended in so well with the surrounding vegetation that Holly hadn't even noticed it when they'd gotten to the house yesterday.

"How long have you lived there?"

"Since I married George. His father was the caretaker for years, and his father before that. It's a family tradition."

Since being orphaned Holly missed out on family traditions, though her foster parents had done their best to give her a somewhat normal childhood. But without a real family it had never been the same. "And will your kids carry on the tradition?"

"Our only child died when he was very small."

Holly's heart ached just thinking about it. She couldn't imagine losing a child. Nor did she want to contemplate it. Some things were better left alone. "I'm so sorry."

"He was born with a genetic abnormality," Faye said. "He didn't even make it to his first birthday. His short life was filled with pain and suffering. My doctor warned us that if I were to have another child there was a chance it would suffer the same condition, so we decided it wasn't worth the risk. They knew so little about genetics back then."

The idea of never having children of her own hurt Holly's heart. She couldn't imagine life without her boys. "That must have been a difficult choice."

"I sank into deep depression for several months. But

then Jason and Jeremy were born and their mother was overwhelmed and needed my help. It wasn't the same as having my own children, but I loved them." Faye paused, looking sad. "If our boy had lived he would be forty this fall."

"What was his name?"

The memory made Faye smile. "His name was Travis. Travis George Henderson."

"It's a nice name."

"Travis was my father's name."

"Did you know when you were pregnant that anything was wrong?"

"We had no idea. And I had a perfectly normal pregnancy. But the minute he was born it was obvious that something was wrong. They couldn't get him to cry, and when he did it was so weak and raspy. Then I saw him. He wasn't normal, that much was obvious, but I thought he was the most beautiful baby I had ever seen. Jason's parents were so good to George and me. Though the Cavanaughs paid us generously, we were helping to support my parents and didn't have money for medical bills. Jason's father paid for Travis to see at least half a dozen specialists, but they all told us the same thing. He wouldn't live past his first birthday, and there wasn't anything anyone could do."

Holly had to swallow the huge lump in her throat so she could speak. "I'm so sorry, Faye."

"It's all a part of God's plan. And it was a long time ago. I just wanted you to know how good the Cavanaughs were to us. They took care of us, and Jason will do the same for you."

Whether Holly wanted him to or not, it would seem. If she'd known that he'd intended to let her sleep all night, she wouldn't have lain down for a nap. But she couldn't deny feeling the most rested she had since the twins were born. Maybe, just in this instance, he did know what was best for her. As long as he didn't make a habit of it.

Holly reached into her back pocket for her phone, realizing when she didn't feel it there that she must have left it upstairs. She'd called one of those credit counselors yesterday in the hopes that they might have some sort of financial solution for her and was waiting for a call back.

She asked Faye, "Can you watch them for a minute while I go grab my phone?"

"Of course, honey. Take your time."

Holly set Marshall back in his car seat and headed upstairs to her room. She found her phone on the bed where she must have dropped it. Aside from a dozen emails and Facebook notifications, there was a missed call from the financial people. She sat on the bed and listened to the voice mail they'd left. Then she listened again. Then once more to be sure she was hearing the agent correctly.

She stuffed her phone in her back pocket, but what she really wanted to do was chuck it at the wall. There was only one explanation for this. And though she rarely cursed, she shook her head and muttered, "Sonofabitch."

Jason waited until he was in his office with the door shut before he answered Lewis's call.

"It's done," he told Jason.

"You're sure you got everything."

"Down to that last penny."

"Thanks, Lewis."

"You may not be so grateful when she learns the

truth. How long do you think it will take her to figure it out?"

Not long enough, Jason was sure. And she would be furious with him when she did. But she would get over it. She would see that it was best for everyone.

"What was her reaction when she saw the house?" Lewis asked him.

"She took it surprisingly well, all things considered."

"Have you asked her to stay?"

"No, not yet. I don't want to rush into anything or overwhelm her. I want to give her time to settle in, to feel comfortable here."

"I wouldn't wait too long. If she's as independent as you claim—"

"Don't forget stubborn."

"Once she finds out you paid all her debt she's probably not going to be happy with you."

Lewis had a point. Maybe it would be better to ask sooner rather than later.

"I almost forgot, Miranda wondered if you two—sorry, make that *four*—would like to meet up for dinner sometime. As you can imagine, she's anxious to meet your nephews. And Holly."

"Sounds good."

"You don't want to ask Holly first?"

"It will do her good to get out with people."

"Okay, but do me a favor and don't tell her that I'm the one responsible for her debt being paid off."

"You were operating under my instructions. She has no one to blame but me."

"Yeah, but she might not see it that way. I'd rather err on the side of caution if it's all the same to you."

Jason opened his mouth to reply but was interrupted

by very firm and insistent pounding on his office door. It was so loud that Lewis heard it over the phone.

"What the heck is that?" he asked Jason.

Before he could respond the door swung open and Holly barged right in uninvited. And she was not happy.

She glared at him, hands propped on what little she had in the way of hips, her ponytail still slightly askew, looking pretty damned adorable. "What the hell did you do?"

"I hate to say this," Lewis said, sounding amused. "But I think she knows."

"Astute observation," Jason said, his tone oozing sarcasm as he watched Holly stomp across the room to his desk. "I have to let you go."

Lewis chuckled. "I'll see you later. If you live that long."

"Thanks for the vote of confidence. I'll see you." Jason hung up, and in an attempt to diffuse the situation, gestured to the chair opposite his desk and said, "Have a seat."

She ignored the chair and propped both hands on the desktop, looking as if she might launch over it and strangle him to death. He had to bite down on his lip to keep from smiling. She looked about as threatening as a field mouse.

"I got an interesting message from my financial guy," she said.

He didn't realize she *had* a financial guy. That would have been good to know. "Did you?"

"Yes, he was supposed to help me figure out a way to consolidate all my debt. Needless to say he was a little confused when he discovered that I have no debt."

She was furious, and all Jason could think about was

pulling her down onto the surface of his desk and kissing that frown off those delicious lips.

Delicious lips? Seriously?

What was wrong with him? This was his sister-in-law he was lusting after. His brother's wife. It was the one thing he swore he wouldn't do. "It must be a relief not to have that hanging over your head," he said.

"Of course it is!" she said, bristling with outrage. "That's not the point."

He liked this bolder, saucier side. He wondered what else she was hiding under that demure outer shell. "Maybe it should be," he said, thinking how sexy she looked when she was angry. "Maybe you should try shelving the pride for five minutes and let someone help you."

"Is that what you think this is about? My *pride*?"

"It's not?"

She fisted her hands and he wondered if she would take a swing at him. "I asked you specifically not to get involved in my finances, and you said you wouldn't. Then you went behind my back and did it anyway."

He rose from his chair and walked around his desk. He thought about putting his hands on her shoulders the way he had that morning, just to calm her down, but she looked so beside herself with anger that he was afraid he might pull back two bloody stumps. "Holly, I only did what I knew was best for you. And the boys."

"What *you* knew was best?" She looked at him as though he was a moron. "Don't you get it? You *lied* to me, Jason. Right to my face. Without batting an eyelash."

She didn't come right out and compare him to his brother, but the implication was clear. The worst part was that she was right. No matter the reason for it, or his misguided good intentions, he *had* lied to her.

The women he usually kept company with would let a lie or two slide if it was materialistically advantageous. Which spoke volumes about his skewed attitude toward the opposite sex, he supposed. But Holly was unlike any woman he'd ever known. Strong and resilient and unwilling to compromise her principles, even if it meant putting herself through undue hardship.

And too damned sweet to be around someone like him.

"You're right," he said, angry with himself for thinking that after all she had been through she could be so easily manipulated. Or that he even had the right to try. Who was he to decide what was best for someone he'd known barely four days?

He'd always swore that no matter what his net worth, he wouldn't let money change him or give him a false sense of entitlement. He had officially become his own worst nightmare.

He really *was* a moron.

"I was wrong to go behind your back," he told her. "I hope you'll accept my apology and my promise that it will never happen again."

She took a few seconds to think about it, and he started to wonder if maybe he'd blown it, if she would pack up and leave and deny him the privilege of knowing his nephews. And could he blame her if she did?

"Apology accepted," she finally said.

She was giving him a second chance, and he'd be damned if he was going to screw it up. His relationship with his nephews depended on it. Besides, he could still take care of them, all three of them. He would just have to be a bit more subtle about it.

"Now that we have that settled, I have something that I need to say to you," Holly told him in an unsteady voice, as if she might burst out crying.

Uh-oh, this couldn't be good.

Making an effort not to wince and bracing himself for the worst, he said, "Let's have it."

"Thank you." She threw herself into his arms nearly knocking him backward. "Thank you so much, Jason."

Wait. Now she was thanking him? As long as he lived he would never understand women, and though he knew it was probably a bad idea, he slipped his arms around her, gently rubbing her back as he held her. Holly clung to him, her face pressed against his shirt. She may have been skin and bones, but she was still soft and warm in all the right places. And being a red-blooded single man, it was difficult not to let his mind wander. Or his hands for that matter. She smelled so good, he wanted to bury his nose in the softness of her hair and just breathe her in. He wanted to fist the silky soft locks, pull her head back and taste her lips.

She hung on tighter and he realized that she was trembling. He tried to see her face but she kept it tucked firmly in the crook of his neck. "Hey, are you okay?"

She nodded, but he could feel her tears soaking through his shirt.

"Then why are you crying?"

She held him even harder. "The past few months have been s-so hard. I was nervous and s-scared all the time. It feels as if the weight of the world has been lifted from my shoulders. I feel like I can breathe again. Like there's hope for me and the boys. I don't know how I'll ever repay you—"

"You don't owe me anything."

"Yes, I do."

Well, if she really thought so…

"Stay here with me. You and the boys," he said, the words leaping out before he could think better of it. She went still and silent, and he winced, wondering if he could have picked a worse time to spring this on her. What the hell was wrong with him? In the business world he was a shark, but this sweet, nurturing woman had him chasing his own tail.

Her words muffled a little by his shirt, she finally said, "You really want us to stay here? With you?"

"Just until you get back on your feet."

She abruptly let go of him and stepped back, sniffling and wiping the tears from her cheeks. "I can get by on my own. I have for a very long time."

Stubborn to a fault.

"I don't doubt that for a second," he said, then he pulled out the big guns. "But don't the boys deserve better than just *getting by*?"

Six

Ouch.

Talk about hitting below the belt. Holly couldn't deny that Jason was right: her boys did deserve better than just getting by. And frankly, so did she.

"I owe this to Jeremy," Jason said, and the pain and loss that flashed deep in his eyes made her heart ache. How could she tell him no when he looked at her that way, with so much sincerity and hurt? This might be just as good for him as it was for her and the boys. It might bring him closure.

"Okay," she said.

He blinked, as if he wasn't sure he heard her correctly, "Okay?"

"I'm proud, but I'm not stupid. Even without all that debt hanging over my head, getting by in the city is going to be next to impossible. I have nothing tying me to New York and living in the country, in a small town, has always been a dream of mine. And here the boys will have family."

"And so will I."

Something in his tone pinched her heart. Until just now it hadn't occurred to her that maybe he was lonely, but she could see it in his eyes. Could it be that he needed them just as much as they needed him? Her foster mother used to tell her and her foster siblings when the budget was especially tight that they should not be fooled into believing that money could buy happiness. It looked as if she'd been right.

"I do have a few conditions," Holly told Jason and his left brow spiked. "When it comes to the twins, I decide what's best for them. And this is non-negotiable."

"I just want to help."

"I know, but there's a fine line between helping someone and trying to control them."

His expression said he knew she was right. "*You're* in charge. Got it. What else?"

She sat on the edge of his desk, which was so clean she doubted she would find even a speck of dust. In that way he and Jeremy were nothing alike. Since the day she'd moved in with Jeremy, until the day he died, Holly had always been picking up after him. Shoes and socks on the living room floor. Dirty clothes and wet towels in the bathroom. He left soiled dishes all over the place when an empty dishwasher sat just steps away in the kitchen. She was tidy by nature, so his slovenly ways used to drive her crazy.

She looked up at Jeremy and realized he was watching her expectantly. Conditions, right.

How about no more touching each other? That would be a good one, because pressing herself against all that rock solid male heat had been a really stupid move.

She'd been fine, right up to the second when she realized how good it felt. She was a new mother, but she was also a woman. One who hadn't had any sort of sexual contact with a man since the fifth month of her pregnancy. But if she was going to stay here they needed to have a strict hands-off rule.

But how was she supposed to say that without tipping Jason off to the fact that she *wanted* to put her hands on him? *All over him.*

Eye contact was a tough one, as well, but she couldn't tell him not to look at her. It wasn't his fault that she practically melted when those intense blue eyes locked on hers. And his voice? The low, deep pitch thrummed across her nerves and sent shivers up her spine. But she couldn't tell him not to talk to her.

Oh man, she was in trouble.

"I guess that's it," she told him.

Looking mildly amused, he said, "You drive a hard bargain."

With herself, maybe. But what else was new?

"You're sure there's nothing else?" he asked her.

She nodded, thinking to herself, *Liar.* "If anything unexpected arises—" *Arises? Honey, don't even go there.* "—we can sort it out then."

"Sounds fair enough." Jason held his hand out and said, "So, we have a deal."

So much for her no-touching rule.

She accepted his gesture, watched as his much bigger hand swallowed up hers. And when he didn't let go immediately, she looked up, her eyes snagging on his. She was instantly mesmerized.

Damn it. Another rule down the drain. She really sucked at this.

He held on several seconds longer and then let her

hand slip from his. Slowly, like a caress. Was he doing it on purpose, or did he just naturally radiate this intense sexual energy? Honestly, she wasn't sure which was worse.

She caught her gaze drifting lower and wondered if he and his brother were truly identical…

She blushed at the depraved direction her thoughts had taken, but thankfully her face was already red and splotchy from crying. Which was another thing she never did, especially in front of other people. So what the heck was wrong with her? She certainly wasn't acting like herself. Maybe she didn't know who that person was anymore. Maybe the events of the past year had irrevocably changed her. So what would it take to change back?

Did she even want to?

"Would it be all right if I brought a few things here from my apartment?" she asked him. "The rest can go in storage."

"Holly, this is your home now. You can bring anything you'd like. I *want* you to feel comfortable here."

Weirdly enough, she sort of did already, as if she was meant to be here. Which she knew was ridiculous. Maybe she was just really, really relieved.

"I'll make the arrangements to have your things moved," he said.

"Thank you, but I can handle that myself."

He opened his mouth—she assumed to argue—then caught himself. "Of course. But if it becomes financially prohibitive—"

"You'll be the first one to know," she assured him.

"And if there's anything else you need, anything at all—"

"I *promise* you will be the first one to know."

He chuckled and shook his head. "I'm sorry. You'll have to be patient with me."

"Lucky for you I have loads of patience." She had the feeling she would need it.

"By the way, we're going to—" Jason stopped abruptly, cursed under his breath and then started over. "What I meant to say is that we've been invited to dine with some friends of mine. I wondered if you would like to go. They're excited to meet you and the boys."

"That sounds like fun." She liked the idea of meeting his friends, getting to know more about his life. And she liked the fact that he had asked her instead of issuing an order. "I'd love to go."

If she suspected he was bringing her along just to be nice, his smile told a different story. It said he was genuinely happy that she'd accepted. She wasn't sure why that surprised her, but it did. She just hoped she didn't make a fool of herself. That she didn't say something stupid and embarrass him. Or stare dumbfounded the entire time, lost in his incredibly blue eyes.

The way she was right now.

And even worse, he was looking at her the same way.

What would he do if she reached up and touched his smooth face, if she traced his lips with her finger? Or her tongue…?

"What's going on in here?"

Holly stepped back guiltily, though technically she hadn't done anything wrong, and spun around to see Faye standing in the doorway to Jason's office. Talk about perfect timing. Faye's presence may have just stopped her from doing something monumentally stupid.

The older woman looked back and forth between

Holly and Jason, brow furrowed, and said, "Is everything okay? I heard shouting."

Yikes, had Holly really been so loud that Faye had heard her all the way in the kitchen?

"And why is Holly crying?" she demanded, shooting Jason an accusing look.

He held his arms up in defense. "We were just negotiating."

She narrowed her eyes at him. "Negotiating what?"

He leaned close to Holly and said under his breath, "Did I mention that Faye can be a little nosy?"

"I heard that," she said, crossing her skinny arms, and tossing her short graying hair, looking pretty tough for someone so tiny. And Jason's wry grin said he loved to tease her. They interacted more like family than employee and employer. After so many years it probably felt as if they were related.

"I am not nosy," Faye said. "I'm curious. And concerned. There is a difference."

"I've asked Holly and the boys to stay here," Jason said. "And she's accepted."

Faye gasped and clapped her hands together, eyes wide. "Oh, that's wonderful!"

Her enthusiasm surprised Holly a little, but she sure did feel welcome, as if she really was home.

"For how long?" Faye asked her.

"That part is still up in the air. Long enough to get back on my feet. But I don't want to be a burden."

Faye waved away the words as if they were a pesky insect. "There is no way that you and those beautiful little angels could ever be a burden. Taking care of people is what I do. And these days Jason doesn't need much care. We need some new life breathed into this old place."

"Still, I'd like you to give me a list of things I can do around the house. Any way I can help out. I want to pull my weight."

"I'll see what I can come up with," Faye said. "Now, come have breakfast, you two, before it's cold."

"We'll be right there," Jason told her, and when she was gone, said to Holly, "I never imagined it would be this easy."

"What?"

"Convincing you to stay. I assumed kneepads and groveling would be involved. Especially after you found out what I did."

She couldn't imagine Jason ever groveling or ever needing to. He was so dynamic and charismatic, and he oozed authority. Obviously *she* had trouble telling him no.

Which had her wondering, as he grinned down at her with that mesmerizing smile, looking sexy as hell without even trying, what the heck she had just gotten herself into.

Seven

"Jason, wake up!"

Jason heard the plea through the fog of sleep, felt a hand shaking him and peeled open his eyes. The room was dark, but he could see Holly's silhouette beside his bed. She was holding one of the twins.

He sat up and switched on the lamp, squinting against the sudden bright light. It was a good thing he'd elected to start wearing pajamas to bed while they were here, or he would have some serious explaining to do. "What time is it?"

"Almost two," Holly said. "I'm so sorry to wake you." She wore an oversize T-shirt that hung to her knees and her ponytail was lopsided. "Marshall is sick."

Jason was instantly awake and on his feet, heart in his throat. "What's wrong?"

The words were barely out when Marshall let loose a throaty cough like Jason had never heard before, and his heart plummeted to the balls of his feet. "Oh, my God. Is he choking? Can he breathe?"

"Relax," she said, sounding calm but concerned. "Contrary to how he sounds, he seems to be breathing okay, but since he's a preemie I don't want to take any chances."

"What's wrong with him?"

"I'm pretty sure it's the croup."

He blinked. "The *what*?"

"The croup. It's a virus that settles in the vocal chords. At least, that's what it said on the internet."

She was trusting the internet at a time like this? What Marshall needed was a doctor. Though Jason had to admit that other than the cough the baby seemed fine, flashing Jason a goofy, toothless smile even as he was hacking. "What can I do?"

"Can you get ahold of Faye? I'm sure she'll know what to do. I would go over to their house, but it's so dark out there I'm afraid I might trip on something or get lost in the woods."

"I'll call her," Jason said, reaching for his cell phone and dialing her number.

Faye answered on the first ring with a sleepy, "It's 2:00 a.m."

"What do you know about the croup?" he asked her. "Holly thinks Marshall has it."

"Does he sound like a collie?"

Marshall started to cough again and Jason held the phone closer to the baby. "He sounds like this."

"Oh, yeah, that's the croup, all right."

"You're sure?"

"Positive. You used to get it when you were a baby."

He told Holly, "She said it's definitely the croup."

Holly exhaled deeply, as if she'd been holding her

breath, and sunk against the bedpost in relief. Maybe she hadn't been as calm inside as she was on the outside. "What does she suggest?" she asked Jason, and he in turn asked Faye.

"What should we do?"

"Take him in the bathroom and turn the shower on as hot as it will go. Then sit in there with him."

Horrified, he asked, "In the hot shower?"

"Oh, for goodness sake, no. In the *bathroom*. The steam from the hot water will help clear the congestion."

That made a lot more sense. "Hot water bad, steam good. Gotcha."

"Keep him in there until the water runs cold or you drop five pounds. Whichever comes first. Then wrap him up in a blanket and take him outside into the cool air. And tell Holly they'll be just fine."

It took him a second to process what Faye had just said. "What do you mean *they*?"

"When one catches something, the other is bound to get it, too."

Again, that made sense. As far back as he could remember it had been that way with Jeremy and him, up until it was just Jason who'd been sick all the time.

"Thanks, Faye. Sorry to wake you."

"Anytime, hon."

He hung up and relayed Faye's instructions to Holly. She stood rocking her son back and forth, patting his back softly. "We'll have to use the bathroom in your room," he told her. "The ceiling in mine is fifteen feet high. It would take an awful lot of steam to fill it."

"Thank you for calling her. I'm sorry I had to wake you."

"It's no problem. Let's go get him steamed."

"I think I've got it from here," she said, clutching Marshall closer. "You can go back to sleep."

He was tempted. He had tossed and turned for an hour or so before finally falling asleep around midnight, but something in her expression said she needed his support. Besides, part of taking responsibility for his nephews might mean a sleepless night here and there, but it was a small price to pay. "I'm already up," he said with a shrug. "It's no problem."

"But—"

"I can keep you company." He put his hand on her shoulder to lead her. There was a slight hesitation before she started walking.

Marshall hacked the entire way there, but seemed no worse for wear. Jason figured that most kids would be crying at this point or at the very least be annoyed. But the baby watched Jason over his mother's shoulder, wearing that goofy, toothless smile. He was a tough little guy.

Jason followed her into the bathroom, shut the door behind them. He turned on the hot water in the shower full blast, leaving the etched glass door of the stall open.

He realized immediately that something wasn't right. But it wasn't Marshall this time. It was Holly who had him worried. Her face had paled several shades, she was breathing way too hard and she was trembling. She was hyperventilating, and looked as if she was probably having a panic attack.

"Are you okay?" he asked, putting a hand on her arm to steady her. She shook her head, and didn't resist when Jason took Marshall from her arms and guided her toward the toilet. He shut the lid and said, "Sit."

Holly sat—collapsed really—and he gently pushed

her head down between her knees. "Take slow, shallow breaths."

"I...can't breathe," she gasped.

"Actually, you're breathing too much. Slow it down." His mother used to get panic attacks near the end of her life, but in her case, she really couldn't breathe. Her heart had lacked the strength to pump a sufficient amount of oxygenated air through her veins, making her winded and weak. A trip from the bed to the bathroom would exhaust her.

The room began to fill with steam. Condensation fogged the mirror and clung to his bare skin. He held Marshall up high, where the moisture in the air was more concentrated, while keeping one eye on Holly. Almost immediately Marshall's hacking began to ease.

"See," Jason told her. "He sounds better already. He's going to be fine."

Holly nodded and continued to breathe slowly, elbows on her knees, head cradled in her palms. When she finally raised her head and looked up at him and Marshall, she was still pale but her breathing had returned to normal.

"Feeling better?" he asked her.

She nodded, looking embarrassed. "I'm sorry. I don't know what just happened."

"You had a panic attack."

"Swell," she said, dropping her head back in her hands with a what-next huff. "I'm stronger than this."

"You've been through a lot," he reminded her as the steam drifted lower and sweat began to dampen his upper lip.

"Thank you," Holly said softly, gazing up at him through the curtain of her lashes, looking so vulnerable and lost that he wanted to take her in his arms and hold her. Tell her that everything would be okay. But he knew that *just* holding her would never be enough. Once he got his arms around her he wouldn't want to let go.

"I was so scared," she said. "If you hadn't been here…"

"You would have managed just fine. You would have called their pediatrician and he would have told you what to do."

"You think so?"

"I know so. You don't give yourself enough credit."

A mixture of steam and sweat trickled down the side of his face, soaking into his T-shirt. Loose strands of pale blond hair stuck to Holly's face in damp ribbons. Damn, she was pretty. He'd always preferred blondes. Natural ones.

"I feel as if I'm flying blind," she said.

"I would imagine that all new moms probably feel that way."

"Yes, but it was so stressful when the twins were born. They spent the majority of their first month in the NICU. I spent every day in the hospital nursery with them."

"What about Jeremy?" Surely he must have been there with her.

"He didn't like hospitals," she said, looking embarrassed by the truth. "Because he spent so much time there as a child. Or so he said."

Had it been Jason's children, he wouldn't have left their side. For a split second he considered telling Holly the real reason Jeremy hated hospitals, but now just didn't seem like the right time. "What kind of father was my brother?" he asked instead, and her hesitation didn't bode well.

"The boys came home with heart and breathing monitors. It was a stressful time. Jeremy had difficulties coping. We were fighting all the time. There were times when he would storm out, and not come home until late at night. A few nights he didn't come home at all. Then he would stroll in the next morning like nothing was wrong. I think in a way he resented the boys for taking up too much of my time. He actually accused me of loving them more than him."

"Did you?"

"Maybe. *Probably*. But I should have realized that something was terribly wrong. I didn't *let* myself see it. I just wanted everything to be okay. I wanted that fairy-tale life he promised me. So I made excuses for him."

"Trust me, we've all done that. Me, my parents, even Faye and George. We all wanted so badly for him to change, and he used that to his advantage."

"He had me fooled," she said, and she looked so sad, as if she thought it was her own failure, but Jason knew better.

The steam began to dissipate as the water cooled. Marshall was awake but limp on Jason's shoulder. Though the baby's coughing had all but ceased, his breathing still sounded raspy.

Jason reached into the shower stall and shut off the water. As the air cleared he could see that Holly was just as soggy as he was, and as a result her shirt clung to her body, accentuating everything underneath. And though she was painfully thin, under the oversize white shirt she was still 100 percent woman. And being a red-blooded man, he couldn't help but look. But only for a second before he forced himself to look away.

"What now?" Holly asked him.

"We take him outside into the cool air." He was about

to hand Marshall over to her, but she still looked a bit unsteady. "How do you feel?"

"A little dizzy, from the steam I think."

In that case it probably would be safer if he carried his nephew downstairs and outside. "Why don't I head out to the back deck while you check on Devon."

She paused, gazed at her son, then nodded and said, "Okay."

He opened the bathroom door, letting in a rush of cool, dry air. "Grab the quilt off your bed and wrap us up in it," he told her.

She tugged the quilt off the bed and draped it over his shoulders. He tucked it tightly around Marshall and himself, so that only his nephew's face was exposed. Jason didn't want him catching a chill and aggravating the virus he already had.

Jason headed downstairs and out the back door into the clear, moonlit night. The thermometer on the back of the house said it was sixty-four degrees, but the air felt cool on his damp face and the deck was slippery with dew. Jason paced in the dark with Marshall cradled in the crook of his arm. His nephew gazed up at him, cooing contentedly. He sure seemed like a happy-go-lucky kid.

The first time Jason had held the boys they'd seemed so small and fragile, but they were far sturdier than he'd imagined and he was starting to get the hang of holding them. What a difference only a few days made.

The back door opened and Holly stepped out.

"How is Devon?" he asked her.

"Sound asleep and breathing fine. But I suppose his catching it is inevitable."

"Faye thought so, too. But this time you'll know what to do."

"And I won't have to wake you."

"But it's okay if you do."

In the pale bluish light he could see her smile, and though it was damned pretty, he caught his gaze drifting lower. Her T-shirt was so damp it clung to the swell of her breasts, and so transparent he could see the pale outline of her peaked nipples. He imagined how good they would feel cupped in his hands, or pressed against his chest. In his mouth…

He lifted his gaze and realized that Holly was watching him watch her. And she wasn't making any effort to cover herself.

"Sorry," he said, keeping his eyes level with hers. "I didn't mean to stare."

She surprised him by shrugging and saying almost the exact thing he had told Faye. "No crime in looking."

No, but looking was like a gateway to touching. Or was she suggesting that she *wanted* him to look?

A gust of wind chilled the air and Holly shivered, wrapping her arms around herself for warmth. Blocking the view that he shouldn't have been enjoying in the first place. "If you're cold you can go back inside," he told her.

She frowned and shook her head. "I don't want to leave Marshall."

"He's fine."

"I don't care," she said, her teeth chattering. "I want to stay. He's my responsibility."

Damn it, she was stubborn. What was he supposed to do? Let her stand there shivering? She was going to wind up making herself sick, too. "You won't be much good to them if you have pneumonia."

She shook her head, refusing to leave. He understood

her need to be there for her children, but she was taking it to the extreme.

"Come here," he said, and held open the blanket, inviting her into the warm cocoon he and her son had created. Holly stepped closer, hesitantly at first, but her need for warmth won out. She let Jason fold the blanket around her and pull her in closer. She stood stiffly, her arms folded, and her skin was so cold it was a bit like cuddling a popsicle.

"You're freezing," he said.

"I—I d-didn't think it was th-this c-cold."

"We really need to warm you up." She didn't resist—though he sort of wished she would have—as he pulled the blanket tighter around them, wrapping his free arm around her narrow shoulders. As his body heat began to warm her, she stopped trembling and relaxed in his arms.

"Better?" he asked.

She nodded, her hair catching in the stubble on his chin, her breath warm against his skin as she tucked her head into the crook of his neck. It felt good. Too damned good.

With the crisis over, the concerned uncle in him took a step back and the part of him that was all man, the part of him that craved her touch, took over. Though he tried to fight it, reminded himself he was holding another man's woman and child, his own brother's wife, his body didn't listen. And if he didn't back away soon it was going to become more than obvious to her.

"This is nice," she said. "It's been a really long time since anyone held me like this."

Another shortcoming on Jeremy's part. If she were Jason's wife, he would have a hell of a time keeping his hands off her. And as far as hugs went, it had been a while for him, too, but that didn't make it right.

It didn't necessarily make it wrong, either.

"Maybe a little *too* nice," she said, flooring him with her honesty. "We can't deny that there's chemistry."

He wouldn't even try. He liked a woman who wasn't afraid to speak her mind. He had grown so tired of the mind games and half-truths. How many times had he dated a woman who swore she had no interest in marriage and kids, only to discover that all the while she'd been picking out china patterns and browsing *Modern Bride* magazine? Though he was sure it was more about the size of his wallet than genuine affection.

But there was such a thing as too much honesty.

"Or maybe it's just me?" she said when he didn't reply. "Maybe I'm misreading the signals."

"It's not just you," he told her, her look of relief making him smile. As if there was any question that he was lusting after her. That or she hadn't the slightest clue how beautiful and sweet she was. Too sweet for someone such as him. How many times would he have to remind himself of that?

As many as it took.

"You're not misreading anything," he said.

She looked up at him, putting her mouth mere inches from his. Was she *trying* to drive him crazy?

"I think we'll agree that anything beyond friendship would be a bad idea," she said, so close he could feel the heat of her breath on his lips.

Jesus. It took everything in him not to kiss her. To keep his libido in check. The only thing giving him the will to resist was the drowsy child lying limp in his arms. He was a much needed buffer. "Are you always this brutally honest?"

"I denied my true feelings with Jeremy and look where it got me. If we have any hope of making this work, if the boys and I are going to live under your roof, we have to be honest with each other. Even if the truth hurts a little."

He could see her point, and her willingness to bare her soul to him said an awful lot about her character. He found himself almost wishing that he had met her before his brother had. But knowing her the way he did now, it was probably better that he hadn't. He could never give her what she truly wanted. What she deserved. Despite Jeremy's betrayal he had given her something real and concrete. Two precious sons. It was more than Jeremy was capable of.

Holly was still watching him, waiting for a response. If she wanted honesty that's what he would give her. "The truth is I really want to kiss you."

Her breath caught and he could swear he felt her pulse quicken, her body go soft.

"Too honest for you?"

"I do, too," she said. "Want to kiss *you*, I mean. Not myself. And no, it's not too honest. We have to be able to talk to each other."

"In that case, do you want to know what else I'd like to do to you?"

She blinked. "Um, well…maybe we don't have to be *that* honest."

"Then this would probably be a good time to go inside." Marshall had fallen back to sleep, and Jason could see a very cold shower in his immediate future.

"I think you're right," she said. He lifted his arm from her shoulders and she backed away from him. "I'd like to carry Marshall to bed."

"Are you okay?"

She nodded. "Fine. Better than fine, actually. It's a relief to get that off my chest."

Her chest was exactly what he was trying not to think about. He handed Marshall over and Holly hugged him close. Jason followed her inside, through the dark house and up the stairs to the twins' room. While she laid Marshall down, he checked on Devon, whose breathing sounded normal as far as Jason could tell.

Holly stood over Marshall's crib stroking his hair.

"We should let him sleep," Jason said.

"I don't want to leave him."

"He sounds fine now." Jason needed to get her out of there and back into her bed, where the light from the hallway didn't make her shirt so transparent. So he could get back to his own bed, before he did something he really shouldn't.

Holly backed hesitantly away from the crib, and Jason put a hand on her shoulder to steer her in the right direction. Though she was all skin and bones, there was a sturdiness about her that was strangely alluring.

"Come on," he said. "I'll tuck you in."

She actually laughed. "Get out. No one has tucked me in for years."

"Well, I've never done it before. If I'm going to be a good uncle I need the practice."

"You make a valid point," she said. She didn't balk at his thinly veiled excuse to insinuate himself into her bedroom, and that was all the invitation he needed.

Her room smelled like flowers and a hint of peppermint, and something inexplicably soft and girly. Like her.

She climbed under the covers, but she didn't lie down. She patted the edge of the mattress instead, inviting him to join her. Though he knew that their being together on a bed in any way, shape or form was a bad idea all around, he sat down anyway.

"Thank you. For your help and your honesty," she said, her appreciation and vulnerability so vivid, so honest, it made his heart skip. She was killing him and she didn't even know it. Turning him into some sentimental fool.

The woman was a total contradiction. Sweet and innocent one minute, enticing and sexy the next. How she managed it was beyond him, but it was screwing with his brain.

"So, how does this tucking thing work?"

"Don't even try to convince me that your mother never tucked you in."

She had, thousands of times. And he knew exactly what to do. But where was the fun in that? What was the point in playing with fire if they didn't get just a little burned? "It was a long time ago, but I'll give it my best shot."

Her smile was a wry one and said that she knew exactly what he was up to. But she wasn't doing or saying a damned thing to stop him, and the power struggle going on in his head, between what he should do—*get the hell out of there*—and what he wanted to do—*crawl under the covers and really tuck her in*—was shorting out his brain. He couldn't recall ever being so enchanted by a woman. By the idea of touching her.

In a word, he was toast.

"First, she would usually read me a book or sing to me," he told her.

"I think we can skip that part."

"Sometimes she would do this." He reached up and touched her hair, stroking back the silky strands that had escaped her ponytail, mesmerized by the desire in her eyes.

"That's nice," she said, humming a soft sigh of pleasure as he brushed her plump lower lip with the pad of his thumb. Her lids hovered at half-mast and her pupils were so dilated they swallowed up all but a narrow band of blue. Her voice was low and husky when she asked him, "Did she kiss you good-night?"

Holy hell, she was killing him. And she didn't have to ask twice. He leaned in and her eyes drifted closed. He intended to brush a kiss against her cheek, the way his mother would have. But she wasn't having any of that. She cupped his face and steered him a little to the left so that he got her lips instead.

It was the sweetest, hottest kiss he'd ever given or received. And when her tongue brushed against his, it was like napalm and fireworks and every other cliché all at once. She tangled her fingers in his hair, her nails scraping his scalp, sending a shockwave of blazing desire down his spine right to his groin. He knew that if he didn't do something to stop this, things were about to get out of hand. But that didn't dissuade him from tugging the elastic band from her ponytail, letting her hair tumble across her shoulders and down her back. He thought she couldn't look any sexier or more desirable, but he was wrong.

Holly's arms went around his neck. When her nails sunk into his back, a groan worked its way up from somewhere deep inside him. She kicked the blanket off and pulled him closer, clawing him through his shirt. One creamy, slender thigh brushed against his leg and the reaction was nuclear. But when she fisted his shirt and tried to pull it over his head, the idea of what she would find underneath instantly cooled his jets.

What the hell was he doing? She would see his scar, then he would have to explain. There was so much she didn't know about him, so many things he needed to tell her. He couldn't help but feel that he was misrepresenting himself somehow. And what if she fell in love with him? Jeremy had done enough damage. Jason couldn't risk hurting her again.

Though it tested the boundaries of his self-control, Jason caught her wrists in his hands, pulled them from around him. "Holly, wait."

She gazed up at him questioningly, sounding a little winded. "What's wrong?"

She looked like pure sex sitting there, her hair messy, her lips swollen and bruised from his kisses. Her shirt had ridden up her slender thighs, revealing the crotch of a pair of transparent pink lace panties. If there was ever a question of whether she was a natural blonde, now he knew.

He cursed under his breath, then cursed again. "We can't do this."

"Did I do something wrong?"

"No, not at all. You did everything right. The problem is with me."

"Could you maybe elaborate a little?"

Not at three in the morning. "It's late. Can we pick this conversation up tomorrow? When we're both a bit more clearheaded."

Looking confused and maybe a little hurt, she nodded and said, "If that's what you want."

"Believe me when I say that it's for the best."

Eight

Holly woke late the next morning, if 8:00 a.m. could be considered late. For the mother of twin infants it was.

The boys weren't in their beds, meaning Faye must have had them with her. She probably figured Holly hadn't gotten much sleep caring for Marshall last night. But her son's illness wasn't the only reason Holly had been awake half the night. She was suffering from a good old-fashioned case of unquenched lust.

She had tried to convince herself that Jason had done her a favor. That sleeping with him would have been immoral somehow, but she just couldn't work up the steam. She wanted him, and he'd seemed to want her, too. Right up until the second he'd shot her down. Though he had looked conflicted, as if the decision had been a difficult one.

She could have insisted they talk about it last night, but something in his eyes told her to back off. Could it have something to do with all the mixed messages she'd been sending him? Telling him one minute that they could only be friends, throwing herself at him the next. Maybe he thought it was too soon after his brother's death. She tried to put herself in his place and imagine how she would feel if she had an identical twin sister and was becoming romantically involved with her widower. Would she always feel as if she had come in second place?

Wanting to get this over with as soon as possible, she took a quick shower, dressed and tugged her wet hair into its usual ponytail, remembering the way Jason's hands had felt tangled in her hair last night, feeling the hot pull of lust all the way to the center of her womb.

Sex with Jeremy had been adequate, but he'd never made her feel this pulse-pounding, panty-drenching arousal. She couldn't recall anyone else who had. Not that she was some sort of sex expert. The list of men she'd slept with was a short one. But she knew what she liked, and she didn't doubt that Jason could give it to her.

She found Faye and the boys in the kitchen. The twins were asleep in their bouncy seats and Faye was loading the dishwasher. She turned and smiled when Holly walked into the room.

"Well, good morning, sleepy head."

She took a peek at Marshall, gently checking his forehead with the back of her wrist. "How has he been?"

"You can barely tell he was sick, and so far Devon hasn't been showing any symptoms."

"Thanks for letting me sleep in," Holly said, even though she hadn't done a whole lot of actual sleeping. And when she had drifted off, she'd been plagued with frustrating dreams. She'd dreamed about the day she found Jeremy, only this time when she found him he was still alive, but unconscious and barely alive. She tried to dial 911, but she couldn't make her hands cooperate. She kept hitting the wrong numbers, or her phone had no reception. And when she finally got through, she and the operator were disconnected before she could ask for help.

Then she was in the backseat of her parents' car, and though physically she was her ten-year-old self, mentally she was an adult with all the experiences she had now had. She knew what was about to happen, but when she tried to get the attention of her parents in the front seat, her vocal cords had frozen and she couldn't make a sound. She tried kicking her mother's seat but it was as if they didn't even know she was back there. She could see the truck coming at them in slow motion. That was always the way she remembered it. She'd read that in the face of an inevitable tragic experience the brain went into overdrive, taking in more information faster, which made the passage of time appear slower. Which she supposed made sense.

In her dreams she never felt pain or heard the sound of metal crumpling like a paper bag until the car was barely recognizable. And while in the dream she knew something bad was going to happen, she didn't feel scared or anxious. She was oddly detached, as if the situation were too surreal for a ten-year-old to process, the concept of death too unfamiliar or distant to imagine. Especially losing both her parents at the same time. And she always woke the instant before the truck hit them head-on.

In real life there had been pain like she'd never imagined possible. At first, when she'd woken in the hospital a week later, she'd had no memory of the accident, but during the following miserable months she'd spent confined to a hospital bed, healing from a plethora of injuries, the memories had slowly begun to resurface. Making her almost wish they hadn't. It had taken more than a year of physical therapy before she could walk without a noticeable limp. And nearly two years of psychotherapy to assuage the guilt of being the only one to survive.

"The boys have been angels, of course," Faye said, dragging Holly back to the present. Where she belonged.

"Have you seen Jason around or is he still asleep?" At the mere sound of his name, spoken from her own lips, her stomach did a backflip with a triple twist. She had nothing to be nervous about, yet she was nonetheless.

"He's out back on the deck reading the paper. Go ahead on out. I'll keep an eye on the twins."

"Are you sure?"

Faye looked at the boys sleeping soundly, then back at Holly. "As you can see, they're quite a handful."

Holly smiled. It did seem that they had been on their best behavior since they'd arrived, or maybe it was the huge financial burden lifted from Holly's shoulders, or the help she'd been receiving from Faye and Jason, that had lifted the pressure. Or a combination of the two.

"I won't be long," she told Faye, then headed out back.

Dressed in running pants and a white T-shirt, his hair wet and a little messy, Jason looked more like a soccer dad than a big shot executive. Straddling the chaise longue, he sipped from a cup of coffee, engrossed in the paper spread out in front of him.

"Good morning," she said.

Looking up, he said, "Good morning."

He wore a smile, but it was guarded and a little uncertain.

Well, no point beating around the bush. "I owe you an apology," she said.

His brows lifted in surprise, as if that was the last thing he'd expected to hear. "No, you don't."

She sat on the chair next to his. It was cool and still damp with dew. "I really do," she told him.

"Because we kissed?"

"No, that part was wonderful. You're a really good kisser."

The instant flash of heat in his eyes could have singed her hair. "So are you."

"I sent you some horribly mixed messages. I tell you that we can only be friends, and not ten minutes later, I practically dragged you into my bed. For all I know you could have a girlfriend."

"I could have a dozen."

She hoped he was joking. Or was he seriously some sort of charmingly rakish sex machine? And why did the possibility only intrigue her further?

"But I don't," he said and she tried not to feel relieved. "I've taken a break from dating. Time to step back and re-evaluate."

"Re-evaluate what?"

He hesitated, then said, "It's complicated."

"I'm smarter than I look."

He rubbed his palms together, as if he was working up to something big. "The thing is. I keep my romantic relationships very superficial."

"So you're only in it for the sex?"

"In a way, I guess. I don't do commitment."

"So you're commitment phobic."

The sun reflecting off the lake made the blue of his

eyes especially piercing. "I suppose you could call it that, but not for the reason you're probably thinking."

He couldn't possibly have any idea what she was thinking. Hell, she didn't even know for sure what she was thinking.

His tone changed, eyes went dark and stormy when he said, "Jeremy told you that he was sick when he was a kid, and that's why no one wanted him?"

"That's what he said." Of course she knew it wasn't true now.

"Jason wasn't sick. I was."

"You?"

"My mom died young of heart disease. A trait she passed on to me."

Holly was almost too stunned to reply. "B-but...you look perfectly healthy. *Better* than healthy. Men don't grow muscles like yours without a fair amount of physical stress."

"I am healthy—" he grabbed the hem of his shirt and pulled it over his head in that purposeful way that men have of undressing, revealing a long scar down the center of his chest "—since I got a new heart."

If he'd claimed to be superhero she couldn't have been more surprised. "You had a heart transplant?"

"Four years ago," he said.

She never would have guessed. And she couldn't help noticing that besides the scar, his body was perfect. Better than perfect and oh, how she wished she could put her hands on him. *All over him.*

"And just in the nick of time," he said. "Another week or two and I wouldn't be standing here today."

"How long were you sick?"

"I was diagnosed just after our twelfth birthday. I always knew there was a chance that Jeremy or I could get it. I just never expected it to hit me so young. As you can imagine, it was a really tough time for Jeremy."

Tough for Jeremy? What about Jason? "And for you. Seeing as how you were the one who was sick."

"It took a while, but eventually I was able to accept the diagnosis and not see it as a death sentence. Jeremy never could. He had already begun experimenting with drugs at that point, but my illness was the catalyst that sent him into a downward spiral."

"Don't tell me you feel responsible."

"Wouldn't you? For a good part of our childhood most of our parents' attention was focused on me."

Maybe at first, until she'd had a chance to approach it logically. Which probably would be tough to do as a sick adolescent. But Jason wasn't a kid any longer. He was a grown man who at some point would have to stop taking responsibility for his brother's shortcomings. "You didn't choose to get heart disease, did you?"

He shot her a look. "No one chooses to get heart disease."

"Exactly. So how can you be at fault for your brother's inability to cope? You could even say that the stress of having the twins pushed him over the edge, but you wouldn't blame the boys, would you?"

"Of course not. As I said, it's complicated."

Actually, it sounded pretty cut-and-dried to her. "If he was already experimenting, have you considered that if you hadn't gotten sick, something else might have set him off? Or perhaps that, tragedy or no tragedy, he would have ended up going down the same path?"

Jason's eyes suggested that he hadn't. "He felt guilty that it was me, and not him who'd inherited the gene."

"I know all about survivor's guilt, believe me."

"The accident with your parents?"

She turned her back to him and lifted her shirt, exposing the scars most people never knew she had. "It was bad."

"What happened?"

She tugged her shirt down and swiveled back to him. "We were hit head-on by a drunk driver. My parents died instantly. I was beat to hell, but I was alive, although barely. I heard the nurses tell my social worker that it was a miracle I survived, but it didn't feel like it at the time. I broke almost every major bone in my body. Including my back. In three places. I was in constant, excruciating pain.

"I was in the hospital for months, and then spent almost a year in a rehab facility learning to walk again. After the pain I endured, labor was practically a cakewalk."

"But you healed. You made a full recovery."

"More or less. I still ache when it rains, or if I let myself get too cold, and having so little body fat left I chill easily."

He'd noticed that last night.

"It also affected my pregnancy."

"In what way?"

"I fractured my hip in the accident so my OB was concerned about my carrying a child. When we found out it was twins, he worried that my bones couldn't handle the pressure of all that extra weight. When I went into early labor in my fifth month he put me on mandatory bed rest. For the next three months I had to rely solely on Jeremy."

"How did that go?" Jason asked, pulling his shirt back on, robbing her of her eye candy.

"It was okay at first. But by the time I had the twins I could tell that his patience was wearing thin. Up until then, in the short time that we were together, I had pretty much taken care of him. I did the cooking and the cleaning and all the shopping. He was a bit like a fish out of water."

"Jeremy could barely take care of himself, much less a wife and two kids."

"Call me old-fashioned, but I wanted to be home with the twins. I didn't mind taking care of him. I've always supported myself, but the jobs I had never gave me much satisfaction. I love being a mom. The thought of passing the boys off to a sitter while I worked nine-to-five had very little appeal."

"I don't think it's old-fashioned," he said. "My mother was a stay-at-home mom. If I had decided to marry, I would want my wife to stay home with the kids. If she wanted to."

"You know, I still don't get why you're relationship phobic."

His look said he thought she was a little left of center. "I'm not exactly husband material."

Huh? He would make some lucky woman an *amazing* husband. Unless he had some hidden horrible trait that scared women off. "You're kind, and generous, and I'm sorry, but have you looked in a mirror lately? Because, *damn*. You break the ceiling on the hottie scale."

He grinned. "Thanks."

"*And* you're a good kisser. Who lives in a *mansion*."

"And can never have children without potentially passing on the gene that caused my condition. A long time ago I made a vow to myself to never have a family."

"But technically you still can, right?"

He shook his head. "I can't. I knew that at some point I might be tempted to have a child despite the risk. That as I got older I might decide out of sentimentality that I want an heir. So I made sure that I could never change my mind. So…" He make a *snip-snip* gesture with his fingers.

She sucked in a quiet breath. "You had a vasectomy?"

"After my transplant. It was the only way to ensure that I would never pass on the disease. It would be cruel to put a child through that because of my own selfish needs."

Wow, talk about taking a radical step. She knew so little about her own family history, but she refused to live her life based on *what-if*s. "That must have been a heartbreaking decision to have to make being so young. I honestly don't know if I could do it."

"My feelings are neither here nor there. I know I did the right thing."

And she could understand why he did it. It was a selfless and responsible decision, but the right one? She wasn't so sure about that.

"Okay, so you can't have children of your own," she said. "There are a lot of women out there who wouldn't care. Not every woman has baby fever."

He sat forward, rested his elbows on his knees. "If you could see into the future when you met Jeremy, and you knew he would die, would you still have married him? Would you have even gotten involved with him?"

Her first instinct was to say yes, of course she would have, but it was a little more complicated than that.

"It's a tough one, isn't it?" Jason said. "I'm essentially a walking time bomb."

"I thought you said you were perfectly healthy."

"I am now. But a week from now?" He shrugged, as if they were talking about the weather or sports, or something equally insignificant. "Who knows? The anti-rejection drugs could stop working and my body would reject the heart. Or it could just give out."

Just the thought tied her stomach into knots. "How long do transplanted hearts usually last?"

"It depends on the person. There's a man in England who has been living with a transplanted heart for over thirty years. Some last only a few years. How can I, in good conscience, knowingly put someone through that kind of loss?"

"But like you said, it could last you thirty years or more."

"Is that a chance you'd be willing to take?"

"My situation is unique. I already buried a husband."

"And that," he said, "is precisely why we can never be more than friends."

As much as she hated to admit it, he was right. The thought of losing a second husband was bad enough. But to lose the twin brother of the first was beyond the scope of her comprehension. Just thinking about the possibility made her stomach clench. No one should have to put two husbands in the ground. But she was so drawn to Jason, so fascinated by everything about him. The thought of never kissing him again, never feeling his hands on her body...

"What if we agree that it's just sex," she said.

He leveled those piercing eyes on her and she felt their intensity to her very soul. "Holly, I think we both know that you and I together would never be *just sex*."

He was right, of course. She would fall head over heels in love with him. "So we'll just be friends," she said, and though it was what he wanted, she saw conflict in his eyes, and even worse, disappointment. It wasn't fair that she should find a man so wonderful, so perfect in every way.

Well, almost every way.

"Are you up to meeting my friends Lewis and Miranda?"

"Sure. That sounds like fun."

"I thought we could have dinner here so they can meet the boys, then go to the yacht club for drinks. Faye already agreed to watch the boys. I'm not sure if you noticed, but she loves having the three of you here."

"I noticed. But there might be a slight problem."

"What problem?"

To her, yacht club meant fancy. And she didn't do fancy these days. "I have a closetful of clothes that are two sizes too big. These jeans are about the only thing I have that fits. And even if I'd had the money to buy a new wardrobe, I haven't had the time since the boys were born. So I literally have nothing to wear."

"That," Jason said with a grin, "is a problem I can fix."

Nine

When the doorbell rang that evening, Holly, who was still in her room getting ready, got a sudden and severe case of the jitters. What if Jason's friends didn't like her? What if she used the wrong fork or slurped her soup and embarrassed Jason? She hadn't exactly grown up on the wrong side of the tracks, but she was no socialite.

Although she sort of looked like one.

Jason had insisted on buying her clothes that actually fit, and after a halfhearted protest, and his insisting that she let him do something nice for her—as if he hadn't done a whole mess of nice things already—she agreed to let him take her shopping for a dress.

He kept fixing her problems, and it always seemed to require that he pull out his wallet. But she had to admit that the sundress she chose for tonight looked pretty darned good on her. With a full skirt and halter bodice, it had a distinct retro feel and made her look a little less like a skeleton. She even took the time to use hot rollers in her hair, so it fell in soft waves down her back. She'd never worn much in the way of makeup, but as a final touch she'd brushed on mascara and applied her favorite peppermint-flavored lip gloss.

The boutique he had taken her to in town had the most beautiful clothes she'd ever seen. All designer labels fit for royalty. And though she knew it must have been ridiculously expensive, after stealthily checking the price on an *eight hundred dollar* purse, she'd stopped looking at the tags altogether. The two sales girls had fallen all over themselves catering to her every request, showering her with compliments. It had been almost like a scene out of the movie *Pretty Woman*. Only she wasn't a prostitute and, no offense to Richard Gere, but Jason was way sexier.

Though they had gone into the boutique with the intention of buying one outfit, he'd talked her into half a dozen, and hadn't even blanched when he'd handed his credit card to the cashier. Holly tried to feel guilty, considering all he'd done for her already, but he just seemed so…*happy*. Giving to others seemed to give him immense pleasure. And she could see where someone with fewer scruples could easily take advantage of that.

She would never come right out and ask him for money or clothes, or if she did, it would be out of sheer desperation. But she figured that if he was offering it wouldn't hurt to indulge him every now and then. And indulge herself.

The knock on her bedroom door drew her away from her reflections, and the butterflies in her stomach went on a violent rampage.

She opened the door to find Jason standing there.

He opened his mouth to speak, but all he managed, as his eyes raked over her, was a mumbled "Oh, my God."

She cringed. "Good or bad?"

"Oh, definitely good. You look..." He shook his head, as if grappling for the right thing to say. "I have no words."

She smiled. She'd rendered him speechless. That was kind of cool. She knew she looked good, but not *that* good. Or was it just that while everyone else saw the plain and ordinary woman who stared back at her in the mirror every morning, Jason saw something special in her. Something unique.

"That dress looked good on you in the store, but with your hair down like that..." He reached over and twisted one silky strand around his finger, then let it slip free. "Just...*damn*."

In a dark shirt and slacks he looked good enough to eat. "You don't look half bad yourself. Are they here?"

He couldn't seem to tear his eyes away. "Is who here?"

She really had thrown him for a loop. "Your friends. I heard the doorbell."

"Oh, right. Yes, they are," he said, still looking a little dazed. "Are you ready?"

"I'm ready, but nervous."

"Don't be. They'll love you."

She would have to take his word for it.

She let him lead her down the stairs, and the butter-flies went berserk. But the couple holding her sons and sitting on the sofa in the family room were not at all what she had expected. Jason made the introductions. Lewis was considerably older than his wife, who Holly guessed was only a few years older than she was. Mi-randa was petite, but a little plump, with jet-black hair she wore long and curly. She was exceptionally pretty, with huge brown eyes, a cute button nose and fire-red pouty lips.

She surprised Holly by pulling her in for a firm hug and saying, in a thick Southern drawl, "Oh, honey, I'm so sorry for your loss."

Holly liked her instantly.

"Your boys are just cute as buttons," she said, bouncing Devon gently on her shapely hip. "I'll bet they're a handful."

"They can be, but Faye has been such an incredible help to me."

"They look just like you," Miranda told Jason, then paused, guilt washing over her face. "I'm sorry, Potter. Was that insensitive of me?"

It took a second for Holly to realize that she was talking to Jason.

"It's okay," Jason answered.

Miranda shrugged helplessly. "You know me. My mouth moves faster than my brain sometimes."

"We were identical," Jason told her. "It only makes sense that they would look like me. And it's all right to talk about him."

Lewis had executive written all over him, from his styled salt-and-pepper hair, to his Italian leather loafers. He had kind eyes, and held Marshall with the ease of a man who'd had children. "How old are they?" he asked Holly.

"Almost four months. Do you two have children?"

"Not yet," Lewis said, glancing over at his wife, who promptly burst into tears.

Stunned and horrified, Holly stood there with her jaw hanging, unsure of what to do. She'd known them less than five minutes and had made the poor woman cry. "I—I'm so sorry. I didn't mean to—"

"Honey, don't you even worry about it," Miranda said with a sniffle, plucking a cotton handkerchief from, of all places, her bra, which was already busting at the seams with her ample bosom. "It's these darned fertility drugs. They make me weepy."

"In vitro," Lewis told Holly.

"One minute I'll be right as rain, and the next inconsolable." Miranda smiled through a sheen of tears and squeezed her husband's hand. "But it will all be worth it when we have our own little angel."

"Pardon the interruption," Faye said from the doorway, sparing Holly the burden of an awkward reply. "Dinner is served."

"Oh, good!" Miranda said, brightening instantly. "I'm starved."

She led the pack out to the deck. A coral sunset served as a backdrop to a mouthwatering meal and lively conversation. Miranda dissolved into tears three more times, but was able to laugh it off afterward. And Holly could tell that Lewis adored her. They talked briefly about their three-year struggle to conceive, but Holly could see that it was a very touchy subject for Miranda. She also kept calling Jason "Potter," which Holly thought was a little strange; she assumed it was a nickname from an inside joke they shared. Maybe Jason liked to garden? Or smoke pot?

After dinner they took the boat across the lake and docked it at the marina. The yacht club was busy, and all heads turned when Jason entered the room. The hostess greeted him by name and led them to a table on the veranda.

They ordered after-dinner drinks and a tray of gourmet bite-size desserts that were to die for, though it was difficult for Holly to eat feeling so self-conscious. No matter which direction she turned her gaze, she would catch someone watching her. At first she thought maybe they were looking at Jason, because he certainly was easy on the eyes and obviously highly respected. But when he and Lewis stepped away from the table briefly to talk to a friend at the bar, the curious looks didn't follow them.

"Why are people staring at me?" she whispered to Miranda, while the men were gone.

"Because you're beautiful, and you're currently shacked up with the hottest catch on the East Coast."

Shacked up? "I'm living with Jason, yes, but there's nothing going on. I mean, he's my brother-in-law. It's totally platonic." Or it was supposed to be. Having feelings for each other didn't mean they should act on them.

"Honey, let's be honest," Miranda said, sipping a glass of club soda and lime. "There is nothing *platonic* in the way Potter looks at you."

There it was again, that strange nickname. "Why do you call him that?"

"Potter?"

Holly nodded and Miranda chuckled. "He's the villain in the movie *It's a Wonderful Life*. You know, Mr. Potter. The richest man in town."

It took a second to connect the dots, and when the picture was clear, the truth hit Holly like a freight train. "Are you saying that *Jason* is the richest man in town?"

"You didn't notice that his house is by far the largest on the lake? I mean, don't get me wrong, the median net worth in town is definitely in the millions. As far as I know Jason is the only billionaire."

Holly blinked, positive that she'd misheard her. "I'm sorry, did you say *bill*ionaire?"

"You didn't know?"

Holly shook her head, and only because she was so dumbfounded her vocal cords had seized right up.

Miranda chuckled. "Honey, you should see your face."

She'd known Jeremy had money, and a lot of it. Hundreds of thousands at least. Maybe even a million. But never in her wildest dreams had she considered that he could be a billionaire.

The enormity of it was almost too much to take in. Her breath backed up in her lungs and her brain immediately started to shut down. Her vision began to go dark, her ears started to buzz and the chair swayed underneath her. Or maybe she was the one swaying.

"Whoa, there," Miranda said, grasping Holly's arm, but the other woman's voice sounded miles away. And she no longer looked amused. "Don't you go fainting on me now."

Jason did seem to have that effect on Holly. She blinked her eyes, willing herself to stay conscious, to get some much needed blood back to her brain. She knew the best way not to pass out was to put her head between her knees, but in the middle of a fancy restaurant?

Would that be any more humiliating than passing out in a fancy restaurant?

Miranda slid a glass of water at Holly and said, "Drink this."

Holly took a sip, then another, leaning against the table for support. Gradually her vision began to clear, the buzzing in her ears faded into the background noise and her chair found its balance.

Miranda was frowning, which made her crimson lips look even more like a bow. "You okay, hon?"

Holly nodded. "I think so. It's just so…huge."

"I take it you don't come from money."

She shook her head. "My parents died when I was ten. I grew up in a foster home."

"I grew up in a trailer park in Georgia, so I can relate. I met my first husband when I was working as a waitress at Hooters and living on a friend's couch. I was only eighteen and he was twenty-seven years older than me with the craggiest mug you've ever seen. But he was sweet as honey and he loved me. He was also rich and I was desperate. The marriage lasted less than a year, but we remained good friends until he passed away."

The sound of Miranda's voice worked like a salve on Holly's frayed nerves. "Lewis is your second husband?"

"Fourth," Miranda said without a hint of shame. "I haven't had the best luck with men, but Lewis, he's a keeper."

Holly had thought the same about Jason, but now she wasn't so sure. "Why didn't he tell me?" she said, and Miranda didn't have to ask whom she meant.

"Jason is a modest man. He doesn't like to flaunt his wealth. He's the least pretentious wealthy person that I've ever met. He appreciates the simple things in life. He just enjoys them in places like Aspen and Cabo San Lucas. He has homes all over the world."

All over the world?

"And he keeps his philanthropy very private."

Of course a man like him would be philanthropic. "I really had no idea."

"He was probably worried you would feel intimidated or uncomfortable. He likes to be treated like a regular guy."

But he was not a regular guy.

"He's a financial genius, you know. A bona fide prodigy. People say that everything he touches turns to gold."

"Did you meet him before or after his transplant?"

"I met him about ten months before. He and Lewis have been friends for years. He was in pretty bad shape back then. He spent most of the last year before the surgery laid up. But that didn't stop him from building his fortune. He worked from his home office and later from his bed. He refused to give up. We were so afraid we'd lose him, then just like that they found a match. But it was hard on him knowing that a sixteen-year-old had to die to save his life. There was a lot of guilt at first." She paused and said, "I'm sorry. Here I am shooting off my big mouth."

"I don't mind." She had learned more about Jason in the past five minutes than she had in the past nine days.

Was that all it had been? In some ways she felt as if she had known him forever, and in other ways she barely knew him at all.

"He was so weak and frail, you would barely recognize him. In fact..." Miranda reached into her purse and pulled out her phone. She scrolled through her photos until she found the one she was looking for, then handed it to Holly. "This was about a month before the surgery."

Holly took the phone and sucked in a quiet breath when she saw the photo. Miranda was right. It hardly looked like Jason, and the idea that he'd been that ill made her feel sick inside. He was thin and gaunt and, sitting next to Lewis in the photo, his skin looked pasty and gray. The only thing that hadn't changed was his eyes. They were full of life. And hope. He had come a long way since then.

She handed the phone back to Miranda, a painful knot in the center of her chest. As his new heart began to wear out, would he look like that again? Would she have to watch him waste away knowing there wasn't a thing she could do about it? And what if her boys had inherited the gene? What if they got sick, too?

Suddenly Holly was the one with tears welling in her eyes.

"Oh, honey." Miranda reached across the table and put her hand over Holly's. "I didn't mean to upset you."

Holly sniffled and dabbed at her eyes with a napkin. "It was just a shock to see him like that."

Miranda gave her hand a squeeze and said quietly, "Does he know that you're in love with him?"

She didn't bother trying to deny it. To Miranda or herself. The past few days, since that amazing kiss, had been absolute torture. She craved his presence, his touch. She loved listening to his voice, hearing him laugh. He was intelligent and funny, and even a little goofy at times when he played with the boys, who also adored him. Even if he had been penniless, he'd be everything she could ever want in a man. "He knows there are strong feelings, but I've never said the words."

"Well, if it makes you feel better, it's fairly obvious the feeling is mutual."

Actually, that made her feel worse.

"If I'm being too nosy I apologize, but I just have to ask…" She leaned in close and lowered her voice. "Have you two…you know…?"

"We kissed, but then we agreed that we should keep our relationship platonic."

Miranda sat back in surprise. "Now why would you go and do that? It's obvious you two are crazy for each other. I could see it when you walked down the stairs together. And all through dinner he couldn't keep his eyes off you."

Holly heard herself using Jason's stock answer. "It's complicated." Which was no answer at all.

"How long has it been since you knocked boots with anyone?"

Holly couldn't help but smile at the euphemism. Far too long. "Seven months, two weeks, four days—" she checked the time on her phone "—six hours and… thirty-two minutes. Give or take a minute or two. Co-incidentally, I figured that out last night." While she was lying in bed, aroused and restless, knowing Jason was a floor above her. But he might as well have been a million miles away.

Miranda clucked. "Oh, honey, that's a *long* time."

"I went into premature labor in my fifth month, so I *couldn't* have sex. And after the boys were born, there just wasn't time." Not to mention that Jeremy had shown no interest in her sexually. Half the time he had been too wrapped up in his own contorted emotions to realize she and the twins were even there. And when he had noticed he had been so full of resentment, especially near the end. She hadn't told Jason the whole story. Hadn't admitted how bitter and cruel Jeremy could be. It had been like living with two different people. One who was sweet and compassionate, the other spiteful and mean. Even if he had wanted to have sex, the idea of him touching her had been almost repulsive at times.

She knew now that it was the drugs, but she didn't want to burden Jason with the truth. She wanted him to remember his brother fondly or as fondly as he could under the circumstances.

"If Lewis and I go more than a week I get cranky," Miranda said.

"To be honest, up until recently, I really hadn't given it much thought."

"And now?"

Now it was all she could think about. And her face must have said it all.

"Might that have something to do with the fact that you're stuck living in the same house with a man you're wildly attracted to and who clearly wants to jump your bones."

Yeah, that might explain it. "Like I said, it's complicated."

"Say no more. I know when I'm sticking my nose where it doesn't belong."

The men returned to the table a second later and the conversation turned to a subject a little less scandalous. Holly put on a good face and pretended that everything was normal, when honestly she didn't even know what was normal anymore. And the longer she sat there, the angrier she felt. A lie by omission was still a lie.

When they got back to the house around eleven, Miranda gave her a big goodbye hug, and then joined Lewis to head home in a black SUV that looked just like Jason's. But not before Miranda promised to call and make plans to have lunch in town and go shopping. She knew so few people back in the city it was nice to know that here she would have friends.

Faye was in the family room, stretched out on the sectional watching a rerun of *The X-Files*.

"How were the boys?" Holly asked her.

"Devon was a little fussy, but he finally went to sleep."

Devon had never gotten the croup like his brother. Instead he wound up with a mild case of the sniffles. "Thank you for watching them."

Faye smiled and stood up, stretching her arms way over her head. "You know I don't mind. Did you have a good time?"

Yes and no. "Miranda is really nice."

"Well, I'm off to bed," Faye said. "You know where I am if you need me."

"I should go check on the boys," Holly told Jason after Faye was gone. They needed to talk, but she hadn't figured out exactly what she was going to say. Odds were good that it would be snarky.

"Do you need help?" Jason asked.

She could tell by his expression that he *wanted* to help. But now that she was over being shocked and confused, she was just plain mad. "I'm just going to peek in and then go to bed."

Without waiting for a response she headed up the stairs to the boys' room. They were both sound asleep in their cribs, and though the urge to lift them out and give them a kiss and a snuggle was strong, she really didn't want to wake them.

She backed quietly out of their room, turned and plowed right into Jason, who apparently had followed her up. It was like walking into a steel wall and the momentum knocked her back a step. Jason caught her arms to keep her from falling against the door.

"Sorry," she said, quickly composing herself. "I didn't know you were behind me."

"Is everything okay?"

"Why do you ask?"

"I'm getting a vibe."

"I'm tired. Maybe that's it." She walked to her bedroom and he followed her.

He didn't look as if he believed her. "Can we talk for a minute?"

Probably not such a good idea. "About what?"

"I heard Miranda invite you shopping," he said, following her into her bedroom uninvited. "I know how you feel about taking money from me, but you and the boys are going to need things. I was thinking that it would be a good idea to give you a monthly allowance. Like I did with Jeremy."

What the heck was she going to do with ten thousand dollars a month?

"Okay," she said, and was rewarded with a look of genuine surprise.

"Really?"

"Sure. That would be what? Ten thousand a month? One hundred and twenty thousand a year?"

The bright look began to fade. "In that ballpark, yes."

"Well, why stop there? How does a million sound? Or what the hell, how about a *billon*? You could afford that, right?"

He actually winced.

"So it's true. You are a billionaire?"

Ten

"You're upset," Jason said.

Thanks, Captain Obvious. Ya think? "Can you blame me? You might have mentioned it."

"It didn't seem that relevant."

"Not *relevant*?"

"What I meant was, I was waiting for the right time."

"When? After the twins finish college?"

In a tone that held more patience than she probably deserved, he said, "You said it yourself our situation is unique, and just like you I'm doing my best to figure it out. I'm not perfect. You're going to have to cut me a little slack."

His words sucked the wind right out of her sails, and her head dropped in shame.

He was right. She was being selfish and immature. Maybe he'd been worried that knowing about the money would change things between them. That she would begin to think of him differently. But as he stood in her room, looking just as perplexed and frustrated by this as she was, he was still just Jason. A real man with feelings and not just a number on a bank statement. And she knew, money or no money, that would never change. "I'm sorry," she said. "I'm not being fair. I guess I just thought that there would be no more surprises between us."

He had every right to be angry with her, or at the very least annoyed, but he wasn't. The man had the patience of a saint. And considering all that he had been through, he'd probably earned it. "We'll figure this all out. It'll just take time."

She knew he was right. "It seems so surreal."

"Well, you had better get used to it. If something happens to me, the twins will get it all."

Huh?

No, that couldn't be right. "But...you said Jeremy was disinherited."

"By our father. It's all mine now, and I can do with it what I choose."

"I—I don't know what to say. The idea of being responsible for that much money... I would be lost. Overwhelmed. I wouldn't even know where to begin."

"I would never let that happen. Arrangements have already been made. You'll have all the financial guidance you'll need."

Arrangements had been made, meaning this was not just a possibility. This was her life now. She was the mother of future billionaires. Her life would never be the same. It was so much to take in all at once.

"If it's any consolation, I don't actually have a billion dollars. My money is spread all over the place."

It was a small consolation and good to know that he

was thinking ahead. Not that she would have expected anything less than that.

The last of her energy drained, Holly sat down on the edge of the bed. "Miranda said you're a financial prodigy. And everything you touch turns to gold."

"She was exaggerating."

Holly doubted that.

Jason sat down beside her, already such a familiar presence. She knew the smell of him, the sharp angle of his jaw, the way his hair fell across his forehead. And then there was the electrical current that seemed to arc between them even if they were yards away from each other. The same energy that she was feeling right now.

She wished she could lean against him, bury her face in the crook of his neck and breathe him in, feel the brush of beard stubble against her forehead. The dark shadow on his cheeks and chin made him look sexy and dangerous. A guilty pleasure. She wanted to take his face in her palms and press her lips to his, feel his hands on her skin. She wanted to know the sweet pressure of that delicious body settling over her, his weight pressing her to the mattress, thrusting between her thighs. She wanted it so badly it hurt. And it wasn't fair that she couldn't have him. It was as if the universe was playing some cruel joke on her. The universe had robbed her of her parents, her security. Had given her two beautiful children who would never know their father. It handed her this wonderful man, and then set him behind an indestructible wall of glass. There was no way over or around it. She was cursed to spend the rest of her life watching him from the other side, so close but just out of reach.

"Are we okay now?" he asked her.

"Yes, we're okay. I'm sorry I overreacted. And I want you to know how much I appreciate all that you've done for me."

He rose from the bed and she did, too. "Is there anything I do can for you? Anything you need?"

All she really needed was him, but she shook her head. "About the allowance, you do what you think is right. Whatever you decide, I'll be good with it."

"Well, then, I should let you get to bed."

Only if you come with me, she wanted to say, but of course she didn't.

Jason reached over and cradled her face in his big hands, pressed a kiss to her forehead, his lips lingering as if he didn't want it to end. If he were to kiss her mouth right now she wouldn't try to stop him. Thankfully neither of them seemed willing to take that first step. But the ache that settled in her chest, the deep longing to be close to him could only mean one thing. Miranda was right, Holly loved him. Not just that, but she was *in love* with him. Totally and completely. It had just happened, and now she had to figure out a way to make it un-happen.

The words *I love you* balanced on the tip of her tongue, but she had neither the right nor the courage to let them slip past her lips.

It wasn't meant to be.

A week later, Jason lay in bed in his penthouse apartment in New York, flipping through the channels on his ridiculously huge television, bored out of his skull and wishing he were back home with Holly and the boys. He used to enjoy these occasional business trips to the city, but until recently, he really hadn't had anything to come home to. She and the twins were so deeply ingrained in his life now. He could hardly remember what it was like when they weren't there.

He would have brought them along, but not only had he been in meetings from 8:00 a.m. to 9:00 p.m. that night, he was supposed to be keeping his distance from Holly. Not that it had been doing any good. After that night out with Lewis and Miranda, something had changed between him and Holly. He couldn't quite put his finger on what it was, but things were different. More intense, maybe. All he knew was that it was getting more and more difficult to keep his distance. He'd been thinking things, impossible things, such as what would happen if they stopped fighting it and let their relationship take its natural course. But he already knew the answer. As much as he wanted her, he couldn't do it to Holly and the boys. It wouldn't be fair when his life expectancy was so uncertain. He'd seen the look on her face when she'd talked about already burying one husband. It would be cruel to put her through that again.

His phone rang and he scooped it up from the bed beside him, hoping that it was Holly. Since he'd left yesterday morning they had spoken on the phone and texted numerous times. He'd come to see her not just as a woman he could fall in love with, but a good friend. She saw him for who he was, and he actually liked that she was unimpressed by his money. Intimidated even. He had a feeling that if he lost every penny she genuinely wouldn't care. Most of his life had been about his career and making more money. But now that he had someone to share that money with, and his brother's sons to carry on the family name, making a mark for himself seemed a little less crucial.

He was disappointed to see that it was Lewis calling

him, probably to ask how the meetings went. Normally he would have been there with Jason, but he'd had some sort of appointment with Miranda that he couldn't miss. According to Holly, she and Miranda had been spending a lot of time together. Miranda had been slowly introducing Holly to the local population and helping her deal with people's perceptions, or misperceptions, of what she and Jason did behind closed doors. For him, privacy and anonymity were precious commodities in short supply. But he was used to the gossip and speculation.

Though he wasn't much in the mood for talking, he answered the phone. After the obligatory hellos, Lewis asked Jason how business was going in New York.

"I was hoping I could get out of here in a day or two, but it's not looking that way. Probably Friday at the soonest."

"You don't sound too thrilled about that."

No, he wasn't. "Don't I?"

"You love a challenging business deal. The riskier the better."

He used to.

When he met his friend's observation with silence, Lewis said, "Why don't you just tell her how you feel?"

"My feelings are irrelevant."

"You say that a lot, but I don't know if you really believe it anymore."

Whether he believed it, or even liked it, wasn't the point.

"You've worked hard all of your life," Lewis said. "Why not take a little time off, give yourself a break? Spend some quality time with Holly and the boys."

Spending more time with Holly was the last thing he should be doing. She and the boys were settled and safe, and that was all that mattered. Well, all that should have mattered.

"Will you be driving down tomorrow?" he asked Lewis.

"I'm sending Preston in my place."

"Is something wrong?"

"No, but Miranda has an appointment with a specialist."

"What kind of specialist?"

"An obstetrician who specializes in high-risk pregnancy."

Jason blinked. "Pregnancy?"

"Oh, did I forget to mention that we're pregnant?"

"I think so!" Jason said with a laugh. "Congratulations. I guess third time was the charm."

"I guess so."

Jason couldn't have been happier for his friend, and was maybe just a little envious. "Miranda must be thrilled."

"She's busting at the seams to tell everyone, but we're going to wait a few months to make the official announcement. You know, just in case."

"How do you feel?"

"Cautiously optimistic."

Jason could understand Lewis's apprehension, given how hard it had been for them to conceive. "Does Holly know?"

"Miranda is on the phone with her as we speak."

Jason's call-waiting buzzed, and it was Holly. "Speak of the devil. She's calling me right now."

"I'll let you go."

"Give me a call tomorrow and let me know how the appointment goes."

They said goodbye, and Jason answered Holly's call. "Hello."

"Did you hear the good news?" she asked excitedly.

"I just got off the phone with Lewis."

"Miranda is so excited. She's wanted this so badly. She's already picking out baby furniture and paint swatches. I want to throw her a baby shower. She's due in early spring."

"Do you want more children?" he asked, the question coming out of nowhere. What the hell would he ask her that for?

She didn't seem to find the question unusual at all. "I'm not against the idea of having another child, but I had such a difficult pregnancy. I guess it would depend on the circumstances."

"But if you knew you absolutely couldn't?"

"I would be fine with that. But I have the boys. It's different for Miranda." There was a slight pause, and then she said, "Why do you ask?"

Good question. "Just curious."

She bought his flimsy explanation, or maybe she was just being polite. Maybe she could see right through him.

"The boys miss you," she said.

"I miss them."

"And I miss you, too."

He closed his eyes and sighed. Damn, why did she have to say things like that? He didn't return the sentiment. But considering the time he'd spent calling and texting her, it was probably obvious. He just couldn't seem to help himself. He could go only so long without hearing her voice.

"I thought that I might take flowers to Jeremy's grave," he said, though to him it was hard to picture his brother lying in the ground. It was just a gesture of respect, because for all Jeremy's faults, Jason loved his brother. And he knew Jeremy was in a better place. A place where he would no longer be tortured by his addictions. Where he would find peace. Call it heaven or the afterlife or maybe even another dimension. Whatever and wherever it was, Jason believed he would see his brother again someday.

"That would be nice," she said. "I haven't been back since the funeral."

"Maybe next month on his birthday we could go together, the four of us." Like a family, but not quite.

"I'd like that. When do you think you'll come home?"

Home. That word had taken on a whole new meaning lately. "Probably not until Friday. Sooner if I can manage it, but I can't make any promises."

"It's supposed to be a beautiful weekend. Maybe we can do something fun with the boys."

"Figure out what you'd like to do and we'll do it." He didn't really care what she chose as long as he was with her and the boys.

"Hey, I forgot to tell you that Devon rolled over today."

"Get out, really?"

"Yep, back to stomach."

"They're getting so big, I can practically see them growing."

"Uh-oh, one of the boys is crying."

"Kind of early for their feeding," he said.

"Yeah, maybe I can get him back to sleep. I have to let you go."

"Okay, I'll see you Friday."

"I look forward to it," she said.

"Oh, and Holly?"

"Yeah?"

"I miss you, too."

Eleven

Holly lay draped on a chaise longue on the back deck, trying to get some sun without burning herself to a crisp. The air was still cool but the sun warmed her pale skin. Her bathing suit hung on her like loose skin, but she had gained about five pounds since she got here. Regardless, she would probably have to buy a new one.

Before he'd left for the city, Jason had given her all the information for her new account, along with a debit card. When she'd logged in and checked the balance online, there already had been ten thousand dollars in the account. But so far she hadn't spent a penny. Pretty much all she had done since Jason left was eat, sleep and lie around and play with the boys. She kept asking Faye for that chore list, but her answer was always, "I'm working on it."

Faye probably didn't have time to write it up, considering the way she had been waiting on Holly and the twins hand and foot. Holly was convinced that Faye was clairvoyant, because she always seemed to know what Holly wanted before Holly even knew she wanted it. She also had the twins' schedule down to the minute, and was always there to help with feedings and diaper changes. And even dispense parental advice. The twins were napping now, and Holly had asked Faye to call her when they woke. But knowing Faye, she would feed them then play with them for an extra hour first.

It went against Holly's very being to let someone take care of her like that, but Faye had a way of making it feel okay. She had been giving Holly the time and space she needed to regenerate, to be a productive human being again, and Holly had no way to express her gratitude.

The alarm on her phone went off, telling her it was time to turn on to her stomach. She flipped over on the soft cushion, the loose nylon of her suit riding up her butt cheeks. It didn't matter really. She could be out there stark naked and no one but Faye would see her. The nearest neighbor was almost a quarter mile down the shore in either direction. Jason had told her his property was the largest on the lake, although at one time, before the Great Depression, his family owned pretty much all of the land on this side of the lake.

George was in town getting supplies, which he transported in Jason's boat, so she would hear him coming and have plenty of time to cover up. Jason wasn't due back until tomorrow night.

On the Sunday before Jason left for the city, he'd driven her and the boys into town for a late lunch at the country club, where everyone knew his name. Then they'd walked the busy streets window-shopping. Everyone seemed to know him, and they fawned over the twins. A few of the younger, seasonal employees in the shops even had offered to babysit. Holly would go so far as to say that they'd been treated a bit like royalty.

In the few weeks she'd spent with Jason, the sexual attraction that she had hoped would fade had only grown more intense, and obvious. He wasn't helping matters in the least. He seemed to take every opportunity he could find to touch her. Be it their fingers brushing as they did a baby exchange, or his muscular thigh touching hers when they sat close—which they shouldn't have been doing in the first place.

Before he left for the city, he'd given her what she'd thought would be a platonic hug, but then as she was backing away he'd brushed his lips across her cheek, so lightly it was barely more than a tickle. But it was a tickle that she'd felt everywhere, and his eyes had said he wanted to do a lot more than kiss her.

That made two of them.

That still didn't change the fact that they couldn't, or at least shouldn't, get involved physically. Logically she understood the repercussions. But logic had nothing to do with this. She was running on pure emotion. So it was almost a relief when he'd left for Manhattan on Sunday night.

For about five minutes.

The dust from the tires of the limo that picked him up had barely settled before she'd begun to miss him.

"The view out here is especially pleasing today."

At the sound of Jason's voice just feet from where she lay—with her butt cheeks still hanging out—Holly's heart kicked into third gear. But when she opened her eyes and looked up at him, she was embarrassed to find him staring at her bare bony ass.

To try to cover herself now would not only be pointless, it also would make it look as if she had something to hide. She'd owned bikinis that showed off a whole lot more than he was seeing right now. So instead of freaking out, she pushed herself up on her elbows and greeted him with a smile, doing what was probably the worst thing she could under the circumstances. She looked him up and down and said, "The view from here isn't so shabby, either."

She was rewarded with a sizzling smile. He looked so distinguished in his dark blue pinstripe suit and paisley tie. "You're early. I thought you wouldn't be back until tomorrow."

Still eyeing her behind he said, "It looks to me as if I got here at just the right time."

The deep thrum of his voice burned her skin more than a dozen suns could. He really needed to stop saying things like that. It was too tempting. She'd forgotten how much fun it could be to flirt. What it was like to feel sexy and lusted after. But that didn't make it okay.

Wearing what she had come to think of as his devilish smile, he took off his jacket, draped it on the back of the chair next to hers and sat down. "Anything exciting happen while I was gone?"

"Not since we talked this morning," she said. They'd shared many calls since he'd left. Most of them had been at night, and some had lasted for an hour or more. She'd learned an awful lot about him during those calls, and now he knew just about all there was to know about her. They never seemed to run out of things to talk about. She no longer looked at him as Jeremy's other half. Jason was truly in a class by himself. His quirky sense of humor kept her laughing, and his smile made her heart beat faster. His big sturdy hands made her long to be touched.

"Anything exciting happen in the city?" she asked.

"Nah, just boring business stuff." He nodded toward her lower half and she braced for a butt comment. "You're getting a little pink."

"Pink?" She wasn't even blushing.

"Your back. You're getting a sunburn."

Oh. "My fair skin is a curse."

"You need more sunblock." He picked up the bottle of sunblock spray that she had set on the ground by her chair. "Would you like me to do it?"

"Sure."

The cool spray felt good on the hot skin of her back and legs.

"I miss the days when people had to rub the suntan lotion on," he said with a sigh.

The thought of his hands sliding over her skin made her lady parts tingle. "Well, technically you still can. Sometimes the spray misses places, and it's better to rub it around and make it even so you don't get random burn spots."

"What are you trying to say?" he asked her.

Good question. What *was* she trying to say? She hadn't meant to imply that she wanted him to rub lotion on her. Or had she?

"I'm merely stating a fact."

One brow rose and he grinned that wicked smile, going in one instant from conservative entrepreneur to devilishly handsome rake.

How did he do that?

Jeremy, she hated to admit, had seemed almost two dimensional in comparison. She could sort of understand why, since he'd had so many secrets to juggle. It must have been complicated trying to keep the lies straight in his own head, especially being under the influence of narcotics. The truth just seemed so much easier. At least she had always thought so.

"So you're definitely not asking me to rub lotion on your back?" Jason asked her.

Okay, so maybe there were times when the real truth was better left unsaid. So she told him what she considered a little white lie. "Definitely not."

"Because I can."

And oh, did she want him to. All the more reason to say no.

"I promise I'll keep it completely platonic," he said.

Nothing about having his hands on her could ever be *platonic*.

"Actually," he said with a frown, "you're awfully red. How long have you been sunning your back?"

"I've been out here around an hour, and every fifteen minutes I flip over. Kind of like a hamburger."

"Well, I think you're done. Maybe a little overdone."

He was probably right.

She pushed herself up in the chair and swung her legs over the side so she was facing him, holding up her saggy suit so she didn't give him another peek at her wares. "I should probably go in and take a cool shower."

"If you need someone to platonically rub aloe on your back..."

She laughed. "You're my guy. I know."

He grinned. "How about we leave the twins with Faye and have dinner out tonight? We could invite Lewis and Miranda. Make it a celebration."

"That sounds like fun." She rose from the chair, slipped her feet into her flip-flops. "Let me check and see if that's okay with Faye."

"You know it will be."

"But it would be rude and presumptuous not to ask."

"That's why I pay them handsomely, so I don't have to ask."

"They work for you, not me. I prefer to ask." And even if they had worked for her, she never would have felt comfortable ordering them to do anything. Although at some point she might have to learn how.

On her way up to the shower she stopped to talk to Faye, who was sitting on the sofa feeding the boys their bottles. Of course she was more than happy to watch them tonight, and while Holly showered. They chatted for a few more minutes, and then Holly went up to take her shower.

She took a long, cool one, soaping herself up to get the sunblock off, wishing it was Jason's hands sliding all over her. But she resisted the urge to slide her hand between her legs for some much needed relief. Maybe tonight after she went to bed.

She stepped out onto the mat, and had just wrapped a towel around herself when she heard a knock on her bedroom door. Figuring it was Faye with the twins she didn't hesitate to pull it open. But it was Jason.

The man did have impeccable timing.

His eyes raked over her. "I came to tell you that Miranda isn't feeling well so they won't be joining us for dinner."

"That's too bad."

"Can I come in?"

"I'm in a towel," she said as if he hadn't noticed.

"That's why I want to come in."

Oh. My. God. "Do you think that's a good idea?"

"No. I think it's an *excellent* idea."

Without waiting for an invitation, Jason stepped into her bedroom and shut the door behind him. He didn't care if it was a bad idea. He didn't care about anything but getting her naked and burying himself deep inside of her.

When he'd seen her lying there, her smooth behind rosy from the sun, it had taken every bit of restraint he had not to throw her over his shoulder and carry her to his bedroom.

"I should go check on the boys."

He took a step closer, and she took one back. "They're with Faye."

"I know, but—"

"That towel is coming off," he said, and her eyes went a little wide. But this time when he took a step closer she didn't move.

A long strand of wet blond hair stuck to her plump lower lip. He reached up and brushed it free, stroking her cheek, and something in her seemed to give. She whimpered softly, leaning into his palm so that he was cupping her cheek.

"I want you so much," she said.

"So take me."

She looked up at him, and he found himself instantly caught up in the soft blue of her eyes, the feel of her smooth, pale cheek against his fingers. Good God, she was beautiful and desirable, and he didn't want to let go, didn't want to stop touching her. Ever. Her wet hair tangled in his fingers as he cupped the nape of her neck, and a soft moan escaped between her parted lips. Lips so full and plump and inviting he had to kiss them. But it was Holly who slipped her arms up around his neck, pulled him down to her as she rose up on her toes. The instant their lips touched he was toast.

He wanted to taste her damp skin, kiss away the droplets of water sliding down the column of her throat.

He wanted to bury his nose in the curve of her shoulder and inhale the sweet scent of her, touch her everywhere.

He broke the kiss, his breath quick and shallow. "What do you want, Holly? I'll do anything."

She took a step back, and he thought for sure that she was going to shoot him down. Instead, with her sleepy eyes locked on his, she grabbed the towel where she'd fastened it above her breasts, tugged it loose and let it fall to the floor. "Touch me."

Holy hell. In his life he had never seen anything so beautiful, had never been so aroused by a woman, so desperate to touch her. As if she had cast a spell over him, and he could be satisfied with no one but her.

And he wasn't leaving this room until he'd made love to her.

He felt an almost animalistic urge to yank her into his arms, to nip her skin with his teeth and drag his nails over her back. To tangle his fingers in her hair.

She stepped back from him, her creamy legs so long and slender, her supple breasts tempting him, begging to be touched and sucked. "Come and get me."

Jason cursed under his breath, eyes raking over her, so hot it was a wonder her skin didn't ignite. She loved the way he looked at her. It made her feel sexy and powerful in a way that she never had before.

He stepped closer, his eyes heavy with lust as he slid his hands down her sides and around her waist, pulling her closer. "Kiss me," he said, and she did. She eased her arms around his neck and rubbed her breasts against the front of his shirt as his mouth ravaged hers. He tasted good, felt incredible pressed against her bare skin, even with his clothes on, but she needed them out of the way. She needed to really feel him. All of him.

She fisted the front of his shirt and gave a good hard yank, surprised how easily the buttons popped free, shooting in every direction.

"You realize that's an eight hundred dollar shirt," he said, though he looked more turned on than angry.

Screw the shirt. He could afford another one.

She tugged it down his arms, her eyes taking in his impressive chest, his small dark nipples, his lean torso. She ran her fingers gently down his scar, leaned in to press a kiss to it. She licked one nipple, then the other, and Jason moaned, thrusting his pelvis against her. Through his slacks she could feel that he was long and thick. The brothers weren't completely identical after all.

She cupped her hand over his zipper, squeezed his erection. He groaned and fisted his hands in her hair, pulling her head back so he could nibble on her neck, run his tongue across the little hollow at the base of her throat.

He seemed happy to take his time, teasing her with his tongue, rolling her nipples between his thumb and forefinger until she could barely stand it. She needed more. Right now. It had been too long and she couldn't wait a minute more. She took one of his hands and guided it between her legs. And he took the hint. He cupped her mound, teasing her with the palm of his hand, then his fingers, parting her slippery folds.

"See how wet you make me?" she said, unfastening his pants and slipping her hand inside. He was long and hard and hot to the touch. She stroked him slowly, squeezing and releasing, sliding her thumb through the bead of moisture at the tip.

"See how wet you make me?" he said with a sleepy smile, catching her clitoris between his fingers, rolling it the same way he had her nipple, making her heart race and her knees go weak. "I've wanted this from the day I met you, when you dropped in a dead faint at my feet. You were so damned beautiful, and I hated my brother for finding you first."

"I'm yours now." She shoved down his pants and he kicked them away. Then he reached down and tugged off his black dress socks. When he was completely naked she took it all in, from his wide shoulders to his lean hips, and the long, thick erection pointing upward and slightly to the left against his stomach. He was perfect. Better than perfect.

He slid a finger inside of her, then another, saying, "You're so tight."

He could thank the C-section for that.

He thrust inside of her and the tips of his fingers bumped her G-spot. A violent shudder rocked through her and her knees nearly buckled.

He lifted his hand to his lips and with a devilish smile tasted his fingers. "Hmm, delicious," he said. "I think I want more."

Not just yet.

"Be patient," she said. She flattened her hands on his chest and pushed him backward toward the bed.

"What's the rush?" he asked as the mattress hit the back of his legs, forcing him to sit.

"No rush at all." She lowered herself to her knees on the rug between his legs. "I plan to take my time."

With her eyes on his face, she ran her tongue around the head of his erection, and then took him into her mouth. She heard him mutter, "Oh, damn," as she took him in deeper. He fisted his hands in her hair, guiding her, thrusting his hips to help her find the right rhythm. He swelled in her mouth and she could feel the hot blood pulsing under the surface. He was getting close, and if he was like most every other man he wouldn't want to be the one to come first.

He stilled his hips, but she kept going without missing a beat. He groaned her name, gripped her hair tighter, resisting for all of about three seconds. His hips caught the rhythm again, and he thrust deeper until she could feel him hit the back of her throat. She dug her nails into the tops of his thighs, dragged them over his skin, and he lost it. With one last thrust he threw back his head and groaned, his body tensing as he found his release.

"Holy cow," he said, falling onto his back, arms over his head, gasping for breath. "Where the hell did you learn to do that?"

She kissed her way up his stomach, rising up on her feet to grin down at him. "You really want to know?"

"On second thought, I really don't care. Just keep doing it exactly like that."

"My pleasure." She knew a lot of women who weren't into giving blow jobs and she never understood why. It turned her on.

Jason's arms went around her, pulling her against his chest. "That's going to be a tough act to follow," he said. Then he rolled her onto her back, grinned down at her and said, "Okay, my turn."

Twelve

Jason lifted her as if she weighed nothing and flipped her onto the center of the bed, crawling up between her thighs, looking like a wild animal on the prowl, with her as his willing victim.

He nipped her stomach, dipped his tongue in the crevice of her navel. "Your skin tastes so good," he said.

And he could have as much of it as he wanted.

He kissed and licked his way upward until he got to her breasts. He sucked her nipple into his mouth, and then moved to the opposite side and sucked that one, too. She felt the sweet tug of desire, the slippery heat between her thighs and it was almost unbearable. If he kept that up he wouldn't have to bother himself between her thighs. She was already sitting on the edge of the precipice.

Tough act to follow, my ass.

He worked his way back down, saying, "Spread your legs."

She did, and he said, "More." She did as he asked, and he pushed her legs way back until her knees were parallel with her ears and her butt was lifted up off the mattress.

He gazed down, watching his fingers as they teased their way between her puffy lips to seek out her clitoris. "Beautiful."

Then he practically dove in, licking from end to end, making her body shudder and pulse. He sucked her clitoris, holding it gently between his teeth as he flicked with his tongue. She arched up, so hot and aroused that she nearly forgot her own name. It felt so good she wanted it to last, but she could already feel her orgasm creeping up, feel her womb contract and release in a pulse-pounding rhythm. Then the world went blurry as intense pleasure crashed over her like waves in a violent storm.

"You are so hot," he said, positioning himself over her. "Look at me, Holly. I want to see your face when I make love to you."

With slightly unfocused vision she looked up at him, and the second her eyes locked on his, he thrust deep inside of her. She cried out from a startling sensation of pain and pleasure. They were joined in a way that was completely new to her. She felt closer to him than she'd ever been to a man—to her late husband or anyone who had come before him. With her heart and her head and her soul. She'd known all along where this had been going, but it hadn't really hit home until just now.

Jason went still above her and for an instant they stared at each other as if they couldn't believe they were really here. That they were making love.

"I hurt you," he said.

Yes, but it only made her feel more aware, more alive. Feeling the pain was better than not feeling anything at all. It was better than longing for his touch but never feeling it.

"It's been a while," she said breathlessly. "And you're huge."

And damned proud of it, his smile seemed to say, but there was a hint of uncertainty in his eyes, as though he thought he'd gone too far. "I don't want to hurt you."

"Don't stop," she pleaded. She didn't think she could stand it. It had taken so long to get here. She didn't want it to end yet.

"I'm not going to stop. I'll just go slow."

"Don't you dare," she said through clenched teeth. "I want it hard and fast."

His brows rose in surprise. "You want me to pound you."

"Yes," she gasped, digging her nails into his perfectly formed, muscular backside, thrusting her hips to urge him on. "Pound me."

He eased back and she held her breath in anticipation. Then he slowly sank in, so slowly she thought she would go mad. She knew pounding and this was not *pounding*.

He pulled out again, a look of concentration on his face. She opened her mouth to protest, and he thrust hard and deep inside so all that came out was a strangled cry. Then he thrust again and again. Pounding into her until a different kind of pain, an ache deep in the center of her soul, began to build. She was so close. She wanted to hold back so they could climax together, but her body was having no part of it. It said *right now*. And an orgasm of epic proportions ripped through her. Jason was seconds behind her, roaring as her contracting walls milked him into ecstasy.

* * *

Jason's heart hammered in his chest. Still buried deep inside Holly, he pushed himself up on his elbows and said, "Damn."

"Ditto," she said, struggling to catch her breath.

He'd always known that making love to her would be good. He'd just never imagined it would be *that* good. She was so hot and so tight and his orgasm so intense that for a second he thought he might actually die from the pleasure.

"Now that," she said, "was a pounding."

He laughed and rolled onto his back. "Yes, it was."

He had just slept with his sister-in-law. The woman he'd sworn he wouldn't touch. The mother of his nephews.

He waited for the guilt to set in. The shame and the regret.

It never came. He couldn't even force it.

"I *really* needed that," she said.

"So did I." More than he realized.

She looked over at him, her cheeks rosy and her eyes glassy. "Is this the part where we say we'll never do it again?"

"I don't know about you, but I *want* to do it again."

"Oh, good," she said, sounding relieved. "So do I. Just maybe not right now."

"No," he agreed. "Definitely not right now."

A firm knock on the door had them both bolting up in bed. "Holly, are you in there?"

It was Faye, and she sounded concerned.

"Did you lock the door?" Holly whispered.

Shit. No, he hadn't.

Faye knocked again. "Holly, is everything okay? I heard banging."

"I'm fine," she called to Faye.

"Can I open the door?"

"No!" Jason and Holly called in unison, probably a lot louder than they meant to. He flung the bedspread over them anyway. Just in case.

Their outburst was met with a long tense silence, and he could just imagine what Faye was thinking.

"Ooookay," she finally said, and left it at that. But he would hear about it later. She would ask him what the hell he thought he was doing, and he would have to tell her the truth. He didn't have a freaking clue. For the first time in his life he was functioning on pure emotion, where nothing made much sense. But damn did it feel good.

Looking confused, Holly asked him, "What was banging?"

"I'm guessing the headboard."

She looked over at it, perplexed. "Huh. I didn't even hear it."

"Neither did I." Next time they would have to be a little more mindful of how much noise they made. Or even better, take it up to his bedroom, two floors away from Faye's bat ears. Or there was always the option of waiting until after Faye had gone home for the night.

"She must think I'm a slut," Holly said.

"It doesn't matter what she thinks. We're consenting adults. It's none of her business." Though that didn't mean she wouldn't make it her business.

Holly and Jason went out to dinner as planned, taking his boat across the lake to the marina.

As they walked the two blocks to Lily's, an upscale seafood bistro and brewery, he caught her hand in his and held it. If he cared what other people thought, he didn't let it show.

They dined on grilled lobster and drank micro-brewed beer, and then strolled down the boardwalk, hand in hand, stopping for ice cream before they headed back to the boat. When she caught a chill he took off his jacket and draped it over her shoulders. She couldn't recall the last time she'd had so much fun on a date. It had been so long since she'd been on one. She and Jeremy had gone straight from casually hooking up into marriage.

If she'd known then what she knew now, things would have been very different.

They got back to the house around eleven. As soon as Faye left, Holly checked on the twins, grabbed the baby monitor and practically bolted up the stairs to Jason's bedroom. She'd only been up there the one time and she'd been so freaked out by Marshall's cough then that she hadn't taken the time to look around.

It was a ginormous suite that took up the entire top floor, with an absolutely incredible view of the lake and the lights from the bay. The bathroom alone was bigger than some of the apartments she'd lived in, and his bed was the most comfortable she'd ever been in.

They made love, but it was a little sweeter, and a little slower.

When the boys woke for their midnight feeding, she and Jason each gave them a bottle. When they were back in bed, Jason made love to her again, and then she fell asleep wrapped in his arms. She slept so soundly that she didn't even hear the boys wake up the next morning. She woke from a dead sleep to find the twins in bed with them. Jason had changed their diapers and was feeding them their bottles, which they both slurped greedily to satisfy their rapidly growing bodies.

"I'm sorry if I hurt you last night," he said, when the boys were fed and lying between them in the bed.

"Only for a second. It was the first time since I had the boys. The first time in a *long* time."

"Because of your pregnancy?"

"In part," she said.

"And the other part?"

She hesitated.

"Holly?"

"After I got pregnant, Jeremy seemed to sort of…" *Sort of what, Holly?* "Lose interest, I guess."

"Lose interest?"

It was embarrassing to admit that her own husband hadn't wanted to have sex with her. Not that it had ever been red-hot. She could count on two hands how many times they'd had sex, and not once had she ever lost herself the way she had last night. Not once had she felt so in sync with another person.

"I felt pretty sick in my second month, so I didn't want to, and by the time I was feeling better, he didn't want to. He said he was afraid it would hurt the babies. I tried to explain that sex was perfectly safe, but he wouldn't touch me. There was one time when he came home drunk from a party. Then I went into early labor and we couldn't risk it. Honestly, I think he was relieved.

"What about after you had the twins?"

"He was in such a downward spiral at that point. I didn't even try. Then he was gone."

The experience had left her feeling as if she would never have sex again. At least not the kind that required another person participating. Especially not if it meant getting herself trapped into another inopportune situation.

"My brother was an ass," Jason said. "He didn't deserve you."

"I tried so hard to make it work. I really did. But the truth is it was one careless encounter that became a surprise pregnancy, and he only married me to do the right thing. I don't think he ever really loved me."

"Holly, Jeremy never once did the right thing. If he didn't have genuine feelings for you, he would have skipped out the second the test turned up positive."

She shrugged. "Maybe."

"No maybe. I know this for a fact."

She blinked. "Are you saying that it happened before?"

"In high school he got a girl pregnant. She was the love of his life, he used to tell me. Then she told him she was pregnant and he dumped her."

Yes, Jeremy had had his problems, but it was difficult trying to imagine him being that cold and heartless.

"She was devastated. And of course she came running to me, the 'good' twin."

"What did you do?"

"She didn't want to have it, but she was afraid to tell her parents, so I did the only thing I could. I went to my father. He took care of it. At that point, cleaning up Jeremy's messes was a regular thing."

"How old was she?"

"Fifteen. My brother was eighteen. At the time, the age of consent was sixteen. He could have gone to prison. Honestly, it might have done him some good. But every time he got into trouble, someone would bail him out. I know it was the drugs making him act that way, and though he did try to get clean numerous times, he always relapsed."

"I feel that if I had known, I could have done something."

"He wasn't always like that. I mean, he was definitely the type to push the limits. Some of the things we got away with as kids…" Jason laughed and shook his head. "Sometimes at school we would go into the bathroom and exchange clothes so people would think I was him and he was me, and then we would go to each other's classes. We were so identical most people couldn't tell us apart, and the ones who could thought it was hilarious. It's how Jeremy managed to pass physics. That and me doing all of his homework."

"So you were kind of a bad kid, too," she said.

"I'll admit I let him talk me into some crazy things. I took the SATs for him so he wouldn't have to cope with my father's wrath, and he got into a good school, then flunked in the second semester. Looking back, I know I wasn't doing him any favors. But I drew the line at the drugs. Not that he didn't try to talk me into doing them with him. But my health being what it was, I couldn't take the risk. It caused a huge rift between us."

"That was his shortcoming, not yours."

"I know."

Maybe the only reason she'd met Jeremy was so that he could lead her to Jason. She'd never been the kind to believe in fate, but maybe in this one instance it was just meant to be. Lying here in bed with Jason, the twins between them cooing and kicking their little legs, it felt as if they were a family. Did that mean she was finally getting everything she had ever wanted? Or was it just another illusion?

God, she hoped not. She wanted to let herself believe

it was real this time. That finally, after a lot of searching, she had found her destiny. The question was how did Jason feel?

His phone rang and he rolled onto his back to grab it from the bedside table. He checked the display and answered, "Hey, Lewis, what's up?"

Holly could hear the rumble of Lewis's voice through the phone, but not what he was saying. Jason's smile dissolved and he sat up in bed, asking Lewis, "When?"

She could see instantly from the look on Jason's face that something was wrong and her heart stalled in her chest. Common sense told her that it had something to do with Miranda's pregnancy, but she hoped she was wrong.

"What can I do?" he asked Lewis.

There was another pause, then Jason said, "Let me know."

He hung up and Holly said, "What is it? What's wrong?"

"Miranda lost the baby."

Thirteen

"No," Holly said, looking crestfallen. "When?"

"He said she started to spot in the middle of the night, so they went straight to the hospital, but it was already too late."

Holly's bottom lip started to quiver. "She must be devastated."

"I asked if there was anything we could do, but Lewis said they just need a few days alone to grieve."

A big fat tear spilled over her lid and rolled down her cheek. Jason's reached up and brushed it away.

"I can't even imagine what she's going through," Holly said. "They've tried so hard and she wanted this so badly. It's not fair."

"No, it isn't," he agreed. "But maybe it was better that it happened now than three months from now."

"For someone like Miranda, who has been hoping for this practically her whole life, there is no better time.

Should we send flowers so they know we're thinking of them?"

"They know. I think we should respect their privacy. They'll tell us when they're ready to talk about it."

"But I want to *do* something."

"All we can do now is be there for them when they need us."

Having no children of his own or even the ability to have any, it was difficult for Jason to put himself in his friends' place, but he did feel awful for them. He knew how important it was, especially to Miranda.

"I'm going to dress and get the boys ready, just in case," Holly said, picking up one twin in each arm, which actually didn't look as complicated as he would have imagined. "Let me know if you hear anything."

"I will. I promise. And, Holly?"

She turned back to him.

"Last night was…" He couldn't even find the words. "Wow."

He managed to coax a smile from her. "Yeah, it was."

He showered and dressed and headed down to the kitchen for coffee. Faye must have heard them stirring because a steaming hot cup of his favorite decaffeinated dark roast was waiting for him beside the *Wall Street Journal* on the kitchen table.

"Good morning," she said as he walked in the room. She left out her usual, "How did you sleep?"

"What would you like for breakfast?" she asked instead.

"Just coffee for now."

Normally she would have lectured him on the fundamental benefits of a balanced breakfast, but this time she said nothing at all.

"Everything all right?" he asked her.

"Of course."

He told her about Miranda's miscarriage and she clucked sympathetically. "That poor woman."

"Lewis said that she's devastated."

"God works in mysterious ways."

Jason didn't buy into that. No one controlled his destiny but him. "Then God is cruel and unkind."

"Things happen for a reason," she said.

That was the sort of thing people liked to tell themselves so they didn't have to face the fact that life was random, and bad things happened to good people. There were no guarantees.

Instead of taking the paper and coffee into his office the way he normally would have, he sat at the kitchen table. Faye was much more somber than usual. Ordinarily by now she would be talking his ear off about one thing or another.

"Everything okay?" he asked again while she busied herself wiping down granite countertops that were already clean.

"Yes."

She only gave him one-word answers when she was upset about something. "How about we save some time and rather than me trying to drag it out of you, you just come right out and tell me what's up?" Though he had a feeling he already knew.

She draped the dishrag over the edge of the sink, and then turned to him. "Are you going to do right by her?"

Do right by her? "You make it sound like I'm a kid who knocked up his high school girlfriend. That was Jeremy's thing, not mine. Are you forgetting that I'm not even physically capable of knocking someone up?"

Faye flashed him that stern and exasperated look he

knew so well. "I just don't want to see her hurt. Anyone with eyes can see that she's in love with you."

"I think you're mistaking sex for love."

"Or are you mistaking love for sex?"

"She flat out told me that she didn't want to bury another husband. I think that speaks for itself, don't you?"

"Women say all sorts of things when they're protecting their heart."

"Holly is a straight shooter and honest to a fault. I've never known her to hold back when something is on her mind."

Faye shrugged her narrow shoulders. "If you say so."

He sighed. Why did she have to make this so complicated? "Is there a particular reason you think that Holly and I shouldn't be together?"

"On the contrary. I think you two couldn't be more perfect for each other. You've been alone for too long."

"I do date."

"Tell me the name of the last woman you dated," she said.

Was it Marla or Marsha? Martha maybe? It definitely had started with an *M*.

He frowned. All right, she'd made her point.

"I won't be around forever, you know. It breaks my heart to think of you being alone," Faye said.

It was true that she and George had been in his life longer than anyone. Longer than his parents even. The idea of them not being around was hard to fathom. Despite what he'd told Holly, they were more than just employees. Aside from Holly and the twins, they were the only family he had. Would ever have. He would never have a wife or child of his own. But with his nephews and Holly to look after he would never be truly alone. It was possible Faye would outlive him, as well.

"I just want you to be careful," Faye told him.

"You don't have to worry," he assured her. "We both know what we're getting into. Everything will work out."

It was five days before Holly was able to go see Miranda, and only because Lewis asked her to. Assuming the presence of the twins might be upsetting, Holly left the boys home with Jason, who surprised her by offering to sit with them instead of Faye, who had errands to run in town.

"I've never seen her like this," Lewis told Holly when she got there. "All she does is sleep. She refuses to eat and I have to practically force fluids down her throat. She hasn't been out of bed since we got home from the hospital, and alternates between sleeping, crying and staring at the wall. I'm afraid to leave her alone for fear that she might hurt herself. And when I'm not here I have the housekeeper checking on her every fifteen minutes. I don't know what to do for her."

"It's not even been a week. Maybe it will just take time." Miranda was the most positive, upbeat person Holly had ever met. She would snap out of it.

"I thought maybe if you talked to her, woman to woman, she might bounce back. She refuses to talk to me."

"I'll do my best," she told Lewis, but even after how he'd described Miranda's condition, Holly wasn't prepared for what she saw when she stepped into their bedroom. Though it was the middle of the afternoon and the sun was shining, the shades were drawn. The room was dark and smelled stale and sour. Miranda lay under the covers facing the wall.

"Hey there, you awake?" Holly said softly and got no

response. She could tell, as she drew nearer to the bed, that Miranda hadn't bathed in a while. Holly walked to the window to get some fresh air in the room, but as she reached for the blinds, Miranda said in a hollow voice, "Don't."

"Some fresh air would do you good."

"I want to sleep."

"How about a shower?"

"Go away."

"Lewis thought you might like to talk."

"I don't. Just leave."

She was starting to see why Lewis was so worried. But who was she to tell Miranda how to grieve? Hating to leave her friend alone, she walked to the chair across the room and sat down, thinking that her presence might be a comfort. Miranda didn't move or make a sound the entire hour Holly sat there.

She came the next day, and was happy to hear that Miranda had taken a few bites of the food from the tray the housekeeper had brought in, but Holly's welcome wasn't any less chilly this time. But she stayed, just so Miranda knew that she cared. When she arrived the following day, Miranda still hadn't showered and the smell in the room was getting unbearable. After another chilly greeting and several minutes at her post in the chair, Holly could no longer stand it.

She got up, walked over to the window and snapped the shades open.

"Hey," Miranda protested from the bed, her voice sounding stronger.

"If you can't be bothered to shower, I'm going to have to have some fresh air. It stinks to high heaven in here. After another day or two I'm going to have to hose you down with Lysol."

Holly opened the window, letting in an intoxicating rush of clean lake air. When she turned around, her friend was sitting up in bed. It was the first time Holly had actually seen her face since the miscarriage, and it was heartbreaking. Miranda looked a million years old.

"If you don't like the smell, then leave. I don't want you here anyway."

"If you don't like it, get up off your ass and throw me out."

Miranda shot Holly a look that was pure resentment, and then flopped back down and pulled the covers over her head.

It went on like that for a week. Then one day, as Holly was in her usual chair reading, she heard a quiet voice say, "It's my fault."

Holly put her book down and walked over to the bed and sat on the edge of the mattress. "Miranda, it's not your fault."

Miranda sat up, her beautiful long hair greasy and matted into dreadlocks. "The first day or two when we found out, I was so excited, but then I started to get this sinking feeling, like something horrible was going to happen. I couldn't shake it. I was terrified that I would feel that way through my entire pregnancy."

"That doesn't mean it was your fault."

Tears welled in her eyes. "That's not the worst part. After it happened, I was almost relieved."

"Oh, Miranda." Holly hugged her and Miranda actually hugged back. The foul stench of body odor burned Holly's eyes but that didn't stop her. "Considering all that you went through, of course you would be scared. I'm no expert, but I went through a pregnancy wrought with complications. I can barely remember a time when I wasn't at least a little frightened."

"Lewis doesn't understand. He has a kid from a previous relationship, so it just isn't as important to him."

"And he's a man. They don't understand." Holly held Miranda at arm's length. "But you have to snap out of this. Why don't you take a shower and I'll put some clean sheets on the bed for you? I promise you'll feel so much better."

"I really smell that bad?"

"You really do," Holly said, coaxing the hint of a smile from her friend.

When she left that day, Miranda was still in pajamas, but she had showered and eaten lunch, and was sitting up in bed watching a rerun of the new season of *The Real Housewives of New Jersey*, one of her favorite shows. It had taken more than an hour and a whole lot of painful tugging but Holly had managed to get most of the snarls from her hair. On her way out to the car Holly ran into Lewis, who had just gotten home from work. When she told him the progress they'd made he hugged her.

"I don't know what I would have done without you," he said. "I don't know how I'll ever repay you."

"I'm here because I want to be. You don't owe me anything."

When she got home Faye was fixing dinner and Jason was just putting the boys down for their afternoon nap. They were down to two naps a day now, and had been sleeping through the night. Which meant Holly should have been getting a lot more sleep, but lately Jason had been keeping her up late.

Faye never brought up the strange banging she'd heard, and if she'd said anything to Jason he never mentioned it. Either way Jason seemed to have no qualms about being openly affectionate in front of Faye. And though Holly was curious as to what Faye thought about the situation, she never asked.

Once Holly and Jason had tucked the boys into their cribs, they went up to his room for their own "nap." Since their first time together it was as if they couldn't get enough of each other, and she had never felt sexier or more desirable in her life. Unlike the men who had come before him, Jason seemed to know instinctively what she liked, and making sure she was satisfied was his top priority.

She was barely halfway up the stairs to his bedroom and already she was wet with anticipation. She told him about her progress with Miranda and he seemed happy to hear it.

"I'm sorry that I've been spending so much time over there. I feel like I'm neglecting you and the twins."

"It's not a problem," he said, tugging his shirt over his head as they reached the top step.

"I think it's actually good for the twins. The last thing I want is for them to grow up feeling cheated. They need a male presence in their life."

"Happy to do it," he said, unfastening the buttons on her shirt and tugging it down her arms. "Have I mentioned how sexy you are?"

She grinned. "About fifty times a day."

He undid her bra and cupped her breasts in his warm palms, pinching the tips lightly, driving her crazy before they even finished undressing. She laid back on the bed, and Jason crawled up the mattress looking like a prowling wolf as he settled between her thighs. If she had worried their first few times were beginner's luck, she needn't have. Every time she thought it couldn't get better, it did.

Fourteen

Over the next few weeks Holly and Jason fell into a comfortable routine. She spent every night in his room, usually waking to find that he'd brought the boys into bed. He spent most days in his office, and she began to get out more, meeting people and making new friends. She'd even begun to spend some of the money that was piling up in her bank account. Holly still visited Miranda several times a week, but gradually, as the summer wore on, Miranda began to recover. She started to see a therapist, and Holly was finally able to coax her out of the house, even if it was only to hang out on the beach or have lunch in town.

"How are things with you and Jason," Miranda asked her one blazing afternoon in August when they sat in the shade in Miranda's backyard, the boys playing in their playpen. They were both sitting up on their own and starting to scoot. Holly knew it was only a matter of time before they were crawling and pulling themselves up on furniture.

"Everything is great." She loved him, and she was sure that he loved her, too, although neither seemed to want to be the first to say the words. But she knew it would happen when the time was right. And even though he hadn't come right out and said he loved her, he'd showed it in so many ways. He wasn't just the twins' uncle. On some level, she had come to think of him as their true father. He treated the boys as if they were his children.

The scar on his chest was a daily reminder that he could be living on borrowed time, but the truth was she cared about that less and less.

"Have the two of you talked about the future?"

"Not specifically."

"And you're okay with that?" Miranda asked, sipping her sweet iced tea and nibbling on snack mix. She still wasn't eating enough, but at least she'd stopped dropping weight. Losing thirty pounds in the span of a few weeks had left her looking sad and haggard. She'd lost all interest in trying to conceive, saying that she just couldn't go through that again. Although on the bright side, she was no longer living in her pajamas, and Holly had even coaxed her out of the house to go clothes shopping.

Holly shrugged. "What's there to talk about? Everything is great. We're both deliriously happy."

"Ignorance is bliss, I guess."

Holly shot her a look. "What's that supposed to mean?"

Miranda sighed, rubbing her temples as if she had a headache. "I'm sorry, I didn't mean to sound so snarky. I'm just worried about you."

"Well, don't be. Jason and I are fine. You need to concentrate on making yourself well."

"Lunch is ready," Miranda's housekeeper called from the patio door, saving Holly from another lecture on her relationship with Jason. Her philosophy was: if it ain't broke, don't fix it.

Holly gathered up the twins and they relocated inside the air-conditioned house. The boys played on the family room rug while she and Miranda ate cucumber sandwiches and sipped sweet tea. Well, she ate and Miranda picked. Unlike her friend, Holly had been ravenously hungry lately. It was probably her nightly dose of exercise in Jason's bed. It was her bed, too, now. She had all but moved into his room. In almost every respect they lived just like a married couple. The only thing missing was the ring.

And maybe the sex wasn't nightly anymore, because sometimes they were just too tired. And he did spend at least one week a month in the city working. He'd invited her to come with him on numerous occasions, but not only did she hate being in the city, she felt wrong leaving Miranda. She wanted to stay close, just in case Miranda had another emotional break.

As if on cue, Miranda said, "You don't have to keep coming here all the time. I'm okay."

"I like coming over," Holly said.

"But you must get bored."

"Not at all," she said, even though it wasn't completely true. "Or are *you* getting sick of *me*?"

"Of course not. I'm just tired of everyone treating me like I'm on the edge of a breakdown. It's like you and Lewis have me on suicide watch. It's okay to leave me alone for a while."

"We're just worried about you."

"I'm *okay*. Yes, I'm sad and I'm angry and I'm hurting, but I've accepted it."

"It's all right to take time to grieve."

Miranda blew out frustrated breath. "I *have* been grieving. It feels like it's all I do. I just want to move on."

"Do you want me to leave?"

Miranda sighed and slouched back into her chair. "No. But I want us to have a real conversation. I want us to talk and laugh like we used to. I don't want you to be afraid you'll say the wrong thing and hurt my feelings. I want to feel happy. Happy for me, happy for you. Happy for *anyone*."

She thought she was helping Miranda, but it sounded as if maybe she had been only exacerbating the problem. "I didn't mean to make you feel bad."

"The truth is I'm a little jealous."

"You are?"

"Well, not just a little. I'm a lot jealous."

"Jealous of what?"

"What you have with Jason. You two are so passionate. So hot for each other. I mean, look at you, you're practically glowing."

"That's just from all the greasy foods I've been eating," she said, patting the slight bump of fat growing under the waist of her shorts. "I really haven't been eating right. I feel so hungry all the time."

"That's what happens when you're happy. I was a size six when I married Lewis."

And she was nearly that small now.

Looking embarrassed—and Miranda wasn't the type to get embarrassed about anything—she told Holly, "Lewis and I used to be that way. Now he won't even touch me. We haven't had sex since before I lost the baby. We haven't even fooled around."

"Maybe he's worried that you aren't ready. Maybe you need to make the first move to get the ball rolling."

"I've tried," she said, looking hurt and confused. She set her plate aside and drew her knees up to her chin. "He always has some reason why we can't. He's tired or he has a headache or he has to get up early. I'm the one who's supposed to be using the I've-got-a-headache excuse. Not him."

"He is older. Maybe he's just slowing down. It's bound to happen."

She shook her head. "No, that's not it. We used to be so close. Now there's just no connection. He's completely shut me out. Half the time when I try to talk to him, he doesn't even hear me."

"Maybe you just need to give it time. He's grieving, too."

"Not really. I mean, I know he was disappointed, but he only agreed to have a baby in the first place because he knew how important it was to me."

"Did he actually tell you that?"

"Not in so many words."

"Then how do you know he feels that way?"

"We agreed that if the last IVF failed we would look into foreign adoption."

"That's a good idea."

"I thought so. I thought it was what he wanted, too. I brought it up last week. I told him I thought that I was ready and that starting the process would give me something positive to look forward to. He said he didn't think it was the right time. And maybe we could think about it next year. *Next year?* I'm thirty-eight years old. He's fifty-two. How long does he think we can wait?"

"Maybe he's just worried about—"

"Stop that!" Miranda shrieked, shocking Holly into silence. She'd heard Miranda raise her voice a time or two, but never like that. "Stop making excuses for him. I'm not imagining this or blowing things out of proportion. Our marriage is falling apart right before my eyes. I don't even know if he loves me anymore." She covered her face with her hands and started to cry.

Holly didn't know what to do. Why *was* she making excuses for Lewis? And by doing so was she suggesting that she thought Miranda wasn't clearheaded enough to recognize her own marriage crumbling?

"I'm so sorry," Holly said, touching Miranda's shoulder. "I didn't mean to be so insensitive. I was just trying to help."

Miranda took a deep breath and composed herself, wiping away her tears with the handkerchief she kept in her bra. Now that she was wearing a bra again.

"I just want things to be normal again," she said. "I want us to be happy. The way we used to be. I want us to be like you and Jason. You're so in love."

Holly was, but was Jason? Though she was pretty good at blocking it out and pretending everything was okay, the harsh reality of her situation was that she didn't really know how Jason felt. And she didn't have the courage to ask him. Maybe she'd been focusing on Miranda so she didn't have to confront her own fears. Maybe she wasn't as happy as she let Miranda think.

"You're frowning," Miranda said. "What's wrong?"

Holly gave her an automatic "Nothing. Everything is great."

"You're lying."

"I am?"

"Yes, and maybe no one has ever told you this, but you're not very good at it."

Miranda was right. As a kid Holly had never been able to get away with anything. It was her darned guilty conscience.

Suddenly feeling close to tears, she asked her friend, "If Jason loves me so much, why doesn't he ever say it?"

"Oh, honey," Miranda said, sounding more like herself than she had in months. "You've got to talk to him about it."

"I'm afraid to. I'm afraid of what he'll say. Or what he won't say. What if he doesn't love me and it's just sex to him?"

"No, it's more than that."

"He did tell me that he would never get married, never have kids. Have I just been assuming that his feelings have changed? That he wants those things as much as I do? And if he does want these things, too, how do I know he isn't going to die on me in six months?" Losing Jeremy had been hard, but losing Jason would destroy her.

"And how does he know you won't die on him? You could get hit by a bus or eaten by a shark."

Holly couldn't help chuckling. It was nice to be the one being cheered up for a change.

"Life is a crapshoot," Miranda said. "You can't go through it afraid. What would you be teaching your boys? To let fear run their lives? That's dumb. And it's incredibly selfish. They deserve better than that."

What Miranda said made too much sense. "What if I tell him I love him and he doesn't love me back?"

"At least you could say you tried. And if it's not Jason, it could be someone else. You can't just give up."

She could if she was scared.

"Say you'd never met Jeremy. You were never married and never had kids. Then you met Jason and he asked you out. Would you go out with him?"

"Yes." There was no doubt in her mind about that. She would have been drawn to him instantly.

"Would you break up with him if you found out he'd had a transplant?"

She could see where Miranda was going with this. It was a question she had asked herself a million times. "But the thing is I *was* married to Jeremy, and he *did* die on me. It's a fact that's never going to change."

"I'm a little confused," Miranda said. "Are you worried that Jason doesn't love you or that he's going to die? Are you saying you do want him or you don't want him?"

"Of course I want him. I love him with all of my heart. When he's in the city I hate it. Even though we text and talk on the phone, I miss him so much. He is the most amazing man I've ever met. But when I think about losing him I can barely stand it."

"So don't think about it."

"That's easy for you to say."

Miranda's brows rose and the look on her face made Holly feel like a big fat jerk. "I'm sorry, I didn't mean that. I don't know what's wrong with me. Why can't I just let myself be happy? Things really are going great. Why can't I just accept things the way they are and enjoy it while it lasts? Whether that's a year or ten years."

"Because as women we need to know where we stand. We need to hear the words. I swear sometimes I wish I was born a man."

"It would make things easier."

Miranda laid a hand on her arm. "Honey, I'm not

going to tell you want to do, it's not my place. But if it were me, I would talk to him. For your own peace of mind. You deserve to get what you want. We both do."

"What if I don't know what I want?"

"Well then maybe it's time you figure it out."

Despite her good intentions, two weeks passed and Holly still hadn't been able to bring herself to confront Jason about their relationship. And it was beginning to wear on her. He gave no sign that he saw their relationship as anything but a permanent one, yet those times when it would have been natural to say I love you, all she ever got was silence. She loved him. She loved him more than she thought it was possible to love another person. Not the way she loved her boys, of course. There was no love, no greater connection than that of a mother and child. She would happily lay down her life for them. They were a part of her, an extension of herself, and that would never change. But that didn't mean her love for Jason was any less intense, any less real. The question was did he share that love? As much as she wanted to know, she was still afraid to ask.

They never talked about the future. Once, in an attempt to introduce the subject, she'd asked him where he saw himself in ten years. He had laughed and said, "Hopefully alive," making a joke out of the question. He liked to keep things light and not bother her with anything regarding his health.

Then she'd found out that he saw his cardiologist on a monthly basis, when he was in the city on business. And until she saw Jason swallow literally a handful of pills one morning, she hadn't even realized he took that much medication. It was a reminder that although he was healthy as a horse now, there might come a time when he wasn't. But as difficult as that would be to accept, she was in this for the long haul. Sick or healthy, she loved him and wanted to be with him.

In early September Jason coaxed her into leaving the boys with Faye for a long weekend and flying with him to his condo in Mexico.

"I want us to have a special weekend together," he'd said. "Just you and me."

Of course her first thought had been that he wanted to get her alone so he could propose. But to spare her heart the possible disappointment, she'd tried to convince herself she was making assumptions. Once the seed of the idea was planted, it began to grow out of control. Then this morning, on the day before they left, he'd told her that when they were in Mexico he had a big surprise for her. What else could it be but a proposal?

She and Miranda went shopping for a few last minute items such as summer clothes that actually fit, and with the summer clearance sales, Holly got them for a steal. She kept telling herself that she needed to get up off her increasingly expanding butt and exercise. And lay off the potato chips. But she couldn't work up the enthusiasm. According to Jason, he liked her body a little fuller, and she was sexy no matter what size. But sexy enough to marry?

"I have some good news," Miranda told her while they were having lunch.

Miranda had finally worked up the courage to confront Lewis about their marriage, and told him to man up or get out. And Lewis had said he wasn't going anywhere. Since then things had been steadily improving, and Miranda was back to being her cheerful, positive self. They had even begun the process for foreign adoption. The last Holly had heard, they had completed the application and were waiting to do a home visit with the agency.

"Did you get an appointment for your home visit?" Holly asked her.

"Not yet, but it's looking as if we might not have to."

"You haven't changed your mind?"

"No, not at all," Miranda said, a huge smile crossing her fire-red bow lips. "And we might be getting a baby a whole lot sooner than we thought."

Holly blinked. "How?"

"One of the partners at Lewis's firm has a granddaughter who is pregnant and looking for a couple to adopt her baby."

"No way!"

"She's eighteen, she graduated high school top of her class and plans to attend college in the fall. Premed at USC. The pregnancy was totally unexpected, of course, and Lewis's partner said she wants to do right by the baby."

"What about the father?"

"Still in high school and definitely not ready to be a dad. His parents are all for the adoption."

"That's wonderful! When will you know for sure?"

"We talked on the phone and they both seem like extremely levelheaded kids. We're meeting the expectant mother and her boyfriend and their parents tomorrow. I've never been so excited or so nervous in my life. If they don't like us—"

"*Miranda*, they are going to *love* you. I can't think of two people more deserving or more qualified to be parents."

"They want an open adoption, meaning we would send them occasional letters and pictures, and they might even meet the baby in the future, which freaks me out a little, but they would leave that up to her to decide."

"Her?"

Miranda smiled, barely able to contain her excitement. "She's having a girl. Four weeks from now I could have a daughter!"

"Oh, my gosh! That is soon."

"But I am so ready. If this does work out and we sign the agreement, I only have a month to get everything I need."

"It sounds like we'll be having that baby shower after all," Holly told her. Which wouldn't give her long to plan, but she would manage.

"I'm afraid to get my hopes up, but I just have a really good feeling about this. We offered to reimburse her for all her medical and living expenses, but she doesn't want money. She just wants to know that her baby will go to people who will love and take care of her."

"In that case it sounds like a perfect match."

"I really hope so."

As they finished their lunch the talk turned to baby matters such as which was the best brand of diapers and what color to paint the baby's room, pink or gender nonspecific.

After lunch they were walking back to Miranda's car when they passed a boutique with bathing suits on sale. "I should really get a new one," Holly told Miranda. The one-piece that had been so loose on her in June was now scandalously small. Not only was her butt expanding, but her breasts were, too, so much so that she'd gone up an entire bra size.

They went into the boutique and the salesgirl, whom Holly had come to know pretty well, helped her find the right sizes. Holly stepped into the changing room and shed her clothes, scowling at her reflection as she pulled on the suit. "I really need to go on a diet."

"Let's see it," Miranda said.

Holly stepped out of the dressing room. "I think it might be too small."

Miranda looked her up and down, and got a weird look on her face. The salesgirl was looking at her a little strangely, too. "Ugh, is it really that bad?"

"Could you go and fetch her a size bigger?" Miranda asked the salesgirl.

"I'll see if we have one," she said, scurrying off, her brows furrowed.

Before Holly could comment, Miranda grabbed her arm and dragged her back into the dressing room. "Is there something you need to tell me?"

Confused, Holly said, "No, why?"

"Is it my imagination or have you gained most of your weight in your stomach area."

Holly sighed. "It's gross, I know."

"Is that how you usually gain weight? In your stomach like that?"

"I'm not sure. I've always been naturally thin. The only other time I gained this much weight is when I was pregnant with the…" She trailed off as the meaning of Miranda's reaction sank in.

"No," Holly said. "I know what you're thinking and it can't be possible."

"Honey, one thing I've learned is that nothing is impossible."

"No, I mean it's really impossible. Jason had a vasectomy. He literally can't get me pregnant."

"It's rare, but vasectomies sometimes fail. My cousin in Louisiana and her husband popped out four rug rats all a year apart and not on purpose. So after baby number four he went in and got snipped. A year later they had baby number five."

"You're kidding," Holly said, but her stomach was starting to sink and her heart had risen up in her throat to somewhere just below her vocal chords. "That didn't really happen."

"I swear on my mother's grave," Miranda said, laying her hand over her heart. "Have you two used protection?"

"No," Holly said. "Why would we bother?"

"What about your periods? Have you missed any?"

She felt a little sick to her stomach. "My periods have always been kind of screwy. Sometimes I'll go a month or two and barely spot."

"How long have you gone without one?"

"Um…" She tried to recall when she'd had her last full period and honestly couldn't. "I don't remember. But I don't feel pregnant. I was sick from my second to fifth month with the boys. I could barely function."

"According to my cousin not every pregnancy is the same."

"But if I were pregnant enough to already be showing, I would have to be past my third month at least."

"My cousin also said that she showed sooner with her later pregnancies. And I've heard that women carrying twins show a lot faster."

Twins? She shook her head. "No, what are the odds that I would have twins again?"

"About the same as they were the first time, considering Jason is a twin."

"It can't be," Holly said. "It just can't."

"When did you and Jason start sleeping together?"

"I don't know. Maybe three months…" She trailed off. No. No way. It wasn't possible.

But what if it is? her inner voice nagged.

"Well, there's only one way to know for sure," Miranda said. "We need a pregnancy test, and we need it right now."

Thinking that this had to be a mistake, that she had more potato chips in her belly than baby, Holly let Miranda walk her to the pharmacy where they picked out a test.

"We should get the two pack," Miranda said.

"Why?"

"Just trust me."

Miranda's fertility struggles were common knowledge in town, so when she dropped the package on the counter the cashier just assumed it was for her.

"Good luck!" the woman said as she dropped it in a bag, giving Miranda a thumbs-up.

Miranda smiled and returned the gesture, mumbling something not so nice under her breath as they were walking out the door, telling Holly, "Sometimes I really hate living in a small town."

Jason was working in his home office today so taking the test there was out of the question. They drove to Miranda's house instead and went straight to the master bath.

"I still think this is a waste of time," Holly said as she had second thoughts about the whole thing. Or did she think that by not knowing for sure there was no way it could be true?

"I'm not letting you back out now. You want me in or out?"

This was all Miranda's idea. There was no way Holly was doing this alone. "Definitely in."

She opened the box and started reading the directions, which Miranda promptly plucked from her hand. "You pee on the stick. It's not complicated."

Holly was so convinced it was impossible that when the word *Pregnant* appeared in the little window after about ten seconds instead of the typical five minutes, she was convinced something was wrong with the test. But when the second test did the same thing, her heart practically turned inside out.

"You're not just pregnant," Miranda said. "You're superpregnant."

"It can't be," Holly said. "They must both be defective."

"Now you're just rationalizing."

It was that or have a full-blown panic attack. "How did this happen?"

"I'm going to assume that's a rhetorical question," Miranda said, a huge goofy smile on her face.

"You're smiling," Holly said in horror. "Don't smile. This is a disaster. What am I going to tell Jason?"

"You could start with *I'm pregnant*, then go from there."

Her legs weak and shaky, Holly leaned against the sink for support. "He got a vasectomy for a reason. He doesn't want kids. Ever."

"Honey, it takes two to tango. Unless you got yourself pregnant, he's just as responsible for this little miracle as you. Or two little miracles if it's twins."

"I never should have taken the test," Holly said.

"Why? So you could be one of those women who has no idea they're pregnant and gives birth on the toilet? I can't imagine anything less dignified. Test or no test, there's no question, honey. You're pregnant."

Fifteen

Holly hung out at Miranda's house for a while, trying to decide what to say, how to approach the topic in a way that wouldn't completely freak out Jason. But around dinnertime Miranda pretty much shoved her out the door. "Stop being such a drama queen and just tell him. It'll be okay, I promise."

Holly didn't believe her, but she went home. She couldn't stay away forever.

When she got there Faye was gone and Jason wasn't in his office. She headed up to their bedroom—yes, *their* bedroom—to look for him. And when she reached the top of the stairs and saw where he was her heart climbed way up into her throat and tears choked her.

Jason was lying in bed dozing with a twin on either side curled up against him, their sweet little heads resting on his chest. Like an adorable Jason sandwich. She found herself wishing that he was their real father or that he at least wanted the job. In her opinion he was born to be a father. It was Jason who could always draw a laugh or a smile from them when they were cranky. It was he who rocked them to sleep when they woke up in the middle of the night fussy and didn't want Mommy. He got up with them nearly every morning when he wasn't traveling, and was almost always there to tuck them in at night. He fed them and changed them. He marveled over each new milestone they reached, beaming with the pride of a real father. In almost every way he *was* their father. Didn't it make sense that he would be happy to learn he would become a father himself? As much as he loved the boys, how couldn't he be?

But what if he isn't? a vicious little voice in her head mocked. *You don't even know if he loves you.*

It was true that he had never said the words, but that didn't mean anything. They were talking about a man who had been hesitant to tell her about his financial status for fear that she would feel intimidated or overwhelmed. Her happiness and well-being obviously meant a lot to him. So much so that she was almost positive the surprise he mentioned today was an engagement ring. He would get down on one knee, maybe in the sand at sunset, and then he would tell her he loved her, and that he wanted to spend the rest of his life with her. Then he would produce the ring and ask her to marry him. However he did it she knew it would be incredibly romantic, because that was just the kind of man he was. He would make sure everything was perfect. And of course she would say yes. She would slip the ring onto her finger—and of course it would be a perfect fit—then throw herself into his arms.

That would be the best time to tell him, she realized. What could be a better conclusion to a romantic proposal? If she told him today, he would probably feel obligated to propose right away, thereby ruining the beautiful event that he had already planned.

Yes, that was definitely the best way to go. She would wait for the proposal and then tell him that she was pregnant. He would be thrilled beyond words, and as soon as they got home he would go with her to the doctor. And if the doctor heard two heartbeats, the way he had with the boys, Jason would be doubly thrilled. She just knew it.

"You're home."

She shook herself out of her daydream and realized Jason was awake and looking up at her.

"I'm home," she agreed.

He looked down at the boys sleeping soundly, sprawled on his chest, and smiled. "They were fussy. I think they're cutting teeth. I guess I nodded off."

"You want me to take them?"

He yawned and shook his head. "That's okay. I like holding them."

In that instant, she loved him even more. Loved him so much it felt as if her heart would burst. She thought back to when Miranda had told her that she couldn't go through life afraid. Maybe her friend was right. It was time to stop living in fear of what could happen and get on with her life. It was time that she let herself have faith in someone. Maybe he was worth the risk.

"Did you get everything you need for the trip?" he asked her.

She sat on the mattress beside them. "Almost everything. I couldn't find a bathing suit that I didn't look horrifying in."

He made a *pft* sound, the way he always did when

she complained about her recent weight gain. Wouldn't he be surprised when she told him the reason behind it.

"You would look sexy in a burlap sack," he said, reaching over to take her hand, drawing it to his lips to kiss it. "I prefer a woman with meat on her bones," he said with a sexy grin, wiggling his eyebrows.

God, he was gorgeous. Though they were identical twins, Jeremy had never looked this good to her. He'd never given her butterflies in her stomach or made her heart race when he'd smiled at her. More and more she had come to believe that she and Jeremy had not been meant to be. That their relationship had been merely the bridge that had brought her to Jason. She was just sorry that Jeremy had had to die to make it happen. And she hoped that from somewhere in the afterlife he was smiling down on them. She hoped he was happy for her. Happy for his children that a man so wonderful had stepped in to take care of them and love them as if they were his own.

"We leave for the airport at 7:00 a.m.," Jason reminded her. "Make sure you're packed and ready."

"Oh, I will be."

"Are you excited?"

Like he would not believe. "A little nervous about the flying part."

"Don't be. It's even safer than traveling in a car, and I know the pilot personally."

She hadn't been at all surprised when he'd told her they would take a private jet to their destination. Jason was a modest man, but he definitely enjoyed the finer things in life.

"I can't wait to get you alone," he said and the heat in his eyes made her shiver.

"And once you have me alone, what will you do with me?"

"Tell you what," he said with a grin. "Let's get these little guys into bed and I'll give you a sneak preview."

Holly lay stretched out in a lounge chair on the resort's private beach, thinking that she could really get used to this. Eating gourmet food, drinking expensive champagne—which she hadn't actually consumed, but instead had dumped in the sand when no one was looking—getting waited on hand and foot and making love until the sun came up.

She glanced over at Jason, who was in the chair beside hers sound asleep. So far they had gone snorkeling and shell hunting. They had visited museums and art galleries. They'd been on an ATV tour, which actually had been a little scary until she'd gotten the hang of it, and wandered through a small village where they'd dined on the local food and danced to a mariachi band until late into the night. And of course there had been sex. Lots and lots of sex.

All of that, and with only one night left, she still didn't have a ring on her finger. But that was Jason. He liked to draw out the suspense. At least, she hoped that was what he was doing. This morning he had asked if she was ready for her surprise and her heart had jumped up into her throat.

Then he'd grinned and told her that she would have to wait a little bit longer, meaning he had to be planning to do it tonight. And then she would be free to tell him the good news. And he would be thrilled, and they would live happily ever after. Though the idea of having twins again had sort of freaked her out at first, the more she thought about it the more she was getting used to the idea. And wouldn't it be perfect if it was identical twin girls? Little sisters the boys could play with, and occasionally pick on of course, because that was what brothers did. But they would love their sisters and they would protect them and beat up anyone who tried to hurt them.

Well, maybe not beat up, but they would be excellent protectors. And though four kids under two years old would be a handful, even with Faye, they could afford a nanny, or even a team of nannies, though she preferred to do the majority of the parenting herself. Whatever the situation, Jason would make sure everyone was taken care of.

"You okay?" Jason asked sleepily from beside her.

"Fine," she said. Better than fine. She was by far the happiest she had been in her whole life.

"You looked like maybe you had a stomach ache."

She looked down and realized she had one hand cupped over the tiny baby bump. It was habit, and something she was sure all pregnant women did, but until she made the announcement later tonight—and it would be later tonight—she would have to be more careful.

"I'm just a little hungry."

"We could go back to the condo and get a bite to eat to hold us over. Or we could do something to distract ourselves until dinner," he said.

"A distraction sounds good." Anything to make the day go faster.

He pushed himself up from the chair and held a hand out to give her a boost. He probably would be doing that a lot in the near future. Especially if she was having twins. Though she had no idea how far along she was yet, she felt really good. Maybe this pregnancy would be easier and she would be spared the disheartening complications of the first time. Maybe being so happy and being with a man she loved, and who loved her back, would make all the difference in the world.

They made love for several hours, and then she must have fallen asleep because when she heard Jason's voice calling to her and she opened her eyes, the room was dark.

She sat up and blinked herself awake. "What time is it?"

"Almost seven."

"I didn't mean to sleep so long."

"That's okay. It gave me time to prepare."

"Prepare what?"

He grinned. "You'll see. Why don't you hop in the shower and get dressed. I'll let you know when it's safe to come downstairs."

"Safe?"

"We're eating in tonight."

So nervous and excited that she could barely contain it, she showered and put on the dress she had bought specifically with this night in mind. She dried her hair and left it loose, the way Jason liked it most, and even put on eyeliner and mascara, which he'd told her he could take or leave because she was beautiful and sexy just the way she was and didn't need any extra help.

She was smoothing on a bit of peppermint lip gloss when Jason returned, dressed in a casual but expensive suit. "Are you ready?"

He had no idea. "Ready as I'll ever be."

He offered his hand and led her down the stairs and out onto the veranda where dozens and dozens of candles flickered in the warm breeze blowing off the ocean.

"Oh, my God," she whispered. "This is amazing."

He gestured to the small round table where they usually had their morning coffee, and it was set for a multi-course gourmet meal. She was so excited and nervous that her hands started shaking and she had no idea how she was going to make it through dinner. Especially one with more than one course.

A waiter from the resort served them, one excruciating course at a time, but she was so nervous she could barely choke down a thing.

"You're not eating much," he said. "You don't like it?"

"It's delicious."

"Maybe you're nervous about your surprise?"

She nodded. "A little."

"We could skip dessert."

Yes, please. "I doubt I would eat much anyway."

After the waiter cleared the table, Jason dismissed him, but not before handing him a hefty tip. Jason always tipped well, even if the service was less than stellar.

When he sat back down Holly was literally on the edge of her seat. Another inch and she probably would fall off the chair.

"Are you ready for your surprise?" he asked and she nodded. She assumed he would want to take a walk on the beach or at least get on one knee, but still sitting at the table he reached into the side pocket of his jacket and she held her breath.

"I know you're not crazy about flashy jewelry," he said with a grin, "and me spending a lot of money on you. But for this I hope you'll make an exception."

In his hand was a small black velvet box, the ideal size to hold a ring. He set it down on the table and slid it across to her, and for a second she just stared. Waiting for him to say something.

"Aren't you going to open it?"

Maybe he wanted her to open it and see it first, then he would get down on his knee to propose. That had to be it.

She reached out and took the box, noting that it felt pretty heavy, which could mean it was a huge rock, though she would have been just as happy if it was a chip.

Heart racing, she slowly lifted the top and on a bed of red satin sat...

She blinked. Then blinked again.

A pair of diamond stud earrings.

Huh?

Mouth hanging open, she looked up at Jason and he smiled, obviously thinking that she was stunned into silence by the beauty of his gift.

"Every woman should have a pair of diamond studs," he said. "They go with everything."

They sure did. And they were exquisitely beautiful, but they were not an engagement ring. Not even close. There had been no proposal, no confessions of true love. Nothing. Just a stupid pair of earrings that probably had cost him a fortune. But that sure didn't mean he loved her.

This entire trip had been a farce. Her happily ever after another figment of her imagination.

"Holly, are you okay?"

She looked up at him and he was no longer smiling.

"If you don't like the earrings—"

"Jason, do you love me?"

He sat back as if he'd been struck. "What?"

"You heard me. *Do. You. Love. Me?*"

He looked baffled, as if he hadn't a clue how to respond or why she was shouting at him.

"It's a simple question," she said so loudly she was sure the people in the neighboring condos could hear her, but she didn't care. She couldn't have helped it if she had. "Do you love me? Yes or no."

"Maybe this is something we should talk about."

"Yes, let's," she said, her voice rising in pitch until she was shrieking. *"Because I'm pregnant!"*

His slack-jawed, bewildered look was more than she could take. The room went fuzzy and her chair began to sway beneath her, and the last thing she heard as she lost consciousness was the thump of her body hitting the floor.

Sixteen

Holly woke from a haze to find Jason kneeling over her, and for a second she thought she was back in her apartment in New York, passed out from seeing Jeremy's ghost, and wondering if it had all just been some strange vivid dream. But as her vision cleared she realized they were still in the condo in Mexico, and it was all very real.

"Are you okay?" Jason asked, and she nodded, even though she was just about the furthest she'd ever been from okay. And she felt embarrassed and stupid and completely heartbroken. How could she have blown this whole thing out of proportion? How could she have been so presumptuous? And she couldn't believe that she hadn't merely informed Jason that she was pregnant, she had screamed it at him. He must have thought she was a loon.

He offered a hand to help her sit up and said, "You know, we really have to stop meeting like this."

In spite of herself she laughed, because the only other option was to cry, and she didn't want to cry. She just wanted to disappear. "I'm sorry I shouted at you."

"You're pregnant?"

"I guess this wasn't the ideal way to break the news." She didn't know if there was an ideal way.

"How? I had a vasectomy."

"That's what I thought, but according to Miranda, they can magically reverse themselves."

He shook his head. "No shit."

She shrugged. "Who knew?"

"Well, thank God for small miracles."

Wait? What? "What does that mean?"

"When I had the procedure done it made sense. Then I met you and fell in love with you, and I began to realize what a huge mistake I'd made."

"You fell in love with me?"

"Pretty much from the minute I met you."

"Then why didn't you say anything?"

"What was I supposed to say? You made it pretty clear that you didn't want to bury another husband. Whether I loved you or not, it didn't seem to make much difference. And to be fair, you never said it, either."

No, she hadn't, but she would say it now. "I love you, Jason. I never knew I could love someone the way I love you."

"Well," he said with a grin, "I'm glad we've got that settled."

"I'm so sorry that I freaked out like that."

"It's okay. And if you really don't like the earrings we can take them back, or exchange them for something else. Like a diamond ring."

She gasped.

"It took you passing out for my dumb ass to figure

out what was happening. The trip and the fancy dinner and the 'surprise' I kept talking about. You thought I was going to propose, didn't you?"

Embarrassed, she nodded.

"Damn," he said, shaking his head. "I am so sorry. If I had known that you wanted me to propose I wouldn't have hesitated. But knowing the way you felt I thought that even earrings would be pushing it. I thought that if I hyped it you wouldn't be able to say no. I guess I went a little overboard."

"You know, it really doesn't matter now. You love me."

"Yes," he said, stroking her hair back from her face. "I do."

"And I love you, too. And I don't care about what might happen in the future. I want to make the best of every minute, whether we have one year or fifty. I want us to be a family."

"I want that, too." He cupped her face in his hand. "You, me, the boys and the baby."

"Out of curiosity, how would you feel if it were two babies?"

"Two?"

"Miranda seems to think that because you're a twin, it's a distinct possibility."

He grinned. "Then we're going to have a *big* family, I guess."

"I've never been one to believe in fate or karma but look at us. I survived an unsurvivable car crash. You got a new heart just in the nick of time, while you were at death's door. You had a vasectomy and still managed to knock me up."

"A failed vasectomy," he said, shaking his head

and laughing. "The possibility never even crossed my mind."

"Is it just me or do you get the feeling the universe is trying to tell us something?"

"Well, if the universe thinks we should be together," he said, cradling her face in his hands, pressing the sweetest kiss against her lips, "who are we to question it?"

* * * * *

Brady laughed, and the transformation was enough to take her breath away.

A handsome man when frowning, he was staggering when he smiled. "You're one of a kind, Aine. I've never met anyone quite like you."

"Thanks for that," she said, then added, "and at the risk of inflating an ego too many women before me have stroked, I'll say the same of you." She tipped her head back to meet the shadowed eyes she felt watching her with tightly restrained hunger.

He gave her a nod. "Then it's good we're not doing this."

"Absolutely. 'Tis the sensible solution."

"This is business," Brady said. "Sex would just confuse the situation."

"You're right again."

He moved in closer. "It's good we talked about it. Cleared the air. Got things settled."

"It is." She leaned toward him. "I'm sure we'll both be better off now and able to focus on our shared task."

Nodding, gaze locked with hers, he whispered, "We're not going to be sensible, are we?"

"Not at the moment, no," she said.

Then he kissed her.

* * *

Having Her Boss's Baby
is part of the Pregnant by the Boss trilogy:
Three business partners find love—and
fatherhood—where they least expect it

HAVING HER
BOSS'S BABY

BY
MAUREEN CHILD

Published in Great Britain 2015
by Mills & Boon, an imprint of Harlequin (UK) Limited,
Eton House, 18-24 Paradise Road, Richmond, Surrey, TW9 1SR

© 2015 Maureen Child

ISBN: 978-0-263-25273-6

51-0815

Harlequin (UK) Limited's policy is to use papers that are natural, renewable and recyclable products and made from wood grown in sustainable forests. The logging and manufacturing processes conform to the legal environmental regulations of the country of origin.

Printed and bound in Spain
by CPI, Barcelona

Maureen Child writes for the Mills & Boon® Desire™ line and can't imagine a better job. A seven-time finalist for the prestigious Romance Writers of America RITA® Award, Maureen is the author of more than one hundred romance novels. Her books regularly appear on bestseller lists and have won several awards, including a Prism Award, a National Readers' Choice Award, a Colorado Romance Writers Award of Excellence and a Golden Quill Award.

One of her books, *The Soul Collector*, was made into a CBS TV movie starring Melissa Gilbert, Bruce Greenwood and Ossie Davis. If you look closely, in the last five minutes of the movie you'll spot Maureen, who was an extra in the last scene.

Maureen believes that laughter goes hand in hand with love, so her stories are always filled with humor. The many letters she receives assure her that her readers love to laugh as much as she does. Maureen Child is a native Californian but has recently moved to the mountains of Utah.

For Bob Butler
Because we remember
And we miss you

One

Brady Finn liked his life just as it was.

So there was a part of him that was less than enthusiastic about the latest venture his company, Celtic Knot Games, was investing in. But he'd been overruled. Which was what happened when your partners were brothers who sided with each other on the big decisions even as they argued over minutiae.

Still, Brady wouldn't change a thing because the life he loved had only happened because he and the Ryan brothers had formed their company while still in college. They'd strung together their first video game with little more than dreams and the arrogance of youth.

That game, "Fate Castle," based on an ancient Irish legend, had sold well enough to finance the next game, and now Celtic Knot was at the top of the video game mountain. The three of them had already expanded their business into graphic novels and role-playing board games. Now they were moving into seriously uncharted waters.

What the hell the three of them knew about hotels could be written on the head of a pin with enough room left over for *War and Peace*. They'd drawn straws to see who would be the first of them to take over an old hotel and turn it into a fantasy. Brady had lost. He still thought the Ryans had rigged that draw to make sure he was up to bat first, but since there was nothing he could do to change the outcome he was determined to take this challenge and turn it into a win. Brady wouldn't settle for less.

The three of them had built this company from nothing. He looked around, silently approving of the workplace. Housed in a Victorian mansion on Ocean Boulevard in Long Beach, California, Celtic Knot's offices were relaxed, fun and efficient. They could have taken over a few floors of some steel-and-glass building, but none of them had liked the idea of that. Instead, they'd purchased the old house and had it rehabbed into what they needed. There was plenty of room, with none of the cold stuffiness associated with many successful companies.

There was a view of the beach from the front, and the backyard was a favorite spot for taking breaks. It was more than a place to work. It was home. The first real home he'd ever had. A home Brady shared with the only family he'd ever known.

"The designs for the new game are brilliant," Mike Ryan insisted, his voice rising as he tried to get through to his younger brother.

"Yeah, for a fifth-grade art fair," Sean countered and reached for one of the drawings scattered across the conference table to emphasize his point. "Peter's had three months to do the new storyboards. He emailed these to me yesterday as an example of what he's got for us." Clearly disgusted, he stabbed the picture with his index finger. "Take a look at that banshee," he said. "Does that look scary to you? Looks more like an underfed surfer than a servant of death."

"You're nit-picking," Mike said, shuffling through the drawings himself until he found the one he wanted. Sliding the artwork depicting a medieval hunter across the table, he said, "This is great. So he's having trouble with the banshee. He'll get it right eventually."

"That's the problem with Peter," Brady spoke up quietly, and both of the brothers turned to look at him. "It's always *eventually*. He hasn't made one deadline since he started with us."

Shaking his head, Brady reached for his coffee, which was already going cold in the heavy ceramic mug. Taking a sip, he listened as Sean said, "Agreed. We've given Peter plenty of chances to prove he's worth the money we're paying him and he hasn't done it yet. I want to give Jenny Marshall a shot at the storyboards."

"Marshall?" Mike frowned as he tried to put a face to the name.

"You know her work," Brady said. "Graphic artist. Been here about six months. Did the background art on 'Forest Run.' She's talented. Deserves the shot."

Frowning, Mike mumbled, "Okay, yeah. I remember her work on that game. But she was backup. You really think she's ready to be the lead artist?"

Sean started to speak, but Brady held up a hand. If the brothers went at it again, this argument could go on forever. "Yeah, I do. But before we do anything permanent, I'll talk to Peter. His latest deadline is tomorrow. If he fails again, that's it. Agreed?"

"Absolutely," Sean said and shot a look at his brother.

"Agreed." Mike nodded, then leaned back in his chair, propping his feet up on the corner of the table. "Now, on another topic, when's our Irish visitor arriving?"

Brady frowned. Both brothers were watching him. The Ryans had black hair and blue eyes and both of them stood well over six feet, just like Brady. They were as close as family, he reminded himself, and he was grateful for both of them—even when they irritated the hell out of him.

He stared at the older of the two brothers from across the gleaming oak conference table. "Her flight lands in an hour."

"It might've been easier for you to go to Ireland—take a look at the castle yourself."

Brady shook his head. "There's too much going on here for me to go to Europe. Besides, we've all seen the castle in the 360-degree videos."

"True," Mike said, a half smile on his face. "And it'll be perfect for our first hotel. Fate Castle."

Named after their initial success, the Irish castle would be revamped into a luxurious modern fantasy resort where guests could imagine being a part of the world that Celtic Knot had invented. Though Brady could see the potential in their expansion, he still wondered if hotels were the way to go. Then he remembered the last Comic-Con and the reaction of the fans when they'd been told about the latest idea rolling out of Celtic Knot. The place had gone nuts with cheers as their fans realized that soon they'd be able to not only visit the darkly dangerous worlds they loved but actually live in them, as well.

Brady didn't have to love the idea to see the merit in it.

"What's the woman's name again?" Sean took a seat and sprawled comfortably.

"Her last name's Donovan," Brady said. "First name, who knows? It's spelled *A-I-N-E*. Don't have a clue how to pronounce it. My best guess is *ain't* without the *T*."

"Guess it's Gaelic," Sean said, gathering up the sheaf of sketches he'd brought with him into the meeting.

"Whatever it is," Brady said, glancing down at the file they had on the castle hotel and employees, "she's been the manager for three years and by all accounts is good at her job. In spite of the fact the hotel's been losing money over the past couple of years. She's twenty-eight, degree in hotel management and lives on the property in a guest cottage with her mother and younger brother."

"She's almost thirty and still living with her mother?" Sean whistled low and long, then gave a little shudder. "Is there a picture of her in the file?"

"Yeah." He pulled it free and slid it across the table to Sean. The photo was a standard employee shot and if it was true to life, Aine Donovan wasn't going to be much of a distraction for Brady.

Which was just as well. He loved women. All women. But even if he hadn't been too busy for an affair at the moment, he had no interest in starting something up with an employee. When he wanted a woman, he had no problem finding one. But the truth was, he was happier burying himself in his work anyway. Far less aggravating to deal with the intricacies of running their company than to deal with a woman who would eventually expect more from him than he was willing to give.

Sean glanced at her photo. "She looks...*nice*."

Brady snorted at Sean's pitiful attempt to be kind.

Even he had to admit that the Irishwoman wasn't much to look at. In that photo, her hair was scraped back from her face, probably into a tidy bun. She wore glasses that made her green eyes look huge, and her pale skin looked white against the black blouse she wore buttoned primly up to the base of her throat.

"She's a hotel manager, not a model," Brady pointed out, for some reason feeling the need to defend the woman.

"Let me see that," Mike said.

Sean passed the slightly out-of-focus photo across the table. Mike studied it for a minute. Lifting his gaze to Brady's, Mike shrugged. "She looks…efficient."

Shaking his head at the two of them, Brady took the picture back, slid it into the file and closed the folder. "Doesn't matter what she looks like as long as she can do the job. And according to the reports we got on the hotel and its employees, she's good at what she does."

"Have you talked to her about the changes we've got planned?"

"Not really," he told Mike. "It was pointless to try to explain everything long distance. Besides, we only just got the finalized plan for the remodel."

Since the construction crews would begin work in a month, it was time to bring Aine Donovan up to date.

"Well, if we're finished with the Irish news," Sean said, "I had a call from a toy company interested in marketing some of our characters."

"*Toys?*" Mike sneered. "Not really who we are, Sean."

"Gotta agree." Brady shook his head. "Our games are more for the teenagers-and-up crowd."

"True, but if they were collectibles…" Sean's voice trailed off even as he gave them both a small smile.

Brady and Mike looked at each other and nodded.

"Collectibles is a different story," Brady said. "We get people excited about owning our characters—that will only push the games themselves higher up the food chain."

"Yeah, that could work," Mike finally said. "Get some numbers. Once we have a better idea of the licensing agreement we can talk it over again."

"Right." Sean stood up and looked at Brady. "You picking up Irish from the airport?"

"No." Brady stood, too, and gathered up the file folder. "I've got a car meeting her and taking her directly to the hotel."

"That's the personal touch," Sean muttered.

Brady snapped, "It's not a date, Sean. She's coming here to work."

"You setting her up at the Seaview?" Mike asked, interrupting Sean.

"Yeah." The company kept a suite at the nearby hotel for visiting clients. It was within walking distance to their business, which made meetings easier to arrange. It was also where Brady lived, in a penthouse suite. "I'll go over there this afternoon to meet with her. Tomorrow's soon enough for us to show her what we've got in mind for the remodel."

Once the three of them explained the situation to Aine Donovan, she could get back to Ireland and, more important, Brady could get back to his life.

"I'm here, Mum, and it's just lovely."

"Aine?"

She winced at the sleepy tone of her mother's voice. Standing on the balcony off the living room of her hotel

suite, Aine stared out at the blue Pacific and finally remembered the time difference between California and
home. Here in Long Beach, it was four in the afternoon
and a warm sun was shining out of a clear sky. Back in
County Mayo, it was…after midnight.

Now that she thought about it, Aine realized she
should be exhausted. But she wasn't. Excitement about
the travel, she guessed, tangled with anxiety over what
was going to happen once she met with Brady Finn about
her castle. All right, not *her* castle, but certainly more
hers than his, despite his having bought the place a few
months ago. What did he know of its traditions, its history
and legacy, its importance to the village where her friends
lived? *Nothing, that's what*, she told herself, though she'd
make him aware of all of it before he began whatever remodeling he had in mind.

It worried her to be sure—what did a video game
maven want with a centuries-old castle in a tiny village
in Ireland? It wasn't as though Castle Butler had ever
been a tourist draw. There were far finer estates, much
easier to get to, dotting the Irish countryside.

Thoughts whirled in her brain, circling each other,
making her mind a jumble that only cleared momen-
tarily when her mother spoke again. "Aine. You've arrived, then?"

"I have. I'm so sorry, Mum. I completely forgot—"

"No matter." Molly Donovan's voice became clearer
and Aine could almost see her mother sitting up in bed,
trying to wake herself. "I'm glad you called. Your flight
was all right, then?"

"More than all right." She'd never flown in a private
jet before, and now that she had, Aine knew she'd never
be happy in coach again. "It was like flying while relax-

ing in a posh living room. There were couches and tables and flowers in the loo. The flight attendant made fresh cookies," she said. "Cooked them up right there on the plane. Or maybe only heated them. But there was a real meal and champagne to go with it and really, I was almost sorry when the flight ended."

A hard truth indeed, because once her travel was over, it meant that she had no choice but to face down the man who owned the company that had the power to ruin her life and the lives of so many others. But, she argued with herself, why would he do that? Surely he wouldn't purchase the castle only to shut down the hotel? True enough that profits hadn't been what they should be in the past couple of years, but she had ideas to change all that, didn't she? The previous owner hadn't wanted to be bothered. She could only hope that this one would.

Although, she had to say, he was setting the scene perfectly to keep her off balance, wasn't he? Sending a private jet for her. Then, rather than meeting her himself, he'd had a driver there holding a sign with her name on it. Arranging for her to stay in a suite that was larger than the entire first floor of the guest cottage where she and her family lived, yet not a whisper of a personal greeting from the man.

He was letting her know, without speaking a word, that he was in charge. Master to servant, she supposed, and wondered if all exceedingly wealthy people were the same.

"It sounds lovely. And now?" her mother asked. "You're tucked into a hotel?"

"I am," Aine said, turning her face into the wind driving in from the sea. "I'm standing on a terrace look-

ing out at the ocean. It's warm and lovely, nothing like
spring at home."

"Aye," her mother agreed. "Rained all day and half
the night. Now, you'll have your meeting with the new
owner of the castle soon, won't you?"

"I will." Aine's stomach fluttered with the wings of
what felt like a million butterflies. She laid one hand on
her abdomen in a futile attempt to ease that stirring of
nerves. "He's left a message for me saying he'll be here
at five."

A message, she told herself and shook her head. Again,
she recalled the man hadn't bothered to meet her at the
airport or give her the courtesy of being here when she
arrived. All small ways to impress upon her that she was
on his territory now and that he would be the one making the decisions. Well, he might hold the purse strings,
but she would at least be heard.

"You'll not be a terrier at the man from the beginning, will you?" her mother asked. "You'll have some
patience?"

Patience was a difficult matter for Aine. Her mother
had always said that Aine had been born two weeks early
and hadn't stopped running since. She didn't like waiting. For anything. The past few months, knowing that
the castle had been sold but having no more information beyond that, had nearly driven her around the bend.
Now she wanted answers. She needed to know what the
new owner of Castle Butler was planning—so she could
prepare.

"I'll not say a thing until I've heard him out, and that's
the best I can promise," she said and hoped she could
keep that vow.

It was only that this was so important. To her. To her

family. To the village that looked to the castle's guests to shop in their stores, eat in their pubs. Now a trio of American businessmen had purchased the castle and everyone was worried about what might happen.

For the past three years, Aine had managed the castle hotel and though she'd had to fight the owner for every nail and gallon of paint needed for its upkeep, she felt she'd done a good job of it. Now though, things had changed. It wasn't only the hotel she had to see to—it was the survival of her village and her family's future she fought for. She hated feeling off balance, as if she was one step behind everyone else in the bloody world. It was being here, in California, that was throwing her. If Brady Finn had come to Ireland, she might have felt more in control of the situation. As it was, she'd have to stay on her toes and impress on the new owner the importance of the responsibility he had just acquired.

"I know you'll do what's best," her mother said.

It was hard, having the faith of everyone you knew and loved settled on your shoulders. More than her mother and brother were counting on her; the whole village was worried, and Aine was their hope. She wouldn't let them down.

"I will. You go back to sleep now, Mum. I'll call you again tomorrow." She paused and smiled. "At a better time."

Aine took the time before the arrival of her new employer to freshen up. She fixed her makeup, did her hair and, since she was running out of time, didn't bother with changing her clothes, only gave them a quick brush.

But when five o'clock came and went with still no sign of her new employer, Aine's temper spiked. So much for her vow of patience. Was he so busy, then, that he couldn't even be bothered to contact her to say his plans had changed? Or did he think so little of her that being late for their appointment didn't bother him? The phone in her suite rang and when she answered, the hotel desk clerk said, "Ms. Donovan? Your driver is here to take you to the Celtic Knot offices."

"My driver?"

"Yes. Apparently Mr. Finn was delayed and so sent a driver to take you to your meeting."

Irritation rippled along her nerve endings. In seconds, her mind raced with outraged thoughts. Hadn't she flown thousands of miles to meet with him? And now, after being ignored by the great man, she was being sent for, was she? Lord of the manor summoning a scullery maid? Had he a velvet rope in his office that he tugged on to get all of his servants moving in a timely fashion?

"Ms. Donovan?"

"Yes. I'm sorry, yes." It wasn't this man's fault, was it, that her new employer had the manners of a goat? "Would you please tell the driver I'll be down in a moment?"

She hung up, then took another moment to check her reflection. But for the anger-infused color in her cheeks, she looked fine, though she briefly considered changing her clothes after all. Aine decided against it as she doubted very much her new employer would be pleased if she kept him waiting.

Thankfully, flying on a private jet hadn't left her looking as haggard as surviving a twelve-hour flight in economy would have. So she would go now to meet the man who clearly expected his underlings to leap into motion when he spoke. And she would, even if it killed her, keep her temper.

Two

"We need the new storyboards by tomorrow afternoon at the latest," Brady barked into the phone. He'd been hung up for the past two hours with call after call and his patience was strained to the breaking point. "No more excuses, Peter. Meet the deadline or be replaced."

Artists were difficult to deal with in the best of times. But Peter Singer was an artist with no ambition and no idea of how to schedule his time. With the best of intentions, the man laid down deadlines, then because he was so disorganized, he never managed to meet the dates he himself had arranged.

His talent wasn't in question. Peter was good at sketching out the boards the programmers would use to lay out the basic story line of their newest game. And without that road map, the whole process would be brought to a crawl. In fact, Peter was good enough at his work that

Brady had given him several extensions when he'd asked for them. But he wasn't getting another one.

"Brady, I can have them for you by the end of the week," the man was arguing. "I'm on a roll here, but I can't get them by tomorrow. That's just impossible. I swear they'll be worth the wait if you—"

"Tomorrow, Peter," Brady said flatly, as he turned in his desk chair to stare out the window behind him. "Have them here by five tomorrow or start looking for another job."

"You can't rush art."

"If I can pay for it, I can rush it," Brady told him, idly watching a blackbird jump from branch to branch in the pine tree out back. "And you've had three months on your last extension to make this deadline, so no sense in complaining now that you're being rushed. Do it or not. Your choice."

He hung up before he could be drawn into more of Peter's dramatic appeals. He'd been dealing with marketing most of the day—not his favorite part of the job anyway—so he admittedly had less patience than he normally would have for Peter's latest justification for failure. But the point was, they had a business to run, schedules to keep and for the past year Peter hadn't been able to, or wasn't interested in, keeping to the schedule. It was time to move on, find another graphic artist who could do the job. Sean was right. Jenny Marshall deserved a shot.

And now, rather than head home for a well-deserved beer, Brady had one more meeting to get through. As the thought passed through his mind, he heard a brisk knock at his door and knew the Irishwoman had arrived.

"Come in."

The door opened and there she was.

Auburn hair and green eyes identified her as Aine Donovan, but there the resemblance to the woman in the employee photo ended. He'd been prepared for a spinsterish female, a librarian type. *This* woman was a surprise.

His gaze swept her up and down in a blink, taking in everything. She wore black slacks and a crimson blouse with a short black jacket over it. Her thick dark red hair fell in heavy waves around her shoulders. Her green eyes, not hidden behind the glasses she'd worn in her photo, were artfully enhanced and shone like sunlight in a forest. She was tall and curvy enough to make a man's mouth water, and the steady, even stare she sent him told Brady that she also had strength. Nothing hotter than a gorgeous woman with a strong sense of self. Unexpectedly, he felt a punch of desire that hit him harder than anything he'd ever experienced before.

Discomfited, he tamped down that feeling instantly and fought to ignore it. Desire had its place, and this definitely wasn't it. She worked for him, and sex with an employee only set up endless possibilities for problems. Even that fact, though, wasn't enough to kill the want that only increased the moment she opened her mouth and the music of Ireland flavored her words.

"Brady Finn?"

"That's right. Ms. Donovan?" He stood up and waited as she crossed the room to him, her right hand outstretched. She moved with a slow, easy grace that made him think of silk sheets, moonlit nights and the soft slide of skin against skin. Damn.

"It's Aine, please."

She pronounced it *Anya* and Brady knew he never

would have figured that out from its spelling. "I wondered how to say your first name," he admitted.

For the first time, a hint of a smile touched her mouth, then slipped away again. "'Tis Gaelic."

He took her hand in his and felt a buzz of sensation shoot straight up his arm, as if he'd grabbed a live electrical wire. It was unexpected enough that he let her go instantly and just resisted rubbing his palm against his pant leg. "I assumed so. Please, have a seat."

She sat down in one of the chairs in front of his desk and slowly crossed one leg over the other. It was an unconsciously seductive move that he really resented noticing.

"How was your flight?" he blurted out, wanting to steer the conversation into the banal so his mind would have nothing else to torment him with.

"Lovely, thanks," she said shortly and lifted her chin a notch. "Is that what we're to talk about, then? My flight? My hotel? I wonder that you care what I think. Perhaps we could speak instead about the fact that twice now you've not showed the slightest interest in keeping your appointments with me."

Brady sat back, surprised at her nerve. Not many employees would risk making their new boss angry. "Twice?"

"You sent a car for me at the airport and again at the hotel." She folded her hands neatly atop her knee. If she was uneasy about speaking her mind, she didn't show it.

He merely looked at her for a long moment before saying, "Was there something wrong with the car service?"

"Not at all. But I wonder why a man who takes the trouble to fly his hotel manager halfway across the world can't be bothered to cross the street and walk a block to meet her in person."

When Brady had seen her photo, he'd thought, *Efficient, cool, dispassionate.* Now he had to revise those thoughts entirely. There was fire here, sparking in her eyes and practically humming in the air around her.

Damned if he didn't like it.

It was more than simple desire he felt now—there was respect, as well.

Which meant that he was in more trouble here than he would have thought.

Aine could have bitten her own tongue off. Hadn't she promised herself to rein in her temper? And what did she do the moment she met her new boss? Insult him was what. An apology was owed him and Aine knew it, though the words stuck in her throat and wouldn't come free. Yes, she shouldn't have spoken to him so, but nothing she'd said was untrue, was it? Oh, she should have taken a moment to calm herself before coming into his office. Instead, she'd allowed her temper to simmer into a fine boil and then spill over the moment she met the man. Now there was an unwanted tension between them and she had to find a way to try to smooth things over.

The trouble was, Aine told herself as she met his steady gaze across the wide expanse of his desk, she hadn't expected him to be so…wildly attractive. On the short ride to his office, she'd told herself to be confident. Then the door had opened and she'd taken one look at the man and gone light-headed enough that all her good intentions had simply dissolved.

His thick black hair fell across his forehead, making her want to reach out and smooth it back. His strong jaw, sharp blue eyes and just the barest hint of whiskers on his cheeks made him seem so much more than a man who made his fortune by inventing games. He looked like a pirate. A highwayman. A dark hero from one of the romance novels she loved to read. Something raw and wild in him teased to life all sorts of inappropriate thoughts in her mind and stirred something warm and wonderful through her blood.

This wasn't something she wanted, or was even interested in, she assured herself. But it seemed she had no choice but to feel that whip of heat and tendrils of desire snaking through her body. When he shook her hand, she'd wanted to hold on to that tight, firm grip just a bit longer, but she was grateful, too, when he deliberately let her go. Well, now she wasn't even making sense to herself. This was not a good sign.

Trying to distract herself, Aine admitted that not only was the man himself unexpected, but his office was, as well. She had thought to find Celtic Knot in one of those eerily modern glass-and-chrome buildings. Instead, the old home they'd transformed into a work space was both charming and surprising. And it gave her just a bit of hope for the castle—if this man's company could modernize an old building such as this and maintain its character, perhaps they could do the same with Castle Butler, too.

With that thought firmly in mind, Aine settled into the uncomfortable chair, swallowed her pride like a bitter pill and forced herself to say, "I'll apologize for biting your head off first thing."

His eyebrows arched, but he didn't speak, so Aine continued on in a rush—before he could open his mouth to say, "You're fired."

"It's the jet lag, I'm sure, that's put me in a mood." Though she wasn't at all tired, she would reach for the most understandable excuse.

"Of course," he said, though it was clear from his tone he wasn't buying that. "And I'll apologize for not meeting you personally. We're very busy right now, with one game being released this week and the next due out in December."

Games, she thought. Wasn't her younger brother, Robbie, forever playing this man's games? Ancient legends of Ireland brought to life so people around the world could pretend to be Celts fighting age-old evil. She didn't yet see why a company that built video games was buying a hotel in Ireland, though, and she was willing to admit, at least to herself, that she was worried about what might be coming.

"There isn't time enough today to get into all of our plans for the castle, but I did want to meet with you to let you know that changes are coming."

Instantly, it seemed, a ball of ice dropped into the pit of her stomach as every defensive instinct she possessed fired up. "Changes, is it?"

"You had to assume things would change, Aine." He sat forward, propping his arms on the desk, and met her gaze. "The past couple of years, your castle has been losing money."

She bristled and felt the first tremor of anxiety ripple through her. Was he saying she was at fault for the hotel losing money? Had he brought her all this way just to fire her? Was she about to lose not only her job but her home? Now it seemed she not only needed to defend her castle but herself, as well. "If you're thinking my management of the castle has been lacking—"

"Not at all," he interrupted her, and held up one hand to keep her from speaking again. "I've gone over the books, as have my partners, and we all agree that your skills are what held the place together the past couple of years."

A relieved breath escaped her, but that sensation didn't last long.

"Still," he continued, and Aine felt as though she were hypnotized. She couldn't tear her gaze from him, from his eyes. There was something pulling her toward him even as her common sense was shrieking a warning. Working with him would have been so much easier if he had been the stereotypical computer nerd—skinny, awkward. Instead, Brady Finn was obviously the kind of man who was used to issuing orders and having them obeyed without question. That worried her a bit, as she'd never been one to blindly fall in line.

"We'll be making some substantial changes both to the castle itself and the way it's run."

Well, that simple sentence sent cold chills dancing through her. "What sort of *substantial* changes did you have in mind?" The words forced their way out of her mouth.

"Time enough to get into all of that," he said and stood up. "We'll get started on it tomorrow."

Tomorrow. She was worried enough that she didn't mind putting off whatever was coming. Yet at the same time, she knew she wouldn't sleep a wink for thinking of it.

Her gaze tracked him. He was tall and broad shouldered, and in his white dress shirt his chest looked as wide as the sky. Her mouth went dry as she stood to face him. His eyes were fixed on her, and there was power in those blue depths. The kind of power only rich men knew. It was a mix of wealth and confidence and the surety of his own convictions. And that kind of man would not be easy to stand against.

"You must be hungry," he said.

"I am, a bit," she admitted, though if he continued to stare at her in just that way, she'd be lucky to swallow a single bite.

"Then, we'll go to an early dinner and talk." He walked to a closet, opened it and pulled out a black jacket. Shrugging it on, he went back to her side and waited.

"Talk?" she asked. "About what?"

He took her arm, threaded it through his and headed for the door. "You can tell me all about yourself and the castle."

She'd no interest in talking about herself, but maybe, she thought, she could impress on him what the castle meant to those who worked there and the people in the nearby village, as well.

"All right," she said, then hesitated, remembering she hadn't even changed clothes since her flight. "But I'm not dressed for it, really."

"You look great," he assured her.

How like a man was all she could think.

"If we could stop by my hotel first," she said, dismissing his words, "I'd like to change."

He shrugged and said, "Sure."

She was worth the wait, Brady thought, looking across the linen-draped tablecloth at Aine. She wore a simple black dress with wide shoulder straps and a square neckline that displayed just the hint of the tops of her breasts. Her skin glowed like fine porcelain in the candlelight, and the candle flames seemed to shoot golden sparks through her dark red hair and wink off the tiny gold stars she wore at her ears.

His insides burned, and watching her smile and sip at her wine was only stoking the flames. She was… temptation, Brady told himself. One he didn't want to resist but would have to.

"It's lovely wine," she said, setting her glass down.

"Yeah. Lovely." He didn't mean the wine and, judging by the flash in her eyes, she knew it. Damn. This upscale restaurant with the candlelight had probably been a mistake. He should have taken her for a nice casual burger in a crowded diner. This setting was too damn intimate.

The only way to keep the want clawing at him in check was to steer this conversation to business and keep it there. A shame that his brain didn't exactly have dibs on his blood supply at the moment. "Tell me about the castle. From your perspective, what needs to be done?"

She took a breath, then another sip of wine, and set the glass down again before speaking. "It's true, there does need to be some remodeling. Bathrooms updated, new paint throughout, of course, and the furniture's a bit shabby. But the building itself is strong and sure as it has been since it was first built in 1430."

Almost six hundred years. For a man with no family, no personal history to talk about, that kind of longevity seemed impossible to understand and accept. But as a man with no roots, changes came easier to him than they would to people like her. People who clung to traditions and tales of the past.

"We're going to do all of that, of course," he said. "And more."

"That's what worries me," she admitted. "The *more*. I

know you've said we'd talk about this tomorrow, but can you tell me some small things that you have in mind?"

Hard to concentrate on the conversation when listening to her speak made that twist of desire inside him curl tighter. But maybe talking about the castle would help give him something else to focus on. Deliberately, he took a gulp of his wine to give himself time to settle. When he could think clearly again, he said, "Our company, Celtic Knot, is going into the hotel business."

She nodded and waited for him to continue.

"Starting with Castle Butler, we're buying three hotels and reimagining them."

"*Reimagine* sounds much grander than a few simple changes," she said, suspicion clear in her tone.

"It is," he said. "We're going to turn them into mock-ups of our three bestselling games."

"Games."

Warming to his theme, Brady said, "The first will be Fate Castle."

"Fate…?"

"Designed after our first successful game."

"I know of it," she said quietly.

His eyebrows shot up, and he couldn't quite keep the surprise out of his voice when he asked, "You've played it? And here I was thinking you didn't look the gaming type to me."

"There's a type, is there?" She ran her fingers up and down the stem of her wineglass, but the movement was anything but smooth and relaxed. "As it happens, you'd be right. I don't play, but my younger brother, Robbie, does. He's mad for your games."

Brady smiled in spite of the coolness in her eyes. "He has excellent taste."

"I wouldn't know," she said with detachment, "for the idea of using a toy to chase down zombies and wraiths doesn't appeal to me."

"You shouldn't knock it until you've tried it."

"What makes you think I haven't?"

"You'd like it more if you had," he said simply. He knew their games were addictive to players. "Our games are more than just running and shooting. There are intricate puzzles to be solved. Choices made, and the player takes the consequences for those choices. Our games are more sophisticated in that we expect our players to *think*."

She smiled briefly. "To listen to Robbie shouting and railing against the game, you wouldn't know it was a test of intelligence."

He smiled again as her voice twisted the knots in his belly even tighter. "Well, even smart guys get angry when they don't succeed at first try."

"True enough," she said, then paused as the waiter delivered their meals.

La Bella Vita was Brady's favorite restaurant. Elegant, quiet, and the food was as amazing as the atmosphere. The walls were a pale yellow, with paintings of Italy dotting the space. Candles flickered atop every one of the linen-draped tables, and soft music sighed through the speakers tucked into the corners of the room. The clink of crystal and the rise and fall of muted conversations around them filled the silence while Aine took a bite of her crab-stuffed ravioli in Alfredo sauce.

"Good?" he asked.

"Wonderful," she said, then asked, "Do you often bring your employees to such a fine restaurant?"

"No," he admitted and couldn't have said, even to himself, why he'd brought Aine here. They could have stopped for a burger somewhere or eaten at the restaurant in her hotel. Instead, he'd brought her here, as if they were on a date. Which they really weren't. Best to steer this back to work. "It's quiet here, though, and I thought that would give us a chance to talk."

"About the castle."

"Yes, and about your part in helping us make this happen."

"My part?" Genuine surprise flashed in her eyes.

Brady took a bite of his own ravioli, then said, "You'll be there on-site, for the day-to-day changes. We need you to oversee the workers, make sure they stay on schedule, on budget, things like that."

"I'm to be in charge?"

"You're my liaison," he told her. "You come to me with problems, I take care of them, then you make sure they're handled right."

"I see." She dragged her fork listlessly across her plate.

"Is there a problem?"

"Have you given thought to who will be doing the work?"

"We've got the best contractor in California lined up," Brady said. "He'll be bringing in crews he trusts."

She frowned a bit. "Things might go easier and more quickly if you hired Irish workmen."

"I don't like working with people I don't know," he said.

"Yet here we are, and you don't know me from the man in the moon."

"True." He nodded. "Fine. I'll think about it."

"Good. But you've yet to tell me what kind of changes you're talking about." She met his gaze. "You said only that you were going to 'reimagine' things. Which could mean anything at all. What exactly are you planning?"

"Nothing structural," he told her. "We like the look of Castle Butler—that's why we bought it. But there will be plenty of changes made to the interior."

She sighed, set her fork down and admitted, "To be honest, that's what I'm worried about."

"In what way?"

"Will I be seeing zombies in the hallways?" she asked. "Cobwebs strung across the stone?"

She looked so worried about that possibility, Brady grinned. "Tempting, but no. We'll go into all the details starting tomorrow, but I'll say tonight I think you'll like what we've got in mind."

Folding her hands on the table, she looked at him and said, "I've worked at Castle Butler since I was sixteen and went into the kitchens. I worked my way up from there, becoming first a maid, then moving on through reception and finally into managing the castle.

"I know every board that creaks, every draft that blows through broken mortar. I know every wall that needs painting and every tree in the garden that needs trimming." She paused, took a breath and continued before he could speak, "Everyone who works in the castle is a friend to me, or family. The village depends on the hotel for its livelihood and their worries are mine, as well. So," she said softly, "when you speak of reimagining the castle, know that for me, it's not about games."

Brady could see that. Her forest green eyes met his, and he read the stubborn strength in them that foretold all kinds of interesting battles ahead.

Damned if he wasn't looking forward to them.

Three

By the following day, Aine was sure she'd stepped in it with Brady at dinner. She'd had such plans to mind her temper and her words and hadn't she thrown all those plans to the wind the moment he mentioned "substantial changes"?

She sipped room-service tea and watched the play of sunlight on the water from her balcony. The tea was a misery, and why was it, she wondered, that Americans couldn't brew a decent cup of tea? But the view was breathtaking—the water sapphire blue, crested with whitecaps, and in the distance, a boat with a bright red sail skimmed that frothy surface.

She only wished the vista was enough to clear her mind of the mistakes made the night before. But as her father used to say, she'd already walked that path—it was useless to regret the footprints left behind.

So she would do better today. She'd meet Brady Finn's partners and be the very *essence* of professionalism…

Not two hours later, she felt her personal vow to maintain a quiet, dignified presence shatter like glass.

"You can't mean it."

Aine had remained silent during most of this meeting with all three partners of Celtic Knot Games. She'd listened as they'd tossed ideas back and forth, almost as if they'd forgotten her presence entirely. She'd bitten her tongue so many times, that particular organ felt swollen in her mouth. And yet, there came a time when a woman could be silent no longer and Aine had just reached it. Looking from one man to the other, she focused on Sean Ryan since he seemed to be the most reasonable.

"You're talking about turning a dignified piece of Irish history into a mockery of itself," she said bluntly.

Before Sean could speak, his brother said, "I understand you feel a little protective of the castle, but—"

"Protective, yes, but it's more than that," she argued, shifting her gaze from one to the other of the three men, ending finally by meeting Brady's gaze. "There's tradition. There's the centuries etched into every stone."

"It's a building," Brady said. "One that you yourself have already agreed needs remodeling."

"To that, yes, I do agree," she said quickly, leaning toward him a bit to emphasize what she wanted to say. "And I'm pleased to hear you're going to make some long-needed repairs to the castle. I've some ideas for changes that would enhance our guests' experiences even while keeping the building's, for lack of a better word, *soul* intact."

Amused, Brady asked, "You believe the castle has a soul?"

She looked almost affronted. "It's been standing since 1430," she reminded him, so focused on Brady alone that the other men in the room might not have been there at all. "People have come and gone, but the castle remains. It's stood against invaders, neglect and indifference. It's housed kings and peasants and everything in between. Why wouldn't it have a soul?"

"That's very…Irish of you to think so."

She didn't care for the patronizing smile he offered her. "As you're Irish yourself, you should agree."

Brady's features froze over. It was as if she'd doused him with a bucket of ice water. Aine didn't know what it was about her simple statement that had turned him to stone, but clearly, she'd hit a very sore spot.

"Only my name is Irish," he said shortly.

"An intriguing statement," she answered, never moving her gaze from his.

"I'm not trying to intrigue you," he pointed out. "I'm saying that if you're looking for a kindred spirit in this, it's not me."

"Okay," Sean said, voice overly cheerful. "So we're all Irish here—some of us more than others. Let's move on, huh?"

Aine stiffened, didn't so much as acknowledge Sean's attempt to lighten the mood. "I'm not looking for a friend or a confidante or a kindred spirit, as you say," she said and every word was measured, careful, as she deliberately tried to hold on to a temper that was nearly choking her. "I've come thousands of miles at your direction to discuss the future of Castle Butler. I can give you information on the building, the village it supports and the country it resides in. All of which you might have found out for yourself had you bothered to once visit the property in person."

Silence hummed uncomfortably in the room for a few long seconds before Brady spoke up. "While I admire your guts in speaking your mind, I also wonder if you think the wisest course of action is to piss off your new boss."

"All right, then," she forced herself to say at last. "I'll apologize for my outburst, as it wasn't my intention to insult you."

"No need to apologize."

"I'll decide for myself when I'm wrong, thanks," she said, shaking her head firmly. "I promised myself I'd keep my temper in check, and I didn't. So for that I'm sorry."

"Fine."

She swept her gaze across all three men, who were now watching her as if she was an unstable bomb. "But I won't apologize for telling you what I think about the castle and its future."

Once again, she met the eyes of all three men before focusing on Brady alone. "I've been nervous about this meeting. It's important to me that the people who work at the castle—including me—keep our jobs. I want the castle to shine again, as it should."

Brady's gaze held hers, and she felt the Ryan brothers watching her, as well. Maybe she should have kept her mouth shut. Perhaps she didn't have the right to say anything at all about their plans for the place she loved. But she couldn't sit idly by and pretend all was well when it certainly wasn't.

Still meeting Brady's gaze, she asked, "Did you bring me all this way to simply agree with your decisions? Is that what you expect from your hotel manager? To stand quietly at your side and do everything you say?"

Brady tipped his head to one side and studied her. "You're asking if I want a yes man?"

"Exactly."

"Of course I don't," he said sharply. "I want your opinions, as I told you last night."

Aine blew out a breath. "Now that you've opened the door, I can only hope you won't regret it."

"I admire honesty," he said. "Doesn't mean I'll agree with you—but I want to know what you really think about what we're planning."

Nodding, she sat more easily in her chair and glanced at the Ryan brothers. "I'll say it's hard to form an opinion with nothing more to go on than these descriptions of your ideas you've been giving me."

"I think we can take care of that," Mike said. "We've got a few drawings that could give you a better picture of what we have in mind."

Brady nodded. "Jenny Marshall's drafted some basic art that should help."

"Jenny Marshall again?" Mike looked at his brother. "What, is she our go-to artist now?"

Aine leaned back in her chair and shook her head. Watching the brothers argue, and Brady following along, was a real lesson. The three men were clearly a unit and yet Aine had the sense that Brady was still holding back, even from his friends. As if he was deliberately standing outside, looking in from a safe distance.

Even while the Ryans' heated discussion amped up, she continued to watch Brady and his reaction to his friends. He seemed completely at ease with their argument, and since the brothers were Irish, she was willing to bet their differences of opinion happened frequently. The mystery for her was why he separated himself from the disagreement. Did he simply not care one way or the other about the artist's work or was it an inborn remoteness that drove him?

"Jenny's good, I keep telling you." Sean shrugged. "You haven't even looked at the mock-ups she's done of the stuff Peter was supposed to have finished five months ago."

"It's Peter's job, not hers," Mike reminded his brother. "Why would I look at what she's doing?"

"So you could appreciate just how good she is?" Sean asked.

Mike scowled at his younger brother. "Why are you so anxious to push Jenny off on us?"

"He just told you why," a voice said as the door opened to admit a petite, curvy woman with short, curly blond hair. Her blue eyes narrowed on Mike Ryan briefly before she looked at Sean and smiled. Crossing the room, she handed him a large black portfolio. "Sorry this took longer than I thought, but I wanted to finalize a few details this morning before bringing them to you."

"No problem, Jenny, thanks."

While sunlight slanted through the wide windows, Jenny and Mike faced each other across the conference table. Aine watched the byplay between the tiny blonde and the older of the Ryan brothers. There was a near visible tension humming in the room as the two of them glared at each other. And yet, she thought, neither of the other men in the room seemed to notice.

In fact, Brady and Sean were so fixed on the portfolio, they never saw the blonde sneer at Mike Ryan before slipping from the room and closing the door quietly behind her. Clearly, Jenny Marshall wasn't afraid to stand up for herself, and though Aine didn't know the woman at all, she felt a kinship with her.

"What the hell, Sean," Mike muttered when she was gone. "You could have told me she was coming in this morning."

"Why? So we could argue about it?" Sean shook his head and spread the series of drawings across the table. "This way was easier. Just take a look, will you?"

Aine was already looking, coming to her feet so she could see every one of the drawings Jenny had brought in. Sean was right about the woman being a wonderful artist. There was real imagination and brilliance in the artwork, whether Aine liked the subject matter or not. She recognized Castle Butler, of course, but the images she was looking at were so different from the place she'd left only a day or two before, it was hard to reconcile them.

"Okay, yeah, they're good," Mike said shortly.

"Wow," Sean said. "Quite the concession."

"Shut up," his brother retorted. "This still doesn't say she should be doing Peter's job."

"It really does," Brady put in, using his index finger to drag a rendering of the castle's main hall closer toward him. "I haven't seen Peter do work like this in, well…ever."

"There you go!" Sean slapped Brady on the back and gave an I-told-you-so look to his brother. "We promote Jenny to lead artist and we'll get back on track and stay there."

"I don't know…" Mike shook his head.

"What do you need to be convinced?" Sean asked.

"Why don't you guys take this argument somewhere

else?" Brady suggested. Both men turned to look at him as if they'd forgotten he and Aine were there.

Shrugging, Sean said, "Good idea. Aine, nice to meet you."

"Thank you," she said, tearing her gaze from the images spilled across the gleaming oak table.

"Right," Mike said. "We'll be seeing you again soon, I know."

"I'm sure," she murmured, lost in the pen-and-ink sketches that were made more vivid by the bright splashes of color added sparingly, as if to draw the viewer's attention to the tiny details of the art itself.

When she and Brady were alone in the conference room, Aine laid her fingertip on the drawing of the great hall. She knew the room well, of course—it was a place the castle rented out for wedding receptions and the occasional corporate function. But this… There were medieval banners on the walls, tapestries that were colorful and in keeping with the era of the building itself. There were torches and candelabra and several long tables that would easily seat fifty each. The fireplace that hadn't been used in years looked as it should, trimmed with fresh stone and a wide mantel that displayed pewter jugs and goblets.

"What do you think?"

Truthfully, she didn't know what to think. Aine had been prepared to be appalled. Instead, she found herself intrigued by the artist's vision for the great hall and couldn't help wondering what else might surprise her. "This is—" she paused and lifted her gaze to his "—lovely."

A flicker of pleasure danced in his eyes and she responded to it.

"Your artist, Jenny, is it? She's very talented. The great hall looks as it might have when the castle was new and Lord Butler and his lady entertained."

"High praise from a woman afraid to see zombies and cobwebs all over her castle."

Hearing her own words tossed back at her only underscored her need to watch what she said in future. But for now, she lifted her chin and nodded in acceptance. "True enough, and I can admit when I'm wrong. Although I haven't seen all of your plans, have I?"

"So you're withholding praise until you're sure?"

"Seems wise, doesn't it?"

"It does," he agreed, then drew a few other images toward him. "So let me show you a few more."

For the next hour, Aine and Brady went over his plans for the castle. Though some of it sounded wonderful, there were other points she wasn't as fond of. "Gaming systems in all the bedrooms?" She shook her head. "That hardly seems in keeping with the castle's lineage."

He leaned back in his chair, reached for the cup of soda in front of him and took a drink. Then he leisurely polished off the last of his French fries. They'd had lunch sent in and Aine had hardly touched her club sandwich. How could she eat when her very future hung in the balance?

He had said he didn't want a yes man, someone to just agree with his pronouncements. But surely he would have a breaking point where he would resent having her argue with him over what was, to him and his partners, a very big deal.

"Even the people in the Middle Ages played games," he pointed out.

"Not on gigantic flat-screen televisions and built-in gaming systems."

Brady shook his head. "They would have if the tech had been around. And the televisions will be camouflaged in crafted cabinets to look period correct."

"That's something, I suppose," Aine said, knowing that she was being stubborn, but feeling as though she were fighting for the very life of the castle she loved.

He was covering her arguments one by one and he was doing it so easily she almost admired it. But she felt it was up to *her* to protect Castle Butler and the people who depended on it, so Aine would keep at her arguments in favor of tradition and history.

"And on the ground floor," she asked, "you want the dining room walls decorated with images from your game, yes?"

"That's the idea. It is Fate Castle after all."

"So the zombies and the wraiths will have their places there, as well."

"Yes."

She ground her teeth together. "You don't think people might be put off their food if they're surrounded by spirits of the dead looking over their shoulders?"

He frowned, tapped one finger against the table and said, "We can move the wall murals to the reception hall—"

Aine took a breath. "And what of the guests who *aren't* coming to be a part of role-playing?" she asked. "We've regular guests, you know, who return year after year and they're accustomed to a castle with dignity, tradition."

"You keep throwing around the word *tradition*, and yet, with all of that dignity, the castle is in desperate need of repair and almost broke."

She took a breath to fight him on that, but it was impossible to argue with an ugly truth. The castle she loved was in dire straits, and whether she liked it or not, Brady Finn was her only hope to save it. So many people depended on the castle and the guests who came to stay there that she couldn't risk alienating the man. Yet despite knowing all of that, she felt as though the castle itself was depending on her to preserve its heritage.

"I admit the castle needs some care and attention," she said, steeling herself to meet that clear, steady stare he'd fixed on her. "But I wonder if turning it into an amusement park is really the answer."

"Not an amusement park," he corrected. "No roller coasters, Ferris wheels or cotton-candy booths."

"Thank heaven for that, at least," she murmured.

"It's going to be a destination hotel," Brady told her and leaned forward, bracing his elbows on his knees. "People all over the world will want to come to Fate Castle and experience the game they love in real life."

"Fans, then."

"Sure, fans," he said, straightening abruptly and leaning back in his chair again. "But not only fans of the game. There'll be others. People who want a taste of a real medieval experience."

"Real?" she asked, tapping one finger on a drawing of a wraith with wild gray hair blowing in an unseen wind. "I've lived near the castle all my life and I've never seen anything like this haunting the grounds."

"Real with a twist," he amended, his lips twitching briefly.

That quick, thoughtless tiny half smile and her stomach did a quick dip and roll. She had to fight to keep her mind focused on their conversation. "And you believe there are enough fans of this game to turn the castle's finances around?"

He shrugged. "We sold one hundred million copies of Fate Castle."

Her mind boggled. The number was so huge it was impossible to believe. "So many?"

"And more selling all the time," he assured her.

She sighed, looked at the drawings spread out over the table and tried to mentally apply them to the castle she knew. It would be so different, she thought. Yet a voice in the back of her mind whispered, *It will survive*. If all went as Brady Finn suggested, the castle and the village it supported would continue. That was the most important thing, wasn't it?

"I suppose you're right, then, about fans coming to the castle. Though I worry about people like Mrs. Deery and her sister, Miss Baker."

He frowned. "Who are they?"

Aine sighed and brushed her hair back behind her ear. "Just two of our regular guests," she said. "They're sisters, in their eighties, and they've been coming to Castle Butler every year for the past twenty. They take a week together to catch up on each other's lives and to be coddled a little by the hotel staff."

"They can still come to the hotel," he said.

Aine glanced again at the drawing of the wraith. "Yes, they can and no doubt will. I just wonder what they'll make of the zombies..."

"It's not just the gaming aspects we're renovating at the castle," he said. "We'll be restoring the whole place. Making it safe again. The wiring's mostly shot. It's a wonder the place hasn't caught fire."

"Oh, it's not that bad," she argued, defending the place she loved.

"According to the building inspector we hired, it is," Brady said. "The plumbing will be redone, new roof, insulation—though the castle will look medieval, it won't feel like it."

Aine took a breath and held it to keep from saying anything else. He was right in that the building itself needed updating desperately. In winter, you could feel cold wind sliding between the stones. Under the window sashes it came through strong enough to make the drapes flutter.

"We're going to modernize the kitchens, install working furnaces and change out the worn or faded furniture. We'll be replacing woodwork that's rotted or ruined by water damage…"

All right, then, she thought, he was making her beloved castle sound like a tumbledown shack. "There've been storms over the years, of course, and—"

He held up one hand for silence and she was so surprised, she gave it to him.

"You don't have to defend every mantel and window sash in the place to me, Aine. I understand the castle's old…"

"Ancient," she corrected, prepared to defend anyway. "Historic."

"And we agree it needs work. I'm willing to have that work done."

"And change the heart of it," she said sadly.

"You're stubborn," he said. "I can appreciate that. So am I. The difference is, I'm the one who'll make the decisions here, Aine. You can either work with me or—"

She looked at him and read the truth in his cool blue eyes. Well, the implication there was clear enough. Get on board or get out. And since there wasn't a chance in hell she would willingly walk away from Castle Butler and all it entailed, she would have to bide her time, bite her tongue and choose very carefully the battles she was willing to wage.

With that thought in mind, she nodded and said, "Fine, then. If you must have the murals, why not put them in the great hall? You've said it's the place where your role players will gather. Wouldn't they be the ones to appreciate this kind of…art?"

His lips twitched again, and once more, she felt that quick jolt of something hot and…exciting zip through her like a lightning strike. *Ridiculous*, she told herself, ordering her hormones to go dormant.

She couldn't keep having these delicious little fantasy moments about her *boss*. Especially a boss who had made it abundantly clear that she was expendable. But it seemed that knowing she shouldn't had nothing to do with reality. Because just being in the same room with Brady Finn made her feel as if every inch of her skin was tingling.

Rather than answer her question immediately he said, "You have to admit that Jenny's sketches are good."

"They are," she said quickly, hoping to take her own mind off the path it continually wanted to wander. "For a game, they're wonderful. But as decoration in a hotel?"

"In *our* kind of hotel, they're perfect," Brady said firmly. "Though you have a point about the reception area. All right," he said, tapping a finger against the drawing of a howling banshee, "murals in the great hall."

"As easily as that?"

"I can compromise when the situation calls for it," he told her.

Nodding, she ticked off one win for herself on her

imaginary tote board. Naturally, Brady had more scores in this competition than she, but gaining this one compromise gave her hope for more. He wasn't implacable and that was good to know. Brady Finn would be difficult to deal with but not impossible.

"But," he added before complacency could settle in, "I will do things my way, Aine."

A warning and a challenge all in one, she told herself. No wonder the man fascinated her so.

The door opened after a soft perfunctory knock and a young woman stuck her head inside. "I'm sorry, Brady. But Peter's on the phone and he's insisting on speaking with you."

"That's fine, Sandy. Put him through." When the woman darted out again, Brady looked at Aine and said, "I have to take this call."

"Should I go?"

"No." He waved her down into her seat. "This won't take long and we're not finished."

Aine watched as he snatched up the receiver. The look on his face was hard, unforgiving, and she could have sworn ice chips swam in the blue of his eyes. She spared a moment of sympathy for Peter, whoever he was, as it looked as though he would regret interrupting Brady Finn.

"Peter?" Brady's voice was clipped, cool. "I'm not interested in more excuses."

A pause while the mysterious Peter babbled loudly enough for Aine to catch snatches of words. *Time—art— patience.*

"I've been more than patient, Peter. We all have been," Brady reminded the man, cutting his stream of excuses short. "That time is past. I told you what to expect if I didn't have those renderings by this afternoon."

More hurried, frantic talking from Peter in a voice that lifted into an outraged shout.

Brady frowned. "I'll have Sandy send you a check for the remainder of what we owe you."

Stunned silence filled the pause that followed that statement, and Aine could almost feel the unknown man's panic.

"Do yourself a favor and remember the confidentiality contract you signed with us, Peter. All drawings you've completed are our property, and if they leak to the competition…"

He smiled tightly and Aine noted the glint of satisfaction in his eyes. "Good. Glad to hear it. You're talented, Peter. If you can become focused, you'll have a solid career at some point. Just not here with us."

Aine felt a cold chill race along her spine and just managed to stifle the corresponding shudder. He had dismissed the unlamented Peter without a moment's hesitation. Would it be that easy for him to rid himself of *her*? That thought gave her pause and made her even more determined to watch her mouth and her temper.

When he hung up, Brady glanced at her and said, "Sorry about the interruption, but it couldn't be helped."

"Who's Peter?"

"An artist with more excuses than work," he said shortly. Maybe he caught the worry no doubt shining in her eyes because he added, "He was given more than one chance to come through. He failed."

"And so he's gone."

"Yeah," Brady said, gaze locked with hers. "Patience

only stretches so far. When it's business, you have to be able to make the hard choices."

But the thing was, Aine thought, firing Peter hadn't looked as if it was difficult for Brady at all. He'd ended the man's employment in a blink and now had moved on already to more pressing business. Aine felt the shaky bridge she stood upon tremble beneath her feet.

Four

Brady hadn't missed the wariness in her gaze as she'd listened to his conversation with Peter. Maybe he should have taken the call privately, but then again, it was probably best that she'd overheard him fire the man. She had to know that Brady was more than willing to dismiss any employee who couldn't do the work expected of them. He didn't enjoy that part of his job, but he wasn't reluctant to do what was necessary, either. He had nothing but respect for a hard worker and nothing but contempt for anyone who tried to slide out of their responsibilities by producing half-baked excuses.

Jenny Marshall would get her shot at being the lead artist on this project, and if she failed, he'd get rid of her, too. Brady and his partners worked hard, put everything they were into the job at hand, and damned if he'd accept anything less from the people around them.

"My brother, Robbie, would love this," she said as Brady steered her into the graphic-art division on the third floor of the old mansion.

There were desks, easels and plotting boards scattered around the big space. Computer terminals sat at every desk alongside jars holding pencils, pens, colored markers and reams of paper. Rock music pumped through the air, setting a beat that had a couple of the artists' chairs dancing, bobbing their heads and mouthing the words to the song. Every time Brady went into that room, he felt like the only earthling on Mars.

Someone had made popcorn in the bright red microwave, and the smell flavored every breath as he walked with Aine around the room.

"Some of our artists prefer doing all of the work on the computer, but most also enjoy the sensation of putting pen to paper, as well." He watched Aine sneaking peeks at works in progress. "It doesn't matter to me *how* they get the job done," Brady added, "as long as they do it well. And on schedule."

She slanted him a look. "Yes, I remember what happened to Peter."

Brady shrugged. "He had his chances and blew them all."

"You're not an easy man, are you?"

"*Nothing's* easy," he said, staring into the cool forest green eyes that had haunted him from the first moment he'd seen them. Then he took her arm and guided her around the room. As they walked, the buzz of conversations quieted. Brady knew that having the boss in the place would slow things down, but he wanted Aine to see all of Celtic Knot so she could appreciate exactly who it was she was working for.

He gave a meaningful glance to the people watching them and they all quickly got back to their work. Aine pulled away from him to take a closer look at a sketch one of the women was perfecting. When she came back to his side, Aine was smiling. "Oh, yes, Robbie would love all of this."

"Your brother?" he asked.

She glanced at him briefly. "Aye, I've told you he's mad for your games, but he's also an artist. A good one, too," she added with a quick, proud smile. "He'd be in heaven here, surrounded by talented people, drawing what he loves to draw."

"He wants to work on games?" Brady asked.

"It's his dream and one he's determined will come true," she said, pausing to look over the shoulder of a young man adding a wash of color to a sketch of a forest under moonlight.

"Lovely," she said, and the man turned to give her a wide grin.

Brady frowned, watching as Joe Dana turned on the charm and aimed it right at Aine. Annoyance—and something else—rose up inside and nearly choked him. He wasn't sure what the hell he was feeling, but he damn well knew he didn't like the way Joe was letting his gaze slide up and down Aine's curvy body.

"You've made the forest look alive," Aine told the man, giving him another smile.

"Thanks," Joe said, "but you haven't seen me add the werewolves yet."

"Werewolves?" She looked at the forest scene again. "But it's so pastoral, really, despite all the wild growth beneath the trees there. Adding monsters to it seems a shame."

"Monsters are what people like about games," Brady said, interrupting before Joe could speak again. At the sound of his boss's voice, the other man seemed to remember Brady's presence and shifted his focus from Aine to the sketch pad in front of him.

"We keep the soul of the art," Joe was saying as he deftly added a few dark strokes with a thick black marker, creating the shadowy outline of a werewolf, complete with dripping fangs. "'The Wolf of Clontarf Forest.' It'll be out sometime next year."

"Well, that's terrifying, isn't it?" Aine said to no one in particular. "And the forest looked so peaceful and dreamlike before…"

"That's one of the things our games are known for," Brady told her.

"Werewolves?"

Joe, the artist, laughed and said, "Not specifically. But the boss is right. We take something beautiful and make it dangerous. That's what makes it creepy. The danger lurking just beneath a placid surface."

Aine nodded and turned her gaze up to Brady's. In her eyes he saw the same danger lying beneath the serene surface she showed him. A different kind of jeopardy than some animated monster, Aine was like nothing he'd ever known before. There were fires within her, waiting to be stoked. Skin waiting to be caressed. And if he gave in to what he wanted, he'd be in even deeper trouble than if he stumbled across a werewolf.

"Clontarf?" she asked suddenly, her eyes narrowed suspiciously on him. "Are you making a game of the Battle of Clontarf?"

"We're using it as a backdrop, yeah. You've heard of it?"

Aine's eyes widened. "Every Irish child learns their history. The last high king of Ireland, Brian Boru, fought and died at Clontarf."

"He did," Brady said, impressed that she knew of it. He and the Ryan brothers did a lot of research into Irish history, not to mention the fact that the Ryans' parents were from Ireland and had raised their sons on the traditions and superstitions they remembered. At Celtic Knot, they preferred using actual historical figures and actions as stepping-off points to give their games another layer of reality. "I think you'll be impressed with the artwork of the actual battle scenes. Kids are going to love the gore factor of fighting with broadswords…"

"And you've turned it into a game?" She was horrified.

Joe Dana whistled low and long and hunched over his sketch pad. A couple of heads turned toward them, but Brady hardly noticed, so caught was he by the fury in Aine's gaze.

"King Brian defeated the Vikings, setting Ireland free, and died in the doing," she said, clearly outraged at having her country's history *borrowed* for entertainment.

"He did, and in our game, he'll do the same," Brady said coolly, taking her arm, ignoring the stiffness of her movements as he guided her through the room. "Only when Brian wins, it'll be because a legion of werewolves helped him. And if a player does well enough, he can be crowned the next high king of Ireland. Look at it this way," he said, "when people play this game, they'll be learning about your history. They'll play a game, fight for the Irish and learn all about King Brian Boru."

"Irish history doesn't include slavering werewolves." Aine shook her head and blew out a breath, obviously trying to relieve the rush of anger at seeing her country's heroes portrayed as part of a supernatural scenario. "I'm not sure if I should be impressed or appalled. Werewolves in Ireland?"

He shrugged and noticed the tension in her body was easing whether she realized it or not. "Why not? You guys believe in banshees, faeries, pookas... The list is long. Why not a werewolf?"

"True," she allowed, then cocked her head and looked up at him. "*You guys?* You still think you're not Irish."

Ignoring that, he frowned and guided her toward another artist's desk. "The storyboards for the games are laid out, checked for mistakes, and the scriptwriters work with the artists to lay in just enough dialogue to explain what's happening."

"So it's as you said, not just running and shooting?" Aine asked.

Her eyes were wide and interested, but he saw playfulness in those depths, too. "Much more than that. There are riddles, puzzles to solve. Mysteries to work out along the way."

"Ah, sure, the thinking man's video game, then," she said, humor evident in her tone.

Brady nodded. "Actually, that's exactly right."

He could see he'd surprised her with his response. But Brady thought her quip was right on the money. He and the Ryans prided themselves on the depth of the games they designed. While most people dismissed video entertainment as mindless, Celtic Knot Games had built a reputation for sophistication of story style and a narrative that, while rooted in fantasy, also boasted realism that drew a player into a role-playing world.

He took her arm and steered her out of the graphic design area and across the wide hall to a room on the other side of the house, where computers ruled.

"This is where our programmers take over," he said, then stepped back and allowed her to enter the room. He watched her as she wandered through the space, stopping at each desk where computer experts worked their keyboards. There were framed images taken from their games dotting the walls, and a sense of humming energy and creativity buzzed in the air. Music churned out, a wild rock beat giving the programmers a rhythm they matched with the rapid typing at the keyboards.

He could see where Aine might be fascinated by the programmers, who were, he noticed with a frown, pausing in their work to explain things to her. Normally, when you walked into this room, you were completely ignored. Like every other computer expert Brady had ever met, the guys in here didn't see anything beyond what was on their screens. Hell, Brady himself had been in here when he'd had to shout to get their attention—but every man in the room had suddenly become focused on Aine Donovan. He couldn't blame them, but damned if he enjoyed watching the scene play out in front of him.

She laughed at something one of them said and Brady's insides fisted at the sound. She let her head fall back, and all that amazing hair of hers seemed to flow down her back like a molten river. She reached out and laid one hand on a programmer's shoulder as she leaned in to see what he wanted to show her on the screen, and Brady's frown deepened. Jealous of a friendly touch? No, he assured himself. The idea was ridiculous. But for completely unrelated reasons, he ended the visit to the programming room and steered Aine back into the hall.

"It's all very impressive," she said, "though I'll admit I don't understand half of what it is you do here."

"That's all right," he said, guiding her down the stairs to the main hall. "I wouldn't know how to manage a castle, would I?"

She sent him a long look. "I've a feeling that you'd find a way to excel at it."

"I would," he agreed, leading her along the hall and toward the French doors that led to the patio and backyard. "But since you're already an expert, I don't need to be."

She stepped outside and walked into a patch of sunlight that dappled through the surrounding elms. A soft ocean breeze rustled the leaves and lifted her hair from her shoulders. Turning to face him, she said, "And as your manager, I'll be in charge of seeing the changes made to the castle."

"That's right."

"And you'll give me a list, I suppose."

"More than that," he said and gestured to a table and chairs. They took seats beside each other and Brady said, "Over the next three weeks, you and I will be working on the plans for the castle—"

"Three weeks?"

Her surprise sounded in her voice even if he hadn't seen it in her eyes. Brady paid no attention and continued, "I'll want your input on some of the changes to the bedrooms, the furnishings, the setup to the new kitchens. There we want the medieval look and feel but naturally all modern appliances..."

"I'm sorry," she interrupted. "Did you say three weeks?"

"Yeah." He looked at her. "Is that a problem?"

"I never thought I'd be here that long."

Brady watched her and could almost see the wheels of her brain turning. She chewed at her bottom lip, and the action tugged at something inside him. Her face was an open book, he thought. There was no artifice there, no poker face. She obviously wasn't as used to schooling her features as he was.

But then, he'd spent a lifetime hiding what he was feeling from the rest of the world.

And over the years that had become easier because Brady had simply avoided feeling anything at all. Friendship was one thing. He couldn't stop caring for the Ryan brothers because they were the only family he'd ever known. Cutting them out of his life would be impossible even if he wanted to. It hadn't been easy, lowering his defenses enough to let them in, but Mike and Sean had simply refused to be shut out of Brady's life. They'd steamrolled over his objections and had drawn him into a circle of friendship he'd never known before them.

They were the only people who saw Brady's laughter or anger or fears. They were the only people he trusted that much. And he had no intention of risking anyone else getting that close. Especially a woman who worked for him.

Didn't mean he couldn't enjoy the rush of desire that came out of nowhere to knock his legs out from under him.

"Three weeks," she repeated, more to herself than to him.

"Is there a problem?" He heard the stiffness in his own voice and didn't bother to soften it. She worked for Celtic Knot, whether she was in Ireland or America.

She responded to his tone and he watched as she squared her shoulders and lifted her chin. Why those subtle movements would affect him as much as a more sensual move would have was beyond him.

"Three weeks is a long time when you're not prepared for it," she said, then she became thoughtful. "I can call home, let the staff know I won't be about, and then call my mother…"

Now she surprised him. "Your mother?"

"She'd worry otherwise, wouldn't she?"

"I wouldn't know," Brady said simply. How the hell would he know what mothers were like? His own had dropped him off at Child Services when he was six years old, with the promise to come back by the end of the week. He'd never seen her again. As for the Ryan brothers, whenever they went home to visit with their folks, Brady stayed away. He'd gone with them once, during college. And though their parents had made every effort, Brady had spent that incredibly long weekend too uncomfortable to accept their open hospitality. He had no idea how to deal with the threads of family and he told himself it was too damn late now to try to understand it. Not that he wanted to.

Aine looked at him in confusion, but that expression quickly faded. "I'm happy to stay, of course," she said a little too tightly to be believable. "I'll help in any way I can, obviously."

"Good." He nodded shortly and refused to acknowledge the fact that the next three weeks with Aine Donovan were going to be a test of the self-control he'd always prided himself on. Hell, even sitting here beside her in the sunlight was making him burn. Watching her eyes narrow on him kindled those slow-moving flames inside him until his skin buzzed with expectation. She was unexpected, but damned if he could regret having her drop into his lap—so to speak.

Maybe he would regret it later. But for right now, that quickening fire was all he could think about.

For the next week, Aine felt as if she was living in a tornado—the Brady Finn Tornado. It seemed he was tireless. They roamed through countless antiques stores—and Brady kept insisting that old furniture was the same, whether European or American. She'd fought him on several tables, chairs and even a bed or two, and to give the man his due, he was willing to be nudged away from his first decision when offered a better choice. But he was monopolizing her time. They were together every day and talked of what still needed to be done over dinner.

And every day it became just a little bit harder to ignore the heat she felt just being around him.

Ridiculous, and she knew it, to feel this way, but it appeared she had no control over her body's reaction to a man she had no business getting dizzy over. He was autocratic, opinionated, and he tended to speak to her as if he were expecting her to pull a steno tablet from her bag and start taking notes.

If anything, she should be infuriated at his domineering attitude. Yes, he was her employer, but he wasn't the Prince of Wales, was he? And even if he were, Aine admitted, an Irishwoman wouldn't be bowing down to him.

But instead of this very rational reaction to being ordered about on a daily basis, Aine spent entirely too much time watching his mouth as he spoke, wondering what his lips would feel like. Taste like. And it wasn't as if she could escape these thoughts when she slept, because her dreams were full of him, as well.

Because, she acknowledged, bossy and controlling wasn't all there was to the man. She'd also seen him stop and hold a door for a woman burdened down with bags of groceries. Whenever they went walking he never failed to drop a bill or two into the open cases of street musicians or to hand money to a homeless man holding a cardboard sign. He was a confusing mixture of rough and kind, of sharp and soft, and he fascinated her more with every passing day.

"I think that takes care of today's business," Brady said, snapping Aine's attention back to him.

The sea wind ruffled his dark hair like fingers running through it and Aine folded her own fingers into her palm to avoid the urge to do it herself. He pulled off dark glasses and laid them on the table in front of him. Lunch at this sidewalk café in Newport Beach had become something of a habit over the past week. Here was where they sat, went over his plans and purchases made for the castle.

"Really? No more looking for just the right linens today, then?"

He slanted her a sardonic look. "You don't want to shop? I never thought I'd hear that particular statement from a woman."

"Allow me to be the first," Aine said, picking up her tea and taking a sip. She winced slightly at the taste and idly wished for a *real* cup of tea. "'Tis fair, I think, to say that my shopping quota has been met for the year, at least."

"Tired of looking at towels, huh?"

"You aren't?"

"I couldn't be more bored," he admitted and picked up his coffee for a long drink. "But it's important that we have everything just as it should be at this new hotel. Even down to the towels."

While she could admire his attention to detail, it surprised her that the owner of a hotel was taking such personal responsibility for every aspect of his business. "I agree," she said, tipping her head to one side to watch him. "It's only that the previous owner never bothered with such minutiae so I'm a bit surprised."

He set his coffee cup down. "But the previous owner ended up losing his hotel to me, didn't he?"

"True."

"I don't lose," he said shortly.

She was willing to bet that Brady Finn had never lost anything important to him. What must it be like, she wondered, to live a life so ruthlessly organized? So completely in your control? Aine smiled to herself at the very idea of being so sure of yourself that you could reorder the world around you to suit your needs. She knew all too well that the wealthy had no idea how the real world lived, and Brady's arrogance only seemed to highlight that opinion. He expected things to go his way, so they did. If he met an obstacle, it was probably his nature to roll right over it. He wouldn't be stopped. Wouldn't be changed. Wouldn't be ignored.

And God help her, she found all of that fascinating. She shouldn't, Aine knew. But how could she ignore what it was that happened to her when he was near—or on those rare occasions when he actually touched her? A casual brush of his hand against hers. His hand at the small of her back when he guided her through one of the innumerable shops they'd been through in the past several days? The flash of pride she felt when he turned and asked her opinion on something. The look in his eyes when he would stop suddenly and stare at her as if she'd simply dropped from the sky.

All of this and more was what fed the dreams that kept her restless every night and woke her feeling on edge, as though she was standing on a precipice and needed only the slightest push to tumble over. It was pointless to have these feelings, to indulge in dreams that would lead nowhere, she knew. The chasm separating them was too wide, and deep. A woman from a small rural village in Ireland had nothing in common with a multimillionaire.

"Is there a problem?"

His voice, deep, low and somehow intimate, tore her from her thoughts. "I'm sorry, what was that?"

"A problem?" he asked. "You went quiet, and the look on your face tells me you're trying to think your way out of something."

Wasn't it an annoying thing, she thought, to not have your thoughts remain your own? "So easy to read, am I?"

One corner of his mouth lifted briefly. "Poker? Not your game."

"Humiliating, but true enough," she said on a sigh. Heaven knew he wasn't the first person to see what she was thinking by studying her expression. Hopefully, though, he wouldn't be able to suss out exactly what it was she felt when he was close. Her humiliation then would know no bounds. "But no, there's no problem. I'm only thinking about home, wondering what's happening while I'm gone."

"You live with your mother and brother, don't you?"

She looked at him and saw speculation in his eyes. "Yes, and you're wondering why at my age I would be."

He nodded and waited for whatever she had to say next.

Sighing a bit, Aine said, "The truth is, I moved out

when I was twenty. Took a flat in the village and loved having my own space." She smiled, remembering. "I love my family, but—"

"I get it," he said companionably.

Her smile widened, then slipped away. "But then, five years ago, my father died."

"Sorry."

He looked uncomfortable, as most people did when faced with something they couldn't change or help with.

"Thank you." Aine smiled at him again, letting him know she was fine. She still missed her father, but the worst of the pain had faded over the years. She could talk about him now, think about him, without a crushing ache settling into her heart. "He was a fisherman and there was a ferocious storm one night. He never came home." She frowned then, remembering how their family had changed so suddenly. "My mother was wrecked. Shattered without him, as he was the love of her life. They'd been together so long and had been true partners in everything. Without him, she was lost and didn't want to be found. So I moved back home to help her care for Robbie, who was only twelve at the time and just as lost as Mum."

"Must have been hard."

She saw a glimmer of understanding in his eyes and responded to it. "It was, for some time. But things are better now and Mum is not so sad as before."

"So you put your life on hold for your family."

She shrugged. "'Tis what you do for those you love."

He frowned a bit at that, and Aine wondered about it. Did he not understand after all? Had he no one in his life to matter so much? Her heart twisted at that thought.

"You miss it?"

"Ireland, you mean?" Surprised at the question, she said, "'Tis natural, isn't it? It's home after all."

"Right." He nodded, set his coffee aside and said, "Tell me about it."

"About Ireland?"

That half smile appeared again and vanished in a blink. "Not all of it, just your part. The village. The castle."

All around them, people laughed and talked. Waiters moved through the cluster of tables with the easy rhythm of long practice. The hum of traffic from the street became a drone of sound that mimicked the ocean just half a block away. Sunlight slanted through a bank of white clouds and glinted off the glass-topped tables.

As lovely as it was, the scene around her was a lifetime and more from what Aine knew and loved. She took a breath, smiled as she drew up the familiar images in her mind and started talking.

"The village is small but has everything we need in it. If you're wanting more of a shopping experience, Galway city is but an hour's drive." Her voice softened as she described the country that seemed so very far away. "As I've always lived there, I might be a bit biased, but it's a lovely village and the people are warm and friendly. The roads are narrow, lined with thick hedgerows of gorse and fuchsia—"

He laughed shortly. "Those are plants?"

She grinned. "Yes, fine, heavy hedges that bloom with yellow and red flowers in spring and early summer. You drive down roads so narrow that sometimes it's a wonder two cars could pass each other. Farms abound, with their stone walls and grazing cows and sheep. There are ruins, of course," she said, bracing her forearms on the warm tabletop. "Conical towers and the remains of castles long fallen stand near stone dances where, if you listen closely enough, you can hear the echoes of voices from the past."

Her gaze caught his and she stared into those deep, guarded eyes as she said softly, "The sky is so blue in Ireland you could weep for it. And when the clouds roll in from the Atlantic, they carry with them either fine, soft rain or storms vicious enough to moan through the stones of the castle until it sounds as if souls are screaming."

A moment of silence ticked past before Brady spoke and shattered the spell she'd woven for herself.

"Souls screaming," he repeated thoughtfully. "That'll go well with the guests at Fate Castle."

"That's what you heard? Something to help with your business?" she asked, wondering if he ever thought of anything else.

"It's not all I heard," he said. "But it's my main interest. It's why you're here, isn't it?" he asked with a shrug. "If not for my buying the castle, you'd still be in Ireland trying to think of a way to save the hotel you manage."

So he'd heard nothing of the magic of Ireland in her description. Only the barest facts as it concerned his latest business. "You've a way of boiling things down to their center, don't you?"

"No point in pretending otherwise, is there?"

"I suppose not," she said, and knew he was probably reading her expression again. This time what he would see was exasperation, and she was comfortable with that. She might be determined to keep her temper, but the fact that the man could so easily dismiss a hotel that had been in operation for decades—never mind the centuries-old castle itself—was still annoying.

He laughed, and the sound was so surprising she forgot her momentary irritation. "What's funny?"

"You. You're insulted on behalf of your castle."

"As you've continually pointed out, 'tis not mine but *your* castle," she said more stiffly than she'd wanted.

"And yet..." He tipped his head to one side and asked, "So in all the descriptions of your Ireland, I didn't hear any mention of a man. No one there for you to particularly miss?"

Now it was Aine's turn to frown as she realized she was the one doing all the sharing and talking here and he was as much a mystery to her today as he had been in the beginning. But maybe, she thought, by opening up herself, she would find it easier to pry information from him.

"No," she said at last, "there's no one now."

"Now?"

"There was," she told him. "I was engaged once. Brian Feeny." She paused and realized that she could remember him now, talk about him now and not feel even the slightest echo of pain or regret. "He's an accountant living in Dublin. I heard he's married and happy."

"Why'd you break up?"

"Why's that your business?"

"It isn't," he said simply.

She laughed shortly. "Fine, then. 'Twas nothing dramatic. It was only that my family needed me and Brian couldn't understand how I would put them before him. Us."

"Most men probably wouldn't," he told her.

"Would you?"

"I know that if the Ryan brothers needed me, I'd be there no matter what anyone else needed from me." He shrugged negligently. "Does that answer the question?"

"Aye," she said, "it does." She took a breath and admitted, "When it ended, I wasn't heartbroken or devastated or even really disappointed. And I knew then that I hadn't really loved him. Not enough."

She'd *wanted* to love Brian, but she simply hadn't had it in her. And maybe she never would know the kind of love her parents had had. But then, loving that deeply, that completely—that carried its own risks, didn't it? She remembered clearly how broken her mother had been at the loss of her love, and Aine had to wonder if the pain of it was worth the loving.

"Or maybe it wasn't you at all, and it was just this Brian being a jackass," Brady said.

Her gaze snapped to his and a slow smile curved her mouth. She'd never really considered it from that angle.

"That's enough depth for today, I think. How about a walk?" He stood up and held out one hand to her.

Surprise flickered through her again. Aine looked from his eyes to his extended hand and back again. She hesitated only a moment or two before laying her hand in his. Exasperation aside, the man was not only her employer but was currently beguiling her. When her hand met his, heat dazzled her and she fought with everything she had to keep him from seeing her reaction to the connection between them. "I'd like that. I feel as if I've been indoors for days."

"We'll walk to the pier, then," he said, folding his fingers around her hand and tugging her along beside him. "You can watch the Pacific and think of the Atlantic."

Five

Aine knew she'd be hard-pressed to think of anything but him as long as he was beside her, but she was eager for the cold sea wind. Maybe it would help douse the fire inside her.

For a woman accustomed to the quiet of a rural Irish village, the constant pound of noise—from traffic and hundreds of people—was distracting. Aine thought she'd become accustomed to the bustle and rush in the past week or more, but when she and Brady walked to the end of the pier, she sighed in relief and smiled to herself. Here there was only the rush of the waves to the beach, the call of seabirds and the creak of the pier itself as it rocked in the water. She took a deep breath of the ocean air and tipped her face back to the sky, letting the sunlight wash over her skin.

"I think this is the first time I've seen you relaxed since you got here," Brady said.

"It's the sea," she answered, sliding a look at him. "The waves here are calmer, softer than at home, where the water can rage, but the sound of it, like a heartbeat, 'tis soothing after all the noise of the main street. I think if I had so many people about me all of the time, I might lose my mind."

"And I think having nothing but quiet around me all the time would do the same."

Another point to show how ill matched they were, Aine thought, as if she had needed more. "Is that why you've not come to Ireland to see your castle in person?"

"Not really," he said, tucking both hands into his pockets. He turned his face into the wind. "There's no need for me to be there with you on scene to report."

"What about the curiosity factor, then?" she asked, plucking her wind-blown hair from her eyes.

He glanced at her. "There isn't one," he said. "Not about this."

Both of her eyebrows flew up. "You'd spend millions on a castle, invest even more in making it into what you've imagined and have no desire to see it yourself?"

"If there's a problem you can't handle, I'll consider it." He cocked his head to one side. "*Is* there a problem you can't handle?"

"I've not found one yet," she said.

"There you go, then. I've got the right manager."

"I like to think so." Yet his attitude still puzzled her. How was it a man could be so involved in a project the size of this one and have no interest in being a part of it beyond writing checks? Then she remembered how he'd denied being Irish in spite of the name that gave away his heritage, and Aine wondered if it was the castle he was avoiding or Ireland itself. The mystery of that question only made her wonder more about Brady Finn.

"I've been wondering…"

"Never good when a woman says that," he mused.

A wry smile touched her mouth briefly. "You said once that the only thing Irish about you is your name."

He stiffened and a rigid look came over his face. "Yeah."

"What did you mean?"

She thought for a moment he wasn't going to answer her at all. His gaze shifted from her eyes to the wide sweep of sea spilling out before them. Aine kept quiet, waiting, hoping that because she had opened up about her own past he would bend and give her a glimpse of the man inside.

"I mean," he finally said, "I didn't grow up with the legends of Ireland like you. Or with Irish music and pride of heritage like the Ryans." His big hands curled over the top bar of the pier railing and he leaned into the wind as it blew his thick dark hair back from his face. "I grew up—" He bit the words off before he could say more. "Doesn't matter. A name's just a name. The Irish thing is as foreign to me as America is to you, I imagine." He was scowling as if he'd said more than he wanted to, even though it was pitifully little as far as Aine was concerned.

"Your family wasn't interested in their roots? Where they came from?" she asked, more curious than ever now, though she could see clearly he'd no wish to speak of his past.

"I didn't have a family," he said shortly, his tone demanding an end to the conversation.

He meant it, that was plain. She couldn't imagine it, having no one to call your own. To not have the solid base of a family to stand upon and build a life. Her heart hurt for him, even though she knew he wouldn't want it to. A proud man he was, and even admitting to that small piece of his past would have torn at him. So she let it go. For now.

"And yet now you own a castle in Ireland," she said softly.

He shot her a look. "It doesn't mean anything."

Or, she thought, he didn't *want* it to mean anything.

"I've noticed a few things about you myself the past several days." He turned to face her, and with the wide sweep of ocean behind him, he could have been a pirate, with his dark good looks and sharp cobalt eyes. The collar of his black bomber jacket was turned up against the wind and his hair blew around his face like a dark halo.

God help her, he took her breath away.

"What is that?" she asked finally, when she knew she could speak without her voice breaking.

"You're as focused as I am," he said, "as determined to get things right. Though it makes you crazy, you're protecting your castle by changing what you think of as the heart of it."

She shifted, still uncomfortable at being read so easily. Why was it, she wondered, that he could see so clearly into her when who he was remained a mystery to her?

"Its heart will still be there," she assured him, "as will its soul. I'll make sure of it. But no, I'm not fighting you on most of it because what would be the point? I work for you. You own the castle."

"And if I didn't?"

"What?" She looked up at him. The sun was positioned right behind him, gilding the outline of his body. His eyes were shadowed, and she wasn't sure if that was good or bad. She couldn't try to figure out what he might be thinking if she couldn't see his eyes—but on the other hand, not being able to look into those deep blue eyes might help her keep from making a fool of herself.

"If I didn't own the castle—" He moved in closer to her, and Aine's heart galloped in her chest. Her mouth was dry, her stomach twisting into knots. Anxious, Aine took a breath and held it.

She could feel the heat of him reaching out to her. They were alone here at the end of the pier, with only the sigh of the ocean waves as they surged toward shore. Sunlight streamed from a sky studded with thick white clouds, and the cool sea breeze wrapped itself around the two of them, as if trying to draw them closer. Aine swallowed hard and forced herself to stand her ground, though it might have been safer all around if she'd taken a step back.

"If you didn't own the castle, I wouldn't be here at all, would I?"

He nodded. "Then, it's good I do own it, isn't it?"

"I suppose." Oh, at the moment, she thought it was very good indeed that he'd brought her here and that they had wandered to this spot of privacy in the middle of the city.

"And this thing between us?" His voice dropped until it became a rush of sound as deep as the ocean. "Do you think that's good, too?"

She flushed. She felt it; she only hoped he couldn't see it. How humiliating to be a woman near thirty and feel heat flood her cheeks. But it wasn't voluntary, was it? Wasn't her fault that he triggered something inside her that made her every reaction to him twice as fast and hot as anything she'd ever known. And he asked if she was glad of the thing burning between them? Whether she was or not, it was there and as each day passed, more difficult to ignore. But that didn't mean she had to speak of it with him.

"I don't know what you mean—"

"Don't pretend," he said, cutting her off before she could tell a hopeless lie. "We both feel it. Have from the first." He laid his hand over hers where it rested on the top bar of the pier railing.

His touch set off sparks and flames that hissed and burned inside her until it felt as if her skin was bubbling with the intensity. Blast him for touching her, for making it impossible to ignore what she felt around him or to hide those feelings from him.

"All right, then, yes," she said and tugged her hand free. "There's something…"

"We've been together every day for more than a week, and it's time we talked about this."

Aine laughed shortly and shook her head. "Talk about it? To what end?" she asked. "We're both of us adults. Just because we feel a thing doesn't mean we'll act on it."

"And we won't," he said. "That's what I wanted to talk about. It would be a mistake to do anything about this. I'm your boss."

"I know that," Aine said, feeling the first flare of anger erupt. "'Tisn't necessary for you to warn me away from you or to tell me I've to keep my hormones in check around you. I'm not planning to have my wicked way with you, Brady Finn. Your honor is safe with me."

He shook his head. "You keep surprising me, Aine."

"Well, I'll say the same to you," she answered, folding her arms across her chest and taking that one all-important step backward. "This is the first conversation of the type I've ever had."

"Me, too," he said. "Usually, when I want a woman, I just go after her."

She cocked her head and gave him a narrowed look. "And she falls gratefully into your manly arms?"

He laughed, and the transformation his face went under was enough to take her breath away. A handsome man when frowning, he was staggering when he smiled.

"Most of the time, yeah."

"It's disappointed I am in my gender," Aine said, then reached up and pushed her windblown hair out of her eyes. "As for being one of the few who've managed to resist your *charms*, I'm doubly glad to take a stand for myself as I'd have no interest in being part of a crowd anyway."

"You wouldn't be," he said and his voice lost all trace of amusement. "You're one of a kind, Aine. I've never met anyone quite like you."

"Thanks for that," she said, then added, "and at the risk of inflating an ego too many women before me have stroked, I'll say the same of you." She tipped her head back to meet the shadowed eyes she *felt* watching her with tightly restrained hunger.

He gave her a nod. "Then, it's good we're not doing this."

"Absolutely. 'Tis the sensible solution."

"This is business," Brady said. "Sex would just confuse the situation."

And, oh, she thought she might really love to be confused by this man. But clearly, he was more interested in backing away from her as quickly as he could. "You're right again."

He moved in closer. "It's good we talked about it. Cleared the air. Got things settled."

"It is." She leaned toward him. "I'm sure we'll both be better off now and able to focus on our shared task."

"Concentration is good."

"A laudable talent."

Nodding, gaze locked with hers, he whispered, "We're not going to be sensible, are we?"

"Not at the moment, no," she said.

Then he kissed her.

The first touch of his mouth to hers turned Brady's world upside down. He'd expected heat, the flash of desire, the hunger that had been building in him for the past week. What he hadn't expected was the compulsion to devour. The frantic need to pull her closer, tighter to him, to feel her body bend to his. Her arms circled his neck; her fingers threaded through his hair, nails scraping along his scalp.

Her mouth opened under his, and the first taste of her staggered him until he was forced to lock his knees to keep from simply sagging to the ground beneath the onslaught of sensations. No woman had ever done this to him before. Hell, he hadn't known he *could* feel like this. Sex was easy. Desire was enjoyable, naturally. But this fire was unlike anything else he'd ever experienced. He fisted his hands at the small of her back and held her with arms of steel.

One taste awakened the need for more, and a wild voice in his mind whispered a taste would never be enough. He wanted to drown in her, feel her legs wrap around his hips and hold his body deeply within hers. Even as those thoughts beat at his brain, he fought against them. Wanting her was okay. *Needing* was something else.

She moaned, and the soft sound whispered into his mind, bringing him to his senses before he could lose his grip on the last tattered threads of his self-control. Hell, they were locked together in broad daylight where anyone could walk up and get an eyeful. It cost him, but he tore his mouth free, then rested his forehead against hers while he caught his breath and tried to find his way back to sanity. It wasn't easy.

What the hell was wrong with her ex-fiancé? What kind of man made the decision to marry a woman like Aine, then gave her up? Brady wasn't looking for forever, but he didn't want to let her go, either.

"Well, then," she murmured, the Irish in her voice singing as she, too, fought for air, "that was an unexpected feast."

He laughed shortly. "It was." Lifting his head, he looked down at her, saw her green eyes shining, glittering, and steeled himself against giving in to the impulse to grab her and taste her again. Give in once and he might never let her go, and that was unacceptable.

"And," he said firmly, as much to himself as to her, "now that we've got that out of our systems, working together will go much more smoothly."

She blew out a breath, then lifted both hands to scoop them through her hair. After a moment, she nodded. "So then, you kissed me, half devoured me, for the sake of the work?"

At the word *devoured*, his body tightened, but he said only, "Yes. We both felt the tension all week. I thought it would be a good idea to just give in and get it out of the way. Now the urge's been satisfied."

Not nearly, his brain screamed. In fact, if he had her over, under, around him for weeks, Brady doubted his hunger for her would be quenched.

"I see." She nodded, turned her face into the wind and stared out to sea for a long moment before speaking. "Then, I'll thank you for being so brave as to throw yourself on a live grenade such as myself—for the good of the work."

Brady frowned. Figured she'd take this the wrong way. Had she even *once* reacted to something the way he thought she would? It wasn't as if he'd sacrificed himself by kissing her—it was only that he didn't want her to get the wrong idea about that kiss. "I didn't say that."

"Aye, you did." She whipped her gaze back to his. Her green eyes flashed, and damned if he didn't want her even more than he had before that kiss. "Why, it was practically *saintly* how you took on the chore of teaching me a lesson. You kissed me for my own good. To make sure I can work with you and stay focused on my job rather than wasting time with idle daydreams of *you*."

With every word she spoke, Brady felt like more of an ass. Which he didn't appreciate. "I didn't say that, either," he ground out.

"Oh, what a trial it must be for you," she continued, tipping her head back to glare at him. "Being so handsome and rich and such a *magnet* for women. Why, you should think about hiring a bodyguard to protect you from those you haven't had time to teach how to control themselves."

"For—" Brady shoved one hand through his hair and muttered, "You're putting words in my mouth, Aine."

"You might as well have said them yourself."

"No. I say exactly what I mean," Brady told her and

shot a quick glare at some tourist who was wandering too close to them. The man immediately turned and walked the other way. Brady refocused on Aine. "I don't need you guessing what I might have meant. You won't have to. I'll tell you exactly what I'm thinking."

"As you have," she said, folding both arms across her chest and then tapping her fingertips against her upper arms. "Well, you'll be happy to know I agree with you. It was a lovely kiss, I'm sure, but you needn't worry I'll swoon into your arms demanding another."

Gritting his teeth, Brady's eyes rolled back briefly. "Swoon?"

"Or throw myself at your feet," she continued as if he hadn't spoken. "As I said, it was a lovely kiss, but it wasn't enough to drive me into a rage of frustrated lust. I'm here to do a job, and I intend to do it and then go home. You're completely safe from my wiles." She paused only long enough to take a breath, then added, "I've been kissed before and managed to hold on to my sanity."

He barked out a sharp laugh.

"'Tisn't funny," she snapped.

Yeah, it was. He knew she was lying because he'd felt her reaction to that kiss. Didn't matter how she tried to bluff her way out of it. She'd been as rocked by it as he was, and hearing her lie about it now made him smile. The woman kept him guessing all the time. Strange how much he was beginning to like it. "Damn. You've got a mouth on you, I'll give you that."

She flushed a bit at that. "What it is about you that makes my temper boil over, I don't know. But I'll not apologize for what I've said, even if you fire me for it."

"Who said anything about firing you?"

"No one, as of yet. Mind, I won't be kissing you again,

Brady Finn, so if it's all the same to you, keep your own mouth to yourself in the future."

"That's the plan," he said, though it wouldn't be easy. But then what the hell else in his life had *ever* been easy?

"Then, we've an agreement on this." While he watched, she turned and started walking away from him.

For a long moment, Brady admired the view. Coming or going, Aine Donovan was a feast for any man's eyes. But, he reminded himself sternly as his gaze dropped to the curve of her behind, he wasn't looking for a feast.

His hands curled into fists as he started after her. The sun was just dipping toward the ocean, the light fading into a soft twilight. In the last rays of the sun, her dark red hair looked alight with fire. She was more than he'd expected. More than he wanted. The only answer, he thought as he caught up to her and took hold of her upper arm in a firm grip that had her turning her green eyes to his, was to finish their business and get her back to Ireland as quickly as possible.

She tried to tug free of his grip, but Brady kept hold of her.

"Let go of me," Aine said, her eyes flashing.

"Trust me, I'll be doing that just as soon as I can," Brady assured her, steering her down the pier and back to the crowds along Pacific Coast Highway.

"How are things at home, Mum?" Aine paced the hotel suite that felt, at the moment, like a lavishly decorated cage. She was tense, on edge, and because she couldn't stop thinking about that kiss she'd shared with Brady just a few hours ago, it was only getting worse. Every cell in her body felt as if it were on fire. Her skin was buzzing and her concentration was simply shot.

She'd always prided herself on her ability to compart-mentalize things in her life. But now her personal life was sliding into her business life, and she didn't know how to stop it. Or worse, even if she *wanted* to stop it. Then there was the problem of forever losing her temper with the man who could fire her with a word. Oh, God help her, life would be so much easier if only she was home again.

"Oh, it's been noisy as ten drums about here lately," Molly Donovan said. "There's lorries coming and going from the castle dozens of times a day. Some American men arrived today, construction people they say they are, only waiting for everything to be readied before they begin fixing the castle."

"American crews?" Aine asked, interrupting her mother before the woman could get on such a roll she wouldn't be stopped. "Are there no local men working there?"

"Not so far, but they've not started as yet. Just cart-ing in half of Ireland in the way of rocks and lumber and what have you." Her mother clucked her tongue and added, "Although Danny Leary is down to the pub telling all who'll listen that it should be Irish workmen bringing our own castle back to life."

Aine sighed, and rested her forehead against the cold glass of the French doors. Danny Leary ran the best construction crews in County Mayo, and if he was un-happy with the work situation, that meant word of this was spreading throughout the county. People wouldn't be pleased. Sure, the idea of Castle Butler being reno-vated was a good one, but if the people at home didn't feel a part of it, how could they support it? And if those in the village wanted to, they could make the work very hard indeed. They could block roads—*accidentally*, of course—and slow down deliveries. All manner of things could go wrong. This could end up being a huge mess, all because Brady Finn wouldn't listen when she'd told him to hire local crews.

"I'm sure it'll all be fine," her mother was saying. "As soon as you tell your Mr. Finn that he'd do better to use Irish hands on the job."

"I've told him, Mum," Aine admitted on another sigh, remembering their conversation about just this not long after she'd arrived. "'Tis clear now he wasn't listening."

"And since when is it that you couldn't make yourself heard, Aine Donovan?" Molly's voice went as firm as steel and Aine winced as she recognized the no-nonsense tone. "You've a place there. And a voice. Your Mr. Finn—"

"He's not *my* anything, Mum," Aine interrupted, ignoring the stir of something inside her, "except my employer, who could fire me at a whim."

"And why would he do that?" her mother countered. "Didn't he fly you to California like a queen on her own plane? Hasn't he kept you there for more than a week already to listen to your ideas?"

"Yes, but—"

"Hasn't he told you more than once that he values an honest opinion and not simply the mindless nattering of a yes man?"

"He has, but—"

"Let me ask you this," Molly continued.

Ask away, Aine thought, and wondered if her mother would let her get a word in to answer whatever question was coming.

"Are you good at your job, Aine?"

"Of course I am." That wasn't in question.

"Do you know what's best for the castle and the village?"

"I do." Aine swallowed her impatience, as it wouldn't do her a bit of good when dealing with her mother. Besides, she thought, Molly was right in all she was saying, but that didn't mean Aine could repeat any of it to Brady. Yes, he'd said he wanted to hear her opinions, but there was a coolness to him, something that kept everyone around him at a distance.

Of course, her mind whispered, there'd been no distance between them at all when he'd kissed her out on the pier, with the waves crashing below and the wind swimming around them in a cold embrace. No, he hadn't held back then, and neither had she, though she nearly cringed to admit that. Though he'd done a quick step away when the kiss ended and had managed to insult her all at the same time.

He was her boss. With the power to dismiss her from the job she loved. He was a wealthy man with all the expectations of the rich, no doubt. If he wanted something, he took it, and be damned to consequences. Well, she was one who had to think of what might be. And kissing Brady Finn again would be another foolish step along a road that could only lead her to regret.

"Then, Aine," her mother said, drawing her attention back to the matter at hand, "you must speak up. You must do what you can for all of our sakes. The man's a businessman. He'll surely see the right of it when you lay it out for him plainly." Then she half covered the phone receiver and said, "Robbie, your sister's in no mind to answer questions from you about the silly games."

Aine couldn't help but smile. Her younger brother was fascinated by computer games, and Celtic Knot's in particular. If he'd had his way, Robbie would have been on the plane with her to visit the offices of his favorite gaming company.

Her mother sighed. "Robbie says to ask you are there zombies in the new game that's coming." Then to her son, she said, "Why would you want zombies? A lot of dead people stumbling about..."

Aine grinned. "Tell Robbie they're all very keen on zombies, and I saw a drawing of a werewolf."

"There, you see," her mother repeated. "Zombies there are, as well as a werewolf or two. Well," she said to Aine now, "you've made him a happy man. Werewolves indeed."

Listening to her family made Aine feel better. Even though they were thousands of miles away, she could imagine them sitting at the kitchen table over tea, and she wished ferociously that she were there. Safely away from Brady Finn and the temptations he presented.

But as that wish was a useless one, she said only, "I'll think on what you've said, Mum. I promise." Aine stepped out onto the deck, where the wind blew and sea-birds cried with a lonesome, mournful sound. "I'll talk to Brady about Danny Leary and then call you again in a day or two."

"Don't worry about calling, love. You do what needs doing and come back to us soon." Her mother paused, then added, "And Robbie says to bring him back a drawing of that werewolf if you can."

"I will." Laughing, Aine hung up, leaned one hand on the cold iron railing and stared out to sea. Right then, Ireland felt a lifetime away, while the lure of Brady Finn was all too close for comfort.

Six

"So what's the deal with you and Irish?" Mike Ryan leaned back in his chair and lifted the bottle of beer for a sip.

"There is no deal," Brady said, studying the label on his beer bottle as if it was a *New York Times* bestseller. The memory of the kiss he'd shared with Aine that afternoon was fresh enough that his blood was still frothing in his veins—not something he felt like sharing. "We're working together on the ideas for the castle and then she goes home. End of story."

"Right," Mike said with a lazy smile. "That's why you go all stone-faced at just the thought of her."

Brady fired a hard look at his friend. Sitting at their usual table in the neighborhood bar, Brady should have been relaxed. Instead, he was anything but. He never should have kissed her, but hell, what man wouldn't have?

Standing there in the wind, that amazing hair blowing about her face and shoulders, those wide green eyes looking up at him. Was he made of granite? Hell no.

Stalling, he looked around the bar. The after-work crowd was all there, with a handful of tourists sprinkled in for good measure. The heavy oak tables gleamed under what was probably a million coats of wax. Overhead lighting made things clear but not overly bright, and the music was low enough that you could enjoy it and still have a conversation. Waitresses in blue denim shorts and yellow T-shirts emblazoned with *Lagoon in Long Beach* weaved in and out of the crowd with the ease of long practice.

He and the Ryans had been coming to the bar since they'd set up shop in the oceanfront Victorian. Right down the street, the location was easy, the bar food was good and they could each catch up on the other's day and compare notes over a cold beer and some hand-cut onion rings. Apparently, though, Brady told himself, work talk wasn't on the menu tonight.

Looking back at Mike, he saw the man's curious expression hadn't abated. He wasn't going to let this go, so Brady made a stab at ending the conversation.

"She's doing the job I want her to do and that's it," he said, grabbing one of the onion rings and crunching down on it.

"Good to know. Okay, then," Mike said, "if there's nothing going on there, you won't mind if I take her out to dinner."

"I mind," Brady said quickly, giving his friend a hard stare. Maybe he was holding back from anything with Aine, but damned if he wanted someone else going after her.

Mike grinned. "Interesting..."

"Stow the grin," Brady told him. "There's nothing going on between us and there won't be with you and her, either. She works for us, Mike."

"It's not the Middle Ages, Brady." Mike laughed and took another sip of beer. "You're not the duke of the castle flirting with the kitchen maid."

Well, that made everything sound ridiculous. Yet he knew that starting up something with an employee was asking for trouble. "Same principle," he insisted.

"Right. With that point of view there'd never be any office romances. Then what would Jamie and Paul in Accounting do?"

"Their *work* for a change?" Brady asked, thinking of the young couple, who were too busy concentrating on each other to pay attention to business half the time.

"Okay, good point," Mike said and leaned forward, snatching one of the onion rings off the platter. "I'm just saying it wouldn't kill you to relax around her a little."

"I'm plenty relaxed." Hell, he was so *relaxed* around Aine he should have been giving off sparks. The only thing that was going to ease the coiled tension in his body was sex. With her. And that was not going to happen.

He'd come here to meet with his partners and maybe take his mind off Aine for a while. So now his only hope was to shift the subject to something Mike didn't want to talk about, either. "Since you're so interested in office romances, what's the deal with you and Jenny Marshall?"

Mike's face went cold and hard. He bit into the onion ring, chewed, then took another swallow of beer before saying, "Like you said about you and Aine. There is no deal. What the hell are you talking about?"

"Sean might be blind," Brady told him, "but I'm not.

I saw the look she sent you when she brought her drawings into the meeting. Hell, your hair should have been on fire."

"Nice. Thanks."

"So what's going on?"

Mike sucked in a gulp of air, scowled at his beer bottle and finally admitted, "About a year ago, we spent some time together, is all."

"Before she came to work for us? Where'd you meet her?"

"At the gaming convention in Phoenix," Mike muttered. "I met her in the bar the night before the con started. Found out the next day she was there running a booth for Snyder's."

"The art program Snyder?"

"Yeah, seems the old man's her uncle." Mike shrugged, but Brady saw the flash of something in his friend's eyes. "She didn't mention that when we met."

"Uh-huh." Okay, good. Subject off Aine and onto something that made Mike look as if he wanted to bite through a rock. Intrigued enough now to take his mind off his own problems for a while, Brady asked, "So what happened?"

"What do you mean what happened?" Mike countered and signaled to the waitress for two more beers. "We met. We said goodbye. Sean hired her and we've been avoiding each other ever since."

"Wow," Brady mused wryly. "It's like a fairy tale."

"Funny." Mike pointed his beer at him. "Don't think I didn't notice how you changed the subject."

"Always said you were the smart Ryan."

"Got that right."

"So why're you avoiding her?"

"Are you writing a book?" Mike asked.

"There's a thought."

"More funny, thanks," Mike grumbled. "Look, it just didn't go anywhere and I don't see the point in pretending we're gonna be friends, because we won't be. I don't like her. She doesn't like me back. Let's leave it at that."

"There's more you're not saying."

"Damn right there is," Mike agreed, then glanced at the door when it swung open and Sean walked in. Quickly, he glanced back at Brady. "As you pointed out, little brother there seems to be blind when it comes to me and Jenny. I'd like to keep him in the dark."

"You quit giving me grief over Aine and it's a deal."

"Done." All smiles now, Mike turned to look at his brother. "You're late and we're out of onion rings. Next round's on you."

"Why's it on me if you two ate them all?" Sean complained, but waved a waitress over.

Brady only half listened to the Ryans as they cheerfully insulted each other. While conversations went on around him, Brady let himself think of Aine again, and had to admit that knowing Mike was having his own problems with a woman made Brady feel just a bit better.

And actually, Mike was in worse shape than Brady. Because Jenny wasn't going anywhere, but soon Aine would be on a plane back to Ireland.

The thought of which didn't make him as happy as it should have.

Two days later, painters were at the office, and so they were holding a meeting in Brady's home. Well, Aine corrected mentally, his penthouse suite in the same hotel she was currently staying in.

She'd never known anyone who actually *lived* in a hotel, and now that she'd seen Brady's place she could safely say she still hadn't. All right, yes, it might be the place he slept in, but there was no real sign of *life*. Oh, the sprawl of rooms was lovely and richly appointed and afforded spectacular views of the coastline. But there was nothing there that indicated it was someone's *home*.

She scrubbed her hands up and down her arms while she wandered the suite. Until they started talking about the castle and what more was to be arranged, she wasn't needed in the conversation. So while the Ryan brothers and Brady argued points of their next game, Aine looked around the palatial space, hoping for insight into Brady Finn. Yet there was nothing. Oh, there was evidence of his wealth in the very fact that he could live here, but there was nothing of his soul. Nothing to scream out, "Brady Finn lives here and these are his things."

Because there were no things. A few books stacked tidily on an end table, three framed photos of him with the Ryans, and beyond that, the place might as well have been standing empty. There were flowers, no doubt delivered by hotel staff. There were lovely paintings on the walls that looked so generic they, too, must have been part of the standard furnishings.

It was lovely but cold. Luxurious but empty. The man had invested nothing of himself in his home. A deliberate choice? She had to wonder if the place he lived was a kind of metaphor for the man himself. Was he only the cold shell he showed the world? Or was there more to the man, hidden away so no one could see?

She thought it was the latter. He was a man who'd closed himself off from emotion, entanglements, and now, knowing he'd had no family to love and be loved by, she could almost understand it. Aine hated that he fascinated her so, because she knew there was no future in it. Beyond the fact that he'd made it clear he wanted nothing more to do with her, she was only in America temporarily. Soon enough she'd be back in Ireland with Brady nothing more than a voice on a phone or a signature on a paycheck.

Yet she couldn't stop thinking about him. That kiss on the pier hadn't helped anything, either. She'd relived that moment countless times in the past couple of days—despite his ridiculous statements after. She'd felt more in those few moments with him than she had with anyone else ever in her life, and so she was left attempting to understand the man who tugged at her heart even when he wasn't trying.

"If the enchanted sword can kill the banshee, then what's the point?" Sean demanded. "It's too easy."

Aine frowned and turned toward the table where all three men stood, bent over the layout of storyboards that Mike had brought to the meeting with him.

"It's not *just* the enchanted sword," Mike argued. "It's not as if you pick it up off the ground and kill the banshee. You have to win the sword first and, you know, the banshee *will* fight back."

"Yeah, but—"

Mike cut his younger brother off. "You also have to navigate through the Burren, avoid the portal tomb, solve the puzzle and find the key that unlocks the damn sword in the first place. It's not easy."

Curious, Aine wandered closer. The Burren was acres and acres of limestone and rock, dotted with grasses and wildflowers. There were rock formations and a view of Galway Bay that drew thousands of tourists a year to the place. Moving in beside Brady so that she could see the drawings spilled across the table, she had the distinct feeling none of the men even noticed her.

"And where's the key going to be hidden again?" Brady asked no one in particular.

Mike sighed. "The key's hidden outside the portal tomb. It's actually *in* the rock itself, but the player has to solve the riddle to find the key or he gets swept into the tomb and transported back to the beginning of the chapter."

"How do you solve the riddle?" Sean asked.

Mike pointed to a series of drawings. "There. John's noted the placement of the clues. There are four. Each clue leads you to a medallion with part of the code. Collect all four, enter the code, get the sword and you can kill the banshee. Otherwise, you're zapped back to the beginning and have to start all over again with no weapons."

"Ooh, that's a nice touch," Sean said, "stripping the player of his weapons."

"It would infuriate my little brother," Aine put in.

Sean grinned at her. "That's what I like to hear."

She shook her head at his obvious pleasure. *What an odd way to make a living*, she thought. Grown men gathered together, discussing banshees and zombies and enchanted swords.

"You can earn more weapons," Mike told her with relish, "but it's going to cost you time, and a real gamer is always looking to set time records."

"I thought Ireland was supposed to be lush and green," Brady said, staring at the images spread before him.

"Mom told us about the Burren," Mike said, "and Joe did the research necessary to make the drawings real. But I think we should let Aine explain the place."

All three men turned to face her, and she reached for one of the drawings depicting the barren moonscape of this little corner of County Clare. "The Burren is about the only place in Ireland that isn't, as you said, green and lush. There's acres of limestone and rock, with many underground caves and tunnels—"

"Hey, we could incorporate caves and tunnels into the player's experience." Sean clapped his hands together and rubbed his palms briskly.

"We could," Brady said. "Let's have Jenny whip up a few bare-bones sketches of tunnels, caves, and how they could tie into the hunting of the banshee."

"Why's it have to be Jenny?" Mike asked.

"Dude," Sean said, "get over it already. She's a terrific artist."

Mike fumed silently and Aine's head whipped back and forth as if she was watching a tennis match as Sean and Brady fed off each other's ideas.

"Anything else, Aine?" Mike asked loudly, getting the other two men to quiet down.

"Nothing specific," she said, smiling. "It's more the feeling you have when you're there, in the midst of that barrenness. It's a haunting place, really. Beautiful in its own way, but raw and wild, as well. Some say if you're there at night, you can hear the cries of the long dead, sobbing into the wind."

"Have you heard them?" Brady asked.

She looked up at him. "I haven't, no. But then I'm not one for crawling about the Burren late at night, either."

Mike grinned. "Haunting. A good description, at least of our version of it. And Sean, let's tell John what Aine just said about the sobs of the dead. See if he can integrate that as background filler through the music."

"So it's sort of a shadow," Brady mused. "I like it."

"Yeah," Sean said. "Me, too. Thanks, Aine. Want a job in the design department?"

"Thank you, no," she countered. "The castle will do me fine. So at the Burren? The werewolves will be there, as well?" she asked, a little sorry to see the stark landscape of the Burren reduced to a habitat for the weird.

"Nah," Sean put in. "Just the banshee, really. Oh, and the ghosts of people she's killed."

"And a zombie or two," Brady put in, pulling another drawing in to show her. "People she's killed but brought back to a half-life to serve her."

Oh, how Robbie would love this, Aine thought, making a face at the image of the rotting zombie. Shaking her head, Aine could only sigh. "Of course, she'd need a servant or two. Even dead ones. And I suppose she rides a pooka?"

"Nice touch," Sean said, clearly loving the idea. He made a quick note on one of the storyboards. "How cool would it be for our banshee to ride a wild pooka? Black horse, red eyes, flames streaming from his mane, black chains hanging off his body just waiting to wrap themselves around unwary travelers…"

Aine laughed and looked up at Brady, charmed to find a real smile on his face as he watched her. How that smile warmed his eyes and touched something deep inside her. Her heart simply turned over in her chest. The man was a mystery, yes, but there was an air about him that made her want to solve the riddle of him. To find what drove him, what touched him. *Foolish woman*, she thought. To want so much from a man she could never have.

For the next few days, Brady focused solely on business and told himself they were both better for it. If he caught confusion in Aine's eyes or regret in his own, he ignored it. Just as he ignored the fact that he wasn't sleeping, because whenever he closed his eyes Aine's features rose up in his mind. Knowing that her hotel room was just five floors down from his wasn't helping the situation.

So he was tired, sexually frustrated and had only himself to blame. If he was anyone else, he'd simply sweep Aine off to bed and release some of the damn tension that had him wired tightly enough to give off sparks. But Brady Finn didn't do complications, and Aine had *complicated* practically stamped on her forehead. She was the kind of woman who would expect happily-ever-after, and since Brady didn't believe in those, he had no business getting involved with her. Besides, she was here temporarily, and when she went back to Ireland, he'd never see her again.

If that thought gave him another pang of regret, he ignored that, as well.

"I've looked at your architect's ideas for expanding the gardens," Aine said, leaning over his desk to point at the sketch she was referring to.

"Problem?" He turned his head to look at her.

Eyes narrowed, she said, "Only that he wants to remove four-hundred-year-old oaks to do the job."

"What?" He scowled at the drawing, then turned to his computer and pulled up the series of photos he had of the castle and the grounds. He was flipping through the pictures looking for the right one when Aine came around his desk and bent down close. Her scent engulfed him and tantalized every breath he drew. Her hair fell, soft and silky against his neck, and he took a short, tight breath in response.

"There, that's it," she said and reached across him,

her breasts pressing against his shoulder as she tapped the computer screen with the tip of her finger. "You see how the trees shade the front of the castle. They've stood centuries, Brady, and to be torn down for a wider lawn, a circular drive, a plot of dahlias and a sign announcing Fate Castle seems a sin."

How the hell was he supposed to care about centuries-old trees when all he could think about was how close she was? How easy it would be to pull her down onto his lap and ease his hunger with another long taste of her? Brady fought down his impulses and focused. She was right. They weren't going to lose the damn trees because a California architect thought a sign would look better in their place.

Because he was speaking through gritted teeth, his voice came out much harsher than he'd meant. "You're right. The trees stay."

"Wonderful," she said, joy in her voice as she straightened up, thank God. She didn't move away, though, merely stood at his side looking down at him.

"Something else?" He hated that his voice sounded strangled and hoped to hell she didn't notice.

"Actually, yes," she said and bit at her bottom lip before saying, "Do you remember when I first got here, we spoke about having Irish workers as part of the crew to do the renovating?"

He frowned, but nodded. "Yeah?"

"Well, a few days ago, I spoke to my mother and she tells me that the people in the village aren't happy with the way things are moving at the castle."

He leaned back in his chair and swiveled around to look at her. Brady felt at a slight disadvantage because he was forced to look up to meet her eyes, so he solved that problem by getting out of his chair to stand. She was close enough to touch, but he didn't. "What're the villagers angry about?"

"It's the American crew, you see," she told him in a rush of words so musical he could have listened to her for hours. "Your man's brought his own people from the States and hasn't made a move to hire locally. The people in the village feel that Irish workers should be having a hand in the work done to our castle."

His eyebrows lifted. "*Your* castle?"

She sniffed and lifted her chin. "As it's been centuries there and you've only just now learned of it, I think it's more ours than yours."

"Except," he reminded her as he perched easily on the edge of his desk, "for the little fact that my partners and I *bought* it."

She waved that aside with a flick of her fingers. "Aye, you paid money for it, but the people in the village and beyond come from those who have fought and died for it. Castle Butler is more than just a hotel to us. It's our past. Our history."

"And if not for me, Sean and Mike, it would be left to rot."

"I'm not arguing that, am I?" she countered reasonably.

"What exactly are you arguing, then? Cut to the bottom line."

"Fine, then. The bottom line, as you put it, is that if you want the support of the village," she said and lifted one finger in a sign to let him know she had more to say, "and you'll *need* that support as you go on, then you'll bend a bit in the remaking of the castle."

"Is that right?" He folded his arms across his chest and said, "Is this some form of Irish blackmail?"

"Not at all," she said quickly, clearly offended. Then her voice softened as well as her eyes. "I'll remind you we talked of this before and you agreed. Brady, don't you see? It's good business. And as you're such an astute businessman, I'm sure you can see the truth of it. If you'll have your man talk to Danny Leary in the village, he can provide as many skilled workmen as are needed."

Brady scowled at her, wondering if all of this was about her securing a job for her boyfriend. "Who's Danny Leary to you? Boyfriend? Lover?"

Stunned, her mouth dropped open and she blinked at him as if she couldn't believe what she'd just heard. Then an instant later, she laughed and shook her head so hard her beautiful hair went flying. "Danny Leary? My lover? His wife would be surprised to hear it—as would his daughter, Kate, who was with me in school."

Well, didn't he feel like an idiot. She was still laughing, and the sound of it dipped inside him and heated him through. The woman was turning him inside out, and the worst of it was she didn't even have to try to accomplish what no other woman ever had.

She was watching him through eyes twinkling with amusement and damned if he could blame her. He was acting like a jealous teenager and he had no right. "Fine," he said abruptly. "I'll contact my crew manager tomorrow and have him get in touch with Danny Leary."

"That's lovely, thanks." She laid one hand on his forearm and he swore he could feel the imprint of her hand burning its way into his skin, right through the shirt fabric. Then her hand dropped away, stealing the heat as it went. "Anyone in the village can tell him where to find Danny."

"I'm sure." For a moment or two, he wondered what it might be like to have the kind of connections that were obviously so important to her. He'd been a loner most of his life—at first through no fault of his own and later by choice. He avoided the very familiarity with people that she seemed to thrive on.

Brady had always felt that life ran much more smoothly when you traveled light. No ties. No strings. The Ryan brothers were the only exception to his rules of living. The only people he'd ever allowed to get close to him. No woman had ever made it past his personal defenses—before Aine.

Desire he understood. Hell, being this close to Aine was pure torture. But love, commitment, those words had no place in Brady's world. And he liked it that way, he reminded himself.

Watching her, Brady asked, "Anything else?"

She pushed one hand through her hair, and Brady tracked that slow, sexy movement. "Not at the moment," she said, "though I was wondering how much longer I'd be here."

Truth be told, she could go home anytime, he thought. They'd done most of what he'd wanted her here for, and the rest could be handled via the internet. But as much as he wanted her gone, he just plain *wanted* her more. So he wasn't ready for her to leave yet, which made no sense at all, since keeping her here was only extending the confusion he felt around her.

"Anxious to be home?"

She turned her head for a quick look out the French doors to the patio beyond. "I'll be sorry to leave this lovely warm weather, but yes. I miss home. Don't you when you travel?"

"No," he said abruptly, stepping back and away from her. "I don't have a home."

"I've never known anyone who lived in a hotel before," she said softly. "Maybe what you need is a place of your own—something less impersonal than the hotel."

He laughed shortly at the idea. Brady just couldn't picture himself mowing a lawn or dealing with nosy neighbors. He wasn't a suburbia kind of guy. "No thanks. The hotel works for me. I can get twenty-four-hour room service, and maids clean the place daily. It's all I need."

"Is it really?"

Defensive now, he said, "We're not all looking for friendly villages." He walked across the room to snatch his jacket off a hanger in the closet. They had a dinner reservation to get to, and he could really use a drink. When she didn't speak, he turned to look at her and frowned when he saw the insult in her eyes.

"No offense," he said, though he knew he'd done just that even without meaning to. "My life is exactly the way I want it to be. How many people can say that?"

"Anyone can say it," she mused, her gaze locked with his. "A better question might be, for how many people is that true?"

He frowned as she passed him and walked through the open door. He didn't much care for the fact that she always got him thinking, reconsidering who he was and what he did. For years, Brady had followed the path he'd laid out for himself, and until Aine Donovan showed up in his life, that path had been straight and smooth. Now there were too many damn bumps.

Staring after her, Brady told himself he'd do well to

not underestimate her, since Aine Donovan had the annoying habit of being able to dig under his skin and stay there. A dangerous woman.

Seven

By the time they left the restaurant after dinner, it was later than Aine might have guessed. Shops were closed, traffic on the street was light and they had the sidewalk to themselves. The air was cool, the breeze brisk, but not as cold as at home. The lightweight dark green sweater she wore over her simple shirt and slacks was enough to keep her warm even as Brady steered her toward his car, parked at the curb.

"Tired?" he asked.

"Not a bit," Aine said. The man nodded but didn't speak. But then he hadn't spoken much during dinner, either. It was the tension, she told herself. As taut as a wire, it hummed between them whenever they were together and only got tighter with every passing day.

"All through dinner you barely spoke," she said as he opened the car door for her. "Is there something wrong?"

"Nothing more than usual," he grumbled, then waved her into the low-slung sports car.

Sighing, Aine slid inside, then buckled her seat belt as she waited for him to join her in the car. The street was nearly empty, which suited her fine. She couldn't quite get used to riding on the wrong side of the street. She was forever flinching or stepping on an imaginary brake.

He climbed in, settled behind the wheel and she asked, "Is it something to do with work?"

"No," he said, jamming the key into the ignition and giving it a twist.

"Is it me, then?" She reached out one hand, laid it on his forearm.

He paused, looked down at her hand, then slowly lifted his gaze to hers. What she saw flaring in his eyes had Aine's heart catching in her chest. Mouth dry, she drew a short, sharp breath and stared into his eyes. She couldn't have looked away if her life had depended on it. For days and days, it had felt as if her blood was at a slow simmer just beneath her skin, and now it began to boil. Slowly, she drew her hand back, and still the raw connection between them remained.

"Yeah," he finally ground out through gritted teeth. "It's you, Aine."

"I don't know what to say."

"Don't say anything," he advised. "Safer that way." He shifted his gaze from her to the street, put the car in gear and it nearly leaped away from the curb. "I promised myself after that kiss that we'd stay away from each other."

"Aye, I remember," she said wryly.

"It's not an easy promise to keep."

Swirls of heat ribboned through her. She liked knowing he was having a difficult time keeping his hands off her. She wished fervently he would stop trying.

Streetlights were a blur as they passed. A light rain left droplets across the windshield that shone like diamonds. The roar of the engine was the only sound and seemed to reverberate through the car. Her fingers curled around the armrest and held on as Brady drove through the night, headed for the hotel.

Minutes later, he was parking his car and holding the door for her. "You don't have to walk me to my room," she said, and her voice sounded rusty, raw.

"I always do. Tonight's no different."

But it was. Everything felt different. She was both nervous and exhilarated. The cool March wind tugged at the edges of her sweater and ruffled her hair, but Brady's hand at the small of her back ensured that she felt nothing but heat. It was a short walk to the hotel and then through the lobby to the elevators.

Once inside the lift, they stepped to opposite sides of the car like opponents in a boxing match, each of them waiting for a bell to ring to bring them together. When the doors opened, Brady pushed away from the wall, took her hand and half dragged her down the well-lit hall to her door. Her skin against his buzzed with sensation. Her stomach swirled and jumped with nerves.

"Key," he said.

She pulled it from her purse and handed it to him as she had every other time he'd brought her home. But this time when her fingers brushed his palm, it was like a match strike against already sensitized skin. She sucked in air like a drowning woman and wondered what would happen once he had her door open.

Was he really planning to leave her? Or would he

come inside? Would he kiss her again? Take her to bed and relieve the nearly painful ache that had been a part of her life for days now?

The door swung open and he didn't move. He stood at her threshold like a man at a crossroads, trying to decide which path to take. After a long moment, he turned his head, looked down at her and said, "I should go."

Disappointment warred with common sense. He should leave, she knew it. To do anything else would be foolish. Crazy even. But, oh, she wanted him to stay.

"Aye," she said at last, surrendering to sanity and putting aside her own wants and needs. "I suppose so."

"Staying would be a mistake," he said, still standing there between in and out.

"It would, no doubt."

"Leaving makes sense."

"It does," she agreed, looking into his eyes, letting him see in hers that she shared the need clawing at him.

He scrubbed one hand across the back of his neck. "Common sense is overrated."

Relief and desire pumped through her all at once, a tangled mix of emotions that left her breathless. "I've thought so myself," she said and went to him when he reached for her.

Sweeping her up in his arms, he held her close, spun them both into her hotel suite and kicked the door shut behind him. Holding her fast, his hands moved up and down her back, sliding low enough to caress her behind and then back up to hold the back of her head while he kissed her until she felt her brain swim.

If they were wrong, Aine couldn't care. Too many days and nights had been spent thinking about this moment. Now that it was here, she didn't want to think at all. This man had slipped into her mind and heart completely, until he was all she thought about. He was cold and generous, lonely and warm and so many confusing things at once that he was mesmerizing.

She held on to him when as a man unhinged, he turned around, leaned her against the wall and ravaged her mouth. Aine gave as well as took, tangling her tongue with his, tasting his breath, his hunger, as well as her own. He threaded his fingers through her hair and held her still as he devoured her. Their heartbeats thundered in time, their bodies burned from the same fire and soon the clothes separating them became a barrier neither could stand for another moment.

He didn't let her go, yet somehow he still managed to strip them out of the clothes that were an irritant. Then they were naked, bodies meshed together while frantic hands swept up and down, exploring, stroking.

Aine'd never felt anything like this. She hadn't known she *could* feel this. Everything that had come before this moment with Brady paled in comparison. She'd had sex before. There'd been Brian, and before him there'd been another, and with both of them the experience had been… pleasant.

Not earth-shattering.

Everywhere Brady touched her, Aine's skin burned, hummed with electricity and energy that pitched and peaked inside her until she thought she might explode with the tension within. And just when she thought she couldn't take it another moment, he made her feel *more*.

Brady's right hand swept down to the juncture of her thighs, cupped her heat, and made Aine's legs collapse. If he hadn't been holding her so tightly, she might have just puddled on the floor. One touch, her mind screamed, just one and she was on the ragged edge of a screaming orgasm. Then he deepened their kiss and at the same time slid two fingers into her heat, stroking and caressing her needy body from the inside.

Impossible sensations flashed into life and she gasped, eyes wide as she let herself go to feel it all. To revel in what he was doing to her. She clung to him, hands curled at his shoulders, mouth fused to his as he pushed her higher and higher. His thumb brushed across the sensitive heart of her and started the cascade of explosions inside her.

That first climax hit Aine so hard, it left her shuddering in his arms and grateful for the strength of him holding her up. She couldn't breathe and didn't care. She was trembling, her skin alive and bristling with the overload of sensations still rumbling through her. And he didn't give her time to savor any of it.

"Again," he murmured, tearing his mouth from hers, dragging his lips along the line of her throat, licking the pulse point in her neck and sending that pulse into a fiercely wild pounding with another touch.

"I can't," she insisted, groaning, tipping her head to one side, to give him better access, to invite more kisses, more nibbling.

"You can." He threaded his fingers through her hair, pulled her head back and stared down into her eyes when he rubbed his thumb across her center.

"Brady!" His talented fingers dazzled her body until every nerve ending was screaming with renewed tension.

He lifted his head to stare down into her passion-glazed eyes. "I've wanted this for days. Wanted *you* for days."

"Me, as well," she said, her voice a strangled whisper.

He pulled her in tightly to him and she felt the hard length of him pressing against her. She groaned, instinctively arching into him, wanting, needing, all of him.

"I can't think about anything but you," he admitted, dipping his head to kiss her shoulder.

Those words floated through her mind like a blessing until he spoke again.

"I don't like it. I don't want to want you." He lifted his head to stare into her eyes. "But I can't stop it."

That should have been a bucket of ice water on her head. Instead, she was contrary enough to take it as a compliment. What better was there than for a strong man to be brought to his knees by a desire he hadn't asked for? Hadn't planned for?

She cupped his face in her palms and gave him her own confession in a breathless voice, and thought what an odd conversation this was to be having while they were naked and his hand was touching her so intimately.

"I'd no more interest in this happening than you, Brady Finn," she said on a sigh. "I'd not thought to find you…this… And yet we're here and I can't find it in me to stop."

"Thank God," he whispered, and took her mouth again like a man seeking the answer to keeping him alive.

She nearly whimpered again when he pulled his hand free of her core, but he gave her no time for thought or regret. Instead, he spun her around and walked her toward the hall. Still kissing, still embracing, the two of them staggered like drunks into the bedroom and fell onto the bed, a tangle of limbs.

She ran her hands up and down his broad back, loving the slide of her skin against his. His body was amazing, strong and yet yielding, and completely and utterly focused on hers. Aine's brain splintered under the onslaught of sensations pouring through her.

He dipped his head to her breasts and took first one then the other nipple into his mouth. His teeth and tongue tugged at her sensitive skin, and she felt the answering pulls deep within her.

He moved up and down her body, tasting, exploring every inch as if he couldn't get enough of her, and she felt the same. She kissed him when he lowered his mouth to hers and felt the fires engulfing her again. Over and over, he stroked her body until she was nearly frantic with the desperate sort of need she'd never known before. It was as if that first heart-stopping climax hadn't happened at all. Her body was raw and frantic for the next release.

He reared back on his heels, gaze locked with hers and grabbed her hips. Lifting her off the bed to position her just right, he swept into her heat in one long, powerful stroke that had her crying out his name.

She stared into his eyes and couldn't have looked away if it meant her life. She watched as reaction to their joining etched itself on his features and thought she'd never seen anything more beautiful than this man in the throes of soul-shattering passion. There was tenderness along with the frantic need. There was intimacy as well as desire.

And that was when it hit her. A wild realization she hadn't expected or wanted, but it was undeniable. She'd been wrong before—it wasn't that she was incapable of love; she simply hadn't met the right man until now. Brady Finn was it for her. But how could the right man be the wrong one, as well?

Oh, God help her, she loved him. It wasn't simply passion and desire she felt. She *loved* this man of contradictions. He'd slipped into her heart and she very much feared he was there forever. Aine bit down on her lip to keep from telling him how she felt, as she knew he'd no wish to hear it. Whenever they were together she had the sense that he mentally kept one foot out the door, ready to make his escape before things could become...messy.

And now, she thought, reaching up to touch him, to run her fingertips over his face, down his neck and across his broad, muscular chest, it was too late for her to back away. Maybe it had been from the beginning. All she knew was that the man she loved was inside her, holding her, and that was enough.

As her body coiled into a tightened spring, Brady set a rhythm that she raced to match. Locking her legs around his hips, she pulled him higher and tighter at his every thrust. She wanted to hold him close enough that she'd never lose him. Her nails scored his back, her breath chugged out of her lungs and her head tipped back into the cool silk of the pillow beneath her.

"Look at me," he ordered, his voice hardly more than a low growl of desperation. "I want to watch your eyes as I take you."

Aine looked up at him, gaze locking with his. It took all she had to keep from whispering, "I love you," as her body simply imploded with another orgasm so strong that shards of pleasure slid brokenly through her veins. She couldn't look away from those shining blue eyes staring into hers. She clung to him, continuing to move her hips in time with his. Then he flipped her over until she straddled him and his body slid even higher into hers.

"Oh, my..." Her head fell back. His hands gripped her hips and guided her as she rocked on him, holding him deeply inside her. The glory of it filled her as completely as he did. There was something here, something rich and meaningful and desperately beautiful.

"Brady…" She looked down into his eyes and saw the flash of passion erupt, and a moment later felt his powerful body arch and tremble as he surrendered to the inevitable and emptied himself inside her.

Brady couldn't remember the last time he'd let himself lose control like that. His body still humming with a damn near electrical buzz, he wrapped his arms around the woman sprawled across his chest. She'd shattered him. Pushed him beyond the edges of control.

His world was in pieces around him. She'd splintered his preconceptions and left him wondering what the hell had happened to him. For the first time in memory, he'd lost every ounce of self-discipline he'd spent a lifetime acquiring. Losing himself in her was something he hadn't counted on. Hell, he hadn't been that careless, that hungry with a woman since he was a kid. There'd been no seduction here. No romance, no soft sighs and tender touches. Just need. Hunger.

"Considering what's just happened, you don't look very happy." She folded her arms across his chest and looked down at him.

"Yeah." His body was plenty happy. It was his mind that wouldn't give him any peace. Brady rolled to one side so she could stretch out on the mattress beside him. "Did I hurt you?"

He'd been rough and hadn't intended to be, and that was lowering. But then, he hadn't intended any of this to happen, so that made sense in a bizarre sort of way.

"Of course you didn't hurt me," Aine said, reaching

out to smooth his hair back from his face. "What is it that's worrying you so?"

The cool skim of her fingertips against his skin was more than he could take. He caught her hand and held it still. If she kept touching him, he'd have her again, because the need for her hadn't ended as he'd hoped, but only grown. His gaze on hers now, he saw her smile and wondered how she could be so easy with what had just happened between them.

"What is it?" Brady went up on one elbow and stared down at her. "I practically forced you to—"

He broke off when she laughed. Ordinarily that musical, Irish-flavored sound would have ignited a fire inside him. Now it just astounded him.

Reaching up, she slid one hand up and down his arm. "I'm sorry, really. But to say I was nearly forced when I tore your clothes off you is really a bit much, wouldn't you agree?"

"Okay, yes. You're right." But that didn't change the fact that he'd broken his own personal creed about getting involved with an employee. Worse, one who was far from home and probably more vulnerable than even she was aware.

It wasn't only that burrowing through his mind, though, and Brady knew it. He'd allowed Aine to get close. Closer than anyone else ever had. She'd blinded him to everything but her, and he was still overwhelmed by all of it.

"I still shouldn't have—"

"What?" she asked, grinning as she pushed her hair back from her face and sighed a little. "Used me so completely and thoroughly? If you think to apologize for that, I'll tell you now there's no need. I don't bruise easily, and if I hadn't been interested, I'm quite capable of saying no." A contented sigh slipped from her. "As it is, I think we both did a fine job of it, don't you?"

He stared at her. This had to be the weirdest after-sex conversation he'd ever had. Of course Aine Donovan would prove to be just as confusing in bed as she was out of it. Just another reason, he thought, to cut ties, to back away. She intrigued him constantly and she was already taking up way too many of his thoughts.

"You've still a frown on your face," she pointed out.

"I don't know what to make of you," Brady admitted, scowling at the admission he hadn't meant to make.

"That's lovely," she said with a pleased smile. "Thank you."

"Wasn't a compliment."

She shrugged. "I'll think of it as one, if it's all the same to you."

Darkness crept into the room inch by inch. Her eyes were in shadow now, so he couldn't try to read them as he shared the real worry about this evening. The cost of his lack of self-control that clearly she hadn't thought of yet. Damn it, Brady had built a life around responsibility, around being in control of himself and everything around him. Never once had he risked the life he'd built by being reckless. Until tonight. Knowing that he'd thrown all of that away in a moment of passion made him furious with himself.

Staring at her, he said, "All right, well, think of this, too. We were both too busy to notice we didn't use protection."

Aine paled, bolted upright, turned to the bedside table and flipped the lamp on. Shadows fled instantly, and when she looked at Brady she could see him blinking at the sudden bright light. He had taken her to heaven only to send her crashing back to earth with a thud.

Seconds ago she'd been thinking that love had sneaked up on her. That falling for Brady Finn had been inevitable. That it didn't matter if she couldn't have him; it was enough just to know that she loved. That she'd found something most people never knew.

Now...there was more. She was both terrified and oddly hopeful. Which went to show, she guessed, just how muddled her thinking was at the moment.

"So," he said wryly, "*now* you see why I'm frowning."

"Aye, I do." Her stomach did a quick flip and her mind raced as she realized the possible ramifications of what had happened between her and Brady. She would be leaving soon. Going home to a job, a family and a country that she loved. And what if she was pregnant? What then?

Oh, she couldn't wrap her mind around it.

Too many thoughts circled her brain like sharks, each taking a nibble, each demanding to be noticed. Yet how could she make sense of anything? *Pregnant?* Sliding off the bed, she dragged the duvet off the end of the mattress to wrap around her naked body. Holding it to her like a colorful, fluffy shield, she walked to the wide windows, then spun around and came back to the bed again. Whatever she might have said went unuttered when he spoke first.

"I wasn't thinking," Brady told her, and looked as though he'd rather bite off his own tongue than say what he added next. "Not since high school have I been so wrapped up in a woman that I forgot a damn condom."

Aine would have smiled at that, because really, it was a lovely compliment. She could say the same, of course, but as he was so busy heaping coals on his own head she didn't think he'd care to hear it. So she would give him what he needed. Calm. Cool. Deliberate.

"Well, then," she said firmly, tightening her grasp on the duvet, "what's done is done, so there's no use fretting over what can't be changed."

"Fretting?" He pushed off the bed and stalked toward her, apparently completely comfortable being naked.

He was magnificent, was all she could think. Tanned and strong, and a ferocious look on his features that had her heart clutching in her chest and her breath staggering in odd little gasps.

Gripping her upper arms, he asked, "That's what you think I'm doing? *Fretting?*"

"Of course not. I understand you're upset. As am I. But what more is there to do about it?" she asked, shaking her head. "The horse is gone, so 'tis useless now to worry about locking the barn door."

"Barn doors and horses," he muttered darkly. "You're damn right it's too late now. But we need to talk about what might happen."

"Don't curse at me," she said and pulled free of his grip. "We both know what might happen. Do you need me to say it? Then I will. I might be pregnant."

Oh, just saying that word aloud made her knees tremble. Wishful thinking be blasted. How could she have been so foolish? So utterly careless? It wasn't as if she were a shy virgin and this was her first time with a man. She was smart, capable and, right now, shaken to the core at what they'd done. But she wouldn't show him just how unsettled she was. She'd her pride after all.

"What else is there to say?" she asked, lifting one hand in an eloquent shrug.

"Plenty," he muttered, then turned and walked out of the room. "A man can't have this kind of conversation naked."

While he was gone, she took several deep breaths to steady her nerves. It didn't really help. Her heartbeat skittered unsteadily, and when he came back he found her exactly where he'd left her. "If you're pregnant…"

"That's a big if, if you don't mind my saying."

"Why aren't you upset?" he demanded, eyes narrowed on her.

She was, but there was a small part of her deep inside that wondered, would it really be so bad if she *were* pregnant? True, it wouldn't be a perfect situation, but she'd always wanted a family. *Crazy.* Looking at Brady, though, she knew he would never see a baby as a happy accident. He was too busy railing against circumstances.

"Because it would do no good to be upset," she said quietly. "Would you rather I weep and wail, perhaps keen a bit like the banshees you seem so fond of?"

"That would make more sense," he admitted, throwing both hands high.

His frustration was nearly palpable. He was a man used to being in control, and so this had to be hard for him. She sympathized, but for her, there was simply no point in anguish before she knew if there was a reason for it. Brady might be used to ordering his world to follow his commands, but Aine was more accustomed to things spiraling *out* of her control.

"To you, perhaps," she said softly. "But it's not my way."

"What *is* your way, Aine?"

"To wait and see, of course. There's no point in worrying a bone before you have one, is there?" She pushed her hair back in an impatient gesture. "There's an old Irish saying. 'If you worry, you die. If you don't worry, you die. So why worry?'"

"What the hell does that *mean*?" he shouted.

"Not to worry! Weren't you listening?" Aine felt her own temper bubble and strain at the leash she had it on. Deliberately, she took another breath and told herself to calm down. "It was only the one time, Brady. I hardly think it's worth this much concern."

"It only takes once," he reminded her tightly.

"Aye," she said, "in books and movies." Shaking her head, she continued, "I've a friend back home who tried for four years to get pregnant. Real life isn't as predictable as fiction, so it's a waste to think it is."

"Wishful thinking's pretty much a waste, too."

Strange, she thought, that his "wishful thinking" was hoping she wasn't pregnant and her own was not as appalled at the idea of a baby as it should be. But planned for or not, a child would be a gift, and she refused to see it as anything else.

He stuffed his hands into the pockets of his slacks, inadvertently tugging them down farther over his abdomen. The man was too handsome by far, and as she watched him, Aine thought again that he could have been a pirate with that sharp gleam in his eyes and the tight scowl on his lips.

The silence between them stretched out into long, uncomfortable seconds that seemed to take on a life of their own. How could they have been so close only minutes ago and now seem as though they were separated by thousands of miles? When she couldn't stand it anymore, Aine took one long step toward him. Reaching out, she laid one hand on his forearm and said, "This isn't helping, Brady."

At her touch, he went as stiff as stone and his features as blank as any marble statue. Why was she suddenly so cold? Was it the ice in his eyes?

Moving away, as if he couldn't bear to be next to her for another minute, Brady began to pace the confines of the room like a trapped animal looking desperately for a way out. Aine's heart hurt at the image. Even after what they'd just shared, he was anxious to be away from her.

"You're right," he finally said. "It's not helping. There's only one thing that will." He pushed one hand through his hair and threw her a quick glance.

Aine buried her hurt. He was regretting what they'd found together. And maybe she should be, too. But Aine knew that no matter what happened next, she would never second-guess lying with Brady Finn. She'd discovered her love for him and found more pleasure in his arms than she'd ever known before. She couldn't regret it, even knowing that nothing could come of it.

Still, she lifted her chin, kept a tight grip on the duvet she still held to herself and waited for him to speak again. She was determined not to let him see what she was feeling. To keep to herself the fact that his reaction to all of this was tearing at her heart.

The man was cool and deliberate, as distant as he'd been when she first met her. It was as if the Brady she'd come to know had vanished. When he spoke, she was sure of it.

"I think it's time you went back to Ireland."

"What?" She simply stared at him.

He stopped dead, crossed his arms over his chest and

braced his bare feet wide apart. "You wanted to go home. I think you should. Right away."

"That's your answer to tonight?" she asked, hardly believing what he was saying. Yes, she would have gone back home in a week or so anyway, but this felt as if he was throwing her out of the country simply to avoid an awkward situation. "To send me away?"

"Don't make this more than it is," he snapped, then caught himself and took a breath. "Tonight's got nothing to do with it. You did a good job. Now it's time to go home. With a raise."

"A raise, is it?" Her voice sounded as thin and sharp as a blade, yet she couldn't seem to change it. With her heart in her throat it was a wonder she could get any words out at all. If he'd slapped her she couldn't have been more shocked.

Rage and pain twisted into tight knots in the pit of her stomach. She was being dismissed, was all she could think. He was throwing money at her as if to buy her silence about what had happened between them. Or worse yet, as if she were nothing more than a passing fancy who could be bought off with the ease of writing a check.

Her cheeks flushed with heat. She felt it and knew it was the result of being treated as if she was disposable. A mistake to be quickly erased and forgotten. Shame rose up to choke her, then spilled out in a rush of words.

"I did a good job?" she repeated. "Where do you mean? On the castle or right here?" She waved one hand at the rumpled bed.

"You're putting words in my mouth again."

"There's no need. You were plain enough. You think I'm to be bought off, is that it?" She didn't wait for an answer, just swept on, riding the tide of her own fury.

"Though I'm your employee, I'm no servant to be sent off for getting too close to the master of the house."

He scowled at her, his brows lowering dangerously. "What the hell are you talking about now? This isn't about us sleeping together."

"Of course it is," she shouted. "Let's be honest here at least."

"How is giving you a raise and sending you home an insult?"

"You know very well," she said, kicking the duvet out of her way and stalking toward him. "You've decided to rid yourself of me in the most expedient way. Am I to be grateful, then, for this *raise* you're dangling in front of me?"

"If you don't want the damn raise, don't take it," he told her, staring down at her. "And you're not a damn servant. Having sex was a mistake. We both knew going in that it would be, Aine. I'm just trying to do what's best for both of us."

How could his eyes be so cold when only minutes earlier they'd burned with passion? And how could she feel so alone standing right in front of the man she loved?

"If you'd calm down and think," he advised tightly, "you'd see that this is the only solution. You were never staying here anyway, and to stay longer now would just be…awkward."

"Aye," she whispered. "It would be, wouldn't it? Having a temporary lover about might be problematic. Especially if you have your eye already on your next temporary lover."

He blew out a breath and scrubbed both hands over his face. "This isn't about the sex. I'm not looking for a lover and I'm not throwing you into a dungeon, for God's sake—I'm sending you *home*. The home you said you missed. Well, now you don't have to miss it."

"Oh, I'm sure I'll be *grateful* as soon as I calm down and think."

He winced when she threw his words back at him. Then Brady reached for her, but Aine scuttled backward, because she knew she couldn't bear it if he touched her. She was sure she would simply shatter like a crystal vase dropped on stone.

"So it's as it was after that first kiss. It's *you* who decides what the 'right thing' to do is."

"Are you actually trying to tell me this wasn't a mistake?" he asked.

"I'll not try to tell you anything," Aine said softly. It hadn't felt like a mistake. It had been a revelation. At least for her. She'd found love, *finally*, and now the man she loved was looking at her as though he regretted ever meeting her. "What would be the point?"

"Aine..."

"Please leave." She wanted—no needed—to be alone. Aine couldn't bear the thought of him seeing her cry, and tears were so close to the surface now it was all she could do to hold them back. "I'll go home, and gladly. I'll send you reports on the castle's progress, and I'll earn every penny of the raise you've offered."

"And you'll tell me if you're pregnant."

His voice was hard now and as distant as the moon. She felt his absence as if he'd already left, because she knew in his heart he had.

"I'll do that." She wouldn't, though. He'd made himself clear enough, hadn't he? He'd no interest in her, so why would he care about a child that came from her? No, this time with Brady was done. Their connection, if they'd ever really had one outside her own idle daydreams, was over.

Without a word more, he walked past her. She watched him leave and didn't speak. She heard him gather his clothes, let himself out of the suite and close the door behind him and still she stood alone in the shadows. She expected the tears to come then, but they didn't.

They were as frozen as her heart.

Eight

Five months later...

"How long are you gonna be in Ireland?"

Brady looked over at Mike and shrugged. "Shouldn't be long. I just want to check on the progress being made."

"Uh-huh." Mike sat back in his chair and lifted his feet to the edge of Brady's desk, crossing his legs at the ankle.

Brady stifled an impatient sigh. It had been five months since he'd last seen Aine. Five months of emails and short, terse phone calls once a week. True to her word, she'd kept him up-to-date on the renovation and according to her, everything was on schedule. So there was no real reason for him to fly to Ireland—and Mike knew it. So naturally, his friend had to rag him about it.

"It's a business trip," Brady said, stacking the last of the papers on his desk before tucking them away in the top drawer. "That's it."

"Right. This from the same man who said a few months back that with the 360-degree videos there was no reason to go to Ireland in person."

"That was before the renovations started," Brady argued.

"Did Aine say there was a problem?"

"No." In fact, she never said much at all. Irritation simmered deep in his gut. Her emails were rarely more than a sentence or two long. She called once a week without fail, and he could feel the ice in her voice despite the thousands of miles separating them. As far as work went, he had nothing to complain about. She was businesslike and organized and so damn far away it was driving him nuts.

The memory of that last night with her rose up in his mind suddenly, and he could see her as clearly as if she were in the room with him. Her eyes wide and wounded, her hair tumbling around her shoulders in a wild dark red tangle and the duvet she'd held to herself while she'd stared at him in shock.

Hell, it had all gone downhill so fast. The next morning, she had come into the offices, said goodbye to everyone and left for home that afternoon. In a blink it was as if she had never been there at all. Except for the fact that he couldn't go more than an hour without thinking about her.

Then there had been the awkward phone call a few months ago when he'd asked if she was pregnant and she'd told him he had nothing to worry about. He'd almost been disappointed—if there'd been a baby, he'd have had an excuse for seeing her again. But the reality was it was better this way since he knew nothing about being a father. How could he know when he'd never *had* a father?

"So there's no problem, but you're still hopping a jet." Mike grinned. "Why don't you just admit you miss her?"

Because he didn't miss her. That was ridiculous. Brady Finn didn't get close enough to women to miss them when they were gone. Maybe he hadn't been with anyone else since she'd left, but that was because he'd been busy. It had nothing to do with the fact that he could still hear her voice, musical with the sound of Ireland. That he could still see her eyes, as green as a forest. That her taste was still inside him, smothering any other needs in his continuing hunger for her. No, he didn't miss her. He just needed to see her again to clear his mind and then he could return to his life. That was what this was about, he assured himself. Closure.

He needed to look into her eyes, say a clean goodbye and then leave again with a clear conscience. He didn't want the memory of her hurt and insult in his mind anymore.

"Missing a woman isn't a crime, you know."

Brady stiffened, then shot Mike another look. "I don't miss her. I talk to her once a week, don't I? Look, she works for us," he said reasonably. "I'm going to check on the hotel I'm in charge of remodeling. It's business, Mike. That's it."

His friend snorted, dropped his feet to the floor and stood up. Shoving both hands into his pockets, Mike said, "If you really believe that, you are some kind of sad, my friend." He turned and strolled to the door. When he got there, he glanced over his shoulder and said, "If you're just lying to yourself, then good luck with that."

Brady didn't need luck. All he was going to do was check out the castle, make sure the work was going well. Seeing Aine—was Mike right? *Was* he lying to himself?

Brady scrubbed both hands over his face and grumbled, "Damn it, Mike, stay the hell out of my head."

His friend's laughter floated to him from the hallway.

Aine loved her family. She really did. But since she'd moved into one of the bedrooms at the castle and had her own space, it was much easier to love them. Her mother and Robbie had been nothing but supportive since her return home. She'd slipped back into her life almost as if California hadn't happened. Almost. She'd been raw and hurt and sick to her soul when she came home and echoes of that pain were still with her.

But working at the castle kept her busy enough that most of the time Aine could push thoughts of Brady Finn to the back of her mind. It was only the nights that were crowded with memories of him. When she couldn't sleep for thoughts of him, Aine would wander the halls of Castle Butler and have to admit that Brady Finn was doing something wonderful here.

Despite the hurt she felt when thoughts of him settled in her mind and heart, Aine could see the difference in the castle and almost see what it would be when finished. The changes were many, some subtle, some outrageous, but the castle itself remained strong, a reminder to her that whatever changes she faced, she, too, could overcome them.

"But don't take that the wrong way, love," Aine said, sliding her palm across the rounded bulge of her belly. "You're a change I'm looking forward to."

Five months' pregnant and unmarried, some might think she'd be in a panic. But she wasn't. Certainly she worried a bit about the future, as being a single mother was a frightening situation. Still, she was twenty-eight years old and didn't care about village gossip a bit. Her family loved her and she had a good job, a place to live and, in a few short months, she would have a living connection to the man she had loved...and lost.

Aine shrugged deeper into the heavy cream-colored Irish-knit sweater she wore and stuffed both hands into the pockets. She walked downstairs to check on the workmen already making a storm of noise, and while she went thoughts of Brady once more drifted through her mind.

Odd that she'd gone her whole life without feeling these conflicting emotions. She'd been engaged, and had never once felt the swift tugs and pulls that Brady engendered in her. Why was it the man she wanted most was the one man she could never have? Why was he so determined to pull away and shut himself off from any kind of real love and connection?

That was why she hadn't told him about the baby. He was so determined to be alone, so convinced he needed no one, she knew he wouldn't want to be a father to her child. Oh, he would do the dutiful thing, she'd no doubt. He had integrity aplenty, and he would once again sacrifice himself because it was the "right" thing to do. But she needed no sacrificial saint to help raise her child. If he couldn't offer love, he had nothing she and her baby needed.

"Aine, love," Danny Leary called to her from the far side of the banquet room. "Have you been to the kitchen yet today?"

Danny was built like the trunk of one of the ancient oaks surrounding the castle, though coming in much shorter. He was thick with muscles gained from years of hard work. His gray hair was cut short, his blue eyes as sharp as diamonds. He was strong as a bear and gentle as a lamb and one of her late father's oldest friends.

"No," she said, determinedly pushing thoughts of Brady aside. "Why?"

"We've a decision to make there." Danny shifted the hammer he held from hand to hand. "The new stove's arrived, and it's too wide to fit."

She sighed and buried a quick flash of temper at the latest annoyance. "Who did the measurements?"

"I did them myself and they were good, but the company's made a mistake. So now," he said with a shake of his head, "you've a choice. We can have them ship it back and send out another, but the time delay will hold off the painting, the new counters and the new flooring, as well."

Not a catastrophe by any means, just one more bump in a road that had proved itself to have plenty of ruts in it. "What has to be done to make it work?"

He grinned. "If we take out one of the lower cabinets, she'll slide in as if the spot were made for her. And this stove's two more burners on it than the one ordered in the first place, so it could be a blessing in disguise."

"Let's have it, then," she said, making the decision on the spot. "I trust you to do the job right."

"There's a girl," Danny said and winked at her. "Now, then, there's something else, as the slate tiles for the roof have been delayed again."

Her shoulders slumped. It had been months now they'd waited for those tiles. They'd had to be specially made, to keep with the medieval feel of the castle. But with this latest delay it pushed back the renovation of the rooms on the top floor. No one could redo floors and walls and then have rain come through the holes in the roof and ruin everything.

"I'll call them again."

"Good. You could also call about the flagstones for the garden, as they arrived broken and will have to be replaced."

"For pity's sake," she muttered, and pulled her phone from her pocket, making notes on who to call next. It seemed always there was one problem after another.

But Danny wasn't finished. "Now, if you've another moment or two, Kevin Reilly could use your decision on the paint color for the washrooms off the main lobby."

Aine nodded and walked off in that direction. It felt as though she walked miles every day, from one end of the castle to the other. Her steps matched the rhythm set by the crack of hammers and the buzz of saws, not to mention the traditional music pumping from a radio tucked on a ladder nearby. Everyone had a purpose, and Brady's dream was happening before her eyes.

The banquet room was nearly finished, with its tapestries hung, the oversize mantel carved and in place over the refurbished stone hearth. There were what looked to be mile-long tables with benches drawn up to them. Leaded windows let in the watery sunlight peeking through storm clouds, and the refinished floors were covered by protective tarps. She felt the castle coming to life in a way she'd never expected. The murals in the banquet room were otherworldly, true, but they were also beautiful. She shouldn't have worried on that score. Brady had been right—she'd have to remember to tell him that when she made her weekly progress report call tomorrow.

Talking to him every week was getting harder, because as the baby grew and stirred inside her, it felt more and more as though she was cheating him. Her heart urged her to tell him he was to be a father, but her mind kept insisting he wouldn't want to know. And Aine couldn't bear to hear him make excuses—or worse yet, offer her duty when what she wanted was love. So she would keep her secrets and her memories to herself.

The road was so narrow that if another car came at him, Brady thought, he'd just have to die. There was no room to pull over. The thick hedges Aine had told him about crouched so close to the narrow track he drove along, they actually scraped against his impossibly small rental car at nearly every turn.

Brady checked the GPS on his phone and knew he was less than twenty minutes from the castle. His blood hummed in anticipation. It wasn't the damn castle he was interested in seeing, it was Aine. The deeper he drove into her country, the sharper the memories of her became. Her voice. Her smile. That quick flash of temper that disappeared as fast as it erupted.

He'd thought that sending her home would get her out of his thoughts, but instead, the opposite had happened. When he couldn't see her, his brain provided a stockpile of images to make sure he didn't forget her. But memory was a tricky thing, he knew, and he was sure that somehow his own brain was making her seem more than she really was. This trip would settle it. Would show him that she was just another woman and then he could move the hell on and leave her behind.

The car crested a hill, and it seemed that all of Ireland opened up in front of him. A wide sweep of valley so green it hurt to look at it. Stone fences threaded through the green like gray ribbon, and a few scattered cottages looked as though they'd been plunked down in the middle of a painting. Cows and sheep dotted the fields, and not far off, a farmer rode a tractor, churning up black earth. Sunlight speared through the clouds and lay like gold across the fields. The sky was as blue as Aine had promised, and the distant sea glittered darkly like a sapphire.

Even better, Brady spotted the hulking shadow of the castle not far off. In a few minutes, he was driving through the entry, making a mental note to have the tall metal gates painted. On the right stood the guest cottage where Aine lived with her family. He almost stopped, then decided to go to the castle first, then find his hotel manager.

It was impressive, was all he could think as he parked the car in front of the wide double doors. The three-story building was gray stone that contained enough mica to make it glitter when the sun slanted across it. He did a slow turn, taking in the whole picture, and had to admit that it was a different thing entirely to actually stand in front of the castle than it had been to see the pictures of it. A cold wind sliced at him, belying the fact that it was August. The wide lawn was trimmed, the ancient oaks provided shade for the castle entrance and flowers in the neatly tended beds dipped and swayed in a wind that carried the scent of the sea.

He hadn't expected it all to be so beautiful. Or to feel almost...*familiar*. Which just went to prove that jet lag had set in.

Behind him, the front door opened and Brady turned around to see a short barrel-chested man with gray hair and sharp blue eyes glaring at him.

"You've come, then," the man said with a brisk nod. "And about time if you're asking me."

"I'm sorry?"

"It's not my pardon you should be begging, is it?"

Irritation stirred. "What're you talking about?"

"I'm talking man-to-man about what's decent, aren't I? You'll be Brady Finn." The man came down the steps like a bull chasing down an intruder in his field. "I know your face from the pictures Aine showed me."

Brady looked down at the much shorter man. "Who're you?"

"Danny Leary," he said and didn't offer his hand. "I'm one of those putting the castle to rights."

So this was the man Aine had gone to bat for. "Aine told me about you," Brady said and didn't add that she hadn't mentioned he was a little nuts.

"Did she, now? Well, she told all of us about you as well, Brady Finn, and as I said, it's high time you showed yourself." Danny propped fists on his hips, scowled up at Brady and said, "As her father, God rest him, was my friend, I'll stand for him now. You've been too long in coming, but as you're here now, we'll settle this for good and all."

"Settle *what*?" Brady was tired, hungry and in no mood for playing games. Besides all that, he wasn't used to having his employees chew him out as though he was ten years old.

A storm cloud settled on the older man's features. "Follow me, then." Danny turned and charged back up the stairs, not bothering to see if Brady came after him or not.

He followed the man into the castle and stopped dead in the entryway. A wall of noise greeted him. Saws, hammers, men shouting, music playing. The place was huge, so the sound ricocheted off the cathedral ceiling and slammed back down to crash into Brady's head. Gray stone walls were dotted with pennants, tapestries and broadswords. Leaded windows allowed sunlight to spear into the open space. He could see the wide staircase off to the right, its ancient stone steps covered by a deep red runner. A highly polished, intricately carved wooden banister gleamed in the light.

"Aine!" Danny shouted from off to Brady's left. "What're you doing on that ladder, lass? You've no business climbing that thing."

Brady walked into what was clearly the banquet hall. In a split second, his gaze swept the room and he was impressed. It was exactly as he'd imagined it. The feel of the Middle Ages and the comfort of the twenty-first century. Perfect. Right down to the paintings of warriors, werewolves and banshees on the walls.

"Come on down now and careful," the man was saying. "Mind your step, lass."

"I'm fine, Danny," she said on a laugh, "I was just putting a new bulb in this sconce. What do you think? A lower wattage looks more like torchlight, but 'tisn't as bright as a higher-watt bulb."

"I like the torch idea myself," Danny answered.

"As do I."

The musical voice that had haunted Brady for five months fisted something inside him. He watched as Danny helped her down the last few rungs of a ladder and couldn't take his eyes off her. She hadn't seen him yet, so he took advantage of the moment to indulge himself by letting his gaze sweep over her. That amazing hair of hers hung loose in waves and curls of dark fire that fell around her shoulders. She wore a thick sweater over jeans and boots, and Brady thought he'd never seen anything so beautiful.

Damn, he'd missed her. Hadn't wanted to. Had tried

to talk himself out of it time and again, yet she hadn't left his mind once over the past five months.

"Danny," she was saying, "you don't have to worry about me."

"I've known you all your life, lass. And if you haven't the sense to know a pregnant woman has no business climbing a ladder, what choice do I have but to worry?"

"Pregnant?"

Aine whirled around so fast, her hair swung out in an arc around her head. Her face was pale, her green eyes wide and startled. But all he could see was the rounded belly defined by a tight yellow shirt exposed when her sweater swung open. "Brady? What're you doing here?"

"You're pregnant?" he demanded. "What the hell, Aine?"

"Don't curse at me," she snapped.

"He didn't *know*?" Danny bellowed. "You've kept it from the man all this time?"

"No," Brady ground out, answering Danny's question himself. "I didn't know. She didn't bother to tell me."

His gaze drilled into Aine's, and he had some small satisfaction in seeing shame flicker briefly in her eyes. It felt as if there was a giant iron band wrapped around his chest, slowly tightening until he could hardly breathe. His brain was racing and was still outpaced by the damn anger that had him by the throat.

"How could you not tell the man he's to be a father?"

Aine shot Danny a look. "I've my reasons."

"I'm sure they're great ones," Brady snapped. "Can't wait to hear 'em."

Danny folded his arms across his broad chest. "I'd like to know that, as well."

"What were you waiting for, Aine?" Brady took a step

closer and forced himself to stop. "When the kid needs college money?"

Little by little, Brady noticed, the noise in the castle was beginning to die off. First it was the saw, then the hammers. Music, though, still pumped through the air, and a few men shouted to be heard over it.

Aine sucked in a gulp of air and fired a furious look at him. "Did I ever ask you for anything?" she demanded, clearly outraged. "How can you say I'd come to you for *money*?"

"Aye, that was a bit harsh," Danny put in.

Brady wasn't listening. "What else am I supposed to think? You don't tell me you're pregnant and I'm supposed to, what? Congratulate you on your integrity and honesty?"

Her incredible green eyes narrowed and a splash of temper appeared on her pale cheeks. "You've no call to question my honesty."

Brady waved one hand at her belly. "Looks as if I've got about five months' worth of reason."

"Well, he has you there, love," Danny said.

Now the quiet in the castle was nearly ghostly. The silence was so profound, Brady was sure he could hear his own heart crashing in his chest.

A *father*? He'd spent his entire adult life avoiding just this situation, and all it had taken was one night of forgetting—one night of incredible sex mixed with a lack of control—to plunk him right in the middle of it. He couldn't sort through the dozens of emotions and reactions racing through him. All he could think was he was a *father*. And hell if he knew what to do about it.

Vaguely, he noticed the banquet room filling with curious people. One by one, men came in from wherever

they'd been working, following the sounds of shouting.
They stood in a wary half circle, waiting for the argument to continue. And for the first time, Brady came to
himself long enough to realize he was discussing damned
private things with a damn audience.

"That's it for the show," he announced, his voice deep
and dark and loud enough to carry throughout the castle.
"You men get back to work—"

"Who's he to be ordering us about?" someone whispered.

"He's your boss, Jack Dooley," Danny said loudly
enough to cover any other questions. "And he's right
and all. Back to work, the lot of you." Then the older man
gave Brady a nod and a wink before joining the rest of
the crew in their slow shuffle out of the room.

Stalking across the few feet of space separating him
from Aine, Brady grabbed her upper arm in a tight grip
and fought to ignore the expected flare of heat that zipped
from her to him and back again. "We'll finish this in
private."

She pulled away and said, "There's nothing to finish."

Brady laughed shortly, but there was no humor in it.
"You can't be serious."

"Fine. We'll go upstairs to my room."

"Your room? I thought you lived in the guest cottage."

"I moved into the castle some time ago, to better keep
an eye on things as they happen." She walked past him,
chin lifted, head held high. Like a damn queen, Brady
told himself and followed after, the sound of his footsteps
echoing loudly in the quiet.

"You'll notice the work on the ground floor's pro-
gressing," she said, voice thin and tight, like a bored tour

guide. "The first floor—second to you—is nearly finished as well, but the top floor's another matter entirely."

He was hardly listening. In spite of the anger rushing through him he was distracted by the sway of her behind as she climbed the stairs. Gritting his teeth, he looked away and when he did, he noticed some of the work done on the place. At the landing, thick bloodred carpets ran the length of the hallway, and pewter sconces chased away gloomy day shadows. Paintings based on the "Fate Castle" game were framed and hung, and he lost a moment or two admiring them.

"It looks good," he said, grudgingly.

"It does." She turned to the right and walked down the hall to the room at the far end, where she opened the door and Brady followed her inside.

The room was big, filled with antiques and boasting a window seat. There was a fireplace, two chairs pulled up in front of it. A heavy wooden chest sat at the end of a massive four-poster bed opposite a wide flat-screen television hanging over the hearth.

Brady walked to the window, pulled the drapes aside and looked down on what appeared to be a maze. He didn't give a damn about the scenery, though—he was only trying to ease the tightness in his chest, get a grip on his anger. But that wasn't working, so he thought, *Screw it*, and turned around to face Aine.

His heart felt as if a tight fist were closed around it, and even with that, his body stirred at the sight of her. Apparently righteous anger wasn't enough to quench the desire he felt for her.

"You should have told me you were coming," she blurted out, crossing her arms over her chest. The edges of her sweater slid back and the rounded bump of her belly was proudly displayed.

Under that steady regard, Aine pulled her sweater over in front of her, disguising the bump.

Anger, betrayal and a whisper of panic rose up inside him and settled in his chest. "I should have told you?" he asked. "Why? So you could be gone when I got here?"

"No," she said, lifting that stubborn chin of hers even higher. "This is my home, I wouldn't have gone, but I might have been prepared—"

"For more lies?" he interrupted.

"I didn't lie to you," she insisted, chin high, eyes flashing. "Exactly."

"Really?" He walked closer and closer until he was just a breath away from her and she was forced to tip her head back to meet his eyes. God, her scent wrapped itself around him and snaked into his brain, where it tangled with memories and lies and secrets and drove him even closer to the edge. "You didn't lie. When I asked if you were pregnant, what did you say?"

"That you'd nothing to worry about," she snapped, pushing away from him. "'Tis no more than the truth. My child is not yours to worry over."

"My child, too, Aine." God, just saying those words out loud gave Brady a jolt that shook him right to the bones.

"You don't want him. I do."

"Him?" Brady asked.

She sighed and her shoulders slumped. "Aye. 'Tis a boy."

A son. He had a son. Hard to wrap his brain around, but knowing what the baby was made this so much more real. More immediate. "And he's healthy?"

"He is," she said, laying one hand protectively over her belly.

He caught the action and his heart gave a hard thump. She'd been pregnant for five months. She'd been here, building a life without him. Planning a future for their child without him. He hadn't suspected. Hadn't sensed anything during all of the conversations he'd had with her. It seemed he should have known somehow. The fact that he hadn't was due to her.

"I had a right to know, Aine."

"You would only have offered me money—"

Stung, mostly because she was probably right, he said, "You don't know that."

"Don't I? When you were in such a rush to get rid of *me*, your first thought was to offer me a raise."

He ground his teeth together in pure frustration. Yes, she had a point, but that didn't negate the fact that she was in the wrong here and had no excuse good enough for what she'd done.

The thought of being a father had never really entered his mind. It wasn't as if he had any notion how to be a part of a family. But now that he was faced with the very real existence of a child he'd created, he could admit to himself that it wasn't only worry and anger charging through his system.

For the first time in his life, he would be a part of something. His child. And he wouldn't let anyone cut him out of the boy's life.

"You made yourself clear in California, Brady," Aine was saying. "You wanted no more from me, so why would I assume you would want my child?"

"Half yours," he corrected. "Half mine."

"Well, short of Solomon's solution to this situation, I don't know what you want of me."

"I want to know my kid," he snapped. "And I want him to know me. I won't have my son wondering where his parents are. Wondering why he wasn't good enough for his father to stick around or why—"

He broke off, appalled at the words rushing from him. He hadn't talked about his childhood to anyone. Not even the Ryan brothers knew the whole story, and damned if Brady was going to spill his guts to the woman who'd lied to him. The woman who stood there looking at him through green eyes shining now with anxiety and curiosity.

"Why would he think that?" she asked quietly.

"He won't. He'll never have to," Brady assured her, moving in close again. "We've got a lot of talking to do."

"I suppose we do, at that." She sighed and walked to one corner of the room. "I've a tea set up here. Would you like a cup?"

"Are we going to be civilized now?" he asked wryly.

She glanced at him. "We can certainly try."

"Right." Nodding, he walked along behind her and tried to let go of the hard knot of anger in his guts. Wouldn't do him any good to stay angry. Aine would just have to learn that he wasn't going anywhere. Not until they figured out what to do from here.

"The tea services will be in every room," she was saying, plugging in a kettle and readying two cups. "It's not proper tea, of course, but bags. Still, it's welcome on a cold summer day."

"Cold summer day," he mused, stuffing his hands into his pockets as he followed after her. "Don't hear that much at home."

"True enough, but Ireland's a different matter, isn't it?" She busied herself with the tea bags and cups, and when the water in the kettle boiled, she poured it. "The kitchen's not ready for use as yet, with the stove not installed." She was talking faster, showing nerves she otherwise would have hidden. "I've been eating sandwiches mostly, since the fridge is working fine, or eating with Mum and Robbie. If you're planning on staying a bit—"

"I am," he assured her.

She nodded. "Then, sandwiches for you as well, or there's the village where you can find pub grub."

"Sounds delicious." He leaned one shoulder against the wall and watched as she finished preparing the tea and handed him a cup.

"'Tis good," she told him. "Mick Hannigan's wife has a way with shepherd's pie."

"I'll keep it in mind," he said and couldn't care less about the pub, the village or pretty much anything else but the woman in front of him and the child nestled inside her. To keep her off balance, he asked, "How's the work on the castle coming?

She gave him a curious glance. "As I've told you every week. Much progress has been made, though we've hit a bump or two along the way."

"What kind of bumps?" he asked.

"No more than you'd expect on such a big job," she said. "We've had some trouble with supplies arriving or being misordered, but we're dealing with them."

He frowned into his cup. "You didn't say anything to me about this."

"What would you do about it from California?" She threw that question over her shoulder as she walked to one of the chairs in front of the hearth and sat down.

"I can make phone calls," he told her as he took the chair beside her.

"As can I," she pointed out. "And have, as it's my job, isn't it? The only real worry now is the slate tiles for the roof. They've been delayed again, and should a storm hit—"

"I'll talk to the supplier tomorrow."

"I don't need your help to do my job any more than I need your help to care for my child," she said.

"For the baby, you can't know yet what you'll need," he countered. "About the roof tiles, it's my castle. I'll call and get the damn things here."

"Because you're a man, of course."

He grinned. "We use what we have."

"And you'll offer them money, as well?"

"Someday," Brady mused, "you're going to have to explain to me just what it is you've got against money."

She sniffed, took a sip of tea and laid her head against the chair back. "You being here will only make things harder, Brady." Her voice was so soft, he nearly missed her words. "Take one of the rooms on this floor, spend the night, check out the castle to your heart's content." She turned her head to spear him with a forest green glance. "Then, for both our sakes, go home."

Well, now he had an idea of how she'd felt when he'd practically pushed her onto a plane for Ireland. The difference between them was he had no intention of leaving.

Brady took a sip of the tea and wished it was coffee. Or better yet, Irish whiskey. Then he met her eyes in a steady stare and vowed, "I'll take a room, Aine. But I'm not going anywhere. Get used to it."

Nine

The next morning, Aine was up and out of the castle early. Yes, it was cowardly to slip away just to avoid Brady, but she simply couldn't deal with another "discussion" about the baby. She knew going to see her mother wouldn't prevent the next confrontation—only delay it. But in the meantime, she needed the space to think.

"He's angry," Aine said over a cup of tea at her mother's kitchen table.

"Of course he is," Molly told her daughter. "The man's just found out he's to be a father. And that you kept the news from him." She smoothed one hand over Aine's hair. "You should have told him, love. He had the right to know."

"Maybe," Aine admitted, remembering the look on Brady's face yesterday when he'd spotted the evidence of her pregnancy.

Molly pushed a plate of sugar biscuits toward her

daughter. "Have one to tide you over until I make breakfast."

Aine was almost too tired to chew the cookie. She
hadn't slept all night. How could she, with Brady just
down the hall from her? Missing him had been hard on
her when an ocean separated them. It was impossible with
only twenty feet between them. Because he was here, in
Ireland, and still not hers.

Seeing him again after five long months had nearly
torn her in two. Her head warred with her heart and too
often came out the loser. Even knowing there was no future for her with Brady, she couldn't stop the yearning.

"What am I to do, Mum?"

Molly reached across the table and patted her daughter's hand. "Follow your heart, always, Aine. You can't
make a mistake if you do."

Wryly, Aine smoothed her palm over her belly. "I followed my heart five months ago..."

"You did." Molly's blue eyes were kind and full of
understanding. "And if you keep doing just that, you'll
perhaps come out the other side with your heart whole
and a future to look forward to."

Not once had her mother been anything but supportive
in the past five months. Aine knew just how lucky she
was in that. Molly was on her side, no matter what. Robbie, on the other hand, had been furious as only a younger
brother could be when he felt his sister had been used
and discarded. Molly, though, had been steadfast without
even a flicker of disappointment in her only daughter.

Aine loved her mother, but Molly was a hopeless romantic. Aine knew the truth. That Brady would never
be in a relationship with her. The manager of his hotel?

No…wealthy men didn't marry women like her. What drove him now were duty and his own sense of honor.

"I don't like that look in your eye, Aine," her mother said.

"Sorry, but you don't know him, Mum." Frowning into her tea, she said, "He'll see the baby—and me, for that matter—as a burden to be carried. A debt to be settled. There's no thought of more from him because he doesn't *want* more."

"Duty's not so far from love," Molly said. "A man feels a responsibility to his child, to the family he's made…"

"We're not a family," Aine interrupted.

"I'm not finished. Duty may drive his actions, but if he felt no duty to the child he made, you wouldn't want him anyway, would you?"

"I suppose not," Aine admitted, and acknowledged silently that she hadn't thought of it like that before. Brady wanting to do the right thing was the mark of a good man. If he didn't care on some level, he'd have left the moment he saw her rounded belly.

"Still, he didn't want me before," Aine admitted, turning her cup between her hands, watching the tea inside slosh against the sides. "He couldn't put me on a plane fast enough the moment we got…close."

"Yet he's here, in Ireland," her mother pointed out.

Shaking her head, Aine said, "He came to check on the castle."

Molly snorted and gave her daughter's hand a hard pat. "Did he? And in all these months, he's never once done that. He bought the castle without seeing it. Began costly renovations without seeing it. Why is it *now*, I wonder, the man's here?"

Hope was a dangerous thing, and even knowing that,

Aine couldn't keep a tiny blossom of it from forming inside her. But if she held to hope, wouldn't she just be crushed all the more when that hope dissolved?

"Do you love him?" Molly asked gently.

Aine had asked herself that question many times over the past several months and the truth was, she'd even tried to talk herself out of what she felt for Brady Finn. But the fact remained. "Fool that I am, yes. I do."

"Love makes fools of all of us," Molly assured her. "And if you love the man, you can't give up on him."

When her mother stood up and moved to the stove, Aine watched her. Molly wore black slacks and a deep green sweater, and her thick auburn hair, now streaked with silver threads, curled under at chin level. Molly tucked her hair behind her ears and reached for a skillet to start breakfast. Turning the fire on under the pan, she moved off to get the fixings from the fridge, which was currently hiccupping noisily in the corner.

Aine sighed and glanced around the familiar kitchen with its white walls, red cabinets and aging appliances. It was neat and clean as a church, but like the castle itself, the guest cottage was in sore need of repair. She'd like to have the cottage renovated at the same time as the castle, but how, she couldn't imagine.

Making the castle over was one thing, but to fix up the cottage where her family lived was something else again. Then she wondered if Brady would continue to allow her family to live on the grounds. What if he didn't? Worry spread in the pit of her stomach like an ink spill, dark and thick. If he chose to rent out the cottage to guests as well, where would her family go? Her mother couldn't afford a higher rent, and with the baby coming, Aine wouldn't be able to help much.

Her head was swimming with this whole new set of worries when she heard a knock on the door.

"Now, who in the world?" her mother asked no one in particular as she left the kitchen to answer the summons.

Aine took another sugar biscuit and had a big bite when she heard the rumble of voices and recognized Brady's. She pushed to her feet, hurried into the main room and saw him step inside, taking her mother's hand.

"Mrs. Donovan, I'm Brady Finn, the father of your grandson."

His dark hair tumbled over his forehead and he wore a black leather jacket over a dark red T-shirt and black jeans. His boots were scuffed and appeared well used. He looked impossibly gorgeous, and when Aine felt a stir inside her she nearly sighed. There was just no getting past what she felt for the man, even knowing she *should*.

Molly threw her daughter a quick glance before shifting her gaze back to Brady with a smile. "Aren't you a handsome one? It's good you've come."

"Well," Brady said, "when I couldn't find Aine at the castle, I remembered she said her family lived in the cottage. I hoped I'd find her here."

"And so she is." Molly tugged him into the house. "Come in, won't you?"

"Why are you here?" Aine asked.

"To meet your family."

He said it as though she should have expected him, which she hadn't. As he'd told her many times, Brady Finn didn't do families.

"I was just making breakfast," Molly said into the silence. "You'll join us."

"Thank you." Brady threw a half smile at Aine over

his shoulder as Molly tugged him in her wake toward the kitchen.

When Aine followed after them, she found Brady already seated at the table and her mother dropping sausages and bacon into a pan to sizzle.

"That smells great," Brady said, fixing his gaze on Aine as she moved farther into the room.

"You'll have tea, as well," Molly told him, then fired a look at her daughter. "Aine, fetch another cup and pour some tea for the man."

Aine caught the gleam of amusement in Brady's dark blue eyes. As she poured tea and then automatically refilled the kettle and set it on to boil again, she asked herself why he was doing all of this. Duty was one thing, but when a woman told a man she didn't want or need his guilt money, why would he stay? Introduce himself to her family? Lay claim to her child?

The luscious scent of frying bacon and sausage sizzled into the air as Molly efficiently cracked eggs into a bowl and whipped them into a froth.

"How long have you lived here, Mrs. Donovan?" he asked.

"Oh, call me Molly, love, as we're in the way of being family now, aren't we?"

He grinned again, and Aine wondered if her mother was doing this on purpose. "He's not family, Mum."

"If he's not, I don't know who is," her mother countered. "Now, then, Brady, the Donovans have lived here five years now, since we lost Aine's father to a storm at sea."

He sipped at his tea, then gave her a solemn nod. "Aine told me. I was sorry to hear it."

"Thank you." Molly gave him a smile that took the

edge off the sheen of tears clouding her bright blue eyes at the mention of the man she still loved and missed. "The cottage was a godsend to us, for sure, as Robbie was so young and Aine was working here at the castle…"

Aine watched Brady as her mother continued to talk, regaling him with family stories while she cooked. And Brady took it all in, looking as comfortable in the shabby kitchen as he had in the plush penthouse that was his home. Anyone looking at him would never think him a billionaire.

Then he smiled at her and her heart turned over in her chest. She'd missed him, damn the man. She hadn't wanted to, but it was hard not to think of the man who had given her a baby. And it was more than that, as well. She'd missed the contradiction and contrariness of the man. She'd missed looking at him and feeling that slow spin of something lovely sliding through her. And she knew that when he left again, the pain of missing him would be even sharper than it had been before.

But of course he had to leave. The fact that she loved him changed nothing. There was nothing between them but a child each of them wanted. He wouldn't stay, so why was he here, charming her mother?

"Is he the one?" Robbie's voice shook her out of her daydream.

Aine stepped to her younger brother and put one hand on his arm. It still amazed her that at almost eighteen, Robbie towered over her. Tall and lanky like their father had been, Robbie's gaze was locked on Brady, and he didn't look willing to be charmed.

Brady stood up and held out one hand to the boy. "Brady Finn. You're Robbie."

"I am," the boy said, whipping his hair back from his face as he took Brady's hand in a hard grip.

The room went quiet as Aine and her mother watched, neither of them knowing quite what to expect. There was a long moment where the two of them stared hard into each other's eyes and seemed to be each taking the measure of the other. Finally, though, Robbie asked, "You've come to see Aine. Why?"

"Robbie…"

"'Tis a question I'd like answered, too," Molly said, ignoring her daughter's sigh.

Brady let go of Robbie's hand and looked the boy square in the eyes, giving him the respect of treating him like an equal. "I didn't know about the baby," he said quietly, "or I would have been here sooner."

Aine felt a twinge of shame that she'd lied to the man, but it was too late to change that now.

Robbie only nodded and waited for Brady to continue.

"I've been doing a lot of thinking since I found out about the baby," he said, looking from one to the other of them. "And I think I've got the solution. Aine and I will get married."

"Wonderful!" from Molly.

"Good," from Robbie.

"We will not," from Aine.

Brady wasn't surprised. He'd known what her reaction would be, and how could he blame her? Not as if he was husband and father material after all. No one knew that better than he did. But all through the long night, he'd considered and rejected dozens of possibilities.

She wouldn't take his money. She'd made that plain enough, and he wasn't about to let her and his son go without whatever they needed. In his whole life, he'd never had anyone rely on him. He'd been alone and he'd liked it that way. Until Aine. After she'd left, the solitude he had always prized hadn't seemed as comfortable as it had before.

He'd missed her laughter, the way her eyes narrowed and her chin lifted when she was ready to argue with him. He'd missed the feel of her, the taste of her. And he hadn't been able to find any damn peace without her.

Now there was a child who was only alive because of him, and he wouldn't fail that boy. The one thing Brady could do for his son was to marry his mother and ensure that the two of them had whatever they needed.

"He's not serious," Aine said, shaking her head.

Brady shifted his gaze to hers, willing her to see in his eyes that he'd never meant anything more.

"He looks as though he is." Molly waved them all into chairs at the table, then brought platters of food and set them down. "Everyone tuck in while it's hot, now."

Brady settled in to eat breakfast with Aine's family and didn't look her way again. He knew what she must be thinking, because he wasn't far from thinking the same thing himself. *Married?* He'd never thought to marry anyone. But times and situations changed, he reminded himself as he took another bite of scrambled eggs.

All night, his mind had raged, going from one possibility to another, and finally he'd even called Mike Ryan to tell him what was going on. While Robbie talked eagerly of zombies and programming and his mother watched him proudly, Brady's mind drifted back to that conversation.

"She's pregnant?"

"Yeah." Brady paced his room, pausing now and

again to stare out the windows at the night beyond the glass. "She says she doesn't want anything from me. Doesn't need me." And wasn't that a kick in the gut?

"And you believe that?"

Brady stopped, frowned and thought about it. No one had ever needed him before, so why would Aine? "I've no reason not to."

"You have every reason not to. She's giving you an out, that's all." Mike sighed and then patiently spoke again. "You told her you weren't interested in a relationship and sent her back home, right?"

"Yeah..." Brady scrubbed one hand over his face at the memory, wishing he could wipe it away.

"So why would she think you'd changed your mind now? She's just saying what she thinks you want to hear, that's all."

"You think?"

"Please." Mike snorted. "The question is, what are you going to do about this? Give her what she thinks she wants, or what she needs?"

Brady looked at Aine and something inside him tightened uncomfortably. Her eyes were hypnotic as they latched on to his, and he felt himself wishing that things were different. That he was a different man. But he didn't belong in this cozy family setting, and he knew it. The best he could do was provide for Aine and their child whether she liked it or not.

"Did you really think I'd agree to marry you when you've made it clear time and again you've no wish for a relationship at all?"

Hadn't taken her long to fight back, Brady thought.

They'd hardly taken more than ten steps from the cottage when she turned on him.

"You will marry me. If not for you, then for our son," Brady said, taking her arm and steering her toward the castle.

"No, I won't," she argued, whipping her auburn hair back from her face when the wind tossed it into a tangle. "I'll not live a lie. Why does this matter to you? In California you made it plain you weren't interested in becoming involved with your hotel manager."

"What?" Brady shook his head and stared at her. "That had nothing to do with anything."

"Oh, aye, it does. You're a rich man. I wouldn't know how to live in your world, and you've no clue about mine." She tugged her arm free of him and started walking faster. "Our son will be just fine without his parents being married."

"No, he won't." Brady pulled her to a stop beneath one of the oak trees and whirled her around until her back was to the gnarled trunk. Dappled shade danced across her features and shone in the eyes that were narrowed on him. "You think times have changed. It's no big deal for a kid to have no father. Well, they haven't changed that much. And my kid's not going to suffer because his parents couldn't get along."

"And marriage between two people who don't want it is better?" she asked.

"We don't have to live together." He braced his hands on either side of her head and leaned in. He'd thought this through and knew this was the answer. "We'll be married and stay married until after our child is born."

"And then what? A divorce?" Shaking her head, she said, "This must be the first proposal in history that comes with a plan for ending the marriage before it begins. You want to marry me, just not live with me, is that it?"

"I want my son to know that his parents were married."

"However briefly, then?"

"Look I'm no good at the day-to-day relationship thing, but that's my son you're carrying, and he's going to know that I cared enough about him to marry his mother."

"How do you know you're no good at it?" she asked.

"You can't live what you don't know. Anyway, that's the deal," he said shortly, stuffing both hands into his pockets.

"Well, isn't that the most romantic thing I've ever heard."

He stalked away from her and then back again, demanding, "Who's talking about romance?"

This wasn't about love and happily-ever-after, Brady told himself. This was about making sure she and their baby were safe. His son would have his name, and even if he and Aine didn't live together, the child would know his father cared.

"Not you," she said flatly.

"Aine, let me do this. For you. For our baby." He'd never asked anyone for anything before, and the words didn't come easily. "It's important to me that you and our son be safe."

"Of course he'll be safe. Brady…" She reached up to cup his cheek, and her touch was so warm, so tender, it shook him right down to the soles of his feet. "What drives you so? What keeps you from wanting to be a part of something? What makes you propose with the promise of an ending rather than a beginning?"

He stepped back because having her touch him was both a blessing and a curse. He couldn't think with her hand on him. Could hardly breathe without her touch. Staring into green eyes looking up at him anxiously, he felt himself bend. Felt himself need, and he fought it back.

There was nothing he wanted more than to pick her up, carry her into the castle and stretch her out on a bed. He wanted his hands on her, wanted to explore her new curves, caress the mound of his child and hold her tightly enough that the ache inside him eased.

But if he was with her again, he'd never let her go. He knew that now, and he *had* to let her go. For everyone's sake. So Brady pushed his own wants aside, burying them beneath the layers of secrets he was already hoarding. And he tried to make her understand.

"Your family's great," he said with a quick look at the cottage. "You grew up with that, so you know how to create it on your own. I don't. And so I don't try because I won't risk failing."

"You're talking in riddles. Tell me what it is that's tearing at you."

He shook his head. "You wouldn't understand."

Brady's campaign to win Aine over was relentless.

For the next few days, everywhere she turned, there he was. He kept his hand at her back when they walked together, made sure she sat down and put her feet up in the afternoon and helped her with the castle's books.

He had tea with her every afternoon, and in the evenings, he insisted on being with her, tempting her too much with the needs and wishes that clamored in her heart. Aine felt as though she was under siege by a gentle warrior determined to win the war with stubborn, relentless attention.

Her body was on fire and there was no relief in sight. He didn't try to make love to her again, and Aine wanted him more every day. Was he intentionally *punishing* her—and himself—for her turning down his plan of marriage and divorce? But what kind of thing was that for a man to offer? Did he not see that by giving her the vow to end the marriage, he was also giving her a reason to never accept the marriage? How could she when she knew the man was only biding his time before he disappeared from her life again?

He went into the village with her to run errands, and everywhere they went, he introduced himself as her fiancé and invited all of the villagers to a wedding that wasn't going to happen. He took over most of her jobs, seeing to the supplies being ordered, the work being done, and even had the makers of the roof tiles complying and promising delivery within the week—which was just infuriating.

He spent time with Robbie, showing the boy the ins and outs of building a video game from the ground up. Then he would spend hours with the boy, playing "Fate Castle" on Robbie's old television.

Molly couldn't say enough about Brady, who fixed a leaky pipe for her, then repaired a broken cabinet hinge. He was winning over her family, her friends—even the workmen at the castle sang his praises.

And every day, Brady proposed to Aine again, leaving her shaken and wishing that he actually loved her and really meant to live with her and make that family she wanted so badly. But she knew it was a lie. She knew it was only his sense of duty that kept him there and her heart hurt with the knowledge.

Even Brian, her accountant, had promised her forever until she'd ended their engagement. And now the man she truly loved body and soul promised her a beginning and an ending in the same proposal.

She buried the longing, the misery, in working on the hotel's books and planning for the grand reopening. In her office off the main lobby, Aine studied the computer screen and tried to push thoughts of Brady out of her mind. She emailed their website manager and arranged for him to send out email announcements about the changes happening at Castle Butler.

Then they set up a plan to run a web contest, with the grand prize being an all-expenses-paid one-week stay at Fate Castle. Brady and the Ryans had already agreed to it, and Aine thought it was a wonderful way to generate interest in the new hotel.

While the sound of work went on around her, Aine buried her personal miseries in her job, and after a couple of hours thought she was feeling better. All she had to do was stand strong against Brady's ridiculous notion of being married only to divorce. Soon enough, he'd tire of the challenge of wearing her down and go back to his life, allowing her to return to her own.

Without him.

Oh, the thought of that made her ache to her soul. Being with him again was so hard, knowing that she would lose him a second—and no doubt *last*—time.

When her phone rang, she grabbed it up, grateful to be drawn out of her own thoughts. "Hello?"

"Aine, come to the cottage," her mother said, voice breathless. "You must see this!"

Before Aine could ask what was wrong, what was happening, Molly hung up. Aine was out the door a moment later, hurrying across the grounds to the guest cottage.

There were three men on the cottage roof, replacing old, worn shingles with new. There were four more men on the outside of the stone cottage, who were busily painting the stones a soft cream color. What was going on?

Her mother met her on the front steps and waved excitedly. "Come in, come in!" She took Aine's hand when she was close enough and dragged her into the cottage. "Isn't it wonderful? Brady said I wasn't to worry about a leaking roof anymore and before I knew it, he had men on the roof fixing the whole thing. And painters, as well. Isn't it a lovely color?"

Molly's cheeks were flushed and a wide grin split her face and danced in her eyes as she handed Aine a manila envelope. "And then this happened!"

Aine opened it, pulled out a sheaf of papers and skimmed them. Then she read it all again, more slowly, then checked the back page and saw Brady's signature. She lifted her gaze to her mother's. "He's signed over the cottage to you."

Tears pooled in Molly's eyes, spilled over and were wiped away again. "He's a darling man, Aine. The note he sent with the papers said he wanted us to have the home we love. Isn't he a darling man?"

"Darling," Aine whispered, stunned nearly speechless. She couldn't believe he'd done something so kind for her mother. Now Molly would never again worry about making a rent payment, and the small house she'd called home for years was really hers.

"I was never so surprised. I had palpitations when I looked at those papers, I can tell you. But the dear man wasn't finished." She tugged her daughter back to the kitchen. "Look, will you just look at this!"

There was a shiny new cherry-red Aga stove installed in the space where Molly's ancient cooker had been only that morning. And in the corner stood a cherry-red refrigerator, shining and new and making hardly a sound louder than a purr of perfection.

"Isn't it grand?" Molly ran one hand across the stove top, then tsked at the fingerprints left behind. Quickly, she grabbed a cloth and rubbed the surface shiny again. "I've never in my life had such a stove as this. And the refrigerator, Aine! So big, so quiet..." She sighed happily. "And he bought them in red, the dear man, as he must have noticed how I love the color."

Clutching her dish towel in one hand, Molly plopped down onto a kitchen chair and looked around her in astonishment. "It's too much by far, but to know that our home is now really *ours*... Well, it's a gift beyond price is what it is."

Aine couldn't speak. All she could do was watch her mother's excited features as she sighed happily over what had happened. Brady had done this without a word to Aine. He'd seen the shape of things in the cottage and had gone out of his way to fix them. A new roof, fresh paint and then this—he'd transformed the heart of Molly's home. And buying *red*, of all things. He'd noticed the red cabinets in the kitchen and had guessed, rightly, that her mother would love the bright and shiny color.

But far more than that, he'd given her mother *security*. A life without worry. Aine's heart gave a twist and she felt the sting of tears burn her eyes.

"And that's not all." Molly pushed out of the chair as if she couldn't sit still. "He's sent a grand new television for Robbie and a new game machine, as well. Oh, and something he said is an art program that all young designers should have. When the boy gets home from school, he'll be beside himself."

"Why?" Aine whispered. "Why is he doing this?"

"Darling, can't you see why?" Molly cupped Aine's face in her palms and said, "He loves you, darling girl. He's no idea what to do about it, though, so he does this instead. He's showing you without words what you mean to him."

Aine would like nothing more than to believe that, but how could she? He'd sent her away, hadn't he? He'd as much as told her he wasn't interested. He'd proposed, but had also planned a divorce. Did a man in love do that?

"You're wrong, Mum," she finally said sadly. "It's only that he's a rich man, and when he finds a problem, it's his way to throw money at it."

"He didn't need to throw it at *us*," her mother said. "He did all of this for *you*."

Was her mother right? Did Brady love her? And if he did, why wouldn't he tell her? It was time, Aine told herself, to get some answers.

Ten

She found Brady in the back of the castle, near the maze. He turned when she came toward him and asked, "Do we really need this maze? Takes up a lot of room and—"

Aine walked right up to him, cupped his face in her palms and went up on her toes to kiss him. The taste of him after so long was soul stirring. Here was what she wanted, needed. Here was love so rich and thick it filled her, body and soul.

She felt his surprise, then his surrender as he fisted his hands at her back and pulled her in tight and close. Pressed against him, she felt the solid thump of his heartbeat, felt the hard strength of him, and knew she didn't want to live the rest of her life without him.

He deepened the kiss and Aine parted her lips for his tongue to sweep along hers, stealing her breath, making her heartbeat gallop and her knees weak. Brady Finn was in her heart and mind, and she needed him to know that. A cold wind whipped around them, binding them closer as watery sunlight filtered through clouds thick and gray. She let go of everything but the moment and gave herself up to the rush of emotions crowding through her.

When he finally raised his head and looked down at her, he gave her a half smile. "What was that for?"

"I've been talking with my mother."

"Ah…" His eyes cooled, and a wall she was too familiar with came up between them, effectively shutting her out. He stepped back, leaving her feeling alone, adrift. Turning to look at the maze again, he said only, "Well, you're welcome."

She wouldn't let either of them back away this time, though. This was too important. Too *real* not to acknowledge. Aine was determined to tell him how she felt and *demand* that he admit the same.

"That kiss wasn't only a thank-you," she said softly, walking around until she stood in front of him again and he was forced to look at her. He needed to know the whole truth and it was long past time she allowed herself to say the three words that meant everything. "It was also an 'I love you.'"

She saw his eyes flash then darken and go cool again, all in the span of a single heartbeat. His features went hard and detached, so she tried again. "Brady. I said I love you."

"I heard you." He stepped around her, again focusing on the bloody maze that Aine couldn't care about at the moment. "But you don't mean it. You're grateful, that's all. Now about the maze…"

"Devil take the blasted maze," she muttered. "And don't tell me what I feel or I don't. 'Tis insulting."

"Then, don't confuse love with gratitude," he snapped, sparing her only a quick look before focusing on the maze again. "If we tore this down…"

She huffed out a furious breath and said, "We'll not tear the maze down." Irritated that the first time she told him she loved him, he couldn't be bothered to believe her. And it was clear he wouldn't listen to her until they'd gotten the maze issue dealt with. "It was laid out by Lord Butler's great-granddaughter in 1565. 'Tis as much a part of the castle as the stone walls and battlements. All it needs is a bit of tending." She shot the raggedy bushes a hard look. "A good gardener will have it looking as it should in no time. Then maybe your gamer people can hunt werewolves in it." She waved a negligent hand. "Or we'll have prizes in the center of the maze for those who find their way in and out again."

"Hmm…not a bad idea," he said, and walked into the maze, quickly disappearing behind the high thick boxwood hedges.

Aine swallowed the bubble of temper threatening to spew and ruin the lovely romantic moment she'd planned. Why was the man so resolved to ignore what she was trying to tell him? With pride pushing her on and love clawing at her heart, she went after him, and when she caught up, she took a grip on his forearm and turned him to her. "You tell me why you don't believe I love you."

He looked at her and his eyes were as dark as the clouds rushing in from the sea. The wind sharpened, and even with the protection of the hedges surrounding them, she felt the chill it brought. But the cold she saw in his eyes went deeper than a harsh sea gust. Worry curled in the pit of her stomach, but she stood her ground, refusing to let him walk away this time. Seconds fell into minutes and those, too, crawled past as she waited. Just when she thought he would never answer her, he did.

"Because no one ever has," he muttered thickly before scrubbing one hand across his mouth as if he could wipe away the taste of the words.

She'd no idea what to make of that, but Aine could see what the words had cost him. Then he laughed shortly, and she winced at the pain in the sound of it.

"Brady," she said, sliding her hand along his forearm in a gesture meant to be comforting. "Talk to me. Tell me what it is that haunts you so."

He looked down at her hand, then lifted his gaze to hers. When he started speaking, his voice was low and strained. "You're always saying we're too different. Well, you're right, but not for the reasons you think." He moved in on her, backed her up against the maze hedge and loomed over her, his gaze sweeping her features as if carving them into his memory. "You want to know why I won't stay married and build a family? Because I've never had one. Never known one." He took a breath and released it. "When I was six years old, my mother dumped me on the state and left. Never saw her again." Old anger, old pain, glittered in his eyes like dark water in moonlight. "Who the hell knows who my father was? I went into the system. They shuttled me from home to home, with me carting my stuff around in paper sacks like trash." He eased back from her, putting at least a few inches between them. Almost as if he couldn't bear to be close to her when reliving his past.

Aine didn't know what to say, how to help, so she stayed quiet and listened, her heart breaking.

"From six to thirteen, I was in five different foster homes. None of 'em worked. None of 'em wanted me to stay." He swallowed hard. "After that, I didn't try anymore. Just lived at the home, went to school and bided my time until I could get out on my own."

"Brady, I'm so sorry..." She reached for him, but he twisted away and her hand fell helplessly to her side.

"I'm not telling you for your pity," he ground out. "Hell, I've never told anyone all of this, not even the Ryans. They know some, not all. But you need to know. You need to understand. You think I'm rich? All I've got is money. You're way richer than I am in every possible way, Aine." He pushed one hand through his hair, took a deep breath and blurted out, "You grew up with Molly, your father, your brother. You had a place. You had... love. You never doubted it—why would you? It was always there." He shoved his hands into his jacket pockets as if he couldn't figure out what to do with them. "I don't know what that's like. Wouldn't know the first thing about being a part of it. So yeah, you're richer than I'll ever be, and damned if I don't envy you for it."

Aine's heart ached for the boy he had been. But... for the man he was, she felt nothing but exasperation. Couldn't he see that he was so much more than he believed himself to be? He hadn't grown up with love, as she had. But there was so much love locked away inside him, burning to get out. She saw it in his friendship with the Ryans. With his generosity to her mother and brother. And she felt it in every touch he'd ever given her.

"I don't do families because I don't know how," he admitted and speared her gaze with his. "And if I tried and failed, that would damage my own kid, and I won't risk that."

Maybe the two of them weren't as different as she'd thought they were. Money, after all, was cold comfort if you had no one to share it with. He thought his worth was measured only by his bank account. That was why, she told herself, he was always offering her money. Because somewhere inside him he couldn't believe that she wanted him for himself.

"The only way you can damage a child is by not loving it," she said softly. "By not being there."

"It's not the only way, Aine," he said tightly. His gaze slipped down to the curve of her belly, then lifted to meet her eyes. "I don't know anything about families, Aine. They are not for me."

"You're the most stubborn of men," she snapped. "And blind, as well."

"What?"

"You do have a family, Brady. The Ryan brothers are your family whether you see it or not, and you do just fine there, don't you?" She moved in closer. "And you've claimed Mum's and Robbie's hearts, as well. You've made a place for yourself with them in such a short time." Tipping her head back, she stared directly into his eyes so there could be no misunderstanding when she said, "And you've mine, Brady. You have my heart."

He shook his head. "You didn't hear a word I said, did you?"

"I heard everything." Aine grabbed his hand and held it to her belly. At their joined touch, the baby kicked as if he knew his father was there within reach. She watched Brady's eyes widen with awe and felt her heart turn over again. How this man touched her. How he moved her. How he infuriated her. "Don't you see, Brady? You've made a family already. You've got me now, and the baby. Our son."

He stroked her belly, bent his head and kissed her, gently, tenderly, his teeth nibbling at her bottom lip and making her insides go soft and yielding. When he broke the kiss, he rested his forehead against hers and whispered, "You say you love me, Aine."

"I do."

"Then, marry me."

"If you stay," she promised.

"I can't," he said. "I can't take the chance of messing up yours and my kid's life. I don't know how to be what you want me to be."

"You *won't*, you mean." Frustration, anger and love circled around inside her, battering at her heart and soul. Every cell in her body cried out for what she couldn't have, and she heard herself say, "So once again, you'll sacrifice what you want for my own good. You'll turn away from what could be and cling to a past that brings you nothing but pain."

"Don't you get it?" His voice was as hard as stone, as merciless as the expression on his face. "I can't have what I want without risking ruining it. I won't do that to you—or the baby."

Hurt and feeling rejected once again by the man she loved and wanted more than anything, Aine moved away from him, though it tore her in two to do it. Until he realized what he had, what *they* could have, all of the words in the world wouldn't make a difference.

Meeting his gaze, she said, "You know what the hardest part of all this is? Mum was right. You *do* love me. You've said it in every way but words. And I'll not accept less from you, Brady. I deserve all. We deserve all. I want the words and the promise of them. When you find them within yourself, I'll be here."

* * *

By morning he was gone.

Two days later he was alone in his office, watching the sunrise. He hadn't been able to sleep since leaving Ireland, so there was no point staying in bed pretending otherwise. He took a sip of coffee and spun around in his desk chair to look out the windows.

The view didn't ease him because he hardly saw it. Instead, his mind dredged up images of Ireland and the castle…and Aine.

Brady didn't see her before he left. Better that way, he assured himself. Easier.

On who? a voice in his mind asked. *Her? Or you?*

The answer was both, of course. He wasn't a coward, ducking out without seeing her for fear he'd change his mind. He was doing the right thing here. Making the hard choice for all of them. Molly understood. He'd stopped at the cottage to see her on his way out, and rather than being angry that he was leaving, she'd hugged him and told him to come back soon. That he'd always be welcome.

He didn't think Aine felt the same way, but he couldn't really blame her for that.

She loved him.

Pain exploded in his chest and radiated throughout his body. Never in his life had anyone ever loved him, and he'd walked away from it. From her.

He couldn't breathe.

Just like he hadn't been able to sleep in his penthouse suite. It had been too…empty. Too sterile.

He had the distinct feeling his whole damn life was going to be empty from here on out. Brady rubbed the center of his chest, hoping to ease the hollowed-out sensation that had been with him since he'd left Ireland. As if his heart had been carved out and the echoing cavern it left behind was filled with ice.

"What're you doing here so early?" Mike spoke up from the open doorway.

"Couldn't sleep." He took another long drink of coffee, hoping to hell caffeine would kick in soon.

"Wonder why." Mike strolled into the office, dropped into a chair opposite Brady's desk and settled in.

"Jet lag." Brady frowned at his friend. He wasn't in the mood for conversation. Hell, he wasn't in the mood for anything.

"Yeah, I don't think so." Mike folded his hands over his abdomen, tipped his head to one side and said, "You want to tell me why you left Ireland in such a damn hurry? When you had a woman like Aine there? And a son on the way?"

He never should have called Mike when he'd first found out about the baby. If he hadn't, then his misery would be private.

"I had to." Brady set his coffee aside, pushed up from his chair and walked to the window. Leaning one shoulder on the wall, he stared blindly out the glass. "She says she loves me."

"A beautiful woman, pregnant with your kid, tells you she loves you. Of *course* you had to leave!" Astonishment colored Mike's voice. "Are you an idiot?"

"No, I'm not. I just know that I don't belong there." Brady spun around and glared at his friend. "How the hell could I be with her and my kid, Mike? I don't know how to do the family thing." God, he was tired of explaining that. Tired of hearing that his past was going to reach out and strangle his future. But facts were facts. "You can't do something you've never done."

"You are nuts. Because what you just said is bull." Mike stood up, planted both hands on Brady's desk and leaned forward. "Everybody does just that every day. First time I went surfing I'd never done it before. First time you did the storyboards for 'Fate Castle,' you'd never done it before."

"That's different," Brady muttered, raking one hand through his hair. He hadn't really looked at it like that, and, okay, Mike had a point. But those things weren't as important as a family, a kid, were they? "Screw up something like that, you get a do-over. Screw up your kid and it's forever."

"What makes you so sure you'd screw it up?"

Brady shook his head. Mike already knew why. At least, he knew enough of Brady's past that he never should have asked that question.

"You've got a shot at something here, Brady." Mike looked him in the eye and continued, "A woman who loves you, a baby who needs you. You've been trying to escape your past your whole life. Well, maybe it's time to stop running. Maybe it's time that you *make* the family that you missed out on."

Sounded so easy, and Brady knew it wasn't.

"How?" He really wanted to know. To think it could be done. Hope was a knife in his chest, sharp and slicing away at his doubts.

"The kind of family you wanted when you were a kid and never had?" Mike asked. "Build that. Build it now for Aine, your son—and yourself. Stop cheating yourself out of what you need and want and make a grab for it instead." He laughed a little and shook his head. "Go back to Ireland. Make the family you missed—before you miss this one, too."

Brady stared at him as hope continued to carve away at the black doubts that had been a part of him all his life. Was it possible? He thought back to when he was a kid and all the dreams he'd had about the kind of family he wanted. It was all there, in Ireland, waiting for him.

If Brady was willing to take the risk.

He took his first easy breath since leaving Aine and thought it all through again. Wasn't trying for something great and failing better than not trying at all? And when, he asked himself, had he *ever* failed when he wanted something badly enough? The answer was never. Why hadn't he remembered that? Hell, he thought, maybe all he really needed was a little faith. In himself. In Aine. In the kind of future he used to dream about.

"Mike," he said, already moving for the door, "I'm gonna need the company jet again."

"Yeah?" Mike grinned. "For how long?"

Brady stopped in the doorway and looked back over his shoulder at his friend. "Just long enough to get me to Ireland."

Mike's grin was even wider now. "So guess you'll be working long-distance from now on?"

"With any luck," Brady agreed. "With the internet and Skype and hell, the *phone*, I can work anywhere. And you guys will come out for the grand opening, right?"

"Wouldn't miss it," Mike said, and walked toward him, hand extended.

Brady took it, then yanked his friend in for a short hard hug. "Thanks, man. For everything."

Mike slapped Brady's shoulder. "We'll want an invite to the wedding, too."

"Count on it." Brady left to pack, then headed to the airport, hoping it wasn't too late.

"He'll be back, love," Molly told her daughter over a cup of tea.

Her mother's kitchen was warm and cozy despite the cold wind battering at the windows. Moonlight pearled on the glass and illuminated the surrounding trees with a pale silver glow. But inside, there was warm light and comfort.

"I don't think so." Aine hoped her mother was right, but when she remembered the stoic look of determination on Brady's features as he told her he couldn't be what she wanted, her heart ached.

Three days he'd been gone, and it felt as though nothing would ever be right in her world again. Three days and she could hardly take a step without thinking of him. How was she supposed to live the rest of her life without him?

"Why don't you move back here to the cottage for a while?" her mother asked, reaching out to take Aine's hand and give it a squeeze. "Truth be told, I could use the company, as I've hardly seen Robbie. Since Brady gave him that art program, the boy's been locked in his room creating all manner of horrible creatures from zombies to slavering hounds—" She broke off and sighed. "I'm sorry to mention his name, then, if it hurts you so."

"No," Aine said, forcing the smile her mother needed. "It's all right. I'm glad Robbie's enjoying the program, as Brady said he had real talent."

He'd even talked about offering Robbie a job once the boy finished school, and now Aine wondered if that promise would disappear. So much had changed with his leaving. She could hardly bring herself to care about the progress on the castle.

The roof tiles had finally arrived and were near to finished being laid. Soon the top floor would be renovated and then the hotel would be open for business. Would Brady come back for the opening?

"Thanks, Mum," Aine said softly. "But I'll stay at the castle still. It's worked out well, me being close at hand for Danny and the rest of the crew. And to be honest, I'm not really good company right now."

She didn't want comfort, no matter how well meant. She wanted to feel the pain of Brady's loss because it kept him near. She needed to be by herself, to get used to being alone. When she stood up, Molly joined her, coming around the kitchen table to envelop her in a hug.

Stroking her daughter's hair, she murmured, "There's always a chance for love, Aine. Never stop hoping. Never stop, because when you do, that's when all is lost."

Eleven

The second time he drove to the castle, Brady knew exactly where he was going.

To the only place he wanted to be.

Moonlight guided his way down the narrow curving track, past the iron gates now painted a bright silver and along the graveled drive. He spared a quick glance at the cottage where Molly and Robbie lived, but drove on to the main castle. It was a dark shadow against a moonlit sky and seemed to loom over him, daring him to step inside, to claim what he'd come for.

Brady was up to the challenge.

Finally, he was ready to leave his past behind and was ready now to reach for more. To take what he wanted, needed. He only hoped he could convince Aine that he was a changed man. That it was *she* who'd changed him. He used his key to open the front door, then quietly closed and locked it behind him. The silence was all encompassing and he did nothing to shatter it, taking the stairs with hardly a breath of sound.

He turned on the landing and headed for her room, praying she was still there and hadn't moved back to the cottage. Her door wasn't locked, and he took that as a good sign. Moving into the shadow-filled room, he stopped at the foot of the wide bed and watched her sleeping. Moonlight was here, too, slanted across the bed, making her dark red hair shine as it picked up threads of gold in the auburn mass. She had one arm crooked behind her head and the other cradling their child.

The heaviness in his chest that had been with him for days lifted. His heart swelled as a rush of warmth spread through him. Everything he wanted in life was there, in that bed.

He stripped out of his clothes and gently eased into the bed beside her. Brady pulled her to him and he marveled to notice that she didn't wake up. Wasn't frightened. Instead, she curled into him, draping one arm across his stomach, as if she'd only been lying there waiting for him to touch her.

For the first time in days, Brady's heart lurched into life and the sensation was almost painful.

The scent of her filled him; the warmth of her sighs against his skin fired his blood as well as his soul. And because he couldn't resist her another moment, he bent his head and kissed her. Sleepily, she kissed him back, sighing as she did so her breath became his, and then she woke, opened her eyes, stared at him and whispered, "Brady?"

When she would have pulled away, he only wrapped his arms more tightly around her, holding her close, half-afraid that if he let her go, she'd remain out of his reach forever. "Aine, I'm back. I'm here to stay, if you'll have me."

She looked up at him, not speaking, just watching him through those moss-green eyes. He didn't have a clue what she was thinking, feeling. This was a hell of a time for her to figure out how to mask her emotions. Worry pealed in his brain like warning bells going off.

Brady started talking, knowing that choosing the right words now was the most important thing he'd ever done. He wanted to be poetic. Romantic. He wanted to tell her that he wouldn't take no for an answer anymore. She was *going* to marry him. He wouldn't settle for less. Yet looking at her made him say only the simple truth. "I want to be here. With you. And I really need you to want me, too."

She opened her mouth to speak, but before she could, he spread one hand flat on her rounded belly and said, "I want to be a father to our baby. I want to be good at it, so I will be. I finally remembered that I've never failed at anything when I really want it. And I've never wanted anything like I want you and the family we can make."

At his words, he felt that small ripple of movement beneath his hands that told him his son was real and alive, and his heart filled even beyond what he would have thought possible.

"I want to live here in Ireland, with you. I can work from anywhere," he told her, words bursting from him as if they'd been dammed up behind a wall of stubbornness and had only just broken through. "We'll build our own house here, on the grounds. Behind the maze, maybe, I don't care. We'll be near your family, because they're almost as important to me as they are to you."

She swallowed hard and blinked back tears.

He hurried on, "I figure we can live here in the castle until the house is built. Any kind you want. We can build it to match the cottage, or even a replica of the castle itself if that's what you want."

She laughed a little, and he took that as hopeful. He had to keep talking because once he stopped she'd make her decision, and he needed to do what he could to make sure it was the *right* one.

"The house doesn't matter to me," he said. "What matters is the *home* we'll make in it."

Aine watched him, and in the moonlight, he could see the cautious hope in her gaze. When she spoke, her voice was soft, and the music that wove through it wrapped around his heart even as she shared her doubts.

"Though I'm so glad to see you, and I want you here more than anything," she said, "I've no wish to be a duty you carry through your life with brave resolution."

"You're not a duty," he interrupted her quickly, desperate now to make her see the truth he'd only realized. "You're a gift. You're the only truly great gift I've ever been blessed with. I don't know what I did to earn you coming into my life, but I'm grateful."

"Brady..." She chewed at her bottom lip and he saw the first glimmer of tears in her eyes. Not sure if they were happy or sad tears, he rushed on, fighting now for the life he'd always wanted. The life that was just out of reach.

"I made myself into what I am," he said, stroking her hair back from her face with his fingertips. "And I did a good job of it. But with you, I'm *more* than I ever thought I could be. With you, I have everything. Without you, there's *nothing*. It's really just that simple, Aine. You're my heart. Without you I'm only half-alive."

Her mouth curved the slightest bit as she reached to cup his cheek in her palm. "And the words, Brady? I told you I wanted the words. And the promise of them."

"I'll give you the promise," he said, and reached around to the bedside table where he'd left the ring he'd carried in his pocket all the way from California. He'd bought it on his way to the airport and had kept it close to him, like a talisman, like the promise she was waiting for. Holding the square-cut emerald that had reminded him of her, he looked from it to her and knew that no gem could ever shine with the beauty and depth of her eyes.

"I want you to marry me, Aine," he said, voice low and steady. "Not for the baby. Not for duty. But because with you I found something I never really believed in." He took a breath, blew it out and grinned at her. "*I love you*. Never thought I'd say those words. Never thought I'd need to say those words. But I do. I want to say them to you for the rest of my life. *I love you, Aine*. I promise you I always will."

Her smile was wide and bright and filled with everything he'd flown thousands of miles hoping to see.

"I'll marry you, Brady Finn, for I love you so much," she whispered, and held out her hand for him to slide the ring home. "I promise you I always will."

"Thank God," he muttered, and dropped his forehead to hers.

She laid one hand atop his so that both of them were cradling the child they'd made, connecting the three of them into a unit.

"I swear," he said softly, kissing her once, twice, "I will never take for granted the family we'll make to-gether."

She laughed, hooked her arm around his neck and

brought him close enough for a long, deep kiss. "And what a family we'll make, my love." She kissed him again and he felt all the love she held for him rush through him, filling all of the dark, empty places inside him.

With Aine curled against him in the moonlight, Brady finally felt like a rich man.

Epilogue

The grand reopening of Fate Castle emptied the village and half the county. They weren't accepting paying guests until the new year, giving Brady and Aine a chance to settle into marriage without zombie hunters underfoot all the time. But having the renovations complete made them want to show the locals just what they'd done to the place. So far, people liked it.

October was too cold to hold the party outside, so the medieval banquet hall was being christened. There was traditional Irish music that had people up and dancing, tables groaned under a mountain of food and there was enough beer to fill a moat, if the castle had had one.

Brady watched the celebration and told himself again that he was a lucky man. He'd found where he belonged. He had a beautiful wife who loved him, and a son on the way, not to mention a mother-in-law and a younger brother. He'd come here to build a hotel and had instead found the kind of life he used to dream of.

Long-distance working was going fine, too. With weekly Skype meetings, not to mention innumerable phone calls with either Sean or Mike, he kept up with everything. His own work had been going better than ever. Maybe, he thought, it was all the atmosphere at the castle, but he'd come up with some great story lines for future games.

And Robbie, Brady thought as he spotted the boy across the hall talking to Celia Hannigan, had been a big help. The kid was talented and eager to start working for Celtic Knot. But now that he was in the big-brother position, Brady was also insisting the kid go to college. Robbie'd work part-time and get real-world experience while learning as much as he could about graphic design.

Molly was supervising the food tables, making sure everyone had plenty to eat. The woman was never happier than in a kitchen, and Brady loved being able to pop into the cottage for tea and some of her amazing cookies whenever he wanted to.

Aine caught Brady's eye as she danced with Sean Ryan. One look at his amazing wife and his heart gave an oh-so-familiar jolt. He doubted he'd ever get past the rush he felt just knowing she was his.

"You look happy."

Brady glanced at Mike Ryan as he stepped up and handed over a pint glass of Guinness. "That's because I am."

"The hotel turned out great," Mike said, sweeping his gaze across the pennants and tapestries on the walls. There were suits of armor in the corners of the room and pewter plates and mugs scattered across the long tables. "I think it's going to be a winner."

"With the web contest we'll be running after the first of the year, you can bet on it," Brady said. "And Aine's getting emails every day from fans of the game wanting to make reservations even though we're not officially open yet."

"Good to know," Mike said. "Oh, we got the final papers on the river hotel last week. We're set to go there for the River Haunt."

"That's great, and before I forget," Brady said, pausing for a sip of his beer, "I got an email from Jenny Marshall with the new drawings she's come up with for the River Haunt hotel."

Mike gritted his teeth. "Yeah?"

Brady laughed at Mike's resigned expression. "What is it with you and her?"

"Nothing." Mike shook his head, brushing off the question. "I already told you. We met, then we said goodbye."

"Yeah, you're a master storyteller," Brady said wryly, then added, "Well, you'd better get over whatever your issue with her is since you'll be working together on the hotel."

"We'll see," Mike muttered. "I'm thinking Joe would do a better job of the murals."

"Joe quit, bud. How do you not know that?" Brady looked at him. "I live in *Ireland* and I know he quit two weeks ago."

"Perfect," Mike grumbled. "Just freaking perfect."

"Relax. Maybe your hotel project will work out as well for you as mine did for me."

"No chance of that if Jenny Marshall's involved," Mike

told him, then smiled and changed the subject. "Enough about the thorn in my side. Here comes your beautiful wife, you lucky bastard."

Brady turned to grin at the woman walking toward him with green eyes shining and a smile curving her delectable mouth. She looked amazing in black pants and a dark red sweater that did nothing to disguise her growing belly. Her hair was loose and curled around her shoulders, her cheeks were flushed and those eyes were sparkling.

"Mike, do you mind? My new husband promised to dance with me tonight, and I've come to hold him to it."

"Just as long as you save one for me, too," Mike said.

"A deal, it is," Aine told him, then threaded her arm through Brady's as they walked to the middle of the floor. The castle was alive with light and color, and the party was a huge success. She'd already had dozens of people say they wanted to come and stay as soon as they were open. Apparently the locals loved the idea of a werewolf chase through the maze!

Brady covered her hand with his as they walked, and the pulse of heat from his touch dazzled her. She supposed it always would. And wasn't that a wonderful thing? Aine hugged her happiness close, smiling at her friends and family as she and Brady strolled to the dance floor.

The musicians slid from a toe-tapping reel into a slow, soft tune that sailed over the heads of everyone gathered and hung in the air like a sigh.

"Have I told you tonight how gorgeous you are?" Brady asked as he guided her into a slow, lazy circle.

"You have," she said, trailing her fingertips through his hair, loving the silky touch of it against her skin. "And have I told you that I love you?"

"You have, but don't let that stop you from saying it again," he said, smiling, then dipped his head down to claim a kiss.

Magic had happened, Aine thought, looking up into her husband's eyes and seeing love shine back at her. The castle she'd fought to protect was safe, the man she loved had come home to her and the child they'd made was healthy. Her mother had her home, her brother had a future and she and Brady had everything. Her baby gave a quick kick as if sharing the joy she felt.

"Then, let me say it again, every day." She cupped his cheek in her palm. "I love you, Brady Finn. Now and always."

He grinned and spun her around, making the colors and people around them swirl into a blur. She felt as if they were the only two people in the world.

Aine laid her head on his chest and as the music wove its spell around them, they danced into the future.

* * * * *

MILLS & BOON®

It Started With…Collection!

1 BOOK FREE!

Be seduced with this passionate four-book collection from top author Miranda Lee. Each book contains 3-in-1 stories brimming with passion and intensely sexy heroes. Plus, if you order today, you'll get one book free!

**Order yours at
www.millsandboon.co.uk/startedwith**

MILLS & BOON®

The Rising Stars Collection!

1 BOOK FREE!

This fabulous four-book collection features 3-in-1
stories from some of our talented writers who are the
stars of the future! Feel the temperature rise this
summer with our ultra-sexy and powerful heroes.
Don't miss this great offer—buy the collection
today to get one book free!

**Order yours at
www.millsandboon.co.uk/risingstars**

MILLS & BOON®

It's Got to be Perfect

* cover in development

When Ellie Rigby throws her three-carat engagement ring into the gutter, she is certain of only one thing. She has yet to know true love!

Fed up with disastrous internet dates and conflicting advice from her friends, Ellie decides to take matters into her own hands. Starting a dating agency, Ellie becomes an expert in love. Well, that is until a match with one of her clients, charming, infuriating Nick, has her questioning everything she's ever thought about love...

Order yours today at
www.millsandboon.co.uk

MILLS & BOON®

Desire™

PASSIONATE AND DRAMATIC LOVE STORIES

A sneak peek at next month's titles...

In stores from 21st August 2015:

- **Claimed** – Tracy Wolff
  and **Maid for a Magnate** – Jules Bennett

- **The Baby Contract** – Barbara Dunlop
  and **His Son, Her Secret** – Sarah M. Anderson

- **Bidding on Her Boss** – Rachel Bailey
  and **Only on His Terms** – Elizabeth Bevarly

Available at WHSmith, Tesco, Asda, Eason, Amazon and Apple

Just can't wait?
Buy our books online a month before they hit the shops!
visit www.millsandboon.co.uk

These books are also available in eBook format!